Acts of Criticism

James P. Lusardi. September 3, 1931-November 10, 2002. Photo courtesy of Lafayette College.

Acts of Criticism

Performance Matters
in Shakespeare
and His Contemporaries

Essays in Honor of
James P. Lusardi

*for Joe Gordon,
with appreciation for your wonderful
remarks at the memorial service for Jim.
Best wishes,
June Schlueter*

6/06

Edited by
Paul Nelsen and June Schlueter

Madison • Teaneck
Fairleigh Dickinson University Press

Associated University Presses
2010 Eastpark Boulevard
Cranbury, NJ 08512

The paper used in this publication meets the requirements of the American National Standard for Permanence of Paper for Printed Library Materials Z39.48-1984.

Library of Congress Cataloging-in-Publication Data

Acts of criticism : performance matters in Shakespeare and his contemporaries : essays in honor of James P. Lusardi / edited by Paul Nelsen and June Schlueter.
   p. cm.
Includes bibliographical references and index.
ISBN 0-8386-4059-1 (alk. paper)
  1. Shakespeare, William, 1564–1616—Stage history. 2. Shakespeare, William, 1564–1616—Contemporaries. 3. Shakespeare, William, 1564–1616—Dramatic production. 4. Shakespeare, William, 1564–1616—Film and video adaptations. 5. English drama—Early modern and Elizabethan, 1500–1600—History and criticism. 6. English drama—17th century—History and criticism. 7. Theater—England—History. I. Nelsen, Paul, 1947– II. Schlueter, June. III. Lusardi, James P.
  PR3091.A27 2006   2005016273

PRINTED IN THE UNITED STATES OF AMERICA

Contents

Acknowledgments

Over the years, many teacher/scholars have contributed to the conversation that forms the basis for this collection. In particular, we are grateful to contributors to *Shakespeare Bulletin*, to members of the Columbia University Seminar on Shakespeare, and to those who sat with us at theater productions throughout the world. The latter includes Paul's wife, Lou, and June's husband, Paul, who always provided intelligent notes and encouraging words.

Special thanks to Paul Schlueter and to the librarians at Lafayette College, who tracked down texts and quotations in our effort to replicate the quality of editing that Jim Lusardi, as coeditor of *Shakespeare Bulletin*, standardized; to Paul Schlueter for preparing the index; and to Marcy Lusardi, Jim's wife, for her good spirits and support.

Harry Keyishian, as Director of Fairleigh Dickinson University Press and as Jim's friend and colleague, shepherded this *Festschrift* through the publishing process, happily associating Fairleigh Dickinson University, once again, with a colleague who was a frequent contributor to the Shakespeare Colloquium Harry hosted on the Florham/Madison campus each year. We express appreciation to Fairleigh Dickinson University Press for its support and to the University Seminars at Columbia University for their help in publication. Ideas presented in this volume have benefited from discussions in the University Seminar on Shakespeare, which Jim attended for some twenty years.

Introduction

"EVERY PERFORMANCE IS AN ACT OF CRITICISM." THOSE OF US WHO worked with James P. Lusardi during his twenty years as coeditor of *Shakespeare Bulletin* know how often Jim spoke these now canonical words. It did not take a hundred productions of *Hamlet*, which he certainly experienced, for Jim to come to this recognition: it took only two. During his undergraduate years at Lafayette College (Jim was Class of 1955) and his graduate years at Yale (Class of 1963), the prevailing approach to Shakespeare was literary, with New Criticism urging a search for the embedded textual meaning. When scholars like Jim became theatergoers, however, it became clear that interpreting Shakespeare was the work of diverse minds, engaged not only in the practical exercise of performance but also in acts of criticism. When one overlaid just one production of a Shakespeare play on the received text of that play, one realized that it was no longer possible to agree with A. C. Bradley's respectful but misguided insistence that *King Lear* was too big for the stage.

Jim never abandoned the rigorous close reading of the New Critics; indeed, some would say he perfected it. But over the course of his thirty-five-year academic career, he developed an uncanny eye for interpretive detail. A textual critic from the start (he edited *The Confutation of Tyndale's Answer* in *The Yale Edition of the Complete Works of St. Thomas More* [1973]), Jim always instructed *Shakespeare Bulletin* reviewers to focus on the details. "We don't want the 'I like parsnips' variety of criticism," he would say; "we want focused, thoughtful observations. Notice the details, collect and connect them, describe them, and determine how they reveal conception and meaning." In the halcyon days of his own theatergoing, before cancer grounded him, Jim would average one hundred plays a year. For him, each production, no matter how it twisted the text, provided yet another angle of vision on Shakespeare; even "bad" productions taught him something about alternative modalities of reading.

Jim developed so nuanced an understanding of the interpretive process in performance that colleagues loved asking his opinion of Shakespeare productions. They also loved testing a memory that could only be described as a gift. For most of us, after seeing, say, four productions of *The Tempest* in a year, the blending process takes over, creating confused recollections of just how Prospero handled, for example, the long story he tells his daughter about his dukedom. For Jim, each production remained discrete, but his commentary on each was always informed by the other three, which provided a rich context of alternative meanings. Jim could recite long passages from Shakespeare on cue and call up the details of how a production ten years earlier treated a scene. His powers of observation and recollection were nothing short of amazing; Jim was the stuff, personified, of performance criticism.

Jim Lusardi spent most of his academic career at Lafayette College, returning to his alma mater as a member of the faculty in 1966, after teaching at Williams, Wesleyan, and Yale. In 1990, he was made Francis A. March Professor of English, a chair he held with special pride. For March had not only been a towering figure at Lafayette College, he was also the first professor of English anywhere. The archives at Lafayette College preserve many of March's pedagogical essays. With Jim's own course materials and scholarship added to the collection, the College has become a repository for two prominent approaches to teaching Shakespeare: nineteenth-century philology and twentieth-century close reading of text and performance. Alongside Jim's papers rests the archive of *Shakespeare Bulletin* materials, documenting the first twenty years of this journal of performance criticism and scholarship.

As a tribute to Jim Lusardi, we offer this collection of performance-oriented essays by scholars who, over the years, contributed generously to *Shakespeare Bulletin*. As editors, we have a special interest in remembering Jim in this way. Paul Nelsen was Jim's student at Lafayette (Class of 1969) and, as Professor of Theater and Drama at Marlboro College, was a long-time colleague. Paul and Jim undertook intensive playgoing jaunts together in London and served on the scholarly team advising on Sam Wanamaker's reconstruction of the Globe playhouse. June Schlueter was coeditor of *Shakespeare Bulletin* with Jim for twenty years. They team-taught courses on Shakespeare, including Lafayette's interim session in London, and co-authored *Reading Shakespeare in Performance: King Lear*. Others in this volume knew Jim and worked with him in various contexts, including the Columbia University Shakespeare Seminar. Each happily accepted our invitation to contribute to a *Festschrift* that would stand as testimony to Jim's long and lasting contribution to the field.

Acts of Criticism assembles a cast of sixteen distinguished theater historians and performance critics, each of whom has contributed significantly to our understanding of issues associated with performing works of Shakespeare and his contemporaries. Their essays, all appearing in print for the first time, are presented in two groupings: a theater history and practice section, in which contributors treat matters related to performance in Shakespeare's time and our own, and a performance criticism section, in which contributors treat modern productions on stage and screen.

Roslyn L. Knutson's essay, "Toe to Toe across Maid Lane: Repertorial Competition at the Rose and Globe, 1599–1600," begins the collection. In it, Knutson explores the 1599–1600 repertory of the Admiral's Men and the Chamberlain's Men, who performed in rival playhouses across from one another in London's Maid Lane. Working with Henslowe's Diary, the Stationers' Register, and other documents from the period, she carefully reconstructs the chronology of plays performed by the two companies during this "high point in their commercial lives." Through generic and topical pairings of plays in the companies' repertories, she lends support to the argument for "competition through simi-

Jim Lusardi and Paul Nelsen at the Globe Theatre, London. Nelsen and Lusardi were on the scholarly advisory team for the reconstruction of Shakespeare's Globe. Photo courtesy of Lafayette College.

June Schlueter and Jim Lusardi with editorial assistant Heather Braun (center). Schlueter and Lusardi coedited *Shakespeare Bulletin* for 20 years. Photo courtesy of Lafayette College.

larity." The charts Knutson constructs in order to earn that conclusion will remain a valuable resource for scholars interested in understanding commercial performance in Shakespeare's time.

Jay L. Halio's method is also comparative. In "The Study of Shakespearean Playbooks," Halio takes parallel looks at surviving playbooks (or "promptbooks") of Shakespeare's plays, beginning with the Smock Alley collection from the 1670s. Halio is interested in how successive generations of actor/managers and directors modified the Shakespearean "original" and in how subsequent productions treated such change. (Nahum Tate's 1681 revised ending of *King Lear*, for example, held the stage for 150 years.) Familiar eighteenth- and nineteenth-century actor/managers and directors appear in Halio's essay, which offers a provocative survey of a performance history that continues to evolve.

Alan C. Dessen's "'The difference betwixt reporting and representing': Thomas Heywood and the Playgoer's Imagination" examines patterns of production with respect to "telling" and "showing." How elaborate a set did early modern audiences expect when they saw a play? How common were verbal substitutions for the sets and properties identifying time and place? How prevalent was the *as if* of theater that invited early modern audiences to participate imaginatively (as the Chorus in Shakespeare's *Henry V* does when he importunes each spectator to "make imaginary puissance" so that "this cockpit" can hold the "vasty fields of France")? From his own extensive compendium of *as if* examples in explicit and implicit stage directions, Dessen selects several from Heywood's plays—in his opinion, "the best place to go for evidence" of the "full stretch" of *as if* dramaturgy.

Andrew Gurr's essay, "'The stage is hung with black': When Did Melpomene Lose Her Identity?", complements the work of these theater historians by examining a convention in early modern theater of hanging the stage with black to signal the audience that the play it was about to see was a tragedy. With *A Warning for Fair Women* as his focus, Gurr teases the implications of such a practice in Shakespeare's time. His analysis engages both theatrical and generic questions: did a distinction develop, for example, between tragedies, where audience expectation was clear, and tragicomedies, where the story might go either way? Gurr makes the point that, despite the apparent currency of the practice of hanging the stage with black from c. 1591 to c. 1607, "nothing survives to say that any writer of plays after 1607 registered the usage as still current." When and why did the practice disappear?

The section on theater history and practice closes with Maurice Charney's "Shakespeare: Rough or Smooth?", a foray into the question of Shakespeare bardolatry, that academic inclination to suppress or "smooth out" the difficulties in Shakespeare's plays. Charney's discussion suggests that such "acts of kindness" on the part of editors and translators do not always serve the text. Noting that Shakespeare has been "overedited" when compared with his contemporary playwrights, Charney turns to examples of modern translations; Yves Bonnefoy's of *Othello*, he observes, yields a "bloodless, classical French" version of the play. Charney's assumptions about Shakespeare's use of popular speech and his challenge to what we commonly think of as "literary" language provide a performative context for Shakespeare's plays, which, Charney argues, are not recognized for their "distinctive mix of styles."

John Timpane's "Privileging the Spiritual: Performers, Shakespeare's Plays, and the Uses of Theater" begins the section on modern stage productions by drawing attention to the recent flood of "spiritual" scholarship related to Shakespeare. Supported by interviews with directors and crew members of productions he has seen, Timpane examines moments that connect the interior individual with a wider universe—either with knowledge of oneself, with the lives of others, with the human race as a whole, or with the divine. Timpane asks whether and how "spirituality" becomes privileged in performance.

Frances K. Barasch's "Performing Apemantus in Shakespeare's *Timon of Athens*" launches the group of commentaries investigating modern productions of individual plays. Barasch assesses the seriocomic role of Apemantus, the "Cynic philosopher" and "master of mockery" in *Timon of Athens*. After surveying historical attitudes toward this often "disposable" character, she offers a reconsideration of Apemantus in terms of the Cynic school of philosophy available to Renaissance satirists, arguing that the purpose of this character—to provide "life-affirming values" and "a comedic alternative to Timon's bleak misanthropy"—is indispensable in performance.

In "*King Lear*, Act 3: Storming the Stage," Charles A. Hallett focuses the scholarly magnifying glass on the storm scene in act 3 of *King Lear*, which has always been a challenge in performance. After familiarizing himself with multiple modern renderings of the scene, he argues that the contemporary tendency toward realism and spectacle detracts from the design and the action of the play. Hallett sees the 2002 Almeida Theatre production as the epitome of an inclination toward realism that has characterized modern productions of the storm. Director Jonathan Kent's saturating of stage and actors with actual showers of pelting rain may have been a technical wonder, but it left the audience clueless about what else was happening in the scene. Similarly, although Jonathan Miller's 2004 production at New York's Lincoln Center returned "to the simplicity of the Elizabethan stage," Hallett contends that Miller's "visual evocation of an earlier time obscures but doesn't negate the realistic underpinnings on which his production is predicated." Those realistic underpinnings, he argues, "assume a finite world in which there is nothing beyond death but a void" and neglect attention to Lear's heart and soul, thus diminishing the belief that "through suffering and love, one can find redemption."

Edward L. Rocklin's essay, "Placing the Audience at Risk: Realizing the Design of Massinger's *The Roman Actor*," moves the conversation to one of Shakespeare's contemporaries, Philip Massinger, and, specifically, to three production elements in Sean Holmes' 2002 production of that play for the Royal Shakespeare Company. Rocklin is interested in how choices made by Holmes, designers, and actors affect the play-audience relationship; in how performance choices and key inventions foreground the pattern of action followed by the enemies of Domitianus Caesar; and in the manner in which Antony Sher physically realized Domitian. Rocklin studies the play's strategies of inclusion, which entail several plays-within-the-play and other techniques to draw the audience into a theatrical world in which tyranny and torture are the norm.

Michael D. Friedman's "'I'm not a feminist director, but . . .': Recent Feminist Productions of *The Taming of the Shrew*" also combines an historical interest in performance with a look at particular contemporary productions of *The Taming of the Shrew*, each with a contrasting feminist slant, namely, Charles Marowitz's, Gayle Edwards', and Michael Bogdanov's. Friedman examines the affective history of modern productions of *The Shrew*, many of which have faced hostile receptions, not only for their perceived distortion of Shakespeare's work but also for their feminist politics. His special interest is in the disavowal common among directors who tackle this troublesome play: "I'm not a feminist director, but . . ."

In "'So What?': Two Postmodern Adaptations of Shakespearean Tragedies," Naomi C. Liebler takes a look at Rome Neal's *Julius Caesar Set in Africa* and Linda Mussmann's *M.A.C.B.E.T.H.*, both staged in 1991. Not only did both reshape the way Liebler understands these two tragedies; so also did they open up provocative questions about productions that move beyond "interpretation" into the arena of radical intervention. In this fascinating essay on two unpublished scripts, Liebler explores questions of adaptation and intertextuality, arguing that "certain kinds of outside-the-box imaginings . . . invite a fresh examination" of Shakespeare's vision "by asking uncomfortable questions." Her essay outlines an approach to adaptation that enables a dynamic referential meeting place for the Shakespeare text and its offshoots.

In "Shakespeare's Body: Robert Lepage's Slippery *Dream*," Samuel Crowl calls the French-Canadian artist's version of *A Midsummer Night's Dream* "the most controversial and daring Shakespeare to open in London in the last decade of the twentieth century." Celebrating Lepage's ability to "release Shakespeare's text into the wonders of three-dimensional space," Crowl speaks of his production of *Dream* in architectural terms, praising its visual power. Crowl ends with an astute commentary on Lepage's relationship to both theater and film.

In "Trevor Nunn's *The Merchant of Venice*: Portia's House of Mystery, Magic, and Menace," Kenneth S. Rothwell explores the visual techniques behind Nunn's television adaptation of his own stage production. Rothwell places special emphasis on Portia's three caskets, each of which "embodies a major trope of the play." These caskets, he argues, provide an interpretive key for Nunn, who brings together the play's several disparate strands in a nuanced cinematic treatment of this problematic script. As Rothwell puts it, "As Ernst Lubitsch became famous in Hollywood for his 'touch' with icons like white telephones on boudoir bed stands, Nunn also focuses his camera on key symbols to suggest far more than meets the eye."

J. Anthony Burton reflects on how screen renditions of Shakespearean performance can conceal and diminish dimensions of character and thematic complexity by limiting the frame of view. In "The Lady Vanishes or, the Incredible Shrinking Gertrude," Burton reviews four screen treatments of Hamlet and contends that the "important" character of Gertrude gets ignored, somewhat dismissively; the camera's eye—and the director's—fails to take account of "Gertrude's capacity to take the initiative or control events."

Miranda Johnson-Haddad's interest is in children in Shakespeare's plays, particularly those that are not scripted to appear on stage. In "Childhood Dreams and Nightmares: Children in Productions of *A Midsummer Night's Dream*," Johnson-Haddad looks at Adrian Noble's 1997 *Dream*, along with a production she saw at Lake Tahoe in 2003, to ask why recent productions tend not only to include the Indian boy but also to expand the role of the child. Extratextual children, she observes, provide opportunities for directors and audiences to see the play through a fresh perspective, "linked with imagination and creativity." Indeed, extratextual children may, finally, not be "extratextual" at all but "the reification of many seemingly disparate elements that are inherent in the playtext and essential to it."

To anchor the collection, Alexander Leggatt tackles two contemporary re-doings of Shakespeare that transfer a Shakespeare play into a modern American high school and then take the liberties one would expect to make the transfer work. Gil Junger's *10 Things I Hate About You* and Tim Blake Nelson's *O* are the subjects of his analysis, which regularly touches base with their respective sources: *The Taming of the Shrew* and *Othello*. Implicitly valuing how Shakespearean film offshoots appeal to the younger generation, Leggatt credits *10 Things I Hate About You* with presenting the "disruptiveness of adolescence as harmless roleplaying" and *O* with touching on "deeper fears about what lies behind the pictures in the yearbook."

Though wide-ranging and evocative, this collection, like any other, is, finally, a tease. But, like any production of a Shakespeare play, it is designed to stimulate further thought and to enhance understanding of how significant a presence the "abstract and brief chronicles" of performance has become on the current landscape of scholarly criticism. Along the way, of course, we mean to memorialize the role that Jim Lusardi played in this historic shift in critical focus. Jim's dictum— "Every performance is an act of criticism"—seems obvious to us now.

Acts of Criticism

I
Theater History and Practice

Toe to Toe across Maid Lane: Repertorial Competition at the Rose and Globe, 1599–1600

Roslyn L. Knutson

For many years, theater historians believed that the Admiral's Men fled the Rose playhouse in Maid Lane in a commercial panic when the Chamberlain's Men moved into their new Globe across the street in the late summer of 1599. Recently, S. P. Cerasano has disputed the role of company rivalry in the move, arguing that "by the late 1590s [Philip] Henslowe and [Edward] Alleyn were knowledgeable, shrewd entrepreneurs" who anticipated the need to replace the aging Rose well before they signed the building contract for the Fortune on January 8, 1600.[1] Nevertheless, the notion persists that the Admiral's Men could not, or would not, stand up to the competition heightened by the Chamberlain's move. Bolstering that notion is a reluctance to equate the repertories of the Admiral's and Chamberlain's Men despite the argument by Bernard Beckerman in *Shakespeare at the Globe* that the companies' offerings were similar in number and commercial appeal.[2] I apply Beckerman's argument in *The Repertory of Shakespeare's Company, 1594–1613,*[3] and Andrew Gurr, in *The Shakespearian Playing Companies*, presents repertorial similitude as the definitive position: "repertories of the [Admiral's and Chamberlain's Men] . . . show clear signs of the close competition they were engaged in. They copied each other, duplicating specific subjects for their plays and the new fashions each introduced."[4] Here I want to provide additional support for the argument of competition through similarity by exploring the repertories of 1599–1600 when the Admiral's Men and Chamberlain's Men went toe to toe across Maid Lane. I believe that this examination will allay lingering suspicion that the Admiral's repertory was not sufficiently competitive and, further, that it will suggest kinds of plays now lost from the repertory of the Chamberlain's Men. At the very least, an examination of the two repertories in 1599–1600 will show both companies at a high point in their commercial lives, fully masters of the theatrical marketplace.

Philip Henslowe, having recorded lists of performances in his busi-

ness diary from February 19, 1592, through November 5, 1597, began
with increasing regularity in October 1597 to enter instead payments
for playbooks and other necessities of staging. Thus, although his entries no longer give the dates of performances, length of runs, and re-
ceipts per performance, they record information on the titles of plays
being purchased by the company, the dramatists' names, the dates and
amounts of dramatists' payments, and the dates and amounts of payments for costumes and "divers thinge*." From this second set of records, even though there are inconsistencies and incomplete entries, it
is possible to recover a close approximation of the repertory of the Admiral's Men for October 1597–May 1603 (at which time the payments
for playbooks cease). On the issue of which plays were brought into
production, I follow the lead of E. K. Chambers, who pointed out long
ago that £4 (80s.) was an acceptable minimum payment in full but that
the "normal" price of a script was £6 (120s.).[5] On the issue of genre, I
use the designations of Alfred Harbage for *Annal* of *Engli*h *Drama*,[6]
with modifications: I classify romances as a subcategory of comedy and
assign classical topics to a generic category according to the nature of
their stories. A table of the payments for scripts, July 1599–June 1600,
is in the appendix. In it, and in the discussion below, I indicate lost
plays by quotation marks and surviving plays by italics.

Nothing comparable to Henslowe's payments exists for the Chamberlain's Men, but some items in their repertory may be identified from
stationers' records, scholars' construction of a chronology for Shakespeare's plays, scholars' conjectures about revivals, and playgoers' comments. Thomas Platter, a traveler from Basel, saw "the tragedy of the
first Emperor Julius Caesar" in London on September 21, 1599, presumably Shakespeare's *Juliu* *Cae*ar.[7] On the flyleaf of Register C of
the Stationers' Register, there is a list of plays designated as "my lord
chamberlens mens Plaies" and dated May 1600; two titles are recorded:
"Cloth Breeches and Velvet Hose" and *A Larum for London* (Q1602).[8] *A*
You Like It is assigned to the fall of 1599 by Shakespearean chronolo-
gers, and *Every Man Out of hi* *Humour* is assigned to 1599 in the 1616
folio edition. Rowland Whyte, in correspondence with Sir Robert Sidney on March 8, 1600, wrote that the Chamberlain's Men had recently
performed "Sir *John Old Ca*tell*" for the Dutch ambassador, Louis Ver-
reyken.[9] For more repertory items, I must conjecture. I am encouraged
to do so by several sets of entries in the Stationers' Register as well as
fresh publications of a few old plays. In a separate entry from the trun-
cated list of Chamberlain's plays on the flyleaf of Register C, dated August 4, the clerk entered the titles of *A* *You Like It*, *Henry V*, *Every Man*

In his Humour, and *Much Ado About Nothing*. The latter three plays are generally assumed to have been new in 1598–99; their entry in the stationers' records invites me to assume that the plays were continued from the 1598–99 repertory into 1599–1600. Further, on August 14, 1600, immediately following an entry with Walter Burre of *Every Man In his Humour*, Cuthbert Burby entered "The famous Tragicall history, of ye Tartarian Crippell Empero^r of Constantinople."[10] And on August 23, in another multiple entry, Andrew Wise and William Aspley entered *Much Ado About Nothing* and *2 Henry IV*. The latter play is usually assigned to the repertory of 1597–98; however, it might have been revived to accompany *Henry V* and continued in production into 1599–1600. Finally, five old Chamberlain's plays were printed in 1600: *A Midsummer Night's Dream* (S. R. October 8, 1600, Q1600); *The Merchant of Venice* (S. R. July 28, 1598, October 28, 1600, Q1600), *The First Part of the Contention of York and Lancaster* (S. R. March 12, 1594; Q1594, Q1600), *The True Tragedy of Richard Duke of York* (Q1595, Q1600); *Titus Andronicus* (S. R. February 6, 1594, Q1594, Q1600). For the sake of discussion, I will consider all of the above as possible revivals in the repertory of the Chamberlain's Men, 1599–1600.

I begin an assessment of the Admiral's and Chamberlain's repertories by comparing their history plays, where I see most similarity:

Admiral's Men	*Chamberlain's Men*
"Robert II, King of Scots"	"Oldcastle" (?new)
1 John Oldcastle	*2 Henry IV* (?revival)
"2 John Oldcastle"	*Henry V* (continuation)
"2 Henry Richmond"	*The First Part of the Contention* (?revival)
"Owen Tudor"	*The True Tragedy of Richard Duke of York*
	(?revival)
"Jugurtha"[11]	
"Strange News out of Poland"	

Since its invention by the Queen's Men, the English history play had been a staple of company repertories,[12] and the Admiral's Men show a commitment to the genre in the rhythm of their acquisitions throughout the year. Clearly, the centerpiece of the fall season was the two-part "Oldcastle" play, for which the team of dramatists was paid a benefit of 10s. in early November. The "Oldcastle" plays illustrate a new source for historical subject matter, John Foxe's *Acts and Monuments*, but an old commercial staple, the serial. "Owen Tudor" and "2 Henry Richmond" may also have been a serial, though perhaps conceived (or

merely paid for) in reverse order.[13] The entry in Henslowe's diary for
"2 Henry Richmond" tells only that Robert Wilson acknowledged receipt on November 8, 1599, of £8 from Robert Shaa, one of the Admiral's players, for "the second part of Henrye Richmond."[14] However,
the Dulwich Library papers include a letter from Shaa to Henslowe
requesting the £8 payment, and on the back is an outline of scenes indicating that the play would have begun early in the reign of Richard III
when he was lobbying Queen Elizabeth, perhaps for her daughter's
hand in marriage.[15] No doubt subsequent scenes would have shifted
focus to the rise of Henry Richmond, who won that hand on his own.
Raphael Holinshed's *Chronicles* say little about Owen Tudor, but his appeal as a theatrical figure must surely have been as second husband for
Catherine of Valois, widow in 1422 of Henry V, and, through their son
Edmund, as grandfather of Henry Richmond. Owen's capture on the
battlefield at Mortimer's Cross in 1461, and his subsequent execution
at Hereford, would have made an ending for the play; the fate of his
grandfather would also have provided additional motive for Henry
Richmond to lead an army against Richard III, whose brother Edward
had won the crown for the Yorkists after Mortimer's Cross and had
ordered Owen's execution.[16]

The history plays that I assign on conjecture to the repertory of the
Chamberlain's Men for 1599–1600 dramatize similar materials similarly. Like the Admiral's Men, the Chamberlain's Men had a history
play based on Foxe's martyrology and serials based on the English
chronicles. The Chamberlain's "Oldcastle," which undoubtedly had
resonance in the company's own repertory due to the *faux pas* that ne-
cessitated the name change in *1 Henry IV* from Oldcastle to Falstaff,
matched the two-part "Oldcastle" from the Admiral's winter repertory.[17] One pair—*2 Henry IV* and *Henry V*—had echoes of the Oldcastle
figure through Falstaff and further anticipated the family line of Henry
Richmond through Henry V's wooing of the French queen, Richmond's
future grandmother. But even more than two of the Henriad, the revivals of the second and third parts of Shakespeare's tetralogy on the Wars
of the Roses made a serial across company lines with "Owen Tudor"
and "2 Henry Richmond." However, there could well have been teasing
differences. For example, the main plot of "Owen Tudor" might have
celebrated the loyalty of Owen to the Lancastrian cause; Shakespeare's
plays present self-serving combatants on both sides. Also, Owen was
executed on the order of the soon-to-be-king Edward in 1461, during
which year much of the *True Tragedy* is set. Shakespeare's play does not
dramatize the battle in which Owen died, but it does present the vision

of the three suns seen by the Yorkist brothers before Mortimer's Cross. In light of Owen's beheading, Edward's offer of mercy to an adversary on a different, northern battlefield in Shakespeare's play—"Friend or foe, let him be friendlie used"—must have sounded hollow to audiences of the Admiral's play at the Rose.[18]

Three additional titles from the Admiral's history plays—"Robert II, King of Scots," "Jugurtha," and "Strange News out of Poland"—have loose parallels with tragedies in the repertory of the Chamberlain's Men.[19] "Jugurtha" presumably recounted events in the life of the Numidian king, 160–104 BCE. Jugurtha used an alliance with Rome to secure his kingdom but lost it in over-reaching; he was imprisoned and executed in Rome. As classical tragical history, "Jugurtha" invites comparison with *Julius Caesar* in the Chamberlain's repertory, as well as *Titus Andronicus*, with which there would have been the additional connection of North Africa through the character of Aaron the Moor. Depending on how wide a net is cast, "Jugurtha" also invites comparison with the conjectural "Tartarian Cripple" on motifs of conquest and exotic warlords. The title of "Strange News out of Poland" suggests little about its content except that it was quasi-historical and foreign. *A Larum for London* in the repertory of the Chamberlain's Men likewise evokes contemporary European history; and, if the "strangeness" of the news from Poland happened to have been reports of unnatural disturbances that presaged death and destruction, the Admiral's play would have struck a chord of political exemplum similar to the warning voice in *A Larum for London*. "Robert II, King of Scots" has no apparent counterpart in the Chamberlain's repertory, and it is hard to imagine what the dramatists might have seen that was potentially dramatic, much less tragic, in the reign of Robert II (1370–90). Holinshed suggested then, and historians agree now, that King Robert himself was noteworthy only for the transfer of his moniker, "the steward," to the status of surname, thus establishing the House of Stewart (Stuart). During his reign, he fought wars against the English through surrogates, namely the Douglases, fending off incursions led by Henry Percy, or Hotspur, and the Northumberlands. Of dubious theatrical and negative political value was Robert II's other main accomplishment, the siring of more illegitimate children than legitimate, with the former succeeding to the throne on his death. Perhaps, as James Shapiro has suggested, the dramatists were looking ahead to the accession of James Stuart to the English monarchy;[20] yet the reign of Robert II offers more topics to avoid than to dramatize.

Unlike the history plays, the tragedies in repertory lists of the Admiral's and Chamberlain's Men in 1599–1600 offer no obvious matches beyond superficially similar motifs; the strongest connection appears to be with an offering in the Chamberlain's 1598–99 repertory.

Admiral's Men	*Chamberlain's Men*
"Page of Plymouth"	*Julius Caesar* (new)
"Troy's Revenge, w/ Tragedy of Polyphemus"	*A Larum for London* (new)
"The Stepmother's Tragedy"	"The Tartarian Cripple" (?new)
"Cox of Collumpton"	*Titus Andronicus* (?revival)
"The Tragedy of Thomas Merry"	
"Ferrex and Porrex"	
"The Spanish Moor's Tragedy"[21]	

"The Spanish Moor's Tragedy" and *Titus Andronicus* share the character of the Moor; "Troy's Revenge" and *Julius Caesar* share the use of classical history and myth. Based purely on guesswork, *Titus Andronicus* and "The Stepmother's Tragedy" may share ghoulish meals. That connection is suggested by the possibility that a ballad, "The Lady Isabella's Tragedy; or, The Step-Mother's Cruelty," was Henry Chettle's source for the Admiral's play.[22] In that ballad, Isabella is sent to the cook, already enlisted as murderer by the stepmother, with a request that a "fair and milk-white Doe" be dressed for dinner. The cook bakes Isabella in a pie, which is served to her father, but he won't eat until Isabella herself comes to the table. The scullery-boy blurts out what happened, crying that he offered his "own heart's blood" to save the girl. The father has the stepmother burned at the stake and the cook boiled in lead.[23] "Ferrex and Porrex" might also have used the motifs of a vengeful mother and dismemberment, precipitated by a brother's murder. The story itself had been dramatized earlier in a play called "2 Seven Deadly Sins," in which Ferrex and Porrex represent the sin of Envy. Based on players' names in the surviving plot, "2 Seven Deadly Sins" has been assigned to Strange's Men in 1592, but David Kathman argues provocatively for an assignment to the Chamberlain's Men in 1597–98.[24]

The Admiral's Men acquired three middle-class crime plays in 1599–1600, and the Chamberlain's Men had nothing comparable unless they were still playing *A Warning for Fair Women*. There is certainly a coincidence of timing in that the Admiral's Men purchased their three in the fall of 1599, just as *A Warning for Fair Women* was appearing in print (S. R. November 17, 1599, Q1599). For "Page of Plymouth," there was also a coincidence in the story of a husband's murder by his adulterous wife.[25] According to a source for the Admiral's play (the second story in "Sundry strange and inhumaine Murthers," 1591), Ulalia Glandfield was married by her father against her will to a wealthy widower named Page. Previously, her father had encouraged a match with young George Strangwidge. Ulalia and George carried on their romance after the marriage, and on her own, Ulalia attempted several times to poison Page. When she failed, the lovers hired Robert Priddis and Tom Stone to do the deed. The murderers slipped into Page's bedroom one night, strangled him with his own kerchief, then broke his neck against the bed. Priddis, being Page's servant, was soon suspected; he gave up Stone, and soon both Ulalia and George were implicated. The four were tried by Sir Francis Drake, found guilty, and executed.[26] The Admiral's Men spent £10 to buy women's gowns for "Page of Plymouth." If this purchase was to clothe Ulalia Page in finery, and thus to suggest her vanity, the Admiral's play could have evoked a shopping scene in *A Warning for Fair Women* in which Anne Sanders cannot buy what she wants because of her tight-fisted husband.[27] "Cox of Collumpton" is a crime play of a different sort. The story survives in an entry by Simon Forman, who saw the play at the Rose on March 9, 1600. Forman was fascinated more by the coincidence that the murders all occurred on St. Mark's Day than by the murders themselves, but he does give some details: Cox started the chain of events by killing his uncle (on St. Mark's Day [April 25]) to get his land. Seven years later to the day, Cox was himself killed. Exactly a year later, two of Cox's sons, Peter and John, drowned their older brother, Henry. And one year after that on St. Mark's Day, the remaining sons killed themselves: Peter, frightened by the apparition of a bear, beat out his brains against a post, and John stabbed himself.[28] The third domestic crime play in the Admiral's repertory must have told much the same story as one of the narratives woven into Robert Yarington's *Two Lamentable Tragedies* (Q1601).[29] In Yarington's play, Thomas Merry, a low-end London seller of food and beer, grows envious of the prosperity of his neighbor, Thomas Beech, a chandler. Luring Beech to his shop, Merry beats him with fifteen hammer-strokes. Merry's sister, Rachel, and his servant discover the crime but promise to keep quiet. To remove a potential witness, Merry murders Beech's servant boy in the candle shop. Merry is caught when his servant, overcome with guilt, confesses to the authorities.[30] Two features of *Two Lamentable Tragedies*, and thus perhaps also of "The Tragedy of Thomas Merry," look back to the Chamberlain's *A Warning for Fair Women*: the crime scene is London, and the hangings are staged. In Yarington's play, both Merry and his sister are hanged onstage.[31] In *A*

Warning for Fair Women, only George Browne is; his accomplices, including Anne Sanders, are executed offstage.

The comedies at the Rose and Globe appear to have the least in common, but given the number of lost plays for both companies, any number of cross-repertorial parallels is possible.

Admiral's Men	*Chamberlain's Men*
Shoemakers' Holiday	*As You Like It* (new)
"Bear a Brain"[32]	*Every Man In his Humour*
	(?continuation)
"Poor Man's Paradise"[33]	*Every Man Out of his Humour* (new)
"Tristram of Lyons"[34]	"Cloth Breeches and Velvet Hose"
	(new)
Old Fortunatus	*Much Ado About Nothing*
	(?continuation)
Patient Grissil	*A Midsummer Night's Dream* (?revival)
"Damon and Pythias"	*The Merchant of Venice* (?revival)
"Seven Wise Masters"	
"Golden Ass and Cupid and Psyche"	
Blind Beggar of Bednal Green	
"Fair Constance of Rome," part one	
"Fair Constance of Rome," part two[35]	

The Chamberlain's plays offer motifs such as the pastoral elements of *As You Like It*, *A Midsummer Night's Dream*, and *The Merchant of Venice;* the cross-dressed Portia and Rosalind; the "humors" character in *Every Man In his Humour*, *Every Man Out of his Humour*, and *Much Ado About Nothing;* and the successful love plots of the Shakespearean comedies, none of which are obvious links with the Admiral's comedies. However, one plausible repertorial connection is *The Shoemakers' Holiday* by Thomas Dekker with the Chamberlain's "Cloth Breeches and Velvet Hose." Dekker's play is famous for celebrating members of the "gentle craft"; "Cloth Breeches and Velvet Hose," if it followed the likely source of Robert Greene's *Quip for an Upstart Courtier*, would have paraded, though not celebrated, a variety of tradesmen. In the last dream sequence in Greene's prose narrative "A Quaint Dispute Between Velvet-Breeches and Cloth-Breeches," the narrator meets two headless figures—one dressed in velvet breeches, the other in cloth—each of whom claims to be superior to the other. The narrator stops passersby to form a jury to decide the matter. Greene uses the impaneling as an opportunity to satirize the trades, including shoemakers who are characterized as "good fellowes [and] spendethriftes."[36] If the play followed

Greene's narrative, it was probably estate satire, broader in its range of trades than *The Shoemakers' Holiday* and possibly darker in view.

The list of comedies for the Admiral's Men illustrates a long-standing repertorial principle: many comedies, with many different comedic formulas. The stories of two lost plays — "Damon and Pythias" and "The Golden Ass and Cupid and Psyche" — are recoverable to some degree from their classical antecedents. The primary plot line of "Damon and Pythias" must have been the loyalty of the men, one standing for the other in place of execution, while the condemned leaves the country to arrange his affairs before his death. Astonished when the condemned man returns, the tyrant who decreed the execution lifts the death sentence as a reward to them both. The primary focus of "The Golden Ass and Cupid and Psyche" was surely the love story of sororal envy and female curiosity, motifs in contrast with the fraternity of "Damon and Pythias" and fratricide of "Ferrex and Porrex." For "The Poor Man's Paradise" as well as "Bear a Brain," I cannot add to W. W. Greg's bleak admission that "[n]othing is known of this play."[37] However, for "Tristram of Lyons," there are two possible story lines. One is the mainstream Arthurian tale of Tristram and Isolde; however, I incline toward the pseudo-Arthurian, pseudo-Spenserian source of Christopher Middleton's *The Famous Historie of Chinon of England, . . . With the worthy Atchiuement of Sir Lancelot du Lake, and Sir Tristram du Lions for faire Laura . . ."* (S. R. January 20, 1596, Q1597), even though the story gives Tristram no solo adventures.[38] The appeal of Middleton's romance is that the Admiral's Men had had a very successful play called "Chinon of England" three years before. The printing of Middleton's text came a bit late for the debut of "Chinon" on January 3, 1596, but it was perfect timing for a spin-off on Tristram in 1599–1600. Another play crafted out of romance materials was "The Seven Wise Masters," one source for which, *The Seven Sages of Rome*, had been printed throughout the early modern period.[39] The playwrights may have focused on the frame story, in which a youthful Diocletian is protected by his seven wise masters, who tell exemplary tales to counteract the vile charges made against the boy by his wicked stepmother.[40] A variation of that motif governs the romance materials about Constance, who, in Chaucer's version of the story, is persecuted by two mothers-in-law. Suggesting a nascent form of the tragicomedy, the evil matrons of "The Seven Wise Masters" and the two-part "Fair Constance of Rome" evoke tragedies in the Admiral's own repertory, "Ferrex and Porrex" and "The Stepmother's Tragedy." In terms of structure, three of the lost comedies had affinities with multipart or serial designs: "The Golden Ass and

Cupid and Psyche," perhaps enfolding the story of the lovers into that
of a man turned into an ass; "The Seven Wise Masters," in the sequential responsiveness of the masters' stories to the stepmother's; and the
trials of "Fair Constance of Rome," spread over two plays. Against all
this guesswork, one conclusion seems sure: the Admiral's Men, by
spending 400s. for its apparel and an additional 360s. on unspecified
purchases, meant for "The Seven Wise Masters" to be a spectacular
offering.

The three comedies surviving from the Admiral's repertory do not
provide significantly stronger connections across company lines than
are suggested by the lost plays. *Patient Grissil* shares a focus on testing,
class, and patient women in its own repertory with the stories of Damon
and Pythias, Cupid and Psyche, Fair Constance, and (in contrast) the
impatient Ulalia Page; but the play in the Chamberlain's repertory to
offer the best match is yet to come, *All's Well That Ends Well* (1602?).
The Admiral's play of *Old Fortunatus* is a grab-bag of popular motifs.
These include its moral-play structure with the focus on avarice, the
semi-dumb shows, the Faustian fall of Fortunatus and his sons, exotic
Eastern settings and characters, magic tricks, the dysfunctional love
plot involving Agripyne (herself no model of virtue and constancy), and
perhaps a hint of the Jonsonian "humors" character in Fortunatus'
doltish sons. *The Blind Beggar of Bednal Green* is also a grab-bag, but the
most notable feature is disguise. This motif drove the Admiral's block-
buster play of 1596–97, *The Blind Beggar of Alexandria* (Q1598).[41] In the
next year, 1598–99, the Admiral's Men acquired *Look About You*
(Q1600), which out-disguises *The Blind Beggar of Alexandria* by extending the device to nearly everyone in the play. In *The Blind Beggar of Bednal Green*, the character of Momford repeats the motif of *The Blind
Beggar of Alexandria* in which a falsely accused nobleman disguises himself as a blind man; but Momford, unlike the tricksteresque Cleanthus/
Irus, rescues both the romantic story line (by protecting his daughter
from rape) and the political one (by exposing the plot that had branded
him a traitor). Though not the principals in the political story, Henry
VI and Humphrey, Duke of Gloucester, are characters in *The Blind Beggar of Bednal Green*, which thereby associates itself with the Chamberlain's plays on the Wars of the Roses, specifically *The First Part of the
Contention*. In the Admiral's play, Gloucester woos and wins Elinor; in
the Chamberlain's play, Gloucester is helpless to prevent her fall, and
he is subsequently murdered.[42] In Bess Momford's near-recognition
scene with her "blind" father, audiences at both playhouses could have
seen parallels between Lancelot and Old Gobbo in *The Merchant of Ven-*

ice; and, in Momford's first disguise as a soldier, these audiences could have seen varieties of real and disguised soldiers in *The Shoemakers' Holiday* (Rafe), *Every Man In his Humour* (Musco), and *A Larum for London* (Stump). Two allusions in *The Blind Beggar of Bednal Green* invoke current Shakespearean plays specifically: Young Playney invokes the fate of Lavinia in *Titus Andronicus*, threatening Bess that he will "turn a *Tereus*," murdering her father, cutting out her tongue, ravishing her, and leaving her "wretched"; two con men attempt to lure the bumpkin, young Tom Strowd, into a bawdy house by advertising its delights, one of which is to see "the stabbing of *Julius Caesar* in the *French* Capitol by a sort of Dutch *Mesapotamians*."[43]

Sometime after October 16, 1600, when Forman saw an "Oldcastle" play at the Rose, the Admiral's Men left London to travel north, where they performed at Hardwick Hall in Derbyshire in the week of November 6.[44] They would return from the tour no later than mid-December to permanent residence at the Fortune. Much of the repertory acquired in 1599–1600 probably made the move with them, particularly plays advertising their new venue such as *Old Fortunatus*. The quality of that repertory in its mix of genres and diverse subjects suggests a commercial appeal that would have served the Admiral's Men well in competition with the Chamberlain's Men, whether across the street at Maid Lane or across the Thames at Golding Lane. The Admiral's repertory may also suggest kinds of plays now lost from the Chamberlain's repertory. One is the domestic play, either of crime or patience. The Chamberlain's Men were to follow *A Warning for Fair Women* with *A Yorkshire Tragedy* (Q1608), the repertory date of which is uncertain. They were to replicate the character of patient Griselda not only in Helena in *All's Well That Ends Well* (?1602–3) but also Anabell in *The Fair Maid of Bristow* (?1603–4) and Luce in *The London Prodigal* (?1603–4). They were to raise the issue of parental abuse in *The Miseries of Enforced Marriage* (Q1607), in which young Scarborrow is forced to abandon his betrothed and marry a woman chosen by his guardian. Another missing play might have combined romance materials and disguise, as does *As You Like It*, but perhaps more in the vein of the two "blind beggar" plays. Also, there might have been another history play. Those in the offing — *Thomas Lord Cromwell* (Q1602), "Stuhlweissenburg" (1602),[45] and *Sejanus* (1603), to be followed by the Scottish plays of "Gowrie" (1604) and *Macbeth* (1605) — show that the Chamberlain's Men continued an interest in historical-tragical plays both domestic and foreign, from times ancient and present. And yet, teasing as these possibilities are in a recovery of the Chamberlain's repertory, there are limits to the reach of conjecture. The texts of surviving plays, the titles of those lost, the identification of source material, a comparison of offerings, and a demonstrable interest in popular stories and formulas provide insight into the logic of a company's repertory, but they cannot explain the ingenuity of its practitioners to identify a subject with theatrical potential and turn it into a stage-worthy play.

APPENDIX
PAYMENTS BY THE ADMIRAL'S MEN, 1599–1600

The following table contains the play titles for which Philip Henslowe made payments on behalf of the Admiral's Men, July 15, 1599–June 20, 1600. I include the names of the dramatists, the range of dates over which payments were made, and the payment total "for the book." The assignment of genre for lost plays is guesswork. The titles of lost plays are in quotation marks; those of surviving plays are in italics. Plays that I consider brought to the stage are in bold.

Comedy	History	Tragedy
Gentle Craft/Shoemakers' Holiday *Gentle Craft/Shoemakers' Holiday* Thomas Dekker 7/15/99, 60s.	**"Robert II, King of Scots"** Thomas Dekker, Ben Jonson, Henry Chettle, "other gent" 9/3/99–9/27/99, 90s.	"Pastoral Tragedy" George Chapman 7/17/99, 40s.
"Bear a Brain" Thomas Dekker 8/1/99, 40s.	*1 John Oldcastle* Anthony Munday, Michael Drayton, Robert Wilson, Richard Hathway 10/16/99, <200s.	**"Stepmother's Tragedy"** Henry Chettle 8/23/99–10/14/99, 120s.
"Poor Man's Paradise" William Haughton 8/20/99–8/25/99, 30s.	**"2 John Oldcastle"** Anthony Munday, Michael Drayton, Robert Wilson, Richard Hathway 10/16/99–12/26, <200s., 80s.	**"Page of Plymouth"** Thomas Dekker, Ben Jonson 8/10/99–9/2/99 160s.
"Tristram of Lyons" (no dramatist named) 10/13/99, 60s.	**"2 Henry Richmond"** Robert Wilson 11/8/99, 160s.	**"Troy's Revenge, with the Tragedy of Polyphemus"** 10/4/99, 8s. (to the tailor)

Patient Grissil
Thomas Dekker, Henry
Chettle, William Haughton
10/16/99–12/29/99, 210s.

Old Fortunatus
Thomas Dekker
11/9/99–11/30/99, 120s.

"Arcadian Virgin"
Henry Chettle, William
Haughton
12/13/99–12/17/99, 15s.

"Truth's Supplication to
Candlelight"
Thomas Dekker
1/18/00–1/30/00, 40s.

"Damon & Pythias"
Henry Chettle
2/16/00–4/27/00, 120s.

"Seven Wise Masters"
Henry Chettle, Thomas
Dekker, William Haughton,
John Day
3/1/00–3/8/00, 120s.

**"Golden Ass and Cupid
and Psyche"**
Thomas Dekker, John Day,
Henry Chettle
4/27/00–5/14/00, 120s.

"Devil & his Dame"
William Haughton
5/6/00, 5s.

*Blind Beggar of Bednal
Green*
Henry Chettle, John Day
5/26/00, 110s.

"Owen Tudor"
Michael Drayton,
Anthony Munday,
Richard Hathway,
Robert Wilson
1/10/00, 80s.

"Jugurtha"
William Boyle
2/9/00, 30s.

"English Fugitives"
William Haughton
4/16/00–4/24/00, 30s.

**"Strange News out of
Poland"**
William Haughton,
Mr. Pett
5/17/00–5/25/00, 120s.

"Judas"
William Haughton
5/27/00, 10s.

"Cox of Collumpton"
William Haughton,
John Day
11/1/99–11/14/99, 100s.

**"Tragedy of Thomas
Merry"**
William Haughton,
John Day
11/21/99–12/6/99, 100s.

"Orphans Tragedy"
Henry Chettle
11/27/99–9/24/01, 20s.

"Italian Tragedy"
John Day
1/10/00, 40s.

"Spanish Moor's Tragedy"
Thomas Dekker, William
Haughton, John Day
2/13/00, 60s.

"Ferrex & Porrex"
William Haughton
3/18/99–4/3/00, 95s.

'Wooing of Death"
Henry Chettle
4/26/00, 20s.

"Fair Constance"
Anthony Munday, Michael
Drayton, Richard Hathway,
Thomas Dekker
6/3/00–6/14/00, 109s.

"2 Fair Constance"
Richard Hathway
6/20/00, 20s.

Other:
John Marston's book,
9/28/99, 40s.
Henry Chettle & John
Day's book, 6/19, 10s.

NOTES

1. S. P. Cerasano, "Edward Alleyn: 1566–1626," in *Edward Alleyn: Elizabethan Actor, Jacobean Gentleman*, ed. Aileen Reid and Robert Maniura, 1994 (London: Dulwich Picture Gallery, 1994), 19.

2. Bernard Beckerman, *Shakespeare at the Globe, 1599–1609* (New York: Macmillan, 1962).

3. Roslyn Lander Knutson, *The Repertory of Shakespeare's Company, 1594–1613* (Fayetteville: University of Arkansas Press, 1991).

4. Andrew Gurr, *The Shakespearian Playing Companies* (Oxford: Clarendon Press, 1996), 287. Gurr is even more confident in *The Shakespeare Company, 1594–1642*: "The two companies quite deliberately staged their stories in parallel": (Cambridge: Cambridge University Press, 2004), 134. Robert Boies Sharpe epitomizes the pre-Beckerman position; he implies that the Chamberlain's Men had a smaller and classier repertory than the Admiral's repertory when he characterizes the latter as "aimed . . . at the tastes of the *older*, less sophisticated, more middle-class types": *The Real War of the Theaters: Shakespeare's Fellows in Rivalry with the Admiral's Men, 1594–1603: Repertories, Devices, and Types* (Boston: D. C. Heath, 1935), 19.

5. E. K. Chambers, *The Elizabethan Stage*, 4 vols. (Oxford: Clarendon Press, 1923), 1:373. I use play titles as specified in the index of *Henslowe's Diary*, 2nd ed., ed. R. A. Foakes (1961; Cambridge: Cambridge University Press, 2002) (for lost plays) and W. W. Greg, *A Bibliography of the English Printed Drama to the Restoration*, 4 vols. (London: The Bibliographical Society, 1970) (for surviving plays).

6. Alfred Harbage, S. Schoenbaum, and Sylvia Stoler Wagonheim, *Annals of English Drama, 975–1700*, 3rd. ed. (London: Routledge, 1989).

7. *Thomas Platter's Travels in England 1599*, trans. Clare Williams (London: Jonathan Cape, 1937), 166.

8. Greg, *Bibliography*, 1:15. These entries are duplicated in Register C for May 27 and 29, respectively.

9. Arthur Collins, ed., *Letters and Memorials of State*, 2 vols. (London: T. Osborne, 1746), 2:175. Scholars used to assume that this "Oldcastle" was one of Shakespeare's

Falstaff plays. Gurr gives guarded support to my identification of it, in *The Repertory of Shakespeare's Company*, 95–97, as a play genuinely on Oldcastle: *The Shakespearian Playing Companies*, 303 n. 47.

10. In "Evidence for the Assignment of Plays to the Repertory of Shakespeare's Company," I argue for the attribution of "The Tartarian Cripple" to the Chamberlain's repertory: *Medieval and Renaissance Drama in England* 4 (1989): 78–84.

11. A dubious case: Henslowe paid only 30s. for "Jugurtha," but his wording—"for a new booke"—suggests payment in full.

12. See Scott McMillin and Sally-Beth MacLean, *The Queen's Men and Their Plays*, for a discussion of the role of the Queen's Men in the development of the English history play (Cambridge: Cambridge University Press, 1998), 32–36.

13. There is no obvious reason why the Richmond play is designated a second part, but one possibility not previously considered is that it was the second part of a projected Owen Tudor–Henry Richmond serial. Robert Wilson is a common denominator, being the payee for "2 Henry Richmond" and one of the foursome of payees for "Owen Tudor." If the 80s. for "Owen Tudor" is added to the 160s. for "2 Henry Richmond," the sum equals 240s., the equivalent of £6 per play. Elizabethan audiences didn't seem to mind if their serials were not all that sequential.

14. Foakes, ed., *Henslowe's Diary*, 126. I silently expand contractions.

15. Ibid., 287–88. See also Greg, ed., *Henslowe's Diary, Part 2: Commentary* (London: A. H. Bullen, 1908), 207–8.

16. History (but not Holinshed) has preserved a theatrical line for Owen's exit: "The head which used to lie in Queen Katherine's lap would now lie in the executioner's basket."

17. Gurr discusses the entanglement of the "Oldcastle" plays with the "Falstaff" plays and patronage, as do I in *The Repertory of Shakespeare's Company*, 95–97: *The Shakespearian Playing Companies*, 245 and 303 n. 47.

18. "The True Tragedy of Richard Duke of York," in *Shakespeare's Plays in Quarto*, ed. Michael J. B. Allen and Kenneth Muir (Berkeley: University of California Press, 1981), C4.

19. Elizabethan playgoers seem not to have made much distinction between tragical histories and historical tragedies. Confusing boundaries more, there are comical-historical-pastorals such as *Look About You* (Q1600), which is peopled by the historical figures of Henry II and his sons (including Richard the Lion-Hearted and John) along with a clutch of earls, but to which are added the quasi-historical Robin Hood and the utterly fanciful trickster, Skinke. The action of *Look About You*—which takes place at court, in the Tower, on London city streets, and in the country—is comical, except for the plot line of Queen Elinor's commissioning of the murder of the king's mistress (Rosamond) and the dispersing of noblemen at the end to various penances and crusades. Any of the lost plays here discussed could have been similarly a stew of generic formulas.

20. James Shapiro, "*The Scot's Tragedy* and the Politics of Popular Drama," *English Literary Renaissance* 23 (1993): 428–49.

21. A dubious case: Henslowe paid only 60s. for it, yet its consortium of dramatists has a good track record for finishing scripts. The play is often considered the same as *Lust's Dominion, or the Lascivious Queen*, but many scholars, including myself, are skeptical.

22. Andrew Clark, *Domestic Drama: A Survey of the Origins, Antecedents and Nature of the Domestic Play in England, 1500–1640*, 2 vols. (Salzburg: Institut für Englische Sprache

und Literatur, 1975), 2:419. Clark cites but does not show enthusiasm for the ballad as the source of the play.

23. *The Roxburghe Ballads*, ed. W. Chappell, 9 vols. (1869; New York: AMS Press, 1966), 6:650–52.

24. David Kathman, "Reconsidering *The Seven Deadly Sins*," *Early Theatre* 7.1 (2004): 13–44. There is not a scene in the surviving plot of "2 Seven Deadly Sins" in which the queen killed Porrex in his sleep and "cut him into small péeces" (Raphael Holinshed, *Chronicles of England, Scotland, and Ireland* [1587; New York: AMS Press, 1965], 1:450), but there might have been one in "Ferrex and Porrex."

25. I use "adulterous" in the loose sense that the women had extramarital suitors.

26. Two ballads, "The Lamentation of Master Page's Wife of Plimmouth" and "The Lamentation of George Strangwidge," serve as scaffold speeches, emphasizing the love the condemned still shared and the cruelty of the wife's father to force her into the wrong marriage: Chappell, ed., *The Roxburghe Ballads*, 1:555–58, 558–60. The tract "Sundry strange and inhumaine Murthers" provides additional details of the crime: for example, Priddis was promised "seavenscore pounds" (B2v) for the murder, and Ulalia was sleeping apart from her husband on the night of the murder because of the "untimely birth of a child . . . dead borne," B3.

27. Thomas Heywood, *A Warning for Fair Women: A Critical Edition*, ed. Charles Dale Cannon (The Hague: Mouton, 1975).

28. Cerasano, "Philip Henslowe, Simon Forman, and the Theatrical Community of the 1590s," *Shakespeare Quarterly* 44.2 (1993): 145–58, esp. 157–58. Forman seems also drawn to the motif of family murders and their discovery because he appends a note to the Cox entry that tells of a Mr. Hammon, slain by his son, who predicted during the murder that the son's laughter would give him away, which it did. Did the Admiral's Men dramatize the story line about the bear? There was precedent in the Chamberlain's popular *Mucedorus* (Q1598).

29. Robert Yarington, *Two Lamentable Tragedies*, Tudor Facsimile Texts (1913; New York: AMS Press, 1970). In *Domestic Drama*, 2:423–25, Clark summarizes the complex arguments by previous scholars on the relationship of *Two Lamentable Tragedies* to "The Tragedy of Thomas Merry," as well as to "The Orphans Tragedy" and "The Italian Tragedy."

30. Yarington's drama provides additional gruesome details of the crime. For example, Merry also beats the servant boy, Thomas Winchester, leaving the hammer stuck in the boy's head; according to the stage directions, it is still there when the comatose boy is brought onstage in a futile effort to identify the murderer: "*Bringes him forth in a chaire, with a hammer sticking in his head*": Yarington, *Two Lamentable Tragedies*, D3v. Merry chops up Beech's body, putting the head and legs in one bag and the trunk in another; he dumps the bags in ditches at Paris Garden, where one is found by two watermen and the other by a gentleman walking his dog. Merry's servant, Harry Williams, gets branded for withholding information on the crime. Merry's corpse, but not his sister's, is hung up in chains at Mile End Green.

31. If the property in Henslowe's inventory lists, "j frame for the heading of Black Jone," is for the play "Blacke Jonne," and if "Jone" is "Joan," the Admiral's Men may have beheaded a woman onstage in 1598 (Foakes, ed., *Henslowe's Diary*, 321, 323; Clark, *Domestic Drama*, 3:421).

32. A dubious case: Henslowe paid only 40s. to Dekker for "Bear a Brain," yet he specifies "in fulle payment" (Foakes, ed., *Henslowe's Diary*, 123).

33. A dubious case: Henslowe paid only 30s. to Haughton for "Poor Man's Paradise," but his wording, "for his Boocke," could mean payment in full (Foakes, ed., *Henslowe's Diary*, 123).

34. A dubious case: Henslowe paid only 60s. for "Tristram of Lyons," but his wording, "for the Booke," could mean payment in full (Foakes, ed., *Henslowe's Diary*, 124).

35. A dubious case: Henslowe recorded only one payment of 20s. for the second part of "Fair Constance of Rome," but additional payments for it could have been made in the hiatus in Henslowe's entries from June 20, 1600, to December 20, a hiatus broken only by one payment on September 6.

36. Robert Greene, *Quip for an Upstart Courtier*, 1592, D4v. I explore possible connections between Greene's *Quip for an Upstart Courtier* and "Cloth Breeches and Velvet Hose" in "Filling Fare: The Appetite for Current Issues and Traditional Forms in the Repertory of the Chamberlain's Men," *Medieval and Renaissance Drama in England* 15 (2003): 60–63.

37. Greg, *Henslowe's Diary*, 2:205, in the entry for "The Poor Man's Paradise." For "Bear a Brain," Greg repeats the convoluted conjectures linking the title to various lost and surviving plays, including the anonymous *Look About You*, but he does not find the connections persuasive: Greg, *Henslowe's Diary*, 2:204.

38. Edmund Spenser invents adventures for the youthful Tristram as squire to Calidore in *The Faerie Queene*.

39. Michael L. Hays, "A Bibliography of Dramatic Adaptations of Medieval Romances and Renaissance Chivalric Romances First Available in English through 1616," *Research Opportunities in Renaissance Drama* 28 (1985): 93.

40. The Admiral's Men had a play called "Diocletian" in November 1594; it received two shows, returning to Henslowe a very respectable average of 48s. 6d.

41. The disguise motif is, of course, an old one, but the Admiral's Men appear to have reinvigorated it with plays such as *A Knack to Know an Honest Man* (Q1596) and "Disguises," which debuted in October 1595. *The Blind Beggar of Alexandria* debuted in February 1596, receiving twenty-two performances through April 1, 1597.

42. The political and romantic plots of *The Blind Beggar of Bednal Green* invite comparison with *Fair Em* (c. 1592), which is identifiable with the Chamberlain's Men but not necessarily in 1599–1600. Like *Fair Em*, in which William the Conqueror is a lustful and foolish suitor, there are royals at play in *The Blind Beggar of Bednal Green*. Like the fickle Manvile in *Fair Em*, Young Playney in *The Blind Beggar of Bednal Green* dumps Bess, then propositions her. For attribution of *Fair Em* to the Chamberlain's Men, see Knutson, *The Repertory of Shakespeare's Company*, 59.

43. *The Blind Beggar of Bednal Green*, in *The Works of John Day*, ed. A. H. Bullen, 2 vols. (1659; London: Chiswick Press, 1881), 1:80, 72.

44. Cerasano documents the Rose performance in "Henslowe, Forman, and the Theatrical Community," 158. Barbara Palmer and John Wasson document the tour performance in an unpublished paper submitted to the Theater History seminar, "Acting Companies," at the Shakespeare Association of America annual meeting in Miami, Florida, 2001; Palmer and Wasson's work has been supported by the REED project and the National Endowment for the Humanities.

45. Duke Julius of Stettin-Pomerania saw "Stuhlweissenburg" on September 13, 1602, at a playhouse unnamed but not the Fortune or Blackfriars. If that playhouse was the Globe, the play gave the company a use for costumes from "The Tartarian Cripple." Jean MacIntyre does not find "suites" of plays that reuse sets of specialty clothing in the Chamberlain's repertory, but she is not taking into account lost plays: *Costumes and Scripts in the Elizabethan Theatres* (Edmonton: University of Alberta Press, 1992), 200.

The Study of Shakespearean Playbooks

Jay L. Halio

THEATER HISTORIANS HAVE KNOWN FOR A LONG TIME THE VALUE OF playbooks[1] when trying to reconstruct or imagine productions long since vanished from the stage. Reviews of productions are helpful to an extent; but insofar as performances may vary—sometimes widely—from one night to the next, one cannot trust them completely, except when reviewers tend to agree with each other on what happened on-stage, and then only when they attended performances of the same production but on different occasions. The memoirs of leading actors, or their biographies, are also useful up to a point, that is, when their memories can be trusted to relate an accurate and truthful account of a production as it actually happened, and not as the writer thought it happened or wished it had happened.

We come back, then, to the playbook, or copies of it, or the preparation books or workbooks on which the playbooks were based. While these, again, may not tell us exactly how a production was staged, they may suggest ways in which the production was at least conceived by the actor/manager or, in today's theater, the director. Fortunately, scores of Shakespearean playbooks survive—not any, of course, from Shakespeare's Globe, which burned down in 1613, perhaps sending many of them to oblivion, but those of a subsequent age. These, beginning with the Smock Alley playbooks of the 1670s, have been preserved in the archives of the Folger Shakespeare Library, the Harvard Theatre Collection, and elsewhere.[2]

The extant Smock Alley playbooks (from the theater in Dublin located in Smock Alley) were made on copies of the third Folio (1663–64) with notations marked in the margins. Unlike later playbooks interleaved with copious notations on opposite pages of the script, these playbooks are rather more sparsely marked up. Nevertheless, they give us some idea of how the plays were staged, especially regarding what parts of the script might have *not* been staged. The Smock Alley playbook of *Macbeth* offers a good example of what may be found and its importance for theater historians. Actors' calls abound, along with a few stage directions written in the narrow margins of the text. More importantly, we can find several passages and even whole scenes marked for deletion, such as most of the Porter's speech in 2.3, much of 3.3, all of 3.6, much of 4.2 and 4.3 (the longest scene in the play, often trimmed in production), and all of 5.2. This being Shakespeare's shortest play, one might wonder why there are so many cuts. Perhaps one reason was to allow time for another short play, a comedy or farce, to follow, and for a change of setting. Movable painted flats were used after the Restoration owing to the influence of the French theater, but the time needed to change these was not nearly so extensive as later on in the nineteenth century, when far more elaborate sets were used, requiring a good deal more time to shift. No, more likely considerations of taste and decorum dictated some of these cuts, such as the omission of the Porter's bawdier lines or the murder of Lady Macduff and her children.

Later playbooks of *Macbeth* also have noteworthy stage directions and other annotations. Edwin Forrest's playbook of the *Macbeth* dating from 1868–69 provides some interesting notations. Scene 1.5 is marked as having "Strong Red Lights streaming from behind the Castle gates," as if to suggest hellgate. When Lady Macbeth greets her husband with "Great Glamis" (1.5.54), she "rushes into his arms L.C." Then, asking when Duncan departs their castle (1.5.59), "Lady Macbeth suddenly grasps his arm & looks him in the eye—a pause—then he says—'as he purposes.'" Later, at 1.7.47–60, many of Lady Macbeth's words are underlined to denote special emphasis. Henry Irving's preparation copy, dated 1888 and based on his own edition of the play, omits 3.5–6 but includes Thomas Middleton's song "Come away" as a separate scene after 4.1. His production was in six acts, with 4.2 also omitted.

If *Macbeth* is Shakespeare's shortest tragedy, *Hamlet* and *King Lear* are among his longest, whether in conflated editions or in the second quarto or Folio versions. Hence, they pose problems for the stage, especially in the nineteenth century, when spectacularly elaborate stage sets had become popular and time was needed to shift scenes. Understandably, then, in many productions of *Hamlet*, passages or scenes involving Reynaldo, Voltemand, Cornelius, and Fortinbras are absent. But some other omissions were also made, a few of them somewhat surprising. For example, in Charles Kean's acting edition, on which his playbook was formulated in the 1850s, a good part of 3.3, the prayer scene, is cut; only 3.3.1–4 and 24–35 are retained. Possibly these cuts resulted from the desire to respect mid-Victorian sensibilities, regarding not only religious scruples but also the gentlemanly qualities of the hero, who in this scene appears as both a bloodthirsty and an irreligious avenger. In John Barrymore's productions (1923–24), all of 4.1–4 was omitted, probably for other reasons, and, in his original staging of the play, the Ghost did not appear in 1.5; instead, a blue light indicated the supernatural presence.

Earlier, in the eighteenth century, David Garrick based his playbook on a 1703 quarto of *Hamlet*. There, following a still earlier tradition, inverted commas were used to mark those passages that were found inessential to the drama and thus not performed onstage. Or so the preface proclaims. But in Garrick's own playbook, some of the passages thus marked were, in fact, used on stage. For example, Hamlet's advice to the Players, 3.2.1–45, which is not necessary to carry forward the action and, therefore, appears marked in inverted commas, was spoken—hardly surprising, after all, as the passage is a favorite among actors and theatergoers and is rarely omitted. On the other hand, the dumb show following 3.2.135, not in inverted commas but obviously regarded as somewhat redundant, is marked for deletion in the playbook. The 1703 quarto omits 3.4.172–79, but these lines are restored by a manuscript hand: they are clearly important as Hamlet's more considered judgment concerning his murder of Polonius, though in some other acting versions they do not appear.

Besides its length, *King Lear* presents other problems. Nahum Tate's rewrite of Shakespeare's great tragedy held the boards for 150 years, beginning in 1681. Tate eliminated the Fool and restored the happy ending of the source play (*King Leir*, 1593), which all of the narrative accounts going back to Geoffrey of Monmouth's twelfth-century history of Britain retain. He even introduced a love relationship between Edgar and Cordelia, ending in their union. From the mid-eighteenth century onwards, some attempts were made to restore at least parts of Shakespeare's original script, but what audiences saw and heard well into the nineteenth century was basically Tate's version. In America, for example, as late as 1868, Forrest's playbook was still based on Tate, though, like others, he began using lines from Shakespeare's text as well as some of his own verse. But the trend away from Tate had begun. In the early nineteenth century, Edmund Kean restored some of Shakespeare's lines and, most notably, the original ending—unsuccessfully at first but later more acceptably. And in 1838, William Charles Macready reintroduced the Fool, played by a woman, Priscilla Horton.[3]

Edmund's son, Charles Kean, not so great an actor as his father, staged a spectacular version of *King Lear* in the 1850s at the Princess' Theatre, London. His stage manager's workbook, which reflects the actual playbook, contains many notes on backstage activity, along with indications of deletions, calls, stage business, blockings, music cues, and the like.[4] Some of the more interesting cuts occur at 1.1.268–69 (Cordelia's leavetaking), all of 3.5, 3.7 (Gloucester's blinding), 4.3, 4.5, and parts of 4.1 (transposed after 4.2). Act 5 in Charles Kean's production began with 4.7, Lear's reconciliation with Cordelia, which, according to William Winter, was Kean's finest scene.[5] Many lines in 5.1 and elsewhere in act 5 are marked for deletion, evidently to bring the play to a speedier conclusion with Lear's final words (5.3.312).

Shakespeare's *Richard III* was largely transformed, if not entirely rewritten, by another Restoration playwright and actor, Colley Cibber, for his production in 1700. It is this version that, like Tate's *King Lear*, held sway for the next two centuries. George Frederick Cooke's playbook, signed and dated 1810, is typical of scripts used during this period and was apparently marked by Cooke for the instruction of provincial managers.[6] It is a mélange of verse, with pieces of Shakespeare's *3 Henry VI*, *Richard II*, *2 Henry IV*, and *Henry V*, as well as a good many of Cibber's own lines. Although nineteenth-century critics ridiculed many of Cibber's alterations, his most famous lines, "Off with his Head; so much for Buckingham" and "Richard's himself again," are still sometimes used in modern productions of Shakespeare's play. Cooke's playbook marks a number of small deletions, some blockings and stage business, and a good many stage directions inserted on facing pages, as at p. 18, which describe the way Henry VI's corpse is brought in. On p. 65 opposite (the ghost scene) appears the notation: "If traps are inconvenient, the Ghosts walk on," directing managers of less fully equipped provincial theaters how to stage the scene.

By the mid-nineteenth century, the restoration of Shakespeare's texts, including that of *Richard III*, had proceeded apace. One of the leading actor-managers of the time, Samuel Phelps, was in good part responsible for this work. His presentation of *Richard III* at the Sadler's Wells Theatre in London is also noteworthy for the fullness of its anno-tations and the set designs for the production. The cast list indicates that Phelps himself played the lead role of Richard III. A number of supernumeraries are included, as, for example, at the entrance of the Duke of Clarence at 1.1.41; where Shakespeare's stage direction simply states "Clarence, guarded," the playbook inserts "by 4 Super Guards." Elsewhere, a good many more extras are indicated. As the play is quite long, many passages of dialogue are shortened by one or two lines or more throughout the text. Some stage directions are altered on interleaved pages and in the margins of the text; for example, at 1.2.144, the original stage direction "spits at him" is deleted, along with lines 144b–47; instead, on the interleaved page opposite appears the direction "She passes to R. but pauses in front of Gloster, and makes a contemptuous action." Mid-Victorian decorum, of course, had to be observed, and spitting would be unladylike. For similar reasons, as well as for shortening, much of the dialogue between Clarence and the two Murderers in 1.4 is deleted, especially 1.4.164–266, and most of what remains is spoken offstage. A number of other lines are deleted, and some additional passages, written in manuscript hand and inserted after 2.1, evidently to replace part of 2.1, are also thus marked, as they are not part of Shakespeare's text. Such additions and deletions appear elsewhere, too, along with transpositions of passages and scenes. For example, long passages in manuscript adapted from 3.5.72–73 are marked for insertion after 3.1.197, altering the structure of Shakespeare's original but preserving most of the language. Since spectacle figured hugely in most Victorian representations, even Phelps', at 3.7.55 the Mayor of London does not simply enter; the stage direction written on the page facing p. 94 reads: "A Barge pushed on. 4 City Bargemen with oars upraised. The Lord Mayor and 4 Aldermen get from the Barge. At the same time, 6 Citizens 2 with City Flags and the Mace and sword bearers . . . 2 Flags at Terrace steps. Barge taken off."

Those who have seen Baz Luhrmann's film *Romeo + Juliet* may have been amazed to see Juliet awaken and speak to Romeo before he dies at the end of the tragedy. In fact, this was hardly an innovation. Garrick's production of Shakespeare's play had long since anticipated Luhrmann. Garrick wrote a lengthy dialogue for Romeo and Juliet just as Juliet awakens after Romeo has drunk his poison draught. Garrick even went so far as to introduce a funeral procession for Juliet at the beginning of act 5, after she has taken the potion provided by Friar Lawrence; the scene was accompanied with dirges composed expressly for the event. These innovations became customary in many subsequent productions, such as John Philip Kemble's in 1811. Others, like Charlotte Cushman in 1852, also based their productions on Garrick's edition but omitted some of his innovations, as Edwin Booth did in 1874 at his theater in New York. Booth deleted the funeral procession, dirges, and the final dialogue between Romeo and Juliet. He then restored the dying speech Shakespeare gave Juliet (5.3.160–70), but he ended the play at that point, as many other productions tended to do (and some still do), eliminating the long dénouement.

Like many of Shakespeare's plays, *The Merchant of Venice* has had a long and fascinating stage history, which the playbooks help to record.

And like *King Lear*, *Richard III*, and several other plays, *The Merchant of Venice* did not escape the "improvements" of eighteenth-century playwrights. George Granville rewrote much of the text in 1701, and this script—which omitted characters, added songs, invented an elaborate banquet scene at the end of an otherwise severely shortened act 2—held the stage for the next forty years, until Charles Macklin restored most of Shakespeare's original. Unfortunately, no playbook for Macklin's performances survives, but we know from other sources that Macklin restored the princes Morocco and Arragon and even Launcelot Gobbo and his father. More songs were added—songs seem to be important for eighteenth-century versions of Shakespeare's comedies—but far more important was Macklin's interpretation of Shylock as a fierce, relentless moneylender, replacing the more comical villain portrayed by his predecessors, like Thomas Dogget.[7]

Kemble continued the tradition of introducing songs, such as those for Jessica in 2.5 and Lorenzo in 2.6, and even had Jessica and Lorenzo sing a duet in 3.5. But he deleted the song in 3.2 for his production in 1797 and eliminated the roles of Morocco and Arragon. When Edmund Kean played Shylock in 1814, he revolutionized the role of Shylock, making him a more sympathetic, even a tragic, character—a man "more sinned against than sinning." He thus became a character more suitable to the romantic taste of the times.[8] Kean's interpretation greatly influenced subsequent nineteenth-century representations and even many later ones. The tradition of adding songs to Shakespeare's script continued as, for instance, the playbooks of Booth and Helen Modjeska reveal. Morocco and Arragon also continued to appear and disappear from productions, while new characters were sometimes added, as in Booth's 1867 playbook, which includes a silent servant to Bassanio named Leonardo. Productions often consisted of six rather than five acts, with the long act 3 divided into two acts, the second one beginning after either 3.1 or 3.2. Sometimes, act 5 was eliminated altogether, if the main focus of the production was on Shylock as a tragic figure.

Henry Irving's *Merchant* at the end of the nineteenth century, with Ellen Terry as Portia, is perhaps the century's most celebrated production of the play, and some of the innovations have lasted till the present day. Irving, who played Shylock, carried the tragic tradition to the fullest extent, going so far as to interpolate a non-Shakespearean scene. This was one designed to evoke considerable sympathy for Shylock, for it showed him returning from Bassanio's banquet in act 2 to his empty house after his daughter, Jessica, had eloped with Lorenzo. As Shylock began to knock on the door, the curtain slowly descended to end the act. This interpolation was widely applauded and has been included well into the twentieth century in productions like the one at London's Royal National Theatre in 1999, with Henry Goodman as Shylock, a production that also followed the tradition, maintained by Irving, of introducing non-Shakespearean songs.[9]

Irving's playbook has numerous, explicit stage directions on the facing pages of the text, indicating not only the blocking but also attitudes and speech inflections for the actors.[10] Some transpositions of lines are also indicated. For example, two of Shylock's lines (3.3.6–7) are written in to be spoken as an aside at the end of 1.3 to show quite clearly Shylock's intention to entrap Antonio, a point left ambiguous in Shakespeare's original script. Although no pictures of the sets accompany the playbook (as they do, for example, in playbooks based on illustrated editions, like Charles Kean's or Charles Knight's), the stage directions mention a gondola in which Lorenzo and Jessica elope. This, along with the bridge over which Shylock returns home and other details, points to elaborate stage sets typical of nineteenth-century productions. The playbook shows that the performance was divided into six acts instead of the usual five; act 4 here begins after 3.1, an arrangement that places emphasis on Shylock's distress.

As these few examples demonstrate, playbooks are extremely useful materials to help scholars visualize the ways Shakespeare's plays were performed down through the centuries. Even where we now have filmed archives of productions, such as those of Royal Shakespeare Company productions in Stratford-upon-Avon housed at the Shakespeare Centre Library on Henley Street, the playbooks, also housed in that library, are essential tools with which to study productions. By comparing the book with the archival film, a scholar can see what the director's intentions were and the ways they might have been modified in actual performances. Lacking archival films or videotapes, as we do for productions in the eighteenth and nineteenth centuries, as well as for most of the twentieth century, we must have recourse to extant playbooks as well as theater reviews to help us reconstruct and analyze productions. When the Gale "promptbooks" become available, these resources will be consulted more than ever before and will prove extremely useful in advancing the study of Shakespeare's plays in performance.

NOTES

1. The term "promptbooks," long in common usage, is doubtless a misnomer, as William B. Long has argued with good reason in a paper presented at the Columbia

University Shakespeare Seminar on September 10, 2004, that "playbook" is the preferred term. Since the former term is more familiar, I myself use it from time to time with the understanding that it does not refer to a book used by someone standing in the wings to "prompt" an actor who suddenly dries or misses lines. The books here referred to are more usually preparation copies, workbooks, directors' copies, etc. that record the design of a production and are retained by stage managers, actors, and others, whether or not they were intimately involved in actual performance.

2. The material for this article derives from photocopies of books, available on microfilm, in the Folger Shakespeare Library and the Harvard Theatre Collection, which Gale Research is preparing to place online for scholars to examine.

3. *The Diaries of William Charles Macready, 1833–1851*, ed. William Toynbee, 2 vols. (New York: Chapman and Hall, 1912), 1:438.

4. Charles H. Shattuck, *The Shakespeare Promptbooks: A Descriptive Catalogue* (Urbana: University of Illinois Press, 1965), 218.

5. William Winter, *Shakespeare on the Stage*, 2nd series (New York: Moffat, Yard, 1915), 426.

6. Shattuck, *The Shakespeare Promptbooks*, 391.

7. *The Merchant of Venice*, ed. Jay L. Halio. The Oxford Shakespeare (Oxford: Clarendon, 1993), 62–64.

8. Influenced by Edmund Kean, William Hazlitt borrowed this line from *King Lear* to describe Shylock in *Characters of Shakespeare's Plays* (1817; London: Oxford University Press, 1970), 212. For Kean's interpretation of Shylock, see F. W. Hawkins, *The Life of Edmund Kean*, 2 vols. (London: Tinsley Brothers, 1869), 1:148–53.

9. The NT's production included a duet between Shylock and Jessica, partly in Yiddish and partly in English. But earlier productions, like Irving's, only included English songs. Booth's, for example, included "Hark, hark, the lark" at 2.6.25.

10. See, for example, directions facing pages 8, 14, 50, 54 in Folger copy no. 35.

"The difference betwixt reporting and representing": Thomas Heywood and the Playgoer's Imagination

Alan C. Dessen

Tʜᴇ ɢᴀᴘ ʙᴇᴛᴡᴇᴇɴ ᴄʀɪᴛɪᴄᴀʟ ᴛʜᴇᴏʀʏ ᴀɴᴅ ᴛʜᴇᴀᴛʀɪᴄᴀʟ ᴘʀᴀᴄᴛɪᴄᴇ in the English Renaissance can be huge. In particular, neoclassical critics and professional playwrights of the period differ significantly as to what should or should not be brought onto the stage (compare Ben Jonson's *The Alchemist* or a play by Jean Racine to *1 Henry VI, Antony and Cleopatra*, and Thomas Heywood's *The Brazen Age*). The best known exposition of the neoclassical position is Sir Philip Sidney's witty and incisive commentary on early Elizabethan drama. In such plays, he observes:

> you shal have *Asia* of the one side, and *Affrick* of the other, and so many other under-kingdoms, that the Player, when he commeth in, must ever begin with telling where he is, or els the tale wil not be conceived. Now ye shal have three Ladies walke to gather flowers, and then we must beleeve the stage to be a Garden. By and by, we heare newes of shipwracke in the same place, and then wee are to blame if we accept it not for a Rock. Upon the backe of that, comes out a hidious Monster, with fire and smoke, and then the miserable beholders are bounde to take it for a Cave. While in the meantime two Armies flye in, represented with foure swords and bucklers, and then what harde heart will not receive it for a pitched fielde?[1]

Consider, however, an alternative, more positive approach to the same onstage activity that builds upon the imaginative participation of the audience in the spirit of *as if*.[2] A sixteenth-century playgoer would infer from "foure swords and bucklers" in combat an army and, in general terms, "a pitched fielde"; given appropriate dialogue and acting, when a monster enters through a stage door, for a moment that door would become a cave mouth; if ladies gather flowers, even if only in pantomime, a spectator would supply the garden; the sighting of a shipwreck

46

would imply a vantage point near the water, Sidney's rock. His terms ("Now . . . By and by . . . Upon the backe of that . . . While in the meantime . . .") adroitly express a witty incredulity that all these events are being presented "in the same place"; but from another, more sympathetic point of view, this chameleon-like flexibility could be seen as a major asset. Like Jonson and George Chapman two decades later, Sidney rejects many popular dramatic conventions (what "the miserable beholders" have to "beleeve" or "accept" if the scene is to work) that *were* shared by less fastidious playgoers.

Sidney concludes his skewering of the excesses of English theatrical romances of the 1570s with the commonsensical comment that "many things may be told which cannot be shewed" if dramatists would only observe "the difference betwixt reporting and representing."[3] With this latter distinction, however, the battle lines between critics and theatrical practitioners are not so clearly drawn. To substitute the *reporting* of a chorus or choric figure for the sweep of onstage action (as with Shakespeare's presentation of the battle of Actium in *Antony and Cleopatra*, 3.10) *is* a stock device throughout the period. Comparable is the use of elaborate dumb shows to bring complex events onstage (often with a chorus or presenter to spell out what the playgoer is seeing)—as in *Edmond Ironside* (1595), where the Chorus would prefer to have the audience "see the battailes Acted on the stage," but since "theire length wilbe to tedious / then in dumbe shewes I will explaine at large / theire fightes, theire flightes and *Edmonds* victory."[4]

Still, most popular drama before and after Sidney's strictures ranged widely in space and time and brought onstage exciting events that would seem either to strain the limits of a playgoer's credulity or to pose insuperable difficulties for the players. In his argument on behalf of the classical *nuntius*, Sidney remarks: "I may speake (though I am heere) of *Peru*, and in speech digresse from that to the description of *Calicut*; but in action I cannot represent it without *Pacolets* horse,"[5] yet in the closing moments of John Day, William Rowley, and George Wilkins' *The Travels of the Three English Brothers* (1607), the dramatists do introduce a version of Pacolet's horse: a perspective glass that enables the three brothers, widely dispersed in different countries, to see and communicate with each other: "*Enter three severall waies the three Brothers; Robert with the state of Persia . . . ; Sir Anthonie with the King of Spaine and others, . . . ; Sir Thomas in England. . . . Fame gives to each a prospective glasse, they seme to see one another and offer to embrace, at which Fame parts them, and so: Exeunt.*"[6] Despite the position taken by figures like Sidney and despite the practical limitations of their stages, Elizabethan playwrights, players, and playgoers clearly relished big scenes and effects that would seem to us to burst the bounds of the Globe.

How, then, did playwrights deal with the challenge posed by theatrical exigency? One response was to provide the audience with an apology or a plea for pardon. Readers of *Henry V* are familiar with the series of appeals to the playgoer to *suppose* or *imagine* what cannot be represented in the wooden O. The Prologue apologizes for the limits of "this unworthy scaffold" in conveying "So great an object" as Agincourt; still, the players can "On your imaginary forces work" if the viewers are willing to "Suppose" and "make imaginary puissance" by dividing one man into a thousand parts, to "Think, when we talk of horses, that you see them / Printing their proud hoofs i' th' receiving earth," in short, to "Piece out our imperfections with your thoughts." Again, the Chorus to act 3 pleads with the audience to "Suppose," "behold," "do but think," "Grapple your minds," "Work, work your thoughts, and therein see a siege," and, finally, "Still be kind, / And eche out our performance with your mind." Before Agincourt, the Chorus to act 4 apologizes in advance for disgracing this great event "With four or five most vile and ragged foils / (Right ill dispos'd in brawl ridiculous)" but asks the audience: "Yet sit and see, / Minding true things by what their mock'ries be."[7] Repeatedly, this choric spokesman asks the audience to accept a part for the whole, to supply imaginatively what cannot be introduced physically onto the open stage.

That same appeal, moreover, is found in comparable if less familiar passages outside the Shakespeare canon. Instructive but atypical is *suppose* used in a stage direction as an imperative verb to set up an *as if* situation: "*Suppose the Temple of Mahomet*" (*Selimus* [1592]).[8] More common is the use of *suppose* or comparable terms to streamline a narrative: "You must suppose king Richard now is deade, / And John (resistlesse) is faire Englands Lord" (Anthony Munday, *The Death of Robert Earl of Huntington* [1598]);[9] "Now let your thoughts as swift as is the winde, / Skip some few yeares, that *Cromwell* spent in travell, / And now imagine him to be in England" (*Thomas Lord Cromwell* [1600]);[10] "Now be pleas'd, / That your imaginations may help you / To think them safe in Persia . . ." (John Fletcher and Philip Massinger, *The Prophetess* [1622]);[11] "Our Sceane lies speechlesse, active but yet dumbe, / Till your expressing thoughts give it a tongue" (*The Travels of the Three English Brothers*, 6); "Imagine now that whilst he is retired, / From Cambridge back unto his native home, / Suppose the silent, sable visaged night, / Casts her black curtain over all the world" (*Merry Devil of Edmonton* [1602]).[12]

As in *Henry V*, such appeals often are linked to events that cannot be represented onstage. The Chorus in *Captain Thomas Stukeley* (1596) notes that three kings died in one battle and adds:

> Your gentle favour must we needs entreat,
> For rude presenting such a royall fight,
> Which more imaginatian must supply:
> Then all our utmost strength can reach unto.[13]

A similar entreaty is provided by Thomas Dekker's Prologue to *Old Fortunatus* (1599):

> And for this smal Circumference must stand,
> For the imagind Sur-face of much land,
> Of many kingdomes, and since many a mile,
> Should here be measurd out: our muse intreats,
> Your thoughts to helpe poore Art, . . .[14]

A Chorus in John Kirke's *The Seven Champions of Christendom* (1635) notes the problems posed by "the shortnesse of the time" and the many exploits of the champions that would "fill a larger Scene than on this Stage / An Action would containe." The solution is to have each champion "beare a little part / Of their more larger History" and to appeal to the playgoer: "Then let your fancies deeme upon a stage, / One man a thousand, and one houre an age."[15] More elaborate is the appeal in the Prologue to *The Travels of the Three English Brothers*:

> Imagin now the gentle breath of heaven
> Hath on the liquid high-way of the waves
> Convaid him many thousand leagues from us:
> Thinke you have seene him saile by many lands,
> And now at last, arriv'd in *Persia*,
> Within the confines of the great *Sophey*,
> Thinke you have heard his curteous salute
> Speake in a peale of shot, . . .

> (6)

Events at sea are particularly difficult to stage. Note this passage from Heywood's *The Four Prentices of London* (1600):

> Imagine now yee see the aire made thicke
> With stormy tempests, that disturbe the Maine:

And the foure windes at warre among themselves:
And the weake Barkes wherein the brothers saile,
Split on strange rockes, and they enforc'd to swim:
To save their desperate lives.[16]

An especially elaborate appeal is found in Fletcher and Massinger's *The Prophetess*, where a Chorus introducing a dumb show notes that "So full of matter is our Historie / . . . that there wants / Room in this narrow Stage, and time to express / In Action to the life . . ." the necessary events but then asks that "Your apprehensive judgments will conceive / Out of the shadow we can only shew, / How fair the Body was . . ." so that the playgoer can "behold / As in a silent Mirrour, what we cannot / With fit conveniency of time, allow'd / For such Presentments, cloath in vocal sounds" (362–63).

Such apologies and appeals to the imagination, especially when coupled with the strictures of neoclassical purists such as Sidney and Jonson, would seem to suggest severe constraints upon what could be introduced onto the Globe or other stages. But given the available conventions or shared assumptions (at least in the public theaters), such limits seem to evaporate. For example, consider battle scenes, among the most difficult to realize effectively on any stage. Sidney could mock "two Armies . . . represented with foure swords and bucklers"; Jonson could sneer at the players who "with three rustie swords, / And helpe of some few foot-and-halfe-foote words, / Fight over *Yorke*, and *Lancasters* long iarres: / And in the tyring-house bring wounds, to scarres" (Prologue to *Every Man in his Humour*).[17] Shakespeare himself, as already noted, was conscious of the danger of lapsing into the "brawl ridiculous" in presenting Agincourt through only "four or five most vile and ragged foils." Nonetheless, rather than avoiding battle scenes, the Lord Chamberlain's Men and the other companies found practical solutions. As Alfred Harbage observes: "The audience did not see the battles so much as hear them. What it saw was displays of skill by two or occasionally four combatants on that small sector of the battlefield symbolized by the stage." In addition, the players made adept use of *alarums* or offstage sound effects ("a gong insistently clanging, trumpets blaring recognizable military signals, then steel clashing, ordnance firing") and *excursions* ("individual pursuits and combats onstage").[18] Thus, from *Captain Thomas Stukeley*: "*Alarum is sounded, diverse excurtions, / Stukly pursues, shane Oneale, and Neale Mackener,/ And after a good pretty fight his Lieftenannt and Auntient rescue Stuklie, and chace the Ireshe out / Then an excurtion berwixt Herbert and OHanlon, and / so a retreat sounded"* (1170–75). Through such theatrical synecdoche, the whole of a battle is to be imagined or inferred through the parts displayed, an approach to mass combat well suited to a large platform stage and limited personnel.

Playwrights and players of this period were, therefore, ready to 1) apologize or beg pardon for their limitations or 2) appeal to the playgoer to imagine what could not actually be represented onstage, but they were also prepared to 3) defy neoclassical strictures and take on what (given the available resources) would appear to be daunting scenes or effects, including moments involving fire and water.[19] Among professional playwrights, the most inventive and adept in responding to the challenge of representing X rather than reporting X is, without doubt, Heywood.

At times Heywood, like Shakespeare, does resort to a Chorus and an appeal to the playgoer's imaginary forces. Thus, the Chorus in *1 Fair Maid of the West* (1610) laments that "Our Stage so lamely can expresse a Sea, / That we are forst by *Chorus* to discourse / What should have beene in action"; the playgoer is then exhorted to "Now imagine" the heroine's passion and "Suppose her rich, and forst for want of water / To put into Mamorrah in Barbary" (2:319). Here, as elsewhere, complex narratives need assistance from a Chorus and from the playgoer's imagination. Another widely used device to economize or sidestep staging problems is the entrance *as from* a shipwreck, battle, dinner, tournament, or other event. As a knowledgeable professional, Heywood regularly resorts to this device. For example, he twice signals a shipwreck by concentrating upon the recently completed action: in *The Captives* (1624), Palestra is to enter "*all wett as newly shipwracke and escapt the ffury of the Seas*,"[20] and in Heywood's *The Four Prentices of London*, a reported shipwreck is followed by dumb-shows that display Godfrey "*as newly landed & halfe naked*," Guy "*all wet*," and Charles "*all wet with his sword*" (2:176, 177).

But Heywood often goes beyond *as from* directions or appeals to the imagination. Consider *Fortune by Land and Sea* (1609), where he brings onto the platform stage a battle between two ships at sea. After "*A great Alarum and shot*," the two pirates, Purser and Clinton, enter with prisoners from their most recent conquest. Once the stage has been cleared, young Forrest appears "*like a Captain of a ship, with Sailors and Mariners, entering with a flourish*"; a boy is told to "Climb to the main-top" to "see what you kenne there"; "*Above*," the boy calls out "a sayl" and shouts down details; Forrest instructs his gunner, steersman, master, and boatswain; "*A peece goes off*" when the pirates raise their colors (as reported by the boy above). Again, with the stage cleared, Purser and Clinton return *"with their Mariners, all furnished with Sea devices fitting for a fight";* they urge on their gunner ("Oh 'twas a gallant shot, I saw it shatter some of their limbs in pieces") and debate strategy. Again, Heywood switches to Forrest exhorting his men not to spare the powder. Finally, *"A great Alarum, and Flourish. Enter young Forrest and his Mates with Purser and Clinton with their Mariners prisoners"* (6:410–18). The key to the effect lies in the combination of alternating scenes and appropriate signals: the boy above, nautical language, costume (e.g., Forrest *"like a Captain of a ship"),* and sound effects, along with the reported action. There is no evidence that shots are actually fired on stage (although there is considerable talk of guns and gunnery), but there is frenzied activity, much noise, and presentation of *"Sea devices fitting for a fight,"* all appropriate for two ships in battle at sea. The players perform *as if* in such a battle, and (if the sequence is to work) the playgoers suppose or imagine the event.

Similarly, Heywood's plays include many night or darkness scenes with a typical emphasis upon silence, stealth, even tiptoeing. For example, in *A Woman Killed with Kindness* (1603), Frankford, about to steal back into his house at night, asks for his dark lantern and tells Nicholas to "Tread softly, softly"; the latter responds: "I will walke on Egges this pace" (2:137). Perhaps the most revealing scene for "playing" night comes from the Trojan horse sequence of Heywood's *2 The Iron Age* (1612). After Synon has called upon "sweet mid-night" to mask "mischiefe and blacke deedes," the Greeks come on stage *"in a soft march, without noise,"* while Agamemnon urges: "Soft, soft, and let your stilnesse suite with night, / Faire *Phebe* keepe thy silver splendor in, / And be not seene to night." After Synon appears above *"with a torch,"* speaking again of "horrid night," Menelaus proclaims: "March on then, the black darknes covers us." The stage direction reads: *"They march softly in at one door, and presently in at another. Enter Synon with a stealing pace, holding the key in his hand."* When Synon unlocks the horse, *"Pyrrhus, Diomed, and the rest, leap from out the Horse. And as if groping in the darke, meete with Agamemnon and the rest: who after knowledge imbrace"* (3:377–80). The *as if* formula spelled out here in *"as if groping in the darke"* is usually implicit in signals elsewhere and is basic to many comparable onstage effects that depend upon a combination of onstage activity and playgoer imagination.

Again, Heywood, like other dramatists, regularly introduces hunt scenes or *as from* hunt situations, as when Hercules enters *"with the Lyons head and skin"* (*The Silver Age* [1611], 3:131), but he also provides the most elaborate such scene in the period, the hunt for the Caledonian boar in *The Brazen Age* (1611). The sequence starts with Venus dressed *"like a Huntresse,"* horns wound offstage as "The summons to the chace," a group of heroes *"with Javelings, and in greene,"* and Atlanta *"with a Javelin."* Then follow: *"Enter Adonis winding his horne";* cries of "Charge, charge"; *"a great winding of hornes, & shouts";* reports of wounds and pursuits; *"hornes and shouts"; "Hornes"; "After great shouts, enter Venus"; "A cry within."* After the dying Adonis is carried on and off and *"The fall of the Boare being winded,"* the successful hunters enter *"with the head of the Boare"* and *"with their javellins bloudied"* (3:184–94). The combination of distinctive sounds, properties, costumes, and entrances creates a sense of the hunt without an onstage forest or a live boar.

In addition to this extensive hunt and a battle at sea, Heywood stages the story of Horatius at the bridge (*The Rape of Lucrece*, 5:242–45) wherein, in order to save Rome from Tarquin, one heroic individual guards a passage against an army while his comrades tear down a bridge. After Valerius urges "Breake downe the Bridge, least the pursuing enemy / Enter with us and take the spoile of *Rome*," Horatius volunteers: "Then breake behinde me, for by heaven il'e grow / And roote my foote as deepe as to the center, / Before I leave this passage." Heywood cannot bring a bridge onstage but can use dialogue to place it just out of sight, as when Horatius challenges Tarquin and his followers: "Soft *Tarquin*, see a bulwarke to the bridge, / You first must passe, the man that enters here / Must make his passage through *Horatius* brest." The actual fight and the offstage activity is described by two opposing figures above (e.g., "passe *Horatius* quickly, / For they behind him will devolve the bridge" versus "Yet stand *Horatius*, beare but one brunt more, / The arched bridge shall sinke upon his piles"). Also important for the effect are offstage sounds: first *"A noise of knocking downe the bridge, within"* and then *"Alarum, and the falling of the Bridge."* The fate of Horatius is displayed by an exit, some dialogue ("Hee's leapt off from the bridge," "And hark, the shout of all the multitude / Now welcomes him a land"), and more sounds (*"Shout and flourish"*).

Two scenes, both from *The Brazen Age*, best demonstrate Heywood's skills and inventiveness in staging difficult, seemingly impossible moments. Consider first his presentation (3:175–76) of the confrontation between Hercules and the shape-shifter Achelous by which the hero wins Dejanira. The narrative fiction requires that Achelous start in his own shape, shift three times, and reappear in his own guise to confess defeat. The actual stage directions read: *"Achelous is beaten in, and immediatly enters in the shape of a Dragon"; "Alarme. He beats away the dragon.*

Enter a Fury all fire-workes"; *"When the Fury sinkes, a Buls head appeares"*; *"He tugs with the Bull, and pluckes off one of his horns. Enter from the same place Achelous with his forehead all bloudy."* The now bloodied figure spells out the results of the confrontation: "No more, I am thy Captive, thou my Conqueror."

Although not all the details can be pieced out, Heywood's solution in his theater to what might seem an insurmountable staging problem is clear. To reenter *"in the shape of a Dragon"* is to establish the shape-shifting not by means of onstage trickery but by means of a rapid transition (*"immediatly"*) that draws upon the playgoer's imagination. The "Dragon" may be thrust forth from a trap or stage door; clearly the "Fury" sinks through the trap (and may arise *"all fire-workes"* in the same fashion); the "Buls head" could appear from a door or the trap (anywhere within Hercules' reach), but a door would be practical if the Achelous-actor is immediately to *"Enter from the same place"* with his bloody forehead. The in-the-theater timing is crucial here: the players provide the rapid actions; the playgoer (in the spirit of *as if*) supplies the continuity that underlies such signals so as to make the connections between Achelous and the three shapes. This combination of strong onstage signals with the imaginary forces of the spectators epitomizes the unspoken contract essential to this (or any) theater.

Consider a second equally revealing moment from the same play, Heywood's rendition of the death of Nessus the centaur (3:180–82). Here, one would suppose, is an event too complex to be enacted on the open stage, for it involves 1) Nessus carrying Dejanira on his back across a river and 2) Hercules then shooting an arrow across that river to kill the centaur. How does Heywood do it? First, after the departure of Nessus and Dejanira, Hercules, alone on stage, describes for the audience their progress through the water ("Well plunged bold Centaure") but then must rage impotently as he witnesses the attempted rape and hears his bride cry for help (four times). Finally, Hercules announces: "I'le send till I can come, this poisonous shaft / Shall speake my fury and extract thy bloud, / Till I my selfe can crosse this raging floud." The stage direction then reads: *"Hercules shoots, and goes in: Enter Nessus with an arrow through him, and Deianeira."* Moments later, "After long struling with *Evenus* streames," Hercules reappears to "make an end of what my shaft begunne." To depict a figure on one side of a river shooting a figure on the other side, Heywood has resorted to rapidly alternating scenes, reported action, offstage sounds, and, most important (in his version of what in our age has become a stock cinematic effect), a presentation of the initiation and then the immediate resolution of the central event (*"Hercules shoots . . . Enter Nessus with an arrow through him"*) rather than the full sequence (the complete flight of the arrow and the striking of its target). If the choric passages from *Henry V* provide the "theory" behind the open stage (e.g., that the audience is expected to use their imaginary forces to "eche out our performance with your mind"), the arrow in Nessus provides a telling demonstration of the resulting theatrical practice. The spectator sees 1) the shooting of the arrow and 2) the result but then must supply 3) the connection between the two (I am assuming that Nessus enters immediately at another door), including any sense of the river and the distance involved. As with Hercules' confrontation with Achelous, for the scene to work the actors must provide the timing and energy, the audience, the imaginative participation.

At first reading, a stage direction such as *"Enter Nessus with an arrow through him"* may seem quaint or silly, worthy only of amused contempt (and readers familiar with Francis Beaumont's *The Knight of the Burning Pestle* [1607] may conjure up *"Enter Ralph, with a forked arrow through his head"* [6:229]). We should remember, however, that Heywood, like Shakespeare, Fletcher, and Massinger, was a working professional linked to a specific theatrical company who not only knew his craft well but also knew his theater from the inside, both its potential and its limits. If we chuckle at the arrow in Nessus, we are (like Sidney) implicitly asserting our superiority to a "primitive" dramaturgy (how could anyone be expected to believe that?) and, in the process, revealing more about ourselves (e.g., how we read playscripts) than about Heywood and his contemporaries. If we are not responsive to this and other such moments (e.g., Jupiter descending on an eagle [*Cymbeline* 5.4.92], Gloucester's "suicide" at Dover Cliffs [*King Lear* 4.6.1–80], or, closer to home, *"Enter Clifford wounded with an arrow in his neck"* [*3 Henry VI*, 2.6.sd])[21] are we not in danger of reconceiving the plays to suit our sensibilities, of rewriting the clues to suit our solutions? Rather, to characterize the theater or theatrical conventions of another age is to face squarely those moments that do cause problems for us (and for neoclassicists such as Sidney and Jonson) and make us conscious of the gaps between then and now. A major key to unlock what is distinctive about drama in the age of Shakespeare, therefore, lies in the anomalies, the surprises, the moments that make us aware of the full stretch of the dramaturgy. And, in my view, the best place to go for evidence of such theatrical range and inventiveness (in the spirit of *as if*) is the canon of plays linked to Thomas Heywood.

NOTES

1. Philip Sidney, "An Apologie for Poetrie," in *Elizabethan Critical Essays*, ed. G. Gregory Smith, 2 vols. (Oxford: Oxford University Press, 1904), 1:197.

2. For a fuller discussion of *as if* staging and assumptions, see "Much virtue in *as*," in my *Recovering Shakespeare's Theatrical Vocabulary* (Cambridge: Cambridge University Press, 1995), 127–49.

3. Sidney, "An Apologie for Poetrie," 198.

4. *Edmond Ironside or War Hath Made All Friends*, ed. Eleanore Boswell, Malone Society (London: Oxford University Press, 1927), 970–73. For the convenience of the reader, I have attached to the non-Shakespeare plays the dates listed in Alfred Harbage, *Annals of English Drama, 975–1700*, 3rd ed., rev. S. Schoenbaum, rev. Sylvia Stoler Wagonheim (London: Routledge, 1989).

5. Sidney, "An Apologie for Poetrie," 198.

6. *The Works of John Day*, ed. A. H. Bullen, 2 vols. (London: Chiswick Press, 1881), 2:90. Subsequent references to *The Travels of the Three English Brothers* are from this edition and are cited parenthetically.

7. *Henry V*, in *The Riverside Shakespeare*, 2nd ed., ed. G. Blakemore Evans (Boston: Houghton Mifflin, 1997), Prologue, 10–11, 18–19, 25, 26–27, 23; Act 3 Chorus, 3, 10, 13, 18, 25, 34–35; Act 4 Chorus, 50–53. Subsequent references to Shakespeare's plays are from this edition and are cited parenthetically.

8. *The Tragic Reign of Selimus*, ed. W. Bang, Malone Society (London: Oxford University Press, 1908), 2021.

9. Anthony Munday, *The Death of Robert Earl of Huntington*, ed. John C. Meagher, Malone Society (London: Oxford University Press, 1967), 903–4.

10. *Thomas Lord Cromwell*, ed. John S. Farmer, Tudor Facsimile Texts (Amersham, 1911), D1v–D2r.

11. John Fletcher and Philip Massinger, *The Prophetess*, in *The Works of Francis Beaumont and John Fletcher*, ed. Arnold Glover and A. R. Waller, 10 vols. (Cambridge: Cambridge University Press, 1905–12), 5 (1907): 364. Subsequent references to Beaumont and Fletcher's plays are from this edition and are cited parenthetically.

12. *Merry Devil of Edmonton*, ed. John S. Farmer, Tudor Facsimile Texts (Amersham, 1911), A3r–v.

13. *The Famous History of Captain Thomas Stukeley*, ed. Judith C. Levinson, Malone Society (London: Oxford University Press, 1975), 2877–80.

14. Thomas Dekker, *Old Fortunatus*, in *The Dramatic Works of Thomas Dekker*, ed. Fredson Bowers, 4 vols. (Cambridge: Cambridge University Press, 1953–61), 1:115, Prologue, 15–19.

15. John Kirke, *The Seven Champions of Christendom*, ed. Giles Edwin Dawson, *Western Reserve University Bulletin*, n.s. 32.16 (1929): 1414–22.

16. Thomas Heywood, *The Four Prentices of London*, in *The Dramatic Works of Thomas Heywood*, ed. R. W. Shepherd, 6 vols. (London: John Pearson, 1874), 2:175–76. With the exception of *The Captives*, subsequent references to Heywood's plays are from this edition and are cited parenthetically.

17. Ben Jonson, *Every Man in his Humour*, in *Ben Jonson*, ed. C. H. Herford and Percy Simpson, 11 vols. (Oxford: Clarendon Press, 1925–52), 3:303, Prologue, 9–12. The date for this Prologue is much in doubt—likely closer to 1616 (when it first appeared in print) than 1598 (the first performance of the play).

18. Harbage, *Theatre for Shakespeare* (Toronto: University of Toronto Press, 1955), 52.

19. Two of the most bizarre examples are Nero looking on while Rome burns (*The Tragedy of Nero* [1624]) and the onstage rescue of a man marooned on a rock by means of a ship (*The Hector of Germany* [1614]).

20. Heywood, *The Captives*, ed. Arthur Brown, Malone Society (London: Oxford University Press, 1953), 653–54.

21. For other comparable moments (two of them from the Heywood canon), see the entrances of Tarquin *"with an arrow in his breast"* (Heywood, *Rape of Lucrece*, 5:249); Achilles *"with an arrow through his heel"* (Heywood, *1 Iron Age* [1612], 3:332); Vespatian *"wounded in the Leg with an Arrow"* (William Hemings, *The Jews' Tragedy* [1626], in *Materialien zur Kunde des älteren Englischen Dramas*, ed. Henrich A. Cohn [Louvain: A. Uystpruyst, 1913], 862–63); and Strozza *"with an arrow in his side"* (Chapman, *The Gentleman Usher* [1602], in *The Plays of George Chapman: The Comedies: A Critical Edition*, gen. ed. Allan Holaday [Urbana: University of Illinois Press, 1970], 4.1.10).

"The stage is hung with black": When Did Melpomene Lose Her Identity?

Andrew Gurr

Some time before its publication in 1599, Shakespeare's company staged *A Warning for Fair Women* at the Shakespeare company's Theatre playhouse. The plays that the company chose to publish in the years from 1597 to 1599, when they were in need of cash to help build the Globe, included Shakespeare's most popular plays. The publication in 1599 of *A Warning* not long after *Richard II*, *Richard III*, and *Romeo and Juliet*, with its ascription to the Chamberlain's Men, argues that it was one of the company's more popular works and, like the others the company chose to sell to the press, had been staged quite recently. From what little we know of the company's full repertoire of plays in that period, it was also innovatory, a new kind of domestic tragedy. Its opening was overtly designed to show how this innovation was meant to displace the other plays that were standard in the repertory, in particular Shakespeare's histories and early tragedies.

To underline the point, it was given an Induction, asserting the individuality of the play it introduced in strikingly explicit ways. A female figure, Melpomene, the Muse of Tragedy, strides onstage. She enters by one door, "in her one hand a whip, in the other hand a knife," while the figure of History, escorted with drum and flag, enters at the other. They meet, and she demands priority: "peace with that drum: / Downe with that Ensigne which disturbs our stage," she orders. Comedy then enters "at the other end" playing his fiddle, and Tragedy attacks him too, with "What yet more Cats guts?", and threatens to whip him off the stage.[1] What follows is, in effect, the company's definition of a new kind of tragedy.

The Induction is an extended and precise argument for a noteworthy innovation on the Elizabethan stage as it seems the company conceived it: domestic tragedy set in London and telling a true story from London's recent history. It was not quite so new as the Induction claims, since *Arden of Faversham* preceded it by some years, but it was evidently

an innovation for the Chamberlain's Men as one of the only two companies officially licensed to perform in the London suburbs. At first, Comedy adopts a strong line against Tragedy in her usual forms, while
History acts as the moderator. Comedy derides the kind of tragedy that
was evidently commonly performed on that stage:

> How some damnd tyrant, to obtaine a crowne,
> Stabs, hangs, impoysons, smothers, cutteth throats,
> And then a Chorus too comes howling in,
> And tels us of the worrying of a cat,
> Then of a filthie whining ghost,
> Lapt in some fowle sheete, or a leather pelch,
> Comes skreaming like a pigge half stickt,
> And cries *Vindicta*, revenge, revenge.
>
> (50–57)

At this Melpomene whips both Comedy and History off the stage, com-
plaining

> T'is you have kept the Theatres so long,
> Painted in play-bils, upon every poast,
> That I am scorned of the multitude,
> My name prophande.
>
> (74–77)

The essence of Melpomene's case is that she is presenting a fresh and
a better form of tragedy in place of the old revenge drama with its
chorus, tyrant, and ghost. It is at this point that History exclaims,

> Looke *Comedie*, I markt it not till now,
> The stage is hung with blacke; and I perceive
> The Auditors preparde for *Tragedie*.
>
> (81–83)

This was the moment for Comedy and History to make their exit. The
players had set up their signal to their audience that they must expect a
play ending in deaths.

In effect, Melpomene's new form was what we would now call a
drama documentary. Its staging was notable in retaining what was evidently at that time the traditional and standard signal for tragedy, a set
of black hangings; but the play's design was new, as they saw it. The
play will, Melpomene claims, give a truthful account of a real murder,

set in London and presented to Londoners. The story itself, she says, is a well-known piece of recent history.[2] "My Sceane is London, native and your owne," she declares, "I am not faind: many now in this round, / Once to behold me in sad teares were drownd" (95, 97–98).[3] For this day, the fictions and feigning of what is alleged to be the old fashion of tragedy are banished along with History and Comedy.

Tragedy's most substantial claim is that she will tell a tale not "faind" but "true." She reaffirms its truth in the Epilogue, returning in order to explain why the play has not concluded with a more theatrical act of revenge.

> Perhaps it may seeme strange unto you al,
> That one hath not revengde anothers death,
> After the observation of such course:
> The reason is, that now of truth I sing,
> And should I adde, or else diminish aught,
> Many of these spectators then could say,
> I have comitted error in my play.
>
> (2722–28)

Such a boast is an extraordinary assertion to have made on the stage of the playhouse in suburban Shoreditch in 1596 or 1597, which is when we must assume the play was first staged.[4] It runs counter to almost everything we know of the Chamberlain's company repertoire in those first years of duopoly command of London playing. It claims to be muscling aside Shakespeare's history plays with their drums and ensigns and his comedies, even the old revenge tradition of *Titus Andronicus* and the ur-*Hamlet*, replacing them with the novelty of a true story set in the audience's own London. As such, apart from the Eastcheap scenes of the 1596–99 *Henry IV* and *Henry V* plays, *A Warning* is unique among the surviving plays of that company as a story set in London. It was also unequalled by any new play that can be identified in Philip Henslowe's lists for the other company of the then-ruling duopoly, the Admiral's Men. Throughout that time, neither company chose to set plays in the city where they were to be acted.[5]

Sadly, in its banal narrative and moralistic sentiments, the play that follows the Induction hardly justifies its boast. What is most obviously notable about *A Warning* is its suggestion that the company seemed to think that its repertoire of plays needed reform. Comedies about romantic lovers and history plays full of battles with flag and drums were the popular mode, along with the old kind of revenge tragedies like *Titus*.

The new fashion trying to take its place among these old reliables, the author admits, was a precarious venture. "But once a weeke if we do not appeere, / She shall find few that will attend her heere" (37–38), says Comedy, dismissively. Melpomene's claim is remarkable because nearly all we have of the Shakespeare company repertory in its most formative years between its establishment in 1594 and becoming the King's Men in 1603 are the plays of Shakespeare, almost all of them histories and romantic comedies except for *Titus Andronicus, Romeo and Juliet*, and the revision in 1600 of the ur-*Hamlet*. These are the varieties of play that Melpomene wishes to turn off her stage.

Her statements are remarkable in three ways. First, they signal a willingness in the company to acknowledge some discontent with the plays that Shakespeare was giving them. Second, they throw a little light on the great loss from that period, the disappearance of almost every one of the non-Shakespeare plays from the company's repertory through its first years. And, finally, something that is said quite casually in the Induction indicates a form of staging, the implications of which run far beyond the 1590s. It is this third point that is my chief concern here.

A Warning's discontent with fiddling comedy and drumming history in the Chamberlain's first years up to 1599 not only sets it against the other plays surviving from the repertory of that early duopoly period (all of them Shakespeare's); it also argues for an innovation that no company appears to have been happy just then to introduce: a play openly set in contemporary London. The concept of a documentary drama about a local murder was distinctive at the time in its absolute need of a specifically London location. No play before *A Warning* used the city in which the playhouses were situated for their locale. When the Shakespeare company first staged Ben Jonson's *Every Man in his Humour* in 1598, it was set ostensibly in an Italian city; its transfer to an obviously London locale did not come until Jonson produced a revised text for his Folio edition of 1616. George Chapman's *An Humorous Day's Mirth* launched the form of London-based comedy at the Rose in May 1597 which was to dominate playing under King James, but even that introduction of the comedy of humors self-protectively gave its leading characters non-English names and set them not in London but in the English country at a great house and its environs. That, along with Jonson's ostensibly setting his first humors plays in Italy, must reflect some feeling that writers needed to be cautious about using contemporary London for their settings, a care that the author of *A Warning* evidently felt could be ignored, if only because it was indeed a true story.[6]

Before *A Warning*, only *Arden of Faversham* (1592) — an intriguing precedent as a domestic tragedy, with its story likewise taken from Holinshed's record of English history — had used an ordinary English domestic setting. A country house in Kent, however, is a long way from the streets of London. *Arden*'s author and company are unknown, and there is little to suggest that it had any link with the Chamberlain's Men unless one tries to conflate the names of its villains Black Will and Shakebags.[7] Earlier plays, like the Queen's Men's *Three Lords and Three Ladies of London*, largely a moralized account of the Armada, had little of local color besides their titles. Moreover, if *A Warning* was an attempt to introduce a new kind of play to the London stages, as Chapman's play did for citizen comedy, it was far less successful, since no other domestic tragedy of a similar kind has survived, apart perhaps from the same company's *A Yorkshire Tragedy* of 1607.

On Melpomene's second point, it is striking that *A Warning* should be the earliest of the company's surviving non-Shakespeare plays in the Chamberlain's repertory in those years, the more so given the nature and genres of almost all the other early Shakespeare plays that remain with us. We must assume that only a small fraction of the full Chamberlain's repertory survives, since through the thirty-one months when Henslowe kept a detailed record of the Admiral's playing (June 1594–January 1597) the plays of the other duopoly company, the Admiral's Men, were preserved in less than a dozen playtexts compared with the more than fifty titles of lost plays, a survival rate of about one in four. From the Chamberlain's through the same period, we have an even smaller number of survivors and must presume a similar or worse proportion of lost plays. Of the few survivors in addition to *A Warning*, three are histories (*Richard II* and the two parts of *Henry IV*), three are comedies (*A Midsummer Night's Dream*, *The Merchant of Venice*, and *The Merry Wives of Windsor*), plus *Titus Andronicus* and *Romeo and Juliet*, which may be a rewrite of an earlier play. If the Shakespeares were the most prominent features of the company's repertory — they were certainly the most celebrated — *A Warning* had good reason to proclaim its innovatory status. The least one can say about its strange Induction is that the company was prepared to down-rate its own best-known plays for the sake of the innovation they claimed in *A Warning*.

Melpomene's third point is about how a play's genre was commonly signaled on stage. The company's unknown writer prepared its innovation as a real story set in London that the audience had to know was marked out as a tragedy, since, in History's words, "The stage is hung with blacke; and I perceive / The Auditors preparde for *Tragedie*" (82–83). This indication, that the stage was routinely prepared to signal the plays ending in death, I find awesome in its implications. The thought that the early modern stages used decorations, hangings, or similar removable features, designed and hung to signal explicitly what an audience should expect from what they paid to witness is frankly alarming. Was tragedy exceptional in demanding a prior warning of its nature to its witnesses? Would a set of more decorative hangings lead the audience to expect a comedy? If a tragedy was signaled by the stage's being hung with black, how might a tragicomedy have been signaled? Why was it thought necessary to remove the element of suspense from a play's conclusion? Was it felt that audiences needed to be mentally prepared from the outset for whichever genre they were to be offered?

The literate among Elizabethan audiences could, of course, learn about the play in advance by reading the playbills stuck beforehand on posts around the city. Audiences used to going frequently to the only two playhouses open between 1594 and 1600 could hardly have expected every visit to have a completely new play for them, and from 1594 an increasing number of the more popular plays became available in print. What Melpomene's Induction seems to presuppose is that the two companies had to cater principally to newcomers and could leave the more habitual playgoers to their own devices. Moreover, such evidence as there is seems to indicate that there was a striking discrepancy between what the players put on stage for their audiences and what the press chose to lay out for their readership.

Advertising practices seem to have changed with time. Hanging the stage with black was an early way of identifying a play's genre that appears to have stopped by the end of the first decade of the seventeenth century. On the other hand, the labeling of plays by publishers in their genres did not grow into a regular habit until the 1630s. To the printers of *A Warning*, if to nobody else, the genre in which a play was written in the 1590s does not seem to have been defined anything like as precisely as its Induction suggests. Its 1599 title page puts less emphasis on the genre than on the story:

A WARNING FOR FAIRE WOMEN.
Containing,
The most tragicall and lamentable mur-
ther of Master George Sanders of London
Marchant, nigh Shooters hill.
Consented unto
By his owne wife, acted by M. Browne, Mistris
Drewry and Trusty Roger agents therin:
with their severall ends. . . .

A tragical murder, with the "severall" ends of the murderers, is an advertisement, the sort of description that might have appeared on the playbill, insisting on the play's value as a drama documentary rather than on its generic status.

Tragedy appears not to have become a selling point among publishers for quite a long time after the issuing of plays in print first became popular. The earliest favorites in the Shakespeare canon were all, apart from *Romeo and Juliet*, his history plays. Rather too much has been made of the variants on the generic term "tragical history" set out on the title pages of several early Shakespeare quartos, the uncertainty evident in the printing of the First Folio with the mis-grouping of plays such as *Cymbeline* and the doubt about where to place *Troilus and Cressida*. The one thing that the widespread use of those odd tragical-comical-historical doublets does appear to indicate is that through the early years of play-printing no clear distinction was made, or was even thought to be necessary, between the genres, even the basic ones of tragedy and comedy. Up to the Caroline period, a play's genre was hardly often identified clearly on play title pages. Of the 168 extant plays the Chamberlain's/King's Men owned and published after 1594, the titles of only twenty-four even bother to say that they are comedies. Fourteen are called tragedies, twelve are labeled tragicomedies, and three (including *The Merchant of Venice*) are said to be histories. That lack of precision in generic identification came to a gradual end in the 1630s. Not until the time when James Shirley became the Shakespeare company's resident playwright in 1640 did the generic spread of the plays that he supplied the company begin to seem prescriptive.

Calculating his writing on an annual basis, Shakespeare seems to have composed for his duopoly company roughly one comedy and one serious play each year. The "serious" plays were chiefly the ones taken from the chronicles of English history, plus the occasional tragedy: a simple divide. In the two-and-a-half years after his return from Dublin to replace Philip Massinger, Shirley wrote two comedies, two tragicomedies, and one tragedy, leaving a second tragedy unfinished when the playhouses were closed.[8] So far as the company was concerned, the genres had enlarged from two to three, the increase making the identification of the genres more specific. While the company might possibly have used distinctly colored hangings to designate a play's genre when it was staged, almost none of the three genre specifications emerged clearly in print until 1630. There are even a few hints of early resistance among the companies to generic labeling, perhaps in reaction against the omnivorous name of "comedians" that administrators and others laid on them. By the 1590s, these "comedians" were playing quite as many tragedies and histories as comedies, and they may well have felt themselves downgraded by the old-fashioned term. One wonders whether the "very tragical mirth" of *Pyramus and Thisbe* was not a comment on this linguistic confusion, let alone Polonius' equally celebrated list of compound names. In the playhouse, the color of the hangings might have served as a more pointed signal of the play's conclusion than any generic name. Perhaps the players at that time felt their primary concern should be with the illiterate.

The key distinctions in genre for the literate followed the rise of tragicomedy. In fact, the first use of "tragicomedy" as a title page description of a play belonging to the Chamberlain's/King's Men did not appear on a title page until 1630, for Massinger's *The Renegado*. John Marston's *The Malcontent* was called one in the 1604 entry in the Stationers' Register, but that then-distinctive nomenclature was ignored when the printer set the play's title page. Of the fifty-two plays in the collected John Fletcher edition of 1679, when the generic distinctions were entirely clear, one (*Four Plays in One*) is a curious morality with no specific designation, ten were labeled tragedies and twenty-four comedies, while ten were designated and another seven were in effect tragicomedies. That division in the Fletcher canon roughly matches the ratio of the other regular writers for the King's Men, Massinger and Shirley, and is not far out of step with the proportion in Shakespeare.

Such a proportion and such distinctions between the genres were not any sort of concern for the first publishers of plays. In the earlier period, *Richard II* and *Richard III* were both called tragedies, while the publishers of *Hamlet* Q1 and Q2 called it a tragical history. The emphasis on distinct genres in the Induction to *A Warning*, printed in 1599, was certainly not recognized on the title pages of other early plays. *A Warning*'s Induction, though not its title page, must mark the company's position over genre in the 1590s. That had to change once the *de facto* Shakespeare practice of writing one comedy and one serious play, tragedy or history, each year in his contributions to his company's repertory broke down after 1603, when he stopped writing romantic comedies (I assume that *Measure for Measure* was written as a comedy, whatever critics have tried to make of it).[9] Three years after that, the new flow of tragicomedies like *Pericles* and *Cymbeline* destroyed even the ostensible parity of serious and comic. Yet Fletcher's generic division of plays written with his various collaborators for the same company, which produced twenty-four comedies against twenty-seven tragedies or

tragicomedies, seems to have remained the pattern of writing for the
Shakespeare company til 1642.

There are some hints that tragicomedy might have developed as a
new genre precisely because it had the capacity to keep the audience
guessing about the play's conclusion. Keeping the audience in suspense
may not have been a priority or even a realistic likelihood in the early
years, so long as there were only the two duopoly companies catering
for the whole of London's audiences. Once five companies were performing regularly, as happened when James added companies patronized by his two younger children to the three that he, his elder son, and
his wife patronized, the staging of plays with an uncertain ending became more possible. From then on, grouping the tragicomedies with the
tragedies could do much more than simply fit into what was probably
the resident writer's contractual obligation, one play of each genre
every year.

Because their endings could go either way, Fletcherian tragicomedies
were designed to keep newcomers to the theater guessing. In contractual terms, they evidently belonged in the "serious" half of Fletcher's
obligation to the company. On the whole, within the context of the entire Fletcher-inspired canon, his comedies did stand distinctly apart
from his tragicomedies, which were plotted in a sufficiently dark mode
to make them appear capable of ending either way. Fletcher's distinctive tragicomic mode was a play that might equally end with life or
death. It had none of the broad and cheerful comedy of his comedies
such as *The Tamer Tamed* or *The Maid in the Mill*. Recognizing that, we
need to ask whether the shift in Shakespeare's and Fletcher's plans for
their plays, starting with *Pericles* in 1607, might not have led to the ban-
ishment of black hangings from the stage and the introduction of suspense as a writer's device, however facile, to enhance the audience's
enjoyment.

As usual, the evidence is not obviously helpful. In her first choric
comment in *A Warning for Fair Women*, Melpomene announces a dumb-
show, saying

> But now we come unto the dismall act,
> And in these sable curtains shut we up,
> The Comicke entrance to our direful play.

(777–79)

This fairly clearly indicates that at the Theatre in 1595 or 1596 when
the play was first staged, the hangings fronting what is now usually

called the discovery space were the site where the black "curtains" hung in evidence. Making these hangings black to denote a tragedy seems to justify a number of comparable though less specific references in other plays and pamphlets of the time. They are all consistent in claiming that sable hangings marked a tragedy. It is their dates that we need to note. They start early, with the opening of the first Shakespeare history play, *1 Henry VI* (c. 1591): "Hung be the heavens with black, yield day to night."[10] They continue with Marston's second play for Paul's Boys, *Antonio's Revenge* (1600) — "Hurry amain from our black-visaged shows[11] — and *The Insatiate Countess* (1607–8) for the Blackfriars boy company: "The stage of heaven is hung with solemn black, / A time best fitting to act tragedies."[12] The same acknowledgment appears in *North-ward Hoe* (1607) — "the stage hung all with black velvet"[13] — and in *Lanthorne and Candle-light* (1608): "But now when the stage of the world was hung in blacke, they jetted uppe and downe like proud *Tragedians*."[14] The dates for these texts are all fairly early, and two of the five are by the same writer for different companies. These references seem to make it clear that, roughly up to the second decade of the seventeenth century, companies regularly used black hangings to signal to the audience that they should expect a tragedy.

From these citations, it does appear possible that it was the tragicomedies Shakespeare and Fletcher wrote after 1607 that brought the use of black hangings to a halt. But that is a likelihood raising many side issues, not least whether black hangings did disappear after 1607. One of the elegies written on the death of Richard Burbage in 1619 urged "Hang all your house with black,"[15] as if that was still the practice when staging tragedies. However, since knowledge of theatrical traditions dies slowly, I think we must recognize the point that nothing survives to say that any writer of plays after 1607 registered the usage as still current.

And a final sidetrack: just where were these emphatic signifiers located? Hangings strung across the central alcove, to be pulled back for "discoveries," were a standard feature of early staging, needed when Nerissa drew them back to show the caskets in *The Merchant of Venice*, when Falstaff was found asleep behind the hangings at the Boar's Head, when Hamlet uncovered the corpse of Polonius behind the arras, and when Volpone hailed the day and his gold. They were opened to show Juliet's and Desdemona's beds before they were pushed out onto the stage. Clowns poked their heads through them to pull silly faces. In Francis Beaumont's *The Knight of the Burning Pestle* at the Blackfriars, the Citizen and his Wife sit on stools on the stage and discuss the picture on the adjacent stage hangings, evidently visible from where they were seated on the stage, certainly if they positioned their stools in front of the flanking boxes. (They conclude that it must depict "Rafe and Lucrece.")[16] The main location for such hangings was across the *frons scenae* in front of the tiring house, if we can believe John Florio's *A World of wordes* (1598), where he defines *Scéna* as "the forepart of a Theater where Plaiers make them ready, being trimmed with hangings, from out which they enter upon the stage."[17] Jonson, in the Induction to *Cynthia's Revels*, has a boy declare "I am none of your fresh pictures, that use to beautifie the decaied dead arras, in a publike theatre."[18] If the standard *frons* structure in the London playhouses incorporated a large central opening between two sets of single doors, as the evidence from examination of the archaeological findings at the Rose indicates, that would be where the tapestry cloth of arras would necessarily have hung. Such a central opening would be wide enough to absorb a bed or Tamburlaine's chariot pulled by four kings and impressive (and central) enough to provide the substantial entry-place needed for authority figures such as kings or the Prince of Verona when he enters to separate the brawling Montagues and Capulets, who would have entered through the opposing doors at the flanks on each side of the *frons*.

But was the cloth of arras strung across the central opening in the tiring house the only location where the players could hang cloths with pictures on them, or black cloths? They could have been stretched all the way across the tiring-house front, concealing both flanking doors and the central opening. And the two references to blackened heavens seem to suggest that there might also have been hangings above the stage, suspended from the "shadow" or cover over the stage, visibly black when viewed from either side. Conceivably, they might even have been hung from the edge of the stage platform facing the yard or pit. When in his *An Apology for Actors*, Thomas Heywood wrote of the glories of the Roman stages, he declared that they were "hung with rich Arras," and his Melpomene lamented:

> Then did I tread on Arras, cloth of Tissue,
> Hung round the fore-front of my stage: the pillers
> That did support the Roofe of my large frame
> Double appareld in pure Ophir gold:
> Whilst the round Circle of my spacious orbe
> Was throng'd with Princes, Dukes and Senators.[19]

We cannot be sure where Heywood thought the "fore-front" of an Elizabethan stage was. At the Blackfriars and the Cockpit, where boxes for

the richer members of the audience flanked each side of the stage, the
stage front facing the bench-sitters in the pit might have been covered
in cloth like the *frons*, but Heywood was not writing for or about the
indoor playhouses when he composed his *Apology*. Despite the idea that
Johannes de Witt's drawing of the Swan c. 1596 might have been intended to show hangings with wide openings around the lower edge of
the stage, I doubt if the players would have risked suspending expen-
sive cloth, or even the much cheaper painted cloth, within easy reach of
the groundlings. It was at the Swan in 1602 that the gentry and others
duped by Venner's trick-show revenged themselves on the hangings
and other playhouse fittings.[20]

This uncertainty in no way discounts all the testimonies that say that
sable hangings were used to signal a tragedy. So we have to ask, if the
stage cloths registered the kind of conclusion the play was to have before the players or the prologue began speaking, what was done to announce the Fletcherian tragicomedies that prevailed from the
Shakespearean late plays onwards, designed to keep the audience in
suspense about how the play would end? Fletcher's tragicomedies were
designed, in that famous phrase, to offer the danger not the death and
to hold the audience unsure how the story would conclude. A prelimi-
nary signal would reveal all, like *Hamlet*'s miming players. Apart from
the first *Tamburlaine*, unique in its time as a tragedy that does not end
in the eponymous hero's death,[21] the technique of either-way conclusions was largely a Fletcherian innovation. In Shakespeare, the only deliberate mystification laid on audiences was at the end of *The Winter's
Tale*, with Hermione's resurrection. The Fletcher plays abound in final
moments like the last-minute discovery in *Philaster* that the page who
has been accused of having sex with the heroine is a girl in disguise and,
what's more, the accuser's daughter. At that point, the audience should
have been as ready for the hero's death as for a happy resolution. A
black cloth would have pre-resolved Fletcher's designed mysteries.

Why, too, should tragedy have been singled out for such a distinctive
signal, and not comedy and history? Many references to stage hangings
speak of the pictures embroidered on their tapestries, although almost
none of the stories they are said to show seem to relate to a specific play.
Nothing suggests the use of any distinctive color like tragedy's black to
announce history or comedy. The genre of tragedy continued to evolve
in stage fashions, as did that of comedy, especially once it became routine to locate the settings of plays inside the city after 1598, when city
or citizen comedy became a popular mode. Tragedies rarely dramatized
recent history in the way that *A Warning* tried to do, but the ostensibly

moralistic form designed to evoke semifarcical pleasure in murders that end in the suitably grotesque death of the murderer, starting with Christopher Marlowe's *The Jew of Malta*, did continue in Italianate tragedy such as Cyril Tourneur's *The Atheist's Tragedy*, Thomas Middleton's *The Revenger's Tragedy*, and some of Middleton's later work. Marston experimented along similar lines with new forms in *Sophonisba* and *The Insatiate Countess*. Fletcher picked up Hamlet's dilemma in 1611 with *The Maid's Tragedy*, where two heroes debate whether to take revenge on their king and resolve the dilemma by one choosing to suffer nobly with Christian patience while the other takes up arms to kill the king. But the majority of Fletcher's subsequent work with his teams of collaborators writing for the King's Men followed the tragic-comic pattern already set by Beaumont and Fletcher's *Philaster*, and, through the 1620s and 1630s, the King's Men became noted more for their tragicomedies than anything else. So the main question about when the companies might have stopped hanging their tragic stages with black depends on the impact of first Shakespeare's and then Fletcher's use of the tragic-comic mode.

Fletcher's first plays written with Beaumont for the King's Men between 1609 and 1612 were an intriguing group of experiments. The first two for the King's Men, *Philaster* and *The Maid's Tragedy*, were in the alternative genres. Their third play, *A King and No King*, was composed like *Philaster* as a clear and popular tragicomedy, the mode that soon took over the King's Men's repertoire and came to dominate it for the next thirty years. Fletcher and his collaborators did go on to write many comedies, but their favorite mode, and probably their best, was tragicomedy. Eugene M. Waith reckons that *A King and No King* is the apotheosis of Fletcherian tragicomedy.[22]

The last tragicomedy that Fletcher wrote before he died in the plague of 1625, *A Wife for a Month*, maintains an exemplary balance as a play that might end up either way, either with deaths or with a happy ending. The same kind of balance appears rather more oddly in the alternative versions of John Suckling's *Aglaura*, played and published as a tragedy thirteen years after Fletcher's death but restaged for Henrietta Maria, at her insistence, as a tragicomedy.[23] The fate of *Aglaura* shows what a knife-edge Fletcherian tragedy and tragicomedy could balance on, between the danger that leads to death and the pleasure of witnessing the hazard relieved. Suckling first wrote his version of the tragic story of Darius, King of Persia, in 1637, and the King's Men staged it as a tragedy in 1638. In the same year, Suckling proudly published his tragic text in a large folio format. The title page simply, and with rare baldness for the 1630s, calls it just "AGLAURA," without any generic label or description. The story centers on the love and marriage of Aglaura and Thersames, with a heavy input from the platonic love mode that Henrietta Maria favored and that Suckling's ally William Davenant had written plays for, notably *The Platonic Lovers* and *Love and Honour*. Aglaura and Thersames share a moderate version of the varieties of love that Fletcher set out in *The Faithful Shepherdess*, a great success at court with Henrietta Maria when it was revived in 1634. Their love is not free from sex but is not driven by it. The third scene in the final act of the tragicomic version actually presents them in bed together after their marriage night—a visual reminder of Shakespeare, although, unlike Desdemona and Othello, they do wake up.

Aglaura was largely derived from the long-running repertoire of Fletcher's plays performed by the King's Men about tyrannical lechers as rulers, enhanced in Suckling's story by an equally lecherous and poisonous queen. In the tragic version, king, queen, and both lovers die. In both versions, Aglaura stabs her lover in the dark, thinking he is the lustful king. But Suckling had to strip his Melpomene of her coloring by royal command. To change the ending so that everyone lived happily ever after took him no more than a further fifty lines of text, although the altered conclusion was done with an economy of effort that reflects Suckling's own dislike of the exercise.

So, if a little cautiously, we can conclude that up to about 1607 there is no reason to question the ample number of references asserting that, when tragedies were to be presented, the stages were normally hung with black, as a mark to the audience of what it could expect. In *A Warning for Fair Women*, the figure of Melpomene makes that announcement as she banishes History and Comedy off the stage for her play. While there is some question about just where the sable hangings were hung, there is no doubt about the signal they were meant to issue. Neither history nor comedy used such a severe warning. We might wish to attribute the abandonment of such a signal to the rise of more literate audiences, to the growing predominance of regular playgoers, or even to the growth of a preference for unpredictable play-endings. Sadly, because of its less than laudatory implication for audience thinking, it seems that the practice died away only when the new mode of tragicomedy with its suspenseful endings began to take control of the repertories.

Notes

1. Thomas Heywood, *A Warning for Fair Women: A Critical Edition*, ed. Charles Dale Cannon (The Hague: Mouton, 1975), [Induction]. The text is from the 1599 quarto. Subsequent references are from this edition and are cited parenthetically; citations follow the through-line numbers assigned by Cannon.

2. Like the similar story of *Arden of Faversham*'s murder by his wife, in print seven years before *Warning*, the story was supplied at length in both editions of Holinshed's *Chronicles*.

3. A remarkable side effect of this claim is the evidence it provides that the company now thought of itself as wholly London-based, not simply doing what the companies that preceded the duopoly set up in 1594 had done, visiting London as one stop in a routine sweep of the whole country. The Privy Council's licensing of the Theatre and the Rose as the duopoly playhouses confirms this new concept.

4. The Chamberlain's Men sold quite a number of their most popular plays to the press, chiefly through their agent James Roberts, between 1597 and 1600. All of them were at least a year or more old when they first appeared in print.

5. Scott McMillin and Sally-Beth MacLean assert that the Queen's Men claimed that their own history plays were distinct from other plays because as history they were telling truths: *The Queen's Men and Their Plays* (Cambridge: Cambridge University Press, 1998), 133.

6. It also signals a major shift in the mindset of the duopoly's players, or at least of those writing for it, namely, the expectation that the duopoly's audiences would henceforth be exclusively made up of Londoners and that the old tradition of using London as only one stopover in the general practice of touring the whole country had now come to an end.

7. Roslyn L. Knutson suggests that, along with several other unascribed plays, it might have belonged to the Chamberlain's Men. She argues as additional possibilities *Fair Em*, performed at the Rose by Sussex's with *Titus Andronicus* in January 1594, *A Knack to Know a Knave*, *Arden of Faversham*, *Edward III*, and the lost *The Tartarian Cripple*. She notes the link between some Pembroke's plays and the duopoly company, including some of Shakespeare's plays that moved from Pembroke's to the Chamberlain's, but there is nothing to link *A Warning* or *Fair Em* with those transfers: "Shakespeare's Repertory," in *A Companion to Shakespeare*, ed. David Scott Kastan (Oxford: Blackwell Publishers, 1999), 349–50.

8. However, Tiffany Stern has pointed out (in conversation) that in the prologue to his tragedy *The Cardinal* (1641), James Shirley wrote "you may / Think what you please; we call it but a Play."

9. Verna A. Foster has chapters entitled "Shakespearean Tragicomedy: *Measure for Measure*: The Duke's Problem Play versus Shakespeare's Tragicomedy" and "*The Winter's Tale*: Tragicomedy of Wonder": *The Name and Nature of Tragicomedy* (Aldershot, UK, and Burlington, VT: Ashgate, 2004), 54–64, 64–79. For obvious reasons, it is easier to slide comedies than tragedies into the tragic-comic mode.

10. *1 Henry VI*, in *The Riverside Shakespeare*, 2nd ed., ed. G. Blakemore Evans (Boston: Houghton Mifflin, 1997), 1.1.7. Subsequent references to Shakespeare's plays are from this edition and are cited parenthetically.

11. John Marston, *Antonio's Revenge*, in *The Works of John Marston*, ed. Alexander H. Bullen, 3 vols. (London: John C. Nimmo, 1887), 1:Prologue. 20.

12. Marston, *The Insatiate Countess*, in *The Works of John Marston*, ed. Bullen, 3:4.5.4–5.

13. Thomas Dekker and John Webster, *North-ward Hoe* (Old English Drama, Students' Facsimile Edition, 1914), 4.1, E3. [Middleton 1605].

14. Dekker, *Lanthorne and Candle-light*, in *The Non-Dramatic Works of Thomas Dekker*, ed. A. B. Grosart, 4 vols., The Huth Library (Printed for private circulation only, 1885), 3:296.

15. See Edwin Nungezer, *A Dictionary of Actors and of Other Persons Associated with the Public Representation of Plays in England before 1642* (New Haven: Yale University Press, 1929), 76.

16. Francis Beaumont, *The Knight of the Burning Pestle*, ed. Sheldon P. Zitner (Manchester: Manchester University Press, 1984), act 2, interlude 2, 11–15.

17. John Florio, *A World of wordes, or Most copious, and exact dictionarie in Italian and English* (London: Arnold Hatfield for Edw. Blount, 1598), 146.

18. Ben Jonson, *Cynthia's Revels*, in *Ben Jonson*, ed. C. H. Herford and Percy Simpson, 11 vols. (Oxford: Clarendon Press, 1925–52), 4:40. Other examples are given in E. K. Chambers, *The Elizabethan Stage*, 4 vols. (Oxford: Clarendon Press, 1923), 3:79.

19. Thomas Heywood, *An Apology for Actors* (1612; New York: Scholars' Facsimiles and Reprints, 1941), B2v.

20. Chambers, *The Elizabethan Stage*, 3:501.

21. With perhaps the sole exception of *Doctor Faustus*, all of Marlowe's earlier plays challenge their ostensible genre with their endings. Tamburlaine's triumph at the end of Part 1 and the enigmatic nature of his sudden death at the end of Part 2 can be matched with the malign triumph of the Christian Machiavel Ferneze over the Jewish would-be Machiavel Barabbas at the end of *The Jew of Malta*.

22. Eugene M. Waith, *The Pattern of Tragicomedy in Beaumont and Fletcher* (New Haven: Yale University Press, 1952), 27–42 and passim.

23. Melissa Aaron gives a full account of John Suckling's changes in *Global Economics: A History of the Theater Business, the Chamberlain's/King's Men, and Their Plays, 1599–1642*, 192–98 (Newark: University of Delaware Press, 2005).

Shakespeare: Rough or Smooth?

Maurice Charney

AFTER YEARS OF LISTENING TO PAPERS AT THE COLUMBIA UNIVERSITY Shakespeare Seminar,[1] the Shakespeare Association of America, the International Shakespeare Association, and assorted other professional meetings, I find myself becoming more and more of a crusader against Shakespeare bardolatry in all of its various forms. This seems an appropriate subject to take up in a *Festschrift* honoring Jim Lusardi, who held similar views although he may have been more passionate and impatient with bardolaters. The most virulent form of bardolatry is to assert, as the anti-Stratfordians do, that Shakespeare the man wasn't good enough to write the works attributed to William Shakespeare, which must have been created by someone of a more exalted social position. These social arguments go to the heart of Shakespeare bardolatry.

In teaching, I always thought of myself as a professor of *comparative* Shakespeare studies. Imagine my dismay when I discovered that this field doesn't exist. At Rutgers, we have at least a thousand students every semester studying Shakespeare—it may be because New Jersey has such a large ethnic population wanting to stake their claim in Anglo-American culture—and probably less than twenty-five students (if that many) studying all of the other dramatists who were contemporaries of Shakespeare. It is obvious, at least to me, that, although Shakespeare tried many different kinds of plays, he wasn't necessarily the best at everything he did. Certainly, Ben Jonson and Thomas Middleton wrote better comedies of London life.

Some years ago, I edited a volume of essays, with the encouragement of Harry Keyishian, called *"Bad" Shakespeare*,[2] which was based on a seminar at the Shakespeare Association of America. I remember how strenuously the publisher of Fairleigh Dickinson University Press insisted that the word "Bad" had to be put in quotation marks to call attention to the fact that I was kidding around when I used the word "bad" for Shakespeare, and that I only wanted to make an ironic and provocative point. I didn't plan to make an ironic and provocative point, but I acceded graciously even though the quotation marks undercut my campaign against Shakespeare bardolatry. The essays in the volume really address themselves to notable weaknesses in Shakespeare. It seems to be that almost the entire Shakespeare industry, led by the academy, is devoted to smoothing out Shakespeare, or to correcting him when he makes unwitting and obvious errors in classical names or in speech prefixes. These are, if you will pardon the expression, "silently" corrected by editors without any textual fuss.

There are some striking examples of this practice in *Julius Caesar*. In editing the play, I was surprised to learn that in his first scene, Caesar consistently calls Antony "Antonio" (in the Folio, which is the only text we have for this play). In the first lines of act 1, scene 2, Caesar advises his wife Calphurnia, whom he thinks of as barren, to be touched by the naked Antony while he is running the course in the Lupercalian games, because "our elders say, / The barren touched in this holy chase, / Shake off their sterile curse."[3] The sexual errand that Antony is asked to perform suggests that he is a close personal friend of Caesar. Maybe that's why Caesar addresses him as Antonio, which is a familiar Italian variant of Antony. Caesar does this consistently, first to Calphurnia: "Stand you directly in Antonio's way / When he doth run his course" (1.2.3–4). Then to Antony: Caesar calls him Antonio, Antony answers "Caesar, my lord," then Caesar delivers his directions: "Forget not in your speed, Antonio, / To touch Calphurnia" (1.2.6–7). There is virtually not a single edition of this play that has Caesar saying "Antonio." It is corrected to "Antonius" or "Antony" in order to show that Shakespeare was not napping when he designed the speech prefixes but was regular, consistent, and rational. Also, that he knew his Latin. A small point, admittedly, but there is an important issue involved about the assumptions that editors make about Shakespeare.

There is no doubt that Shakespeare has been overedited when compared to all the other Elizabethan and Jacobean dramatists. The point that Shakespeare is regular—and maybe also a regular guy—is also brought home forcefully in modern translations of Shakespeare. André Gide's *Hamlet* is a notorious example, but the wonderful new translations—they are actually bilingual—of Shakespeare by the poet Yves Bonnefoy are also a case in point. For all their excellence, they present Shakespeare in what seems like a bloodless, classical French that avoids grappling with Shakespeare's vivacious colloquial and slang. Perhaps in this sense, Shakespeare is literally untranslatable, because colloquial and slang have a different status and function in the French language than they do in English. This is also true of other modern European languages. Most non-English speaking readers have in translation an awfully smooth Shakespeare that does not accurately render his Elizabethan English. I am not speaking of errors but of differences in the level of usage that distort Shakespeare's style in English.

For some samples of what I mean, I would like to look at Bonnefoy's translation of *Othello*.[4] The soaring lyric and dramatic speeches are beautifully done—they are very poetic. The problems arise in the cruder and rougher aspects of *Othello*, especially in the part of Iago. Honest Iago presents himself as a man of the people, an ordinary Venetian, unlike the exotic Othello, who is African, and the better trained Cassio, who is a Florentine. Iago's insidious and sardonic plot begins when he comments to Othello on Cassio's leaving Desdemona: "Ha? I like not that" (3.3.35). "Ha" is a so-called meaningless interjection in English, a harsh and crude sound unlike the "ha's" associated with laughter. Bonnefoy translates Shakespeare's "Ha" by the colorless word "Ah," and has Iago say "Ah, je n'aime pas cela." One would think that the colloquial "ça" would be more appropriate than "cela" for Iago at this point. Iago's distinctive "Ha" echoes throughout this scene and throughout the play.

When Emilia first offers Iago Desdemona's handkerchief, she says, "I have a thing for you" (3.3.301), which Iago interprets in a purely vulgar and sexual sense: "A thing for me?" (3.3.302). The French "quelque chose" doesn't have quite the same sexual innuendo as "thing," but Emilia's "Ha?" (3.3.303) echoes Iago's word earlier in the scene. The effect is entirely lost in Bonnefoy's "Quoi donc?" Later in the same scene, Othello's "Ha, ha false to me?" (3.3.333) is rendered as "Ah, elle m'aurait donc trompé," with Bonnefoy's "Ah" replacing Shakespeare's "Ha."

I don't want to dwell on the "Ha's" in *Othello*, but "Ha" is a distinctly Iago word. Let me give a few other examples. At the beginning of the play, Iago wants to provoke Desdemona's father, Brabantio, into some radical response to his daughter's elopement with Othello. Iago cultivates much vulgarity: "Even now, very now, an old black ram / Is tupping your white ewe . . ." (1.1.88–89). Bonnefoy's translation is twice as long as the original: "Oui, juste exactement en cette minute, / Un vieux bélier, la nuit ténébreuse en personne, / Cherche à saillir votre blanche brebis." "Saillir," although it refers to the breeding of horses, is a pretty tame equivalent for "tupping," which is much closer to the English "fucking."

Similarly, Othello's explanation in the final scene, "Cassio did top her" (5.2.136), doesn't have the same connotations as "Cassio l'a possédée" in Bonnefoy. I have many more examples where Shakespeare's English seems vivid and pungent and Bonnefoy's French much more proper. In the brothel scene, for example, when the grieving Othello says to his wife, "Pray, chuck, come hither" (4.2.24), "chuck," or little chick, doesn't seem properly rendered by "mon petit." That seems pallid. Or, for a final example, Iago's colloquial "Why, go to, then" (3.3.208) about Desdemona and her betrayal of her father doesn't seem properly translated by "Faut-il chercher plus loin?" ("Do we need to look any further?"), which seems altogether too formal.

Julius Caesar is an even better play than *Othello* from which to draw examples about Shakespeare rough or smooth because it has the most limited vocabulary of all of Shakespeare's plays. It is definitely an experiment in what Shakespeare conceived as the Roman style. When Brutus responds to his wife's emotional entreaties that he should share his secrets with her—if she were left out, she would be "Brutus' harlot, not his wife" (2.1.287)—Brutus says in a confessional tone: "You are my true and honorable wife, / As dear to me as are the ruddy drops / That visit my sad heart" (2.1.288–90). Brutus' Roman blood makes "ruddy" not "red" drops; it is a homely, countrylike fluid, and this is a distinction that translators are likely to miss. How to render "ruddy" in French? Brutus' heart's blood is personified in a plain way because it pays a visit to his "sad" or serious heart. It is one of the most moving speeches that Brutus makes in the play. Admittedly, Brutus is not Romeo, but this is pretty passionate for a legendary Roman Stoic.

Hamlet alone could provide all of the examples I need to make my point about Shakespeare's cultivation of a rough style. By "roughness" I mean literally quick and sudden changes in the level of usage from formality to coarseness, from oratorical loftiness of diction to a crude and harsh slanginess. Harold Jenkins,[5] in his Arden edition of *Hamlet*, objects to a lot of the Folio additions as mere "actors' interpolations," which should be stricken from the true text. For example, in the closet scene, Jenkins omits Hamlet's anguished cries before he enters: "Mother, Mother, Mother!" (3.4), which he speaks from offstage. This is from the Folio text (Q1 has only two "Mothers"), and Jenkins, as we know, wants to purify his Q2 text from Folio excrescences. As it turns out in the closet scene, and as is abundantly evident in the soliloquy that ends act 3, scene 2, Hamlet is steeling himself not to kill his mother, whom he considers Claudius' accomplice in the killing of his father. Behind Hamlet's offstage cries of "Mother, Mother, Mother!" lies the uncertain resolve: "let not ever / The soul of Nero enter this firm bosom" (3.2.393–94).

If it is indeed an actor's interpolation that didn't exist in Shakespeare's original text, what a pity not to include it in the text of *Hamlet* that John Heminge and Henry Condell gave to the printers for the 1623 Folio edition. It is dramatically effective, even startling, as a way to set the tone of the closet scene before Hamlet even enters. Bravo for Richard Burbage for perhaps being Shakespeare's unacknowledged collaborator on *Hamlet*. The harshness of "Mother, Mother, Mother!" has a curious relation to contemporary American slang. These words, or at least half words, make an unanticipated link for up-to-date audiences, who would have no trouble understanding the connection—at least for those audience members who listen to rap music.

We remember the climactic words in *Coriolanus*, when the protagonist capitulates to his mother and decides to spare his native city of Rome:

> O mother, mother!
> What have you done? Behold, the heavens do ope,
> The gods look down, and this unnatural scene
> They laugh at. O my mother, mother! O!
>
> (5.3.182–85)

Unlike Hamlet, Coriolanus is an inarticulate hero who cannot deliver a comprehensive oration on his own undoing.

While I am on this tack, I would like to look at another example of highly frantic and not very smooth Hamlet from the play scene. Hamlet is overly nice here because he thinks he has Claudius in a trap to prove his guilt as a murderer. He emotes with Ophelia in a series of sexually charged exchanges. Poor Ophelia is not in a position to reply to her lover's humiliating taunts:

> *Hamlet.* Lady, shall I lie in your lap?
> *Ophelia.* No, my lord.
> *Hamlet.* I mean, my head upon your lap?
> *Ophelia.* Ay, my lord.
> *Hamlet.* Do you think I meant country matters?
> *Ophelia.* I think nothing, my lord.
> *Hamlet.* That's a fair thought to lie between maids' legs. (3.2.112–18)

The point is not exactly subtle here.

I'd like to look at one single word, "country," as an imagined adjectival form of "cunt." There is some support for this in Jenkins' note, but better support is in Iago's lascivious speech about ladies in Venice like Desdemona:

> I know our country disposition well:
> In Venice, they do let God see the pranks
> They dare not show their husbands.
>
> (*Othello* 3.3.201–3)

A few lines further, Iago speaks of Desdemona's "country forms" (2.3.237) connected with her rank "will" (3.3.232). In *The Comedy of Errors*, Dromio plays sexually on the "countries" he can find in Nell the kitchen wench (3.2.115).

The Hamlet that emerges from these examples is not the smooth Hamlet, rationalizing about the revenge which he has difficulty in carrying out but, rather, a rough Hamlet full of humiliating and vulgar sexual thoughts and sexual words. In the closet scene, I firmly believe that Hamlet enters with the idea of killing his mother. He kills Polonius instead, but there is a triviality about this murder that is disturbing. He kills the old counselor the way Pyrrhus kills Priam in the player's scene and the savage way in which Laertes intends to kill Hamlet in the fencing match. As Hamlet draws his sword, he exclaims: "How now? A rat? Dead, for a ducat, dead!" (3.4.23). "Dead for a ducat, dead" is a gambler's oath, not a characteristic utterance for the romantic Hamlet who thinks too much, beloved by nineteenth-century critics and actors and by no means extinct. For better or for worse, Hamlet is homicidal in this scene, as he certainly was in the previous scene when he refused to kill Claudius because he was looking forward to a more damnable opportunity. The very use of the aphetic form "a" for "he" is a marker for the swaggering Hamlet: "A took my father grossly, full of bread" (3.3.80). "Bread" doesn't mean money, as it does in contemporary slang, but it is still a colloquial way of referring to his living and beloved father right before the deadly poison was poured in his ear.

Hamlet's gross sexuality in the closet scene has often been noted, but critics generally fail to draw the obvious conclusions. When Hamlet shows his mother the pictures of her late husband and of Claudius, her present husband, he drives home what seems to us the clouded vision of an inflamed adolescent:

> Ha! Have you eyes?
> You cannot call it love, for at your age
> The heyday in the blood is tame, it's humble,
> And waits upon the judgment.
>
> (3.4.67–70)

"The heyday in the blood" means specifically sexual excitement, and Hamlet is drawing on what is already a myth in Shakespeare's time that

menopausal women have surrendered their sexuality. Hamlet's "ha" is
a tricky interjection with a wide range of emotional meanings in Shakespeare, many of which are picked up in *Othello*.

From this point on, Hamlet torments his mother with his own sexual
imaginings, despite the fact that it is obvious that the sexual issue is the
least of Gertrude's concerns in this scene. Hamlet luxuriates in disgust-
ing images:

> Nay, but to live
> In the rank sweat of an enseamed bed,
> Stew'd in corruption, honeying and making love
> Over the nasty sty!
>
> (3.4.91–94)

"Seam" is a word for fat, especially the fat used in roasting meat, and
Gertrude and her new husband are wallowing in sensuality like a couple of pigs in the "nasty sty." What is most disturbing in this scene is
that Hamlet can't stop his flow of revolting sexual accusations even
when his repentant mother begs him to be quiet:

> O, speak to me no more!
> These words like daggers enter in my ears.
> No more, sweet Hamlet!
>
> (3.4.94–96)

But Hamlet is by no means finished, even when the ghost of his father
entreats him: "O, step between her and her fighting soul" (3.4.113).
This is like the Ghost's earlier admonition:

> Taint not thy mind, nor let thy soul contrive
> Against thy mother aught. Leave her to heaven,
> And to those thorns that in her bosom lodge
> To prick and sting her.
>
> (1.5.85–88)

If we get back to the text of *Hamlet* and try to understand it fairly
without all the baggage that accompanies it from the theatrical and critical tradition, I think we are in for some surprises. For example, the recent movie by Michael Almereyda, with Ethan Hawke as Hamlet,[6] was
revealing in many interesting ways. It was set in New York in the present and used architectural features of the city to create an uncanny anxiety. Hawke is an unheroic, unimposing, postmodern Hamlet trying to

stay alive in an increasingly threatening environment. This unconventional movie forces us to think about *Hamlet* in new ways.

If we want to be provocative, another thing that has occurred to me is that we need a singing Hamlet to integrate with his speaking role at least a dozen snatches of song he sings at various times in the play. A singing Ophelia has been traditional for the part, but a singing Hamlet is just as important dramatically. Shakespeare relied on a familiar intertextual context supplied by popular tunes—many of them what we would consider folk songs—of the day. The excellent musicological research of such critics as Peter Seng and Frederick Sternfeld has not been well incorporated into the theatrical tradition of the play.

Hamlet's most familiar speech in the play, the "To be, or not to be" soliloquy (3.1.55–56), is full of simple, everyday, homely words that should surprise us in context. The speech may be lofty and philosophical, but it is also plain in its painful utterance. It's this mixed discourse that particularly interests me. For example, Hamlet questions himself eloquently on the value of continued life:

> who would fardels bear,
> To grunt and sweat under a weary life,
> But that the dread of something after death,
> The undiscover'd country, from whose bourn
> No traveller returns, puzzles the will,
> And makes us rather bear those ills we have,
> Than fly to others that we know not of?
>
> (3.1.75–81)

"Fardels" is a medieval, Romance word, perhaps of Arabic origin, meaning "pack; a parcel." It is definitely an unheroic word, only used again in *The Winter's Tale* for the parcel the shepherds find with the infant Perdita, whom the ill-fated Antigonus leaves on the seacoast of Bohemia.

Hamlet is speaking of "fardels," a diminutive object quite unlike the exaggeratedly large objects in his ridiculous flyting with Laertes at the grave of Ophelia:

> And if thou prate of mountains, let them throw
> Millions of acres on us, till our ground,
> Singeing his pate against the burning zone,
> Make Ossa like a wart!
>
> (5.1.280–83)

Hamlet is topping Laertes' hyperbole about Mount Pelion—in classical legend, giants in their conflict with the gods sought to reach heaven by piling Mount Pelion and Mount Ossa on Mount Olympus. There is no grandeur in fardels, which is part of the grind of daily life that stimulates in Hamlet thoughts of self-destruction. It is like

> Th' oppressor's wrong, the proud man's contumely,
> The pangs of despis'd love, the law's delay,
> The insolence of office, and the spurns
> That patient merit of th' unworthy takes.
>
> (3.1.70–73)

All of this is deliberately nonheroic and mundane, perhaps even trivial. The implication is that everyone must bear his fardels, like the fleeing Christian with his pack on his back in Bunyan's *Pilgrim's Progress*.

Also in this context, there are two other noteworthy homely words: "quietus" and "bodkin." One can escape from the annoyances of daily life, "the whips and scorns of time" (3.1.70), quite easily, but there are consequences that prevent you from making your "quietus" "With a bare bodkin" (3.1.74–75). "Quietus" occurs only once in Shakespeare's plays (but it is used in "Sonnet 126"). The *OED* defines it, in its first meaning, as "A discharge or acquittance given on payment of sums due, or clearing of accounts; a receipt," but, in its extended meaning, it is a "Discharge or release from life; death, or that which brings death." The *Hamlet* passage is cited for this meaning.

"Bodkin" in this passage is defined as "A long pin or pin-shaped ornament used by women to fasten up the hair." A bodkin can also be "A short pointed weapon; a dagger, poniard, stiletto, lancet," although this meaning became obsolete in the seventeenth century, whereas bodkin as a hatpin is still current. "Bodkin" is a diminutive, and a "bare bodkin" suggests a meaning like a "mere" bodkin, indicating that even with a hatpin one can kill oneself. This is like Richard II's discourse about Death's sudden extinction of the player king. He is allowed "To monarchize, be fear'd, and kill with looks" (*Richard II* 3.2.165), and then the antic, or clownlike, Death comes "and with a little pin / Bores thorough his castle wall, and farewell king!" (3.2.169–70). Death is deflationary and unheroic, both in *Hamlet* and in *Richard II*. It is not a smooth and easy transition from this life to the afterlife.

Hamlet offers a rich showcase of examples to demonstrate Shakespeare's plainness, or even his crudity or roughness. If we turn from this play, we can find the best examples of Shakespeare's roughness of style, extending to vulgarity and violence, in Shakespeare's villains. Aaron in *Titus Andronicus* is underrated as an experimental, early version of Iago in *Othello*, and the two plays clearly reverse the black and white polarities. Like Iago, Aaron is sardonic and self-dramatizing, in the tradition of the comic Vice figure. He is the archetypal black comedy villain, whose laughter is more disturbing than his wicked deeds. For example, Aaron later confesses his uncontrollable merriment when he persuades Titus to chop off his hand in the hope of freeing his sons:

> I play'd the cheater for thy father's hand,
> And when I had it, drew myself apart,
> And almost broke my heart with extreme laughter.
> I pried me through the crevice of a wall,
> When, for his hand, he had his two sons' heads,
> Beheld his tears, and laugh'd so heartily
> That both mine eyes were rainy like to his.
>
> (5.1.111–17)

Aaron is enormously clever, diabolically so, and his "extreme laughter" is an hyperbole for his "extreme" sport.

It is obvious that he thinks very well of himself, which is seen in histrionic exclamations of superiority. When the Nurse announces that Tamora has given birth to his black baby, he kills her at once with an astonishingly jokey imitation of her death cries: "Weeke, weeke!—so cries a pig prepared to the spit" (4.2.146). Aaron, a specialist in "extreme laughter," must be laughing here in a boastful, vaunting way. Earlier, Aaron is the first spokesman for the black-is-beautiful doctrine, when he upbraids the Nurse for calling his black baby "as loathsome as a toad" (4.2.67). He insults the white Nurse as "sweet blowse," defined in Johnson's *Dictionary* as "a ruddy, fat-faced wench." Then Aaron launches a crushing sexual pun, with proverbial roots, on Chiron's "Thou hast undone our mother" (4.2.75). Chiron is wrong, as Aaron patiently explains: "Villain, I have done thy mother" (4.2.76). This is a vulgar use of "do" as in the contemporary expression, "to do drugs." Aaron is nothing if not vigorous in his speech, and his social status as a captive barbarian makes vulgar slang appropriate for him. In his advice to Tamora's sons, Chiron and Demetrius, early in the play about how to woo Lavinia, he sees clearly what they are after: "Why then it seems some certain snatch or so / Would serve your turns" (2.1.95–96). We don't need a footnote for "snatch" to understand this passage.

The resourceful and inventive Iago masterfully shifts style so that he can appear all things to all men. In his asides and in his conversations with Roderigo, Iago speaks bluntly and plainly. With Othello, his style is somewhat more elevated, but he always aims to appear as the straight-talking, ineloquent military man. Cassio's gallantry with Desdemona really irks Iago, and all of the upper-class social gestures of Cassio are translated by Iago into crudely sexual terms. His long aside in act 2, scene 1, when Iago seems to be sportively jesting with Desdemona and Emilia, is revealing. He already understands how he can ensnare "as great a fly as Cassio" (2.1.169):

> If such tricks as these strip you out of your lieutenantry, it had been better you had not kiss'd your three fingers so oft, which now again you are most apt to play the sir in. Very good, well kiss'd! an excellent courtesy! 'Tis so indeed. Yet again, your fingers to your lips? Would they were clyster-pipes for your sake! (2.1.171–77)

A clyster-pipe is an enema tube, and it makes for an ironic contrast that, right at this moment, Iago hears Othello's trumpet.

I have been trying to argue that there is something distinctively mixed in Shakespeare's style that makes it devilishly difficult to translate. His broken discourse and broken syntax imitate speech and thought in a manner quite unlike Pierre Corneille and Jean Racine, or John Dryden for that matter, or any other so-called classical author. By the workings of Shakespeare bardolatry, however, Shakespeare has been made to seem a much smoother, a more regular and "classical" dramatist than he actually is. Remember that one of the aims of later seventeenth-century and early eighteenth-century adaptations of Shakespeare was to make him seem more of a gentleman.

Of course, bardolatry works much more vigorously for the Shakespeare we read on the page than for the Shakespeare we see in the theater. It is hard to reconcile the page and stage dichotomy, since there are good things to be said on both sides. But I think the postmodern sensibility is moving away from the idea of a final, corrected, and perfected text as the author would have wanted to see it. This old-fashioned idea is particularly unsuitable for plays, which have notoriously unstable texts that keep changing in rehearsal and performance. Thus, there is no way at all of "cleaning up" *Hamlet*, as if there were some ideal text lurking beneath different versions. Q2, the Folio, and even the much maligned Q1 are three different texts of the same play presented at different times and in different circumstances. Like Stoppard's *Rosencrantz and Guildenstern*, we should be set on edge by

Shakespeare's play and what all of its different versions could possibly mean.

NOTES

1. I presented an earlier form of this paper on April 12, 2002, at the Columbia University Shakespeare Seminar.

2. Maurice Charney, ed. *"Bad" Shakespeare: Revaluations of the Shakespeare Canon* (Madison, NJ: Fairleigh Dickinson University Press, 1988).

3. *Julius Caesar*, in *The Riverside Shakespeare*, 2nd ed., ed. G. Blakemore Evans (Boston: Houghton Mifflin, 1997), 1.2.7–9. Except for *Othello* (see note 4 below), subsequent references to Shakespeare's plays are from this edition and are given parenthetically.

4. William Shakespeare, *Othello*, trans. Yves Bonnefoy (Paris: Gallimard, 2001). Subsequent references to *Othello* (in English and in French) are from this edition and are given parenthetically.

5. Harold Jenkins, ed., *Hamlet*, The Arden Edition of the Works of William Shakespeare (London: Methuen, 1982), Introduction, esp. 62–64.

6. *Hamlet*, VHS, prod. Andrew Fierberg and Amy Hobby, dir. Michael Almereyda (2000, Burbank, CA: Miramax Home Entertainment, 2003).

II

Plays in Performance (Stage and Film)

Privileging the Spiritual: Performers, Shakespeare's Plays, and the Uses of Theater

John Timpane

Do DIRECTORS AND PERFORMERS OF SHAKESPEARE'S PLAYS PRIVI-lege "the spiritual"? That is the question I wish to ponder in this essay. At the moment, it is an important question for Shakespeare studies in general and for performance studies in particular, with the "spiritual" dimension of Shakespeare's plays—variously defined, and, I promise, I will offer my own definition below—receiving renewed attention among literary and academic critics.[1]

It is not clear what's behind the movement. Did the anarchic, skeptical energy of deconstruction and postmodernism leave a desert taste in the mouth? Has interest in the spiritual rushed to irrigate this dry place? Or does this renewed interest more nearly concern the increasingly contentious place of religion in American civic and political life?[2] Questions worth asking. In the last fifty years, there have been times when a professor would have been hooted out of some academic departments for professing an interest in religion and spirituality—and yet other times when such an interest was expected. As a moment's reflection suggests, in most cases these shifts of interest involve life outside the academy just as much as life within it.

The question of the spiritual in performance is a fitting one for a chapter in a book celebrating James Lusardi. As a scholar not only of Shakespeare but also of Thomas More and as a powerfully committed teacher of the history of English literature, Professor Lusardi was deeply interested in matters of the spirit, of belief, of transcendence. These were his motivators, the sauce to his feast of the intellect. I believe and hope he would be, and perhaps is, very interested in the notion that we might write about spiritual values in performance. I am writing this essay to acknowledge his mentorship.

GROUNDWORK

While almost all professional students of Shakespeare have written about spirituality in the plays, far fewer have examined the role of the spiritual in the performance of those plays. It is easy to see why. A text—or, at least, the agreed-upon "text of Shakespeare"—is a sitting target (or a critic can pretend it is), whereas performance, much like choreography, is far more elusive, since each director directs, say, *King Lear* differently, and each performance within the run is likely to have its singular, distinct character.

But it would be invaluable to understand what professionals in the theater do with the spiritual and to compare that with their handling of other kinds of issues.

Here, I would like to ask what directors and actors are thinking about as they approach spiritual issues in the performances in which they are engaged. Do they think or do anything differently? Sitting here as a naïve nonactor, yet as a person who has studied and reviewed Shakespearean performance for more than twenty years, I find it difficult to believe that, faced with Lear's or Gloucester's questioning of the gods, Hamlet's ironic acquiescence to the divinity that shapes our ends, or Macbeth's fatal self-deception, directors and actors would not give special thought to performance issues. *Lear* is a famous play with a famous history. Audiences often are awaiting the presentation of the play's themes with special avidity and attention. Many people are challenged and distressed by the extreme suffering Lear and others endure. You will have believers in the audience who will be distressed by the death of the "good" characters and the triumph (however momentary) of the "bad" characters, who, while they themselves are destroyed, manage to destroy Lear and Cordelia first. In almost every audience will be many people struggling in their own lives with belief, fate, and the point of existence. Audience members no doubt see the appropriateness of the questions Lear and Gloucester and other characters ask about the divine and the nature of good and evil. It would be an odd director who did not give special thought to these sensitive and emotional issues.

What kind of thought? Do directors and actors "gear up" in some special way? Do they, as I put it above, somehow privilege the spiritual?

A further question: As of 2004, when the spiritual so pervades American politics, when it is a realm of such intense debate—seen in controversies over abortion, prayer in the schools, gay marriage, stem-cell research, the separation between church and state, and many other issues—does the supercharged field of spirituality take on any special urgency in the mind of director or actor?

The essay below is based on interviews with directors and actors in-

volved in productions I have witnessed. In further honor of Jim Lusardi, I have chosen productions that either I or other reviewers have
discussed in *Shakespeare Bulletin*. In these performances, I have identified moments that seemed fraught with the spiritual, and I have asked
the actors and directors involved to explain what they were doing. At
the end of the essay, I suggest some overarching considerations, and I
hope this first gesture will encourage other writers to build on it.

Defining the Spiritual

I am far from satisfied with the use of the word "spiritual," in American parlance generally and in literary studies specifically. In both
realms, it is used as a synonym or stand-in for, or an avoidance of, the
word "religious." The two terms often are simply mixed up, bespeaking
delicacy, reluctance, hesitancy.

The spiritual comprises emotional, psychic, and intellectual states of
transcendent connection — e.g., between oneself and oneself, between
oneself and other individuals, between oneself and humanity, between
oneself and reality, between oneself and aesthetic or erotic experience,
or between oneself and the divine.

What the spiritual "transcends" are putative separators such as time,
distance, gender, class, race, point of view, politics, the body, even
(where the divine or deceased are involved) ontological status. The
transcendence makes the connection possible. The spiritual involves
conviction, revelation, ways of thinking or feeling in which these divi-
sive things disappear or cease to matter.

Some impediments are political (gender, class, race); some are physical (time and distance); some are biological (age and death); many are
psychological and emotional. To be sure, some can be used against
themselves, as vehicles of transcendence, especially in the political
realm. What do the impediments prevent? Very broadly, the varieties
of human connection and unity: alliances between or among persons
that create a third state, larger and other than any of the parties to it.
Onstage and in human experience, there is a singular psychic reward
in overcoming these impediments, in the triumph over unlikeliness.
There is massive fulfillment of many kinds of conscious and unconscious wishes: my father is dead and I want to feel close to him; I want
to understand the thought of Einstein; I hope my coworker and I can
get along in spite of our age difference. Achievement of such states is
pervaded by the spiritual. There is also a release of uncanny energy, an

expansion of the human ambit. Our worlds literally are made larger, our possibilities enhanced.

Are these states of transcendence always worldly, always grounded in the historical? To say, "No—sometimes another world is involved" would strike some as naïve, others as inevitably right. Let me confine my discussion to performance and observe that in the theater transcendence always begins in the world of the play but may sometimes extend well beyond it.

Let me also stress that not all emotional highpoints in a production are spiritual. Most uses of humor affirm impediments rather than transcend them, as in Falstaff's self-deception about his "in" with Prince Hal or Malvolio's fantasies about Olivia's love. Many uses of irony, which can be profound, concern themselves with conflicts, contradictions, the swerve of events against expectation. Sadness, while often compelling, often does not transcend its occasion; indeed, it often indulges in it.

So the moniker "religious experience," as used in Freud's *Civilization and Its Discontents*, is misleading—as well as irritating.

While it can include the spiritual, the religious more nearly concerns loyalty to and observance of strictures left behind by others who have established an institution. "Religiosity" thus has to do with obedience and observance, of being mindful of ways and rules. Those ways and rules are meant to lead to and enhance the spiritual, to make us more mindful (and more capable!) of the kinds of transcendent connections listed above.

Religions present themselves as ways into the spiritual; they institutionalize the spiritual. They furnish names and accesses to sacred texts, actions, and figures that themselves are presented as routes of access. So a spiritual experience need not be a religious one. While religious experience often is spiritual, much religious experience is institutional and technical (how to take the host, for example, or how to perform the Walking Meditation), having more to do with community, correctness, precision, conformity, sincerity, and ex- and inclusion than with the results or consequences of those attributes.

THE SPIRITUALITY OF READING

Transcendent connection in spite of obstacles—surely this is what people read for, write for, and attend plays to behold. What we often think of as the emotional "high points" of plays are very often their most spiritual moments. In light of this definition, we find that spiritual values permeate performances of Shakespeare.

In fact, by the time we witness a performance, a series of spiritual reckonings has always already taken place. Suppose you are seeing *Lear*. Someone, often the director, had to choose this play to perform. Granted, the director's reasons may involve finances (the need for a hit) or prestige as much as aesthetics. But many spiritual negotiations already have taken place between text and director. As Carmen Kahn, artistic and executive director of the Philadelphia Shakespeare Festival, puts it:

> Night and day, you wake up at two o'clock in the morning *in that play*. We're doing *Hamlet* in April, and I'm already obsessed and waking up in the play. In David Mamet's *True and False*, he talks about the character taking over the actor. Well, the same is true about the play taking over the director. I live and breathe it for about six weeks. And it's not very pleasant always. It's nicer when you're doing a comedy.[3]

There may be other reasons, too, reasons that evoke connection or the need for connection. Later in this essay, a director will explain that she chose *Romeo and Juliet* as a way to explore the political crisis in the Middle East and how the production became a response not only to that crisis but also to the terror attacks of September 11, 2001. Another director may feel, as artistic director Bonnie J. Monte of the Shakespeare Theatre of New Jersey did, that she had never done *Macbeth* very well and needed to revisit the play.

Then the process of persuasion begins. Whoever made the first choice often had to persuade other people—perhaps shareholders or the board of trustees, or perhaps just a few other actors—to do this play. These people, many of them for reasons much like those of the first chooser, reached a consensus, inherently spiritual, that the play should be performed. Then they fanned out and began to prepare for the performance. Some raised funds. Others did publicity. That involved more conviction, persuasion, connection. Others scheduled auditions and chose actors—who attended the auditions for their own reasons. Still others designed the stage, the set, the lighting, the costumes. And, after a period of reading and mastering the text, the actors and director began rehearsals. In each of these phases, all occurring before you sat down to watch *Lear*, many spiritual reckonings had to take place.

Kahn told me she is well aware of what draws her to certain plays and that she regards this transaction as definitely spiritual:

> Yes, I do pick the plays because they resonate in a transcendent way with me. . . . As an artist, there's an initial draw to a certain play, and as a person there are certain plays I am most drawn to. The father-daughter plays resonate with me, and it's all about a reconciliation, a forgiveness after a great breach. . . . As a person, that interests me, and I know there are many families that must endure breaches, and that resonates with many people. I hope that as an artist I am in touch with the pulse of the community.

Actors begin as readers, reading much as anyone reads, for his or her own purposes and resonances. The director, for personal reasons, is drawn to a text by a complex set of motives, many of which involve spiritual values. Kahn all but echoes our definition of the spiritual as she discusses the family dramas in Shakespeare: breach, forgiveness. And that should remind us that reading, especially reading of imaginative literature, is a spiritual endeavor, connecting us imaginatively to characters, situations, and themes that do not exist in our lives.

Even at this early stage, there is something more. The director is making a calculation. What will the audience like? Are my resonances in touch with theirs? In deciding to do this play, am I connecting with them or not? Kahn decided she was—a decision full of spiritual values, seeking and hoping for a connection with people one is only imagining.

That hope for connection is spiritual. It is also commercial. You have to fill the seats; theater is a business. In choosing *Lear* or *Hamlet*, you hope people will come because they have been moved by these plays before, or wish to be moved now. Other motives also exist. As Gary Taylor discusses in *Reinventing Shakespeare*, prestige plays a huge role in the perpetuation of Shakespeare.[4] *Lear* and *Hamlet*, not to exaggerate matters, are two of the most prestigious plays in history. And that will attract people, too. But the first chooser of the play must ask some profound questions of connection, and then he or she must sell the idea to others, who decide in the same way, according to the emotional impact of the play, the cost, the probable audience appeal, and so on.

Actors audition for plays not just for the sake of work but also for what they have seen as readers of the play. Other motives certainly are important—what acting in *Lear* will mean for their careers, for example. But much of what brings them to the audition is what Kahn calls "the overarching thing of us being artists, being in touch, being open." Actors already have sensed transcendent connections in the text and, by showing up at the audition, indicating a belief that they have the tools to embody those spiritual moments; they, like the director, already are hoping for connection with the audience through the performance. And all of this happens before the practical work of stagecraft.

In fact, it *has* to happen for the stagecraft to make sense. Spiritual values are the context of the choices made in stagecraft. It sounds banal, as in "well, of course," but it is crucial. Stageworkers base their craft on openness to experience, to emotion. The practical work of creating a performance would have no direction unless myriad spiritual connections like the ones Kahn describes already have happened.

ANTONY AND CLEOPATRA'S KISS

In 2000, the Shakespeare Theatre of New Jersey presented a production of *Antony and Cleopatra*, directed by the company's artistic director. Viewers were treated to two dynamic actors in Robert Cuccioli as Mark Antony and Tamara Tunie as Cleopatra. The familiar tensions were there; the contrast between Rome and Egypt, Occident and Orient, reason and passion; the irrational drive to love and be destroyed by love; the cosmic, colossal self-deception among the main characters. I was struck by the remorseless view of political reality in the performance. Antony's dealings in Egypt transpire in the languorous half-light of mysticism, sensuality, and self-deception, but when he returns to Rome in 2.2, his encounters with Caesar are bathed in a painfully bright light. Lighting master Steve Rosen's choice was more than a simple way of contrasting the two locales, as most productions do anyway; it was a signal that Antony's time is past. As the Soothsayer makes clear, Caesar, not Antony, is the man. Fate already has passed Antony by, and, for the rest of the play, in a sense, he goes down swinging.

Fascinating use was made of an area behind the main stage, separated from the main action by a dark scrim. Here is where the great battles of the play took place in shadow and slow motion. Here is where armies marched, navies clashed, wars were decided.

That scrimmed area was especially charged with the spiritual, since it enacted the great events that hem the protagonists in. Tragedies are explorations of the spiritual, since tragic protagonists pit themselves against fate and their own limitations. The fear and pity Aristotle celebrated arise from watching the great man or woman battling these limits and losing. King and queen seek to transcend the demands of custom, politics, and position. They fail, and when they realize they are cornered, they end their lives. The search for transcendence itself is what fails. That search has been willful, arbitrary, destructive—yet, in this production, it seemed to be the most authentic thing about Cleopatra and her lover.

Tamara Tunie as Cleopatra and Robert Cuccioli as Mark Antony in the Shakespeare Theatre of New Jersey's 2000 production of *Antony and Cleopatra*, directed by Bonnie J. Monte. Photo by Gerry Goodstein.

That scrimmed area presented what the protagonists could not will away: the facts of history, of victory and defeat, the consequences of bad decisions, breaches of faith, and failed strategy. At the end of the New Jersey Shakespeare production, after Octavius has his final, cold say and bears the future offstage with him, the play ends with a surprise.

In the scrimmed area, we beheld, just for a moment, the dead general and dead queen locked in an abandoned, carefree embrace, loosed of the chains of fate.

It was a bold move on many levels. To be sure, it risked sentimentality. It also read the play against the play. After an entire play that demonstrates how the protagonists cannot avoid the forces of history, this moment, nowhere in the text, presents them as beyond those forces. In that scrimmed area of elevated awareness, instead of being in the realm of history, we were in some other world, apart from it.

Monte agreed that this was a spiritual choice. Her reasons for this move are interesting:

> As a director, I get to the end of many Shakespeare plays, and they seem to end too abruptly. He's worked you up into an emotional peak, and the central figures die, and the remaining high-ranking figure comes onstage and says, "Okay, we're done." And you're left, at least I am, with dissatisfaction. This is truer of the tragedies than of the comedies, where you often have an elaborate ritual of endings, as in marriage. Every time I direct one of the histories or tragedies, however, even some of the comedies, the spiritual button isn't pushed hard enough. The absence of the central figure has created an unsatisfying vacuum, denying us a last connection. Maybe I'm talking about what a contemporary audience needs. I'd love to know whether that's what an Elizabethan audience wanted. We want a different kind of closure that's more spiritual.[5]

She reported finding Antony and Cleopatra "particularly troubling" in this regard and feeling that "there needed to be a moment of seeing them in their pure state, see what made them this couple to begin with, and so—because the moment took place in that odd scrimmed space, between the shades of time and place and dimension—we get just a glimpse of the pure heart of what made them such a dynamic and mythic couple." Worried about the impact of this final scene, she and the company sat through it repeatedly in rehearsals: "We tried it 500 different times, different ways, different timing, and I ultimately said, 'Let me just watch it in rehearsal, see it at the end as it happens,' and I did feel spiritually satisfied with it. It gave me a breath of them."

Directors and actors make choices based on their reading and their sense of their audience, hoping for connection. You could see Monte's choice as a commercialistic pandering to the audience or as a final presentation of the apotheosis of these two lovers. What saved it from sentiment, I think, was the roughness of Antony and the orgasmic surrender of Cleopatra. It gave us a view of these two as they wanted to be, as they and others often speak of them, indeed, as we imagined them, yet as they never are (or can be) in the play.

Where were we in that last moment behind the scrim? The realm of desire, and not just of ours as audience; we were in the world of the characters' desire, an image of transcendence of flesh and time.

OPHELIA AT THE FORE

The 2001 season at the Shakespeare Theatre of New Jersey featured a *Hamlet* directed by John Gilroy. Reviews made much of the fact that famed Irish actor Richard Harris would play the Ghost in a special video projection, and that Jared Harris, his son, would play Prince Hamlet, thus giving a special verisimilitude to their interactions. Like the other directors mentioned in this essay, Gilroy took an active stance with the text. He cut almost all of Hamlet's references to God, presenting Hamlet as a skeptical young man with, as I said in my review, "a nameless disaffection with existence."[6] Gilroy also cut Fortinbras right out of the play, so there are no attempts, even verbal, at closure at the end; the final words were "Why does the drum come hither?" from a half-mad Horatio.

This approach eliminates many of the redeeming values often stressed in other productions. This Hamlet is existentially at odds with the universe and with the audience. As I asked in my review: "What saves the tragedy from emptiness?"[7]

The answer: Ophelia. Gilroy's *Hamlet* emphasized the centrality of her tragedy to Hamlet's motivations and actions in the second half of the play. In too many *Hamlet*s, Ophelia gets lost in the whirl of the prince's language. Her part is of few lines, and her past with Hamlet is only sparsely mentioned. If productions do not take care with Ophelia, her tragedy will go overlooked. But, as directed by Gilroy and realized by Lili Taylor, Ophelia assumed a central cohering force, a spiritual force.

As Monte did with *Antony and Cleopatra*, creating a scene not called for in the text, Gilroy went to great lengths to give some backstory to the Hamlet/Ophelia liaison. The production opened on a dimly-lit love nest strewn with pillows and coverlets. Through a transparent screen (another screen!), we saw Ophelia and Hamlet embracing. Hamlet fixes a chain to Ophelia, and they dance. At last, Hamlet pulls down a curtain and leads Ophelia away.

Although a trifle obvious, the scene established crucial things about the Hamlet-Ophelia connection. The relationship is indeed sexual; it is mutual (Hamlet is deeply involved and not just leading Opheila on); all the power and advantage are on Hamlet's side. Hamlet leads her off-stage, implying that the relationship will destroy both parties and con-tribute to the tumble of lethal confusions to come.

Taylor was an Ophelia with attitude, as I wrote, "Hard as stone, yet showing propensity both to love and to be hurt by love."[8] She stands up skeptically to Laertes' warnings to guard her (already lost) virginity. In many productions of 3.1, Hamlet orbits an immobile Ophelia who is holding her head and reeling with the amphibologies spouted by the verbal prince. But Taylor's Ophelia lets us know at every turn what she thinks, "projecting wordless responses—outrage, objection, determina-tion to stand up for herself, disappointment, shock—to Hamlet's self-canceling utterances."[9] Having chosen Hamlet with eyes wide open, she will fight for him, despite the constraints woven around her by Polon-ius, Claudius, and Hamlet himself.

Taylor's Ophelia is fighting for the very notion of meaning. Meaning, indeed, may be the most directly spiritual thing of all, a connection that, if it does not transcend all obstacles in its path, transcends enough of them to seem miraculous. For me to intend something, express it, how-ever roughly and readily, and for you to receive it, despite all the ways it may be garbled, misconstrued, redirected, or deflected, and for us to come to a consensus of two, to agree that for our purposes the meaning has reached home, is close to miraculous sometimes. In *Hamlet*, with the smeared utterances of the Ghost, the evasions of Gertrude, the careful verbal flowerets of Polonius, with Rosencrantz and Guildenstern trying and failing to play Hamlet's stops, with the disheartening solo of Osric, meaning—the possibility of connecting with anyone—faces constant defeat. Taylor's Ophelia, even in her madness, insists that meaning ex-ists, if only between her and Hamlet. Her death plays a crucial role, for it seems to wake Hamlet up: "He seems to realize the injustice he has dealt and the depth of their mutual love; he also appears to accept that he is in a universe with permanent consequences."[10] Ophelia's death is what gives Hamlet a reason to care.

In this production, Hamlet's other reasons are less than compelling.

The Ghost is a blunted, confused figure, without sufficient force to goad
Hamlet to closure. Hamlet, although outraged at Claudius the fratricide
and usurper, is cynical about the kingship and the claims of honor. But
Ophelia's death, in awakening him to what he does value, clarifies his
resolve. Without such an Ophelia, this production would have served
up a bloodbath without significance.

Gilroy and Taylor craft Ophelia as a human answer to the play's
greatest question. We act not out of duty, obligation, fear of the afterlife,
or belief in deities we imperfectly understand, but out of a sense of what
others have deserved through their sacrifice. Ophelia embodies the one
possibility for spiritual values in this nonspiritual production, the one
sign of transcendence in a production that denied transcendence.
Again, there were risks: some might object that this approach boils
Hamlet down to a love story and minimizes its cosmic impact. But again,
Gilroy and Taylor show that in fighting for Hamlet's love, Ophelia is
fighting for an epiphany, a motive for action. Even if one thinks Gilroy's
approach with the text was a little too slash-and-burn, he—and especially the superb Taylor—may well have discovered the true Ophelia.

A Man and Daughter Afraid: Decisions About *Lear*

From February 15 to March 24, 2002, the Philadelphia Shakespeare
Festival presented a production of *King Lear*. Reviews praised the
strength of the performances and the emotional impact of the production. In my review for *Shakespeare Bulletin*, I wrote the following:

> By the time Lear makes his "God's spies" speech in 5.3 . . . both he and
> Cordelia know they are being led away to their deaths, and both are terri-
> fied, but each tries to rally the other to maintain dignity, each pretending for
> the other's sake not to be scared. . . .
>   Cordelia and Lear teach each other what Edgar and Gloucester teach
> each other: the will to hold on in the face of hopelessness. And that is enno-
> bling and meaningful—though it does leave one with survivor's anger.[11]

The decision to portray Lear and Cordelia as afraid was made, I assume, by Kahn in concert with the actors under her direction. It was a
choice. Not all productions portray the king and the princess this way.
In some, father and daughter emphasize dignity over all, and it is hard
to see any fear in them. In others, father and daughter are portrayed as
unsuspecting of a doom the audience knows is waiting. In still others,
Lear is still not in his right mind and is really looking forward to a long

life in prison with her. But in Kahn's production, they know their lives will not be long, and they are frightened, and they help each other stand up to face what's coming. Each reminds the other of what they are. They teach and learn.

This choice emphasizes the very kind of transcendence-in-spite-of-barriers we are defining as "the spiritual." It stresses and strengthens what we see in Edgar, in Kent, and also—wavering, but then re-gained—in Gloucester: the will to endure, even when there seems to be no point. Endurance becomes its own value. Goneril's suicide, as a fail-ure to endure, thus indicates her lack of humanity. This value tran-scends and unites individual characters; they have connected with one another and made their several progresses more meaningful to the be-holders.

Why was it important to show fear and weakness in Lear and Corde-lia in 5.3? Was Kahn consciously aware of the teaching aspect of their relationship—that Cordelia and Lear teach each other just as Edgar teaches first Lear and then Gloucester? This theme seems crucial to the play. If the young and old don't connect in this manner, their lives and deaths mean less. How consciously was Kahn working toward what seemed (to me, at least) to be a clear, transcendent meaning in the pro-duction?

Kahn agreed that the moment was "spiritual" as per our definition, and she also agreed that she had seen the teaching aspect and the paral-lels with Edgar and Gloucester. For her, the question was not so much theme, however, as it was the practical work of presenting that theme. Getting to transcendence, in her words, is "a very practical affair":

> And so, I would not talk to actors about a moment being a spiritual moment, because that would send them into fits of confusion. If I were directing you as Edgar, we would talk about the actual action and language of the play, and what you're doing. There is a particular thing I want to try to reveal, but the actual way to reveal it is a very practical thing, after which we have to hope that the audience gets it. We don't go into great conversation about these things. So [in 5.3] with Cordelia and Lear, what we talked about was that the language was mostly Lear talking, that there were many feminine endings, indicating a very emotional frame of mind, and so on. What was revealed to the audience, and to you when you noticed the fear in Lear and Cordelia, was achieved through that work.

Once an actor is off-book, once the text is mastered, hard, practical work remains. Actors look for structure. Kahn and company were aware that "that moment in 5.3 grew up out of a series of many other moments—and to make sense of it, we had to keep track of them all and express that in our performance." They were especially aware of parallelism and antithesis. Edgar as Mad Tom with Lear, then Edgar with Gloucester, leads to Lear with Cordelia. In each case, a person with perspective on suffering teaches someone else to endure suffering. Cordelia says, "For thee, oppressed king, I am cast down," and Lear hastens to assure her that she should not be: "Wipe thine eyes" (5.3.24). Repeated throughout the play, then, are scenes of teaching. Kahn has a quintessentially practical point: if you do not do justice to the parallelisms in the play, the audience won't see the ways in which spiritual values connect these different scenes.

Director and actors were keenly aware of the impact of time and space. Lear and Cordelia, for example, do not see each other at all from 1.1 until 5.3. In some productions, that may be as long as three hours. Their meeting in 5.3, with its many ironic parallels with 1.1, is inevitably extremely emotional. Lear does most of the talking because, for one thing, he usually does, and, for another, he is trying to atone with Cordelia ("When thou dost ask me blessing, I'll kneel down / And ask of thee forgiveness" [5.3.10–11]), very much to speak what he feels, not what he ought to say. In this production, since they cannot save themselves (and they know it), they can at least be father and daughter. This is the only time in the play we see Lear and Cordelia as they would want to be, as a father, talking in family prattle to his scared daughter. Kahn implies that the practical work of theater leads to spiritual effects—indeed, that those are the intended and ideal results of that work.

BEYOND THE END: SPIRITUALITY AND THE USES OF THEATER

People do privilege the spiritual in performance. Monte stresses that, since the plays are so rich with spiritual opportunity, performance boils down to a process of exclusion and focus, of choosing the moments you believe you can achieve and, as for the ones you can't, hoping for the best:

For me, the spiritual issues of the play are *the* issues of the play, and if you have ignored them, you have missed the play. All issues in Shakespeare that are worthwhile, if rightly understood, are spiritual. You need to choose the most important, and then aim your focus at them. . . . You have to choose, eliminate, hone in on which of the spiritual issues you can emphasize, focus on that, and then you create a landscape or environment in which the spiritual can thrive and be illuminated.

At least one other consideration involves the spiritual: the uses of the performance in the world, what this *Lear* or that *Twelfth Night* or this *Comedy of Errors* will do or say in the world outside the theater. We are speaking of performance as statement, as instrument of change.

A range of critical thinkers scoff at this notion. For them, there are too many problems and hazards in assuming one's performance can have any effect beyond the theater walls. Theoretically, there probably are. But performance is only intermittently theoretical; what once was theoretical becomes practical. Once they are assembled and rehearsing, once the money has (or hasn't) been arranged and the run has been advertised and there *will* be a play, actors and director must face, always do face, this question: Why this play now? What are we trying to say or do with it?

At some moments in history, the question is all but inevitable. In the United States, *Lysistrata* has been surfacing regularly, with each major war of the last one hundred years. And more localized social and political events can make performances *seem* to be statements when perhaps they were not meant to be.

In 2003, the Shakespeare Theatre of New Jersey presented a production of *King John* that the audience, in a spirited postproduction discussion, insisted was a commentary on the presidency of George W. Bush, even though director Paul Mullins said he'd had no such intention. Sometimes playgoers will ascribe uses to a production whether the director wanted them or not.

Then we have the production that is intended to speak to the moment and to change hearts and minds. From September 9 to September 30, 2001, Emily Mann's production of *Romeo and Juliet* at the McCarter Theatre Center in Princeton, New Jersey, offered a spare, streamlined production that focused as much on the social forces swirling around the lovers as on the lovers themselves. Reviewer Barbara Ann Lukacs noted Mann's determined way with the text, cutting almost a third of the lines, "paring the text down to a little over two hours of stage traffic"[12] in favor of a powerful depiction of the family and political conflicts enfolding and dooming the teenagers—who, by the way, were played by very young actors, a move that emphasized the hopelessness of their quest, very much from the beginning.

Lukacs also noted something that immediately struck me and many other audience members: this production brought out, in Lukacs' words, "a striking resemblance between elements in the play and several trouble spots in today's world."[13]

Boldest of all was the final scene. In the traditional text, Lady Capulet, Juliet's mother, dies offstage. Her death is announced, almost as an afterthought, at 5.3.210–11. Lady Capulet's part is tiny in terms of lines. But in Mann's production, both mothers take on a new importance, which Lukacs' memorable conclusion aptly captures:

> As in Shakespeare, the Prince delivers the final lines in the play, but only he and his entourage exit. The Capulets and the Montagues remain in the tomb as the stage lights darken. Significantly, Lady Montague does not die offstage as in Shakespeare's text, with Montague announcing that event on entering the tomb (5.3.210). In Mann's production, she is a presence in the closing scene at the tomb, and she extends her hand to Lady Capulet over the bodies of their deceased children. This gesture of reconciliation reaffirms and echoes Mann's vision at the opening of the play. Mothers lose their male and female offspring to senseless violence. It is fitting that those from whose wombs the innocent victims spring should make the first gesture at reconciliation and truce. Now, the tomb becomes the womb of future peace and sanity.[14]

As Lukacs implies, the bureaucrats, after mouthing the necessary public words of rapprochement, are rendered almost irrelevant; they almost have to leave because they are no longer the point. The fathers of the dead children must be restrained by bystanders; they're still full of anger and ready for violence. It is left to the mothers to take the first step. This was a scene that asked: "How, when violence has existed for so long, can violence end?" Bureaucratic platitudes and the promises of golden statues seem hollow next to this gesture. We have to find a way out of this, and it begins with our own willingness to connect.

Here was yet another choice by director (and, as we will see, actors) to honor another spiritual moment, indeed, to see an opportunity for one, in the play if not in the text, and to make it happen. Lady Montague seeks transcendent connection with Lady Capulet, a way to begin a process of social change, to create a new world in spite of obstacles of family loyalty, the habit of violence, and the drive for revenge.

When asked what was most important to her in theater, Mann told me, without hesitation:

> How the piece touches the world, because I care so much about what's going on in the world. That's a big part of my life, and my work reflects that. There are certain stories that have an incredible need to be told at cer-

tain moments in time. They've existed for centuries because human beings keep doing the same thing over and over again. We are stuck in certain stories that we keep on living.[15]

In the summer of 2001, tensions in the Middle East once again had escalated. This, Mann told me, was much of her original reason for choosing *Romeo and Juliet* at that time: "It provided that sense of urgency, of necessity to do this play here and now. I was looking at the cycle of violence in the Middle East, a cycle of violence that just keeps going but that has to end somehow. It escalates into murder, mayhem, chaos, just as we see in *Romeo and Juliet*."

Mann said she was aware that "in most productions, it's all about the lovers, but I saw their affair in a historical and political context." She was led to place more emphasis on the parents, the families, and their responsibility for the persistence of the "ancient grudge" in Verona. Somehow, these families have let themselves be brought to a point at which, in Mann's words, "Their hatred for one another becomes more important than the welfare of their children." She saw many parallels between the Veronese feud and the Israeli-Palestinian conflict, the scene of suicide attacks by women and young people.

"It became essential to show how the parents respond to the devastating destruction of their children in the feud," Mann said. This guided her to have both mothers present in the tomb. (Indeed, she was critical of the text: "I didn't think it added anything to have Lady Montague die offstage.") The future now depends on the parents' ability to bridge the ancient hatred.

The idea of the mother reaching out had long been in Mann's mind:

> From the beginning, as a company, we had been driving at the notion of breaking the cycle of violence. I had even written in a comment in my copy of the script: "Does one of the mothers try to reach over the divide to the other mother?" Then one day, it just seemed like the inevitable thing to do, and I whispered this to [Susan Tenney, who played Lady Montague], who told me later that she had almost been on the verge of doing that herself.

Mann already had been noticing how Tenney was interpreting the needs of Lady Capulet, as in 5.3 when the men nearly come to blows over the deaths of the children. Wordlessly, Tenney-as-Montague had "looked across at Lady Capulet, and I could see on one mother's face that *she* knew that the *other* mother was involved in a moment of grief." Knowingly or not, Tenney was investing in her character an expression of empathy, a will to transcend hatred. From there, the gesture seemed inevitable and right.

A final, unsuspected irony awaited, one that would reinforce the significance and aims of the performance. The run opened on September 9, 2001, meaning that the second preview took place on the evening of September 11. Now a changed political environment awaited the words, actions, and vision of the company. Now the nameless, reasonless feud of supposedly civilized people in Verona, a feud that reaps a bloody harvest of innocent life in Romeo, Mercutio, Tybalt, and Juliet—now all this commented not on a struggle in foreign lands far away but on the trauma and anger at home, freshly provoked by terror. All was invested with, in Mann's words, "a weird prescience," a new resonance that seemed to clarify the direction and purpose of the performers. "To see it that night, and then to see it on September 12, to feel the change, to see what that did to the company, how it felt to be doing that in the theater, how the audience's reactions changed—I was really feeling how the piece touches the world."

In a November 4, 2004, dialogue with playwright Tony Kushner, reported to me by Michael Robertson of The College of New Jersey, Mann engaged in a vigorous debate about theater as a social force. Both she and Kushner were quite candid about the quest for connection and transcendence in their work, as well as their intentions to address social issues from a standpoint of protest and a demand for social change. Characteristically, Mann declared that her aim was not simply to present arguments but also to "convert" those who did not agree or did not understand. Kushner disagreed, saying that he realized, especially in the political atmosphere of 2004 America, that there were millions he could never convert and that he chose instead an eloquent depiction of the issues and their consequences and hoped for the best among a diverse audience.[16] Neither side persuaded the other, but both made clear that, for them, no performance can be limited to its aesthetic or verbal tropes; no performance takes place in a vacuum.

We arrive at the very nature of performance. Performers assume, as a central part of their professions, that something important always is at stake in acting out a Shakespeare play. As Kahn told me, adult dramatic theater is "very much like children at play—they're playing, but they're not pretending." Adults at play take huge, real risks; they explore the universe of human experience and emotion. Courage is involved:

You have to be brave to really go to some of the places Lear goes to. For an actor to really go through that rage and endure what he endures and have the audience get it and not "be pretend"—not all actors can do it. You have to risk something personally. You're not even thinking of audience, or how you look—you just have to leap into it with all the work you've done.

If spirituality is to mean anything at all, it must involve a stake—our highest aspirations, our sense of groundedness outside ourselves, ways of being, thinking, imagining, and feeling that expand our understanding of ourselves, one another, and the world we share. It is spiritual to read love letters between one's grandparents; to hear Beethoven's Fifth Symphony; to recite the Lord's Prayer at Sunday Mass; to behold people greeting one another as passengers disembark from an airplane; to watch Verona sacrifice its young to violence and then to be reminded of the violence endangering ourselves. In all of these, we are establishing or sharing or hoping for connections, commonalities, shared ground, that enlarge the clearing of our own lives.

It would be nice to think that organized religion always is a good steward of the spiritual. Since too often that's not the case, however, let's ask whether the theater—which grew out of religion, out of ritual, the need to perform public actions with cosmic significance—may not be the better steward. One may well be skeptical of its social efficacy. Theater can seem a peripheral institution, on the margins of the fiery world of politics and mass persuasion. Yet when we consider the thousands of plays performed on any one night in the United States and the millions who attend a Shakespeare play each year, we might well ask where is the periphery and where the center. Kushner grants the problem: not everyone will connect. But connection is the object, whether the director is trying to convert the audience, as Mann is, or present the issues, as Kushner is.

Monte gave a masterful peroration (though she did not know she was doing it) in response to my direct question: "So, do you think performers privilege the spiritual?"

I can't speak for anyone else, but for me, I do feel we do do something different, that we do privilege the spiritual. First of all, facing spiritual issues in Shakespeare's plays forces me, personally, to face those issues in my life and ask, "Well, others are facing these issues, too—that's a good reason to maybe put this play on." And when I see other people's productions, I am not particularly compelled by those that do not face the spiritual issues. Many don't, and therefore they miss the whole point of any play. If you did *Romeo and Juliet* as *only* a love story, you'd miss the play. Somebody could direct *Macbeth* and do it for the politics, which are there. But I don't find those as interesting. My interest in that play would be what creates the victory of evil in people, a question that bears great impact on the whole human world, the whole fabric of society. Most of the plays deal with these larger issues, and it's rare that they aren't a huge part of what we're doing. Bringing forth these signature spiritual moments—it's a huge responsibility. You can change people with theater. Theater is a force of change, and you can't take that lightly.

Theater—especially Shakespearean theater—is one powerful means by which society works out its problems. That work involves anguish, terror, crisis, heroism, failure, and elation. Because of their familiarity; their tradition and prestige; their verbal, intellectual, and emotional density, Shakespeare's plays become especially potent tools of transcendent connection, between actor and drama, actor and audience, theater and world, and beholder and humanity.

NOTES

1. I wish to thank Eric S. Mallin of the University of Texas for his generous insights regarding the increased critical interest in spiritual values in Shakespeare. In August 2003, Mallin presented "*Titus Andronicus*, the Slasher Film, and the Violence of Unbelief" at the inaugural conference of the British Shakespeare Association at De Montfort University in Leicester, as part of a series of papers on "Shakespeare, Theory and Spirituality." Various deconstructionist and postmodern thinkers have sprinkled their work with invigorated concern for questions of spirituality. Slavoj Žižek's *On Belief* (London and New York: Routledge, 2001) explores a "suspension" of the ethical category in favor of certain brands of religious fervor. In *Specters of Marx* (London and New York: Routledge, 1994), Jacques Derrida reads *Hamlet* for both its tragic vision and its possibilities as a site of ethical thinking, of a species of tragic hopefulness. As of this writing, René Girard's rereadings of Shakespeare plays (see *A Theatre of Envy: William Shakespeare* [Oxford: Oxford University Press, 1991]) have energized critical discussion of the spiritual values in them. Stephen J. Greenblatt has continued his study of Shakespeare's spiritual background in *Will in the World: How Shakespeare Became Shakespeare* (New York: W. W. Norton, 2004), which joins the long-sustained critical battle over putative strains of Protestant and Catholic thought in the playwright's works. Also, at the 2005 meeting of the Shakespeare Association of America, Robert S. Miola led a seminar on "Shakespearean Catholicities." Ewan Fernie's *Shame in Shakespeare* (London and New York: Routledge, 2002) offers a masterful view of the spiritual value of shame as Shakespeare understood it and recommends that understanding as a touchstone for a construction or reconstruction of contemporary moral values. I also admire Graham Ward's discussion of the word "religion" in *Romeo and Juliet* in *True Religion* (Oxford: Blackwell, 2002) and the work of Simon Palfrey, particularly his essay "Macbeth and Kierkegaard" in *Shakespeare Survey* 57 (2004): 96–111. Older hallmarks of this interest include E. M. Howse, *Spiritual Values in Shakespeare* (Nashville, TN: Abingdon Press, 1955) and Ivor Morris, *Shakespeare's God: The Role of Religion in the Tragedies* (New York: St. Martin's Press, 1971).

2. Apparently, there is some sense of the present moment as constituting a "postsecular" age. See Derrida, *Acts of Religion*, ed. Gil Anidjar (London and New York: Routledge, 2001). Also see the brilliant work of John D. Caputo, *On Religion* (*Thinking in Action*) (London and New York: Routledge, 2001). In a celebrated e-mail exchange with Edith Wyschogrod in *Cross Currents* 48.3 (Fall 1998): 293–310, Caputo noted that the past year had seen two books edited by English theologians—Graham Ward, ed., *The Postmodern God: A Theological Reader* (Oxford: Blackwell, 1997) and Philip Blond, ed., *Post-Secular Philosophy: Between Philosophy and Theology* (London and New York: Routledge, 1998)—that pressed the claim that "postmodern" must be understood to mean or at least to include "postsecular." He also noted that Derrida's work had "taken a turn toward what he calls 'religion without religion,' that is, to a thinking that involves a certain repetition of basic religious structures, most notably the 'messianic'":

> Derrida now analyzes in detail notions like the gift, hospitality, testimony—and most recently, forgiveness—that have always belonged to classical religious discourse. As you well know, on the continent this renewal is very much the effect of the impact [Emmanuel] Levinas's work has had. . . . This is especially true of Derrida himself and also of Jean-Luc Marion, who speaks of a God "without being," without the "idols" of what Heidegger calls "onto-theologic." As these thinkers have been arguing, it seems that God is making a comeback.
>
> This is a fascinating development, and one that sends shock waves through certain American "postmodernist" writers . . .
>
> This development raises many questions. What does "God" mean if one speaks of a "postmodern God"? What does reason and philosophy mean? What can we say today of the most ancient religious motif of all, the desire for God? (293–94)

Are the spiritual and the religious opposed? Some writers feel they are. This opposition usually is portrayed as that between a more "authentic" personal experience of the spiritual and a less authentic imposition of it in institutionalized religion. The poet Robert Haas sums up this notion in his informal talk "Raiding the Inarticulate: A Talk on Poetry & Spirituality" (*Poetry Flash* 293: Summer/Fall 2004, 1 +.): "I'm inclined to say . . . that serious spirituality has absolutely nothing to do with morality, and, for that matter, neither does religion" (11). To his credit, Haas admits that such facile dismissal of religion is driven largely by youthful rebellion and selfishness. As I acknowledge in this essay, there certainly are tensions between the spiritual and the religious, and it is distressing how often religion disappoints. Yet billions of human beings have led their spiritual lives within religious institutions, have looked to those institutions for guidance, succor, and identity. Perhaps, in some hands, religion does do what it's supposed to do.

3. John Timpane, Interview with Carmen Kahn, October 23, 2004. Transcript available.

4. Gary Taylor, *Reinventing Shakespeare: A Cultural History, from the Restoration to the Present* (New York and London: Weidenfeld & Nicolson, 1989).

5. Timpane, Interview with Bonnie J. Monte, October 26, 2004. Transcript available.

6. Timpane, Review of *Hamlet*, Shakespeare Theatre of New Jersey. *Shakespeare Bulletin* 20.2 (Spring 2002): 8.

7. Ibid., 9.

8. Ibid., 8.

9. Ibid.

10. Ibid.

11. Timpane, Review of *King Lear*, Philadelphia Shakespeare Festival. *Shakespeare Bulletin* 20.2 (Spring 2002): 13.

12. Barbara Ann Lukacs, Review of *Romeo and Juliet*, McCarter Theatre Center. *Shakespeare Bulletin* 20.2 (Spring 2002): 10.

13. Ibid.

14. Ibid., 11.

15. Timpane, Interview with Emily Mann, November 3, 2004. Transcript available.

16. Tony Kushner and Emily Mann, "An Evening with Tony Kushner," Richardson Auditorium, Princeton University, Princeton, NJ, November 4, 2004. In a 1993 *Village Voice* interview with Don Shewey, Kushner had these thoughts on spirituality. They show him trying to plot a course that embraces both religious spirituality and the restrictions on that spirituality embodied in Marxist dialectic. Kushner seems to be trying to create a personal, postsecular spiritualism via the theater:

> Since I was a very little kid, I've always had an affinity for the supernatural. That's the side of me that's attracted to the theater. I've always had some sense of God. I find deep spiritual faith enormously attractive. People I've been involved with always turn out to be religious in one way or another. After my mother died, I really began to feel connected to something not bounded by the temporal world. I don't know if that's an ardent desire for her that can't accept her real loss.
>
> On some very deep level, I find repugnant the idea that there is such a thing as the eternal and the unchanging. The biggest intellectual breakthrough of my life was my last year at Columbia, when I read Brecht and Marx and took a class in Shakespeare with a professor who was really into dialectical analysis. Suddenly, the world made sense to me. Almost all deep religious thought is dialectical that way. It's never monolithic. It contains subtlety and sophistication, which only fundamentalist morons read out of it. But I'm also enough of a Marxist and a humanist to believe that the material world is of tremendous consequence and there is nothing that overrides it or is free of it. If there is a spiritual dimension, it's in constant interaction with the material.
>
> Which is why I feel very comfortable expressing a certain kind of spirituality in the theater. ... The cloud of unknowing has to be part of the deal of spirituality. You have to be willing to live in the unknowing. Part of faith is leaping over the chasm of doubt. If you're not afraid, you're not brave: Don Shewey, "Tony Kushner's Sexy Ethics," *Village Voice* 38.16 (April 20, 1993): 31–32.

Performing Apemantus in Shakespeare's
Timon of Athens

Frances K. Barasch

I

SHAKESPEARE INHERITED TIMON THE MISANTHROPE FROM PLUT-
arch, Lucian, and his literary predecessors, but, on a bare hint from
these sources, he originated the seriocomic role of Apemantus as a
Cynic philosopher, master of mockery and corrector of mankind. Often
treated as a disposable in theatrical adaptations, Apemantus' significance has been misunderstood almost from the start: in Thomas Shad-
well's period revision (1678), for instance, he was reshaped as the
humble adherent of a repentent Timon, while in Trevor Nunn's modern
setting (1991), he was made the homeless victim of the greedy rich.[1]
Robin Phillips (1983) presented him as an Edwardian photographer;[2]
Penny Metropulos (1997) marginalized him as a woman;[3] and Richard
McCabe (1999) portrayed him as a satirical entertainer.[4] Others have
skirted problems with the role by drastic revision.[5] Given the inconsis-
tent and probably unfinished text of *Timon of Athens*, literary critics too
have been at odds over Apemantus' role: some wisely grant him philosophical vision and an attitude of "half-amused tolerance";[6] others believe Apemantus misunderstands Timon's nature; still others claim he
was meant to serve simply as a counterpoint to the Misanthrope's
spleen and scurrility.[7] A reconsideration of Apemantus in terms of the
Cynic philosopher Diogenes suggests that Apemantus is a key figure in
the play, intended to provide Shakespeare's audience with life-affirming
values and to offer a comedic alternative to Timon's bleak misanthropy.
As such, Apemantus is indispensable to the performance of what some
have mistakenly presented as a grimly nihilistic play.[8]

Laurence Lerner put it best when he wrote of *Timon of Athens*: "The
one inevitable line, that the play could hardly exist without, is Timon's
claim 'I am Misanthropos, and hate mankind . . . .'[9] Everyone knew this

about Timon, and they were probably waiting to hear him say it."[10] Elizabethan/Jacobean literature abounds in references to Timon. According to H. J. Oliver, Shakespeare would have found allusions to Timon in "Lyly, Greene, Nashe, Lodge, Dekker, Marston" and many continental sources.[11] They, in turn, would have learned of Timon's misanthropy from Cicero (fl. 106–43 BCE), Plutarch (c. 46-c. 120 AD), Lucian (c. 115-c. 180 AD), and the Greek biographer Diogenes Laertius (early third century AD), who cited an even earlier source, which named both Timon and Apemantus as "misanthropes."[12]

Apemantus is mentioned briefly in Thomas North's widely read translation of Plutarch's "Life of Marcus Antonius." In this account, North alluded to Timon, who lived a solitary life by the sea during the latter half of the fifth century BCE:

> This Timon was a Citizen of Athens, that lived about the War of Peloponnesus, as appeareth by Plato and Aristophanes Comedies: in which they mocked him, calling him a viper and malicious man unto mankind, to shun all other mens companies, but the company of young Alcibiades. Apemantus wondering at it, asked him the cause what he meant to make so much of that young man alone, and to hate all others: Timon answered him, I do it, said he, because I know that one day he shall do great mischief unto the Athenians. *This Timon sometimes would have Apemantus in his company, because he was much like of his nature and conditions, and also followed him in manner of life.* On a time . . . that they two then feasted together by themselves, Apemantus said unto the other: O here is a trim Banquet Timon. Timon answered again: Yea, said he, so thou wert not here."[13]

Plutarch assigned causation to Timon's misanthropic behavior by comparing him with Marcus Antonius, whose friends were ungrateful after he had done them much good, but he gave Apemantus no motive to explain his association with Timon's nature and lifestyle. Others writing under Plutarch's spell also made no distinction between Timon and Apemantus. In addition to North, William Paynter mentioned Apemantus simply as having "the very same nature, different from the natural kind of man, and lodged likewise in the middle of the fields."[14] For the most part, Elizabethans tended to mock Timon and ignore Apemantus. Even Shakespeare referred to the joyless "critic Timon" without reference to Apemantus in *Love's Labor's Lost* (4.3.168).

II

The skeptic Michel de Montaigne was no exception. An admirer of Plutarch, Montaigne adopted his view of Timon as "the hater of all mankind" and paid no attention to Apemantus, perhaps because he accepted that their natures were the same. In his essay "Of Democritus and Heraclitus," Montaigne explored his own indifference toward the society of men. Considering the question of human judgment, he examined the disparate attitudes attributed to the two philosophers Democritus and Heraclitus:

> the first of which, finding and deeming human condition to be vain and ridiculous, did never walk abroad but with a laughing, scornful, and mocking countenance. Whereas *Heraclitus*, taking pity and compassion of the very same condition of ours, was continually seen with a sad, mournful, and heavy cheer, and with tears trickling down his blubbered eyes.[15]

Montaigne embellished this distinction with the Juvenalian quip: "One from his door, his foot no sooner passed, / But straight he laughed; the other wept as fast."[16] Of the two philosophers, Montaigne preferred Democritus, explaining his own cynical bent with real or seeming humility: "I like the first humor best, not because it is more pleasing to laugh than to weep, but for it is more disdainful and doth more condemn us than the other.[17] Montaigne's essay continues with a similar distinction between Timon and the Cynic philosopher Diogenes:

> We are not so miserable, as base and abject. Even so *Diogenes*—who did nothing but trifle, toy, and dally with himself, in rumbling and rolling of his tub, and flirting at *Alexander*, accounting us but flies, and bladders puffed with wind—was a more sharp, a more bitter, and a more stinging judge, and by consequence, more just and fitting my humor than *Timon*, surnamed the hater of all mankind. For look what a man hateth; the same thing he takes to heart. *Timon* wished all evil might light on us; he was passionate in desiring our ruin. He shunned and loathed our conversation as dangerous and wicked and of a depraved nature. Whereas the other so little regarded us that we could neither trouble nor alter him by our contagion; forsook our company, not for fear, but for disdain of our commerce. He never thought us capable or sufficient to do either good or evil.[18]

As in Montaigne's remarks on Heraclitus, Timon's judgment in Shakespeare's play is marred by too much feeling, mirrored not only in his compassionate gift-giving and brotherhood speech but, more specifically, in the tears with which he toasts his beloved friends: "Mine eyes cannot hold out water, methinks. To forget their faults, I drink to you" (1.2.106–8). In this context, Apemantus' scornful comment, "Thou weep'st to make them drink, Timon" (1.2.109), registers the same indifference Montaigne attributed to Democritus and, similarly, to Diogenes the Cynic, who treated all men with equal disdain.

John Leon Lievsay has demonstrated that Renaissance writers were fascinated by the legendary figure of Diogenes, representing him variously by a "low view" of him as a scurrilous wit, a jester, an ill-tempered brute, or by a "high view" that perceived him as a serious philosopher whose eccentric behavior exemplified his admirable moral stance.[19] For better or worse, English writers frequently associated Diogenes with Timon, and Peter Pauls, while granting disparities between them, has argued that Shakespeare's Timon is ennobled by his implicit association with the better Diogenes.[20] Alternately, Geoffrey Bullough has proposed the witty philosopher of John Lyly's *A moste excellent Comedie of Alexander, Campaspe, and Diogenes* as a source for Apemantus.[21] On the other hand, Willard Farnham's proposal that Montaigne may have suggested Diogenes as a model for Apemantus carries considerable weight.[22] Russ McDonald has argued persuasively that, although other philosophical writers held Shakespeare's attention, none did so "so firmly as Montaigne."[23] Shakespeare certainly read John Florio's 1603 translation of *Essais*, which he may have owned, and it offered him "not stories or characters but ideas and philosophical viewpoints."[24] Among the intertexts that may have inspired Shakespeare's play, it is clear that Plutarch was not entirely useful to him, for he contradicted Plutarch's claim, as noted above, that Apemantus was "much like of [Timon's] nature" and cast him in a different mold. "Do not assume my likeness," Apemantus warns Timon (4.3.218). It seems likely that, on hints from Montaigne, whom he read and admired, Shakespeare found the subtle distinctions that differentiate Apemantus' philosophy from Timon's self-absorbed misanthropy.

Shakespeare would have been as familiar as Montaigne with Diogenes' reputation for theatricality, his trifling, toying, and rumbling about. Diogenes was often depicted in art and literature as going about in daylight with a lighted lantern in search of an honest man. According to tradition, Diogenes once attended a banquet, where seemingly genteel guests threw bones at him. He responded by calling himself "dog" and romping about, coming to rest by lifting his leg on the guests.[25] Apemantus recalls the anecdote in the first scene of Shakespeare's play:

2. Lord. Thou art going to Lord Timon's feast?
Apem. Ay, to see meat fill knaves and wine heat fools.

·   ·   ·   ·   ·   ·   ·   ·   ·   ·   ·   ·   ·   ·   ·   ·   ·   ·   ·

2. Lord. Away, unpeaceable dog, or I'll spurn thee hence!
Apem. I will fly, like a dog, the heels a' th' ass. (1.1.260–61, 270–72)

Another legend recounts Diogenes' meeting with Alexander, who asked what he might do for him; Diogenes replied, "Only step out of my sunlight."[26] The rejection of kindness from a great lord is echoed in Apemantus' refusal to feast with Timon's guests:

Tim. O, Apemantus, you are welcome.
Apem.   No,
You shall not make me welcome.
I come to have thee thrust me out of doors. (1.2.23–25)

Popular stories of Diogenes' antics earned Cynics the reputation for audacious behavior of the sort exhibited by Shakespeare's Apemantus, whose motive, like his ancient model, is to follow an ascetic life in order to achieve virtue in its highest form.

Diogenes of Sinope (c. 412–323 BCE) was a student of Antisthenes (c. 444-after 371 BCE), founder of the Cynic sect, who taught that virtue is attained by the simple life and "the cultivation of freedom from wants, cares, and desires,"[27] desiderata embodied in the name "Apemantus," which may mean "to be free from misery and not to be affected by the evils of the world."[28] That Apemantus, like Diogenes, lived by these life-affirming tenets is implicit in his comment on Timon's nihilism: "Thou shouldst desire to die, being miserable" (4.3.248). Setting an example for his beliefs, Diogenes chose a beggar's life, ate scraps, and wore a threadbare cloak. He made his home in an earthen tub near the marketplace of Athens, where he delivered diatribes and snarled at passersby regardless of their birth or class. Counting free speech "the most beautiful thing in the world," he used it to challenge conventional values, excoriate the corrupt, and encourage reform.[29]

Apemantus speaks in the same vein as Diogenes, although more relevantly to the action of the play, as when he attacks Timon and his flatterers: "I scorn thy meat, 'twould choke me; for I should ne'er flatter thee" (1.2.38–39). Shakespeare's Apemantus, like Diogenes, is a Cynic philosopher. As such, he maintains a philosophic distance from mankind, whom he disdains without personal reasons for hatred. Like Diogenes, he does not shun society and live in seclusion. Rather, he is a public figure; men know him for his chiding. He appears in act 1 on Timon's cue: "Well mock'd" (1.1.173), words that announce the immediate entrance of the arch-mocker of Shakespeare's play. In the prosperous milieu portrayed in act 1, Timon is amused by Apemantus' insulting manner, tolerates his presence, and invites his guests to share his amusement: "Look who comes here; will you be chid?" (1.1.176).

When Apemantus offers to exchange courtesies with "Timon's dog" (1.1.180), insults the Painter, and is told, "Y' are a dog" (1.1.200), he is immediately associated with the "Cynics or Dog-Philosophers," so called after Diogenes, their most prominent member.[30]

Montaigne's distinction between the "passionate" misanthrope and the "thought" of Diogenes was not lost on Shakespeare. It reappears somewhat altered in the wilderness dialogue of act 4. Although others have considered this scene as a contest in satirical scurrility, with both men "equally matched in the linguistic skills of curse and invective,"[31] I see it as an uneven discourse between the two, in which Timon rationalizes his behavior emotionally, while Apemantus reasons calmly: "This is in thee a nature but infected" (4.3.202). Apemantus is amused by Timon's conversion and tries to dissuade him from his misanthropic exile. His is the cool attitude associated with Lucianic cynicism, that "man is an actor, and the world is his stage."[32] Offering reasoned advice, Apemantus tells Timon to play the flatterer, a role he has surely learned from his false friends. But Apemantus underestimates Timon's obsession. Not yet aware that Timon has found new gold, Apemantus incorrectly predicts, "Thou'dst courtier be again, / Wert thou not beggar" (4.3.241–42). On the other hand, he correctly forecasts that "hadst thou wealth again, / Rascals should have't" (4.3.217–18). As soon as Apemantus leaves, the Banditti passing by are given gold. Indeed, as Apemantus complains, Timon has donned a "sour cold habit" (4.3.239) and indulges in diatribes as would *seem* to be the manner of Apemantus, but the difference between them is wide: "Do not assume my likeness," Apemantus warns.

Although adhering to the Cynics' view that all men are fools, Apemantus, nevertheless, projects compassion. He shows concern for the human condition when he vexes Timon for exposing himself to the elements and chides him for assuming a beggarly guise that would be warranted had it been donned out of philosophical commitment, "To castigate thy pride" (4.3.240). Timon's distress, he argues, has come "enforcedly" and is not chosen out of a philosophical acceptance of human folly nor from a desire to cultivate virtue. Rather, Timon assumes the outer manner of the Cynic, while perverting his philosophy: hating rather than judging, motivated not by thought but by his personal loss of "the world as my confectionary" (4.3.260).

Apemantus also reveals himself as a skeptical thinker when he admonishes Timon for his excesses: "The middle of humanity thou never knewest, but the extremity of both ends" (4.3.300–1). In calling for balance, once again Apemantus recalls Montaigne, in this case the essay

"Of Moderation": "We may so seize on virtue that if we embrace it with an over-greedy and violent desire, it may become vicious. . . . A man may love virtue too much, and excessively demean himself in a good action."[33]

Indeed, Timon's immoderation was ever his practice, as the false friends well knew: there was "no gift to him / But breeds the giver a return exceeding / All use of quittance" (1.2.277–79). In the performance of the fourth act dialogue, Timon is angry and dismissive, while Apemantus, although responding to insults in kind, maintains philosophical indifference. Timon demonstrates immoderation in the diatribe that compares Apemantus with beasts, but his irrational discourse has little effect on his companion, who, seeing all men as fools, finds Timon "the cap of all the fools alive" (4.3.358). Finally, at a loss for further words, Timon offers to stone Apemantus. In the give and take of the fourth act debate, Timon's threat of violence marks him as the loser. The Cynic has bested the Misanthrope.

III

Shakespeare's Apemantus is not simply a serious philosopher; he is also a comic satirist, a wise fool whose serious pronouncements are sometimes rendered in cacophonous interplay with the utter fools of the play, sometimes in mock-prayer as in Apemantus' Grace, in the wit contest, or the slanging match. Although his quips recall the Roman satire of Juvenal or Horace, Apemantus is better understood as a Greek or Menippean satirist, whose chief method of moral teaching is to question all manner of men through mockery of their conventional values and social institutions.[34] In his encounters with Apemantus in 1.1–2 and 4.3, Timon may be viewed from the perspective of the "Menippean" Cynic, Lucian of Samosata. Lucian's "Dialogue of Timon the Misanthrope"[35] has been recognized since the nineteenth century as an important source for plot details in Shakespeare's play.[36] Oliver has pointed out some of the similar elements: references to Timon's unwise waste of his former wealth; his kindness to friends, such as his assistance to an imprisoned debtor and a father in need of a marriage dowry; the encomium on gold; the hypocrites' offer of money to Timon when he no longer needs it; and Timon's rejection of the parasites who seek his new-found gold.[37] The Lucianic satire of Apemantus further distinguishes him from Timon the man-hater.

Born in Syria, Lucian studied Greek, became a traveling lecturer, and settled in Athens, where he entertained sophisticated audiences at banquets or symposia with a new type of dramatic dialogue in which contemporary types, including courtesans, were subjected to seriocomic critiques of the Cynic.[38] Following the teaching of the ancient Cynics, Antisthenes, Diogenes, and Menippus, Lucian represented man as a puppet or mindless creature, not far removed from the beasts. In Apemantus' cynical words, "The strain of man's bred out / Into baboon and monkey" (1.1.250–51); and if the world lay in his power, Apemantus would "Give it the beasts, to be rid of the men" (4.3.323). Lucian's seriocomic works, among the few Greek satires that survived over the centuries, was one of the earliest books printed in fifteenth-century Italy, both in Greek and in Latin translation. Through Lucian, much of the Cynics' countercultural use of diatribe, the mock lecture and mock encomium were rediscovered. His *Dialogues*, in particular, became an influential source for Renaissance dramatists from Boiardo to John Heywood and Shakespeare.[39] By 1521, Lucian's works had reached England in Latin translation by way of Erasmus, Thomas More, and his circle and soon entered humanist curricula of sixteenth-century England. Lucianic satire inspired Erasmus' mock-encomium *The Praise of Folly* and Heywood's early Tudor interludes, which, in turn, influenced the development of English comedy.

Heywood adapted Lucian's dialogues in brief interludes, such as *Witty and Witless* (n.d.), in which a witless fool is made to agree with a witty fellow and then reverse his position when another wit argues the opposite position: the issue of debate is whether it is better to be a wise man or a fool. This tradition of pleasantries, usually with coarse overtones, occurred in dramatic interludes for at least a century and accounts for the comic interval in *Timon of Athens*, in which Apemantus banters with the usurers' servants. In the latter scene, the Fool is said to be in "wise company" (2.2.74) and, in a manner becoming Apemantus, proceeds to satirize seemingly reputable citizens as "whoremaster[s]" (2.2.105ff). Heywood's popular *The Play of the Wether* (1533) is another example of Lucian satire, which features Merry Report, a wise fool of English vintage who serves as Jupiter's usher. Merry Report enjoys vexing a procession of self-serving petitioners from various occupations, who present contradictory pleas concerning the weather. Jupiter grants each wish, so that, in the end, as the wise fool observes, the weather remains exactly as it was.[40] In the same Lucianic tradition, representatives of various occupations—painter, poet, merchant, jeweler, lord, et al.—are taunted by Apemantus, who is also pleased to "vex" Timon in his misery (4.3.236). In these ways, Apemantus plays wise fool, mocking others for their folly and causing the audience to perceive them from his Lucianic perspective.

Apemantus is not included in Lucian's Dialogue, "Timon the Misanthrope," but his viewpoint appears directly and indirectly in a number of speeches by the gods, by Timon himself, and by one of the flatterers. In Lucian's *Dialogue*, Timon is a misanthrope from the start; already impoverished, he is engaged in hard labor to earn his way. Addressing Zeus, he recounts his former life of privilege and his generosity to false friends and complains that the wicked are no longer punished. As protector of friendship and hospitality, Zeus expresses sympathy for Timon's misfortune and asks how it came to be. Hermes supplies two answers: the first, to please Zeus, is that "kindness and generosity and universal compassion . . . ruined him"; the second is grotesque in the "Menippean" manner:

> it would be nearer the truth to call him a fool . . . ; he did not realize that his protégés were carrion crows . . . ; vultures were feeding on his unfortunate liver, and he took them for friends . . . So they gnawed his bones perfectly clean, sucked out with great precision any marrow there might be in them, and went off, leaving him as dry as a tree whose roots have been severed; and now they do not know him . . .[41]

Both views reflect Apemantus' opinions. The first, that Timon was kind and generous, is implicit in his caution to Timon: "Methinks false hearts should never have sound legs. / Thus honest fools lay out their wealth on curtsies" (1.2.234–35). The second is Apemantus' often quoted cannibal metaphor:

> O you gods! what a number of men eats Timon, and he sees 'em not! It grieves me to see so many dip their meat in one man's blood, and all the madness is, he cheers them up too. I wonder men dare trust themselves with men. Methinks they should invite them without knives. (1.2.39–44)

Lucian's version continues with Plutus, who is reluctant to obey Zeus' order to restore Timon's wealth. When Zeus assures him that Timon has mended his ways, Plutus is skeptical and responds sarcastically, characterizing Timon as Apemantus has seen him during his extravagant days:

> Oh, of course! he will not do his best to let me run out of a leaky vessel before I have done running in! oh no, he will not be consumed with apprehensions of the inflow's gaining on the waste and flooding him! I shall be

supplying a cask of the Danaids; no matter how fast I pour in, the thing will not hold water; every gallon will be out almost before it is in. . . ."[42]

Plutus, like Apemantus, is certain that Timon would waste his wealth if it were restored. Despite his objections, Plutus is obliged to obey Zeus, but he does so ungraciously, reviling Timon and accusing him of treachery: "You prostituted me vilely to scoundrels, whose laudations and cajolery of you were only samples of their designs upon me. . . ."[43]

Shakespeare recalls Timon's blasphemous misuse of Plutus' gifts in the remarks of the Second Lord: "He pours it out: Plutus, the god of gold, / Is but his steward (1.1.276–77). And, when he refuses the offer of a gift, Apemantus reinforces the idea that Timon's waste is sinful: "No, I'll nothing; for if I should be brib'd too, there would be none left to rail upon thee, and then thou wouldst sin the faster" (1.2.238–40). Although Lucian's Timon rejects Plutus' offer to restore him and claims to prefer poverty, he reverses himself when he finds the buried gold, resolving to "keep his wealth to himself, scorn all men, and live in solitary luxury."[44] In another self-contradiction, Timon then expresses the wish that his fortune might become known so that his enemies "would all be fit to hang themselves over it." Immediately, the former friends "come running from every point of the compass," only to be insulted and stoned.[45]

Most suggestive of Apemantus is the last of the flatterers in Lucian's satire. This is Thrasycles, a philosopher, as greedy as the rest, who makes the typical claims associated with the Cynic school:

> I am not come like the rest of the crowd; *they* are dazzled by your wealth; they are gathered together with an eye to gold and silver and high living. . . . As for me, you know a crust is all the dinner I care for . . . My drink is the crystal spring; and this threadbare cloak is better than your gay robes. . . . What brought *me* was concern for you; I would not have you ruined by this same pestilent wealth, this temptation for plunderers . . . Take my advice, and fling it bodily into the sea; a good man, to whom the wealth of philosophy is revealed, has no need of the other.[46]

But Lucian's hypocritical Thrasycles then advises Timon to distribute his wealth to the poor and give him only "as much as my scrip would hold; it is something short of two standard bushels."[47] No one is spared in Lucian's satire.

Shakespeare's Cynic philosopher Apemantus, however, is sincere. Like Thrasycles, Apemantus scorns Timon's meat, prefers to "eat root" (1.2.71), drinks "Honest water" (1.2.59), and probably wears a beggar's cloak. Unlike Lucian's philosopher, Apemantus certainly cares for Timon's well-being. More than once, he offers Timon advice. In their final dialogue, Apemantus offers kindness along with insults and tries to reason with him. Apemantus has attempted to persuade Timon to embrace poverty philosophically or else leave the wilderness, but their exchange degenerates into stone-throwing and name-calling. Finally, Apemantus departs on the ambiguous note: "Live, and love thy misery" (4.3.395). Although line 395 is often taken as a parting curse, the words, in fact, restate Apemantus' earlier life-affirming *sententia*:

> Willing misery
> Outlives incertain pomp, is crown'd before:
> The one is filling still, never complete;
> The other, at high wish.
>
> (4.3.242–45)

These difficult lines surely mean that contentment is sooner possible in a life of poverty chosen by design than in the extravagant life, which, like the leaky vessel of Danaids, is ever in need of refilling: such is the essence of Cynic thought. The sentiment begins and ends the fourth act dialogue and epitomizes Apemantus' role. Since his first appearance, Apemantus has consistently "rail[ed] on society" (1.2.244), refused to feast, and rejected gifts. But to Timon, all along, he has expressed tough love: "O that men's ears should be / To counsel deaf, but not to flattery!" (1.2.249–50). His parting counsel, as I read it, is uttered with the same philosophical compassion and resignation: "Live, and love thy misery." Perhaps in 5.3, Apemantus silently returns to Timon's tomb and leaves the so-called first epitaph that the Soldier finds: "'Timon is dead, who hath outstretch'd his span: / Some beast read this; there does not live a man'" (5.3.3–4), words that echo Apemantus' declaration that "Athens is become a forest of beasts" (4.3.348).

IV

Accepting Plutarch's account of Timon as a cultural given, Shakespeare portrayed him as an unredeemable misanthropist owing to his shattered belief in brotherhood and his betrayal by false friends. The question for Shakespeare was why did Plutarch's Apemantus share his "nature and conditions"? Lacking no strong popular tradition for Apemantus, Shakespeare was free to develop him by allusion to Dioge-

nes the Cynic. An intertextual reading of Montaigne's meditations and
Lucian's satirical dialogue in terms of Apemantus' role helps to clarify
Shakespeare's intention to distinguish misanthropy from Cynic philosophy. Like Diogenes, Apemantus chooses poverty and eccentricity as a
path to virtue and responds to the beastly world with satirical indifference. Neither recluse nor absolutist, he participates in society, as a satirical preacher like Diogenes and a seriocomic philosopher-entertainer
like Lucian. Like the Democritus of Montaigne's essay, Apemantus is
the "sharper judge" of men; from the start, he perceives Timon's lack
of judgment and ultimately sees him as "the cap of all the fools alive."
Observing Timon's immoderation, he recognizes that in Timon, the virtue of generosity has become vicious through excess and indicates that,
although Timon has learned to hate flattery and hypocrisy, he has de-
meaned himself by excessive hatred. As wise fool, Apemantus stands
outside the plot and directs the audience by his comic mockery to shun
the waste and greed of the social types paraded before them at the banquet and in the wilderness. Within the plot, he is Timon's uninvited
moral adviser who first warns him, out of fondness, against the flatterers and later admonishes him to leave the beggarly life to those philosophically equipped to be content with poverty. In the Cynic tradition
of Diogenes and Lucian, Apemantus' witty critique of vanity, folly, and
greed contradicts Timon's bleak misanthropy.

Productions of the play that trivialize Apemantus' role (most eliminate his scene with the Fool, for instance) deprive the play of his comic
development and philosophical import, leaving only Timon's darkness
as a lasting impression. Such productions, as Ninian Mellamphy wrote
of Robin Phillips' 1983 repertory production, create a "theater of frustration" that keeps audiences away.[48] In stagings where Apemantus has
been given a significant role, on the other hand, productions have
achieved a greater measure of success. Played as a woman by the actress Tamu Gray at the 1997 Oregon Shakespeare Festival, Apemantus
conveyed "philosophical cynicism rather than psychological misanthropy," and Timon's dark mood in 4.3 was leavened by hints of tenderness behind her tough love.[49] Similarly, McCabe's interpretation of
Apemantus as "half-entertainer, half philosopher" in the 1999 production of the Royal Shakespeare Company at Stratford-upon-Avon featured him as a master of ceremonies who presided over the banquet
revels and concluded them, significantly, with his prophetic allusion to
Timon's folly.

Apemantus' reappearance at Timon's seaside retreat in 4.3 was "a
highlight of the production" in Nick Walton's view; dressed as a sun-
bather in straw hat and rolled trousers, his appearance, in contrast to

David Kelly as Timon and Tamu Gray as Apemantus in the Oregon Shakespeare Festival's 1997 production of *Timon of Athens*, directed by Penny Metropulos. Photo by David Cooper.

Timon's rags, was "comically absurd," and the "quick-fire slanging match" delighted the audience.[50] The scene, A. R. Braunmuller agreed, was "wholly affecting—tenderness amidst the ruins of Timon's generosity and . . . Apemantus' blanket condemnations."[51] In these performances, as in Shakespeare's text, Apemantus fails to impart his philosophy to Timon, who remains "To counsel deaf" (1.2.250), but his witty jibes, comic anger, and tough love serve to deflate the bitter rhetoric of the unredeemed Misanthrope. Rather than reduce his role or assign his lines to others, directors would do well to convey the playwright's seriocomic intent with Apemantus on the stage, reinforcing his philosophical stance, perhaps with an indifferent shrug as he silently lights Diogenes' famous lantern to mark the close of the play.

NOTES

1. Murray Biggs, "Adapting *Timon of Athens*," *Shakespeare Bulletin* 10.2 (1992): 5–10.
2. Ninian Mellamphy, "Wormwood in the Wood Outside Athens: *Timon* and the

Problem for the Audience," in *"Bad" Shakespeare: Revaluations of the Shakespeare Canon*, ed. Maurice Charney (Madison, NJ: Fairleigh Dickinson University Press, 1988), 170.

3. Alan Armstrong, "The 1997 Oregon Shakespeare Festival," *Shakespeare Bulletin* 16.2 (Spring 1988): 35–36.

4. A. R. Braunmuller, "*Timon* at the Royal Shakespeare Theatre 1999," in *Timon of Athens*, The New Cambridge Shakespeare, ed. Karl Klein (Cambridge: Cambridge University Press, 2001), 47–52.

5. Apemantus' lines were severely reduced in Michael Benthall's 1956 production at the Old Vic, according to *Timon of Athens*, ed. Klein, Introduction, 40. Similar reductions occurred in Stephen Oliver's opera *Timon of Athens*, first performed May 1991: Biggs, "Adapting *Timon of Athens*, 8; and in Michael Langham's 1991 production at Stratford, Ontario, discussed in Royal Ward, Review of *Timon of Athens*, *Shakespeare Bulletin* 9.4 (Fall 1991): 28–31.

6. *Timon of Athens*, The Arden Shakespeare, ed. H. J. Oliver (London: Methuen, 1959), Introduction, l.

7. *Timon of Athens*, ed. Klein, Introduction, 21–23. Also see Alice Lotvin Birney, *Satiric Catharsis in Shakespeare: A Theory of Dramatic Structure* (Berkeley: University of California Press, 1973), 122–40.

8. Klein supposes that the play may be "nihilistic to its depths, incapable of offering any life-affirmation": *Timon of Athens*, ed. Klein, Introduction, 13, while Marianna da Vinci Nichols finds in Timon's rhetoric "the mad language of his utter nihilism": "*Timon of Athens* and the Rhetoric of *No*," *Cahiers elisabethains* 9 (April 1976): 30.

9. *Timon of Athens*, in *The Riverside Shakespeare*, 2nd ed., ed. G. Blakemore Evans (Boston: Houghton Mifflin, 1997), 4.3.54. Subsequent references to Shakespeare's plays are from this edition and are cited parenthetically.

10. Laurence Lerner, "Timon and Tragedy," in *Shakespearean Continuities: Essays in Honour of E. A. J. Honigmann*, ed. John Batchelor, Tom Cain, and Claire Lamont (New York: St. Martin's Press, 1997), 155.

11. *Timon of Athens*, ed. Oliver, Introduction, xl.

12. *Timon of Athens*, ed. Klein, Appendix, 198.

13. Plutarch, "Life of Marcus Antonius," reprinted in *Timon of Athens*, ed. Oliver, Appendix A, 141. Emphasis is mine.

14. William Paynter, *Palace of Pleasure*, reprinted in *Timon of Athens*, ed. William J. Rolfe (New York: American Book Company, 1898), 130.

15. Michel Eyquem de Montaigne, "Of Democritus and Heraclitus," in *The Selected Essays of Montaigne*, ed. Lester G. Crocker (New York: Pocket Library, 1959), 154.

16. Ibid., 155. The reference is to Juvenal's *Satire* x:28.

17. Ibid., 155.

18. Ibid.

19. John Leon Lievsay, "Some Renaissance Views of Diogenes the Cynic," in *Joseph Quincy Adams Memorial Studies*, ed. James G. McManaway, Giles E. Dawson, and Edwin E. Willoughby (Washington, DC: The Folger Shakespeare Library, 1948), 449–51.

20. Peter Pauls, "Shakespeare's *Timon of Athens* and Renaissance Diogeniana," *The Upstart Crow* 3 (1980): 54–66.

21. Geoffrey Bullough, *Narrative and Dramatic Sources of Shakespeare*, 6 vols. (New York: Columbia University Press, 1966), 6:240–41.

22. Willard Farnham, *Shakespeare's Tragic Frontier* (Berkeley: University of California Press, 1950), 65–67.

23. Russ McDonald, *The Bedford Companion to Shakespeare* (New York: St. Martin's Press, 1996), 112.

24. Ibid., 111.

25. John R. Clark, *The Modern Satiric Grotesque and Its Traditions* (Lexington: University Press of Kentucky, 1991), 32.

26. http://www.encyclopedia.com/html/D/Diogenes.asp. Columbia Encyclopedia, 6th ed., 2004.

27. Clark, *The Modern Satiric Grotesque*, 32.

28. M. C. Bradbrook, *Shakespeare the Craftsman: The Clark Lectures 1968* (Cambridge: Cambridge University Press, 1969), 157.

29. Clark, *The Modern Satiric Grotesque*, 32–33; D. R. Dudley, *A History of Cynicism From Diogenes to the 6th Century A.D.* (Hildesheim: Georg Olms, 1967), 37; W. Scott Blanchard, *Scholars' Bedlam: Menippean Satire in the Renaissance* (Lewisburg, PA: Bucknell University Press, 1995), 27.

30. Clark writes that the Cynics were named "after their gathering-place at the Cynosarges, or 'white dog', a gymnasium outside the walls of Athens," but also because of their snarling manner of behavior: *The Modern Satiric Grotesque*, 31.

31. Birney, *Satiric Catharsis in Shakespeare*, 131.

32. Blanchard, *Scholars' Bedlam*, 17.

33. Montaigne, "Of Moderation," in *Selected Essays*, 131.

34. Blanchard, *Scholars' Bedlam*, 16.

35. Lucian, "Dialogue of Timon the Misanthrope," reprinted in *Timon of Athens*, ed. Oliver, Appendix C, 144–51.

36. *Timon of Athens*, ed. Rolfe, 17–21.

37. *Timon of Athens*, ed. Oliver, Introduction, xxxvi.

38. George A. Test, *Satire: Spirit and Art* (Tampa: University of South Florida Press, 1991), 57.

39. On Boiardo, see Nancy Dersofi, "Staging Timon the Misanthrope," *Fortune and Romance: Boiardo in America*, ed. Jo Ann Cavallo and Charles Ross (Tempe, AZ: Medieval and Renaissance Texts and Studies, 1998), 329–38.

40. Vicki K. Janik, "Merry Report," in *Fools and Jesters in Literature, Art, and History*, ed. Janik (Westport, CT: Greenwood Press, 1998), 308–15.

41. Lucian, "Dialogue of Timon the Misanthrope," reprinted in *Timon of Athens*, ed. Oliver, Appendix C, 145.

42. Ibid.

43. Ibid., 146.

44. Ibid., 147.

45. Ibid.

46. Ibid., 150–51.

47. Ibid., 151.

48. Mellamphy, "Wormwood in the Wood Outside Athens," 172.

49. Armstrong, "The 1997 Oregon Shakespeare Festival," 36.

50. Nick Walton, Review of *Timon of Athens*, *Shakespeare Bulletin* 19.1 (Winter 2001): 24.

51. Braunmuller, "*Timon* at the Royal Shakespeare Theatre 1999," 52.

King Lear, Act 3: Storming the Stage

Charles A. Hallett

[I]n *King Lear*, Shakespeare is far from concerning himself with naturalistic illusion. Not only are there bold improbabilities . . . there is
an almost complete rejection of verisimilitude in the portrayal of the
characters and their setting, of anything that might seem to keep us
in close touch with a familiar—or at all events an actual—world.
                                                              —L. C. Knights[1]

MADNESS AND REDEMPTION: TRAGIC SUFFERING IN ACT 3

"THERE ARE DIFFERENCES OF OPINION AS TO HOW REALISTIC THE
storm needs to be" in productions of *King Lear*, muses Richard David,
contemplating the staging of a 1976 Royal Shakespeare Theatre *King
Lear*, codirected by Trevor Nunn with John Barton and Barry Kyle.
David felt that "the thunder that punctuates Lear's tirades was artistically 'managed,'" but he was less satisfied when

> "real" rain poured onto the stage from an upper level, the storm-driven fig-
> ures appearing and disappearing through a misty curtain of water. This,
> though effective, was a little distracting, and made redundant, and therefore
> tedious, the introductory scene between Kent and the Gentleman whose sole
> purpose is to create the foul weather in the audience's imaginations.[2]

In recent decades, actors playing Lear and audiences experiencing
Lear's tragic exodus into the tempestuous night could be fairly certain
that the special effects crew would engender a spectacular and meteoro-
logically realistic storm. The determination to impose the precepts of
twentieth-century realism upon a play in which there is, as Knights suggests, "an almost complete rejection of verisimilitude," a deliberate disregard of "naturalistic illusion," seems almost perverse. The overlay of
realism often almost cancels out those most significant elements of
Lear's inner storm that the heath scene asks us to perceive.

When the doors to Gloucester's castle slam shut behind the retreating

126

king at the end of act 2, Lear is a man consumed with righteous indignation. He is in no mood to be told that he himself had unwittingly precipitated the situation that now grinds against every fiber of his being. What rules his consciousness is a keen awareness of the calculated, premeditated effronteries inflicted on him by those to whom he had been most generous. And we are inclined to agree with him; he has been deeply wronged, and those who have wronged him are evil. Still, we cannot totally empathize with Lear. Though, now, perhaps, more sinned against than sinning, he remains the obstinate, willful old man who disinherited Cordelia and banished Kent—only now, the tables have been turned on him, and the thought of it fills him with the rage and fury of unappeasable anger. "I will do such things— . . . they shall be / The terrors of the earth!"[3] He enters act 3 the least introspective of Shakespeare's protagonists but leaves it a man who, immersed in the cauldron of internal and external turmoil, develops, or at least discovers, his soul.

In act 3 of *Othello,* Shakespeare set himself the awesome task of rendering the transformation of a man from devout and loving husband to savage murderer merely by subjecting him to the skillful use of innuendo. In act 3 of *King Lear,* Shakespeare set himself no less awesome a task. In fact, Shakespeare's achievement in act 3 of *Lear* is so stupendous it is practically incomprehensible. Here the focus is on a man who is at odds with and isolated from the world, simmering in his injured pride, frustrated and humiliated by his impotence to exact a full measure of vengeance upon his oppressors. Nothing about Lear as he enters act 3 has the least relish of salvation about it. Yet Richard Sewell speaks for many in his appraisal of the Lear we find in act 4:

> The scene of his awakening and reconciliation with Cordelia is as close to redemption as tragedy ever gets. Christian images and spirit pervade it. Lear mistakes his daughter for "a soul in bliss" and starts to kneel for her benediction as she asks for his. All is repentance, forgiveness, harmony. Here, if ever in tragedy, we are in the presence of the peace that passeth understanding. But it is wrought out of the dialectic of experience and through no conversion or doctrine or miracle—except it be the one miracle that tragedy witnesses, the miracle of the man who can learn by suffering.[4]

Redemption is, of course, a Christian term, and had Shakespeare set his play within a Christian context, I believe we would be justified in likening the events in act 3 to a pilgrimage and Lear to a saintly figure. But Shakespeare wasn't writing hagiography. He deliberately set his drama outside Christianity in the pagan past. There, there wasn't the question of grace to be dealt with. Aeschylus had the Chorus in *Agamemnon* say, "Why have the gods ordained that man must suffer to know?" Shakespeare wanted to show how unsought-for suffering (not the suffering of the seeker for enlightenment—John of the Cross' dark night of the soul, for example—but, rather, the suffering that comes unexpectedly streaming in to the most prosaic and worldly lives) may carry the individual beyond himself into realms of illumination he not only never anticipated but had never set out to find. The saint sets his sights on finding meaning. Lear's highest aspiration was revenge. Yet before his journey is over, he is granted a degree of enlightenment denied to most, even to many who long for it. But Lear will have to suffer to know.

This is the impact of the series of storm scenes. They are to convey the experience of suffering that will, in both a positive and a negative sense, take the protagonist out of himself. If the outcome of Lear's contending with the storm is both his madness and his redemption, these scenes must be staged in a manner that will allow them to resonate with their full symbolic force. To drench Lear with buckets of real water in imitation of rain, to drown his voice with a cacophony of noisemakers in imitation of thunder, to jolt him with flashes of burning electricity in imitation of lightning so that by the end of the storm scenes we are left with the remnant of a formerly cantankerous old man, the stuffing thoroughly knocked out of him, can only have the effect of diminishing Lear. Such realistic staging certifies that the storm has accomplished what was beyond the capacity of Goneril and Regan—Lear is now broken, both physically and mentally. If he doesn't look like an escapee from *Endgame* in such productions, he is at least more reminiscent of J. Alfred Prufrock than Prince Hamlet, more an attendant lord than a king and nothing at all like a tragic protagonist.

In several of his earlier plays, Shakespeare was at some pains to establish a sense of actuality. Take, for instance, the tavern scene in the second act of *I Henry IV*. The sole purpose of Prince Hal's opening sequence with Francis is to create the flavor of the tavern that is to prevail throughout the rest of the scene. Yet even here, it would falsify the drama to have the stage carpenters build a realistic tavern on the stage. How much more inappropriate to impose the trappings of modern realism on the storm scene, a scene so obviously conceived as highly symbolic. It is no wonder that productions that seek to graft realistic meteorological conditions onto the actions of act 3 end up disjointed. Look what they have to work with—three scenes portraying the interactions of a Fool, a pretended madman, and a king who is increasingly unhinged. The scene is a heath where, we are told, there is hardly a shrub standing, during a storm that rivals the one from which only Noah and his crew survived, all of this rendered in dialogue that is a mixture of poetry, prose, and song.

Everything about the scene screams out to us that we must be willing to experience it on multiple levels simultaneously, of which the realistic level, an old man caught in a bad storm, is the least important. That is the level at which Goneril and Regan are operating when they slam the doors on him: "O sir, to willful men, / The injuries that they themselves procure / Must be their schoolmasters" (2.4.302–4). If the main effort in the staging of the storm scene is to show an old man buffeted by wind and rain, then what we get is the storm to which Lear's daughters mean to subject him. But certainly Harley Granville-Barker was right when he pointed out, decades ago, that to create a successful production of *King Lear*, "we must master and conform to the stage-craft on which it depends":[5]

> How [does Shakespeare] give [the storm] enough magnificence to impress [Lear], yet keep it from rivaling him? Why, by identifying the storm with him, setting the actor to impersonate both Lear and—reflected in Lear—the storm. . . . [The "Blow, winds, and crack your cheeks" speech] is no mere description of a storm, but in music and imaginative suggestion a dramatic creating of the storm itself, and there is Lear—and here are we, if we yield ourselves—in the midst of it, almost a part of it. Yet Lear himself, in his Promethean defiance, still dominates the scene. . . . [Shakespeare] has no other means of keeping the human and the apocalyptic Lear as one . . . [If the storm effects are separated from Lear, he will seem] physically ridiculous by comparison with them; [if the two are united, he is] invested with their dynamic quality.[6]

Granville-Barker's warning against a staging that transfers power from the fragile but imperial Lear to a raging cosmos cannot lightly be ignored.

The flexibility—one might say the fluidity—of Shakespeare's stage allowed for rapid transitions between levels of actuality. In *Hamlet*, for instance, we jump from the court at Elsinore into Hamlet's mind and back to the court without the benefit of any transition at all. In the storm scene in *Lear*, Shakespeare has pushed this fluidity even further. Several levels of actuality are present on the stage simultaneously. On the quotidian level, we have Kent and Gloucester, who are functioning within the storm that Lear's daughters have cast him out into. They keep that level of actuality before us while everything else on stage continually passes from this level into various chambers of Lear's being. As Granville-Barker says of the storm, it must be both outside and inside of Lear. And Lear himself traverses these realities moment by moment. At just what level the Fool exists has been problematic from his first entrance in 1.4. Now it seems he is even more absorbed into Lear's fabric. As Ben Brantley said of the Fool as played in 2004 at Lincoln Center by Barry MacGregor, "Lear's Fool . . . might be an imaginary friend, a conscience summoned by what is best in the king's character . . . The uncanny rapport is always evident: the Fool gives Lear his grounding in reality, with the servant articulating the master's unspoken and unconscious thoughts."[7] Like the storm, the Fool is both outside *and* inside of Lear. So, too, with Poor Tom. Many view Poor Tom as a raisonneur, though in the storm scenes this is only true of him for one brief moment in 3.6 when he throws off his disguise and soliloquizes in the role of Edgar. Otherwise, as with both the storm and the Fool, Poor Tom seems to exist on multiple levels. On one level, he is yet another creature exposed to the storm. But Shakespeare didn't need another witness to the severity of the weather. Nor is he there as Edgar disguised. Primarily, Poor Tom in 3.4 is a series of experiences Lear undergoes. And in this regard, rather than being a raisonneur, analyzing for the audience the significance of the action, he portrays for us facets of Lear's disintegrating being. Shakespeare was attempting to render something that cannot be explained but must remain mysterious. How is it that suffering can both destroy and illuminate? Here we confront the very nature of the tragic vision, which implies the presence of the mysterious in the human condition.

Unlike in *Hamlet*, where the mysterious intrudes itself into the mundane world before the characters have time to complete the exposition, in *Lear* the action is never interrupted by any visitation from the beyond. Not that the play's pagan setting precludes the divine: it has been noted that there are more references to the gods in *Lear* than in any of Shakespeare's other tragedies. Yet the gods themselves remain offstage. This is one of the reasons they are so frequently spoken of. While no one doubts their existence, their exact nature is dubious. The very gods who in Gloucester's estimation "kill us for their sport" (4.1.37) are later seen by him as "You ever-gentle gods" (4.6.217). And though both Edmund and Lear pray to Nature, they hardly seem to be praying to the same divinity.

Mysterious as the gods may be in this play's primitive universe, Lear confronts a different mystery in the storm scene, and his inability to comprehend it will drive him mad—that is, the mystery of the nature of evil. By this time, Lear has passed beyond what Goneril and Regan can do to him. Confounded and perplexed as he is, what now consumes him isn't what they did to him. He is asking what is in them that makes it possible for them to act this way: "Then let them anatomize Regan; see what breeds about her heart. Is there any cause in nature that make these hard hearts?" (3.6.76–78). He wants to look inside these daughters to locate the hidden causes that have diseased their being.

The madness itself has mysterious dimensions as well. The divinities have constituted human suffering in such a fashion that it can become a gateway into another realm. But you cannot merely endure the suffering; you must push against it or it will not yield. The Lear who exits from the storm is very different from the Lear who entered it; and while he is in it, he is in the state of becoming. We may think of Keats' statement that the world is a vale of soul-making. Surely this has relevance to Lear's journey through the storm, where his mind is shattered like a mirror, with whole areas going dark while other fragments momentarily catch the light and flash glimpses of himself back to himself and occasionally reveal other landscapes as well.

My purpose in this essay is not to ally myself with Charles Lamb in maintaining the impossibility of rendering such profundity on stage. In my view, Shakespeare has so adroitly blended the multiple dimensions of this drama together, so grounded the poetic dialogue in the structure of the action, that these, if allowed to flow unimpeded, have the capacity to render a vivid emotional experience in the theater. I propose, rather, to call attention to specific impositions of verisimilitude that have become a standard part of contemporary staging of the play and to show how these elements of modern realism inevitably work against the profound emotional experience that might otherwise be conveyed to the audience. Jonathan Kent's 2002 Almeida production of *King Lear*, with its drenching rain, illustrates one kind of realistic overlay. Jonathan Miller's 2003–2004 staging of the play with Christopher Plummer as a Lear suffering from dementia manifests another and an equally prevalent form of our age's fascination with verisimilitude.

Storming the Stage, or "Rain, Rain, Go Away . . ."

The impediment I shall focus on initially is the unfortunate circumstance that production teams are convinced that for modern audiences they can more precisely render King Lear's mental storm by staging a tangible storm that reproduces the convulsions of nature graphically on the stage. The standard practice, particularly in screen versions of the play, where the Lears of Paul Scofield, Michael Hordern, Laurence Olivier, and Ian Holm[8] endure as much weather as any real heath can produce, but also in theater productions—the standard practice is to establish a quintessential unity between Lear and the storm by conjuring up a spectacular tempest for the actor to rage against. Because "raging storm" plus "raging actor" are believed to coalesce into a theatrical image of "Lear gone mad," every director feels challenged to demonstrate the creativity with which he can inflict act 3's cataclysmic storm on his stage Lear. What happens is exactly what Granville-Barker predicts will happen: Lear seems "physically ridiculous" in comparison with his imposing rival.

It seems that each successive producer of this play strives to render with every bit of technology that modern machinery can offer a realistic depiction of the storm that Lear's verbal images picture to our imagination. In a book deploring the "naturalism [that] is persistent everywhere" in contemporary theater, a naturalism that has "over-spent itself," has "lasted too long,"[9] Michel Saint-Denis tells a charming story to illustrate a major drawback of putting real rain on the stage:

> In my view, one typical blemish did harm to the production. One scene in the play takes place during a storm. It was the most admirable storm! The thunder was unforgettable. And on top of it was the rain. Through the window on the right I could watch the rain go through all its phases: we had fast rain, slow rain, and at the end, remarkably, dripping rain. You could not only hear but *see* the rain, so much so that it was quite impossible to hear or see the play, which is not written in a realistic style."[10]

Saint-Denis was talking about a production of Nikolai Gogol's *Dead Souls*, and the rain was outside, seen through a window only. In the *King Lear*s of the past half-century, the simulated rain often cascades across the entire stage. The startling Almeida production went even further: its storm was "most admirable" for occurring not outside on the heath but inside an elegantly furnished room.

We have all experienced the rain-drenched *Lear*s on film. The Olivier video version is typical. The old king is discovered standing on a hilltop. Rain is pouring down excessively. The camera focuses mostly on Lear's dripping face; one can follow the raindrops as they move from his brow over his cheekbones down toward the chin, all to the accompaniment of some rather shrill music that competes with his voice. The relationship between Lear and the Fool, who kneels at his feet, clinging to him as he longs for a "dry house," is most touching. John Hurt's Fool has been described as "one whose inalienable compassion has grafted him on to the fate of his master."[11] But what captures our attention is the tempestuous weather. How the actors are being battered by it!

The storm shares star billing with Holm in the filmed version of Richard Eyre's Royal National Theatre's stage production of *King Lear*. Again we see tempestuous rain, but in this storm, winds are featured. So fierce are the winds that Lear and his Fool have trouble keeping on their feet. The Fool, speaking his lines into the camera, is not just *shoved* but almost *blown* off the screen, which the rain dominates.

In Peter Brook's conception, the frigid setting translates rain into snow. A blizzard of cosmic force brutally oppresses Lear as he moves from Gloucester's castle to the heath. We see the storm scattering the king's followers, wrecking his carriage, felling his horse, and, finally, dumping Lear and the Fool on their backs in the snow, thoroughly pummeled, with Lear rising defiantly out of this destitution to deliver his lines. But it is not Lear's verbal creation of the storm that interests Brook's camera; it is the impression that chaos has come again. At points in the Brook film, notably during Lear's "Blow, winds, and crack your cheeks" speech (3.2.1), the storm is quite literally a blinding storm; there is no picture, no view on the film—the raging elements obliterate all (one suspects for a moment that the projector has gone amuck).

Do we not find that what attracts those who choose to produce the play is, first and foremost, the opportunity to make a statement by creating their personal version of "the perfect storm"? The temptation seems irresistible. Those of my readers who have seen the screen versions mentioned above or the most touted productions at the Royal Shakespeare Theatre—Trevor Nunn's *King Lear* in 1976 (with Eric Porter as Lear) or Adrian Noble's in 1982 (with Michael Gambon as Lear), for example—can testify to having had the experience of finding oneself concentrating not on the emotions that Shakespeare's action, Shakespeare's characterization, and Shakespeare's dialogue can generate when intelligently orchestrated but rather on the distracting spectacle of water dripping down a face, characters slogging through a marsh, actors being discomfited, costumes saturated and soggy.

The point can be further illustrated by the reactions noted by so many of the reviewers who witnessed the conception worked up on the stage of the Almeida Theatre for the 2002 production of *King Lear*, billed as another of the triumphs of the director/designer team, Jonathan Kent and Paul Brown. This is the production in which the storm was so fierce that, as one reviewer marveled, during the twenty-minute interval "approximately fifteen staff mop the drenched set."[12]

The storm was magnificent. The problem was that the first two acts were set in a paneled executive suite (corporate headquarters apparently for what was obviously Lear International, Ltd.), with elegant furnishings that had the most refined aura, and the storm took place with no change of setting. One's first impression was that the sprinkler system had malfunctioned in the ceiling of the theater building, as, after Lear exited from his fractious interview with Regan and Goneril, water began to drip onto the splendid Edwardian mahogany desk from which Lear had orchestrated the dividing of the kingdom, onto the upholstered Queen Anne wing chairs that had stood for Gloucester's home, onto the sconces and mirrors that adorned the paneled walls. Then, as Nicholas de Jongh reported in the *Evening Standard*, "in a thrilling coup de théâtre, the huge set begins to split, break and fall as the storm starts. Rain pelts down upon the collapsed palace study, which becomes the blasted heath, and on a Lear reduced to his underpants and impassioned mania: a nightmare tempest in the monarch's mind." And a powerful storm it is. Unremitting! But does the pelting rain serve to

Anthony O'Donnell as the Fool and Oliver Ford Davies as King Lear in the Almeida Theatre's 2002 production of *King Lear* at its temporary King's Cross venue, directed by Jonathan Kent. Photo by Donald Cooper/Photostage.

heighten the drama? Does it increase the majesty of Oliver Ford Davies, the actor playing King Lear? Alas. Susannah Clapp expressed it
this way: "It can't be a good sign when the climactic moment in a
Shakespeare play is a synchronized collapse of the set" (*The Observer*).
Georgina Brown's impression was that "while Ford Davies is an actor
of tremendous power, physically and vocally, there is no contest between him and all this weather. He shouts with all his might but he may
just as well be whistling in the wind. . . . All the storming and the shout-
ing has a steadily deadening effect, like winter in England" (*Mail on
Sunday*). John Nathan lamented that Ford Davies' curse on Cordelia
"chills the blood, but thereafter he's in competition with the elements,
and sometimes the weather wins" (*Jewish Chronicle*). And James In-
verne: "Water plays a decisive role: the storm blasts through the pan-
elled walls of an all-purpose palace (there is only one set), rain soaks
the floor and furniture. It's a riveting moment in a *Lear* that belongs
very much to its director rather than to its leading man" (*Sunday Telegraph*). If the rain, the lightning, and the thunder do not totally distract
one from the plight of the much-abused king, there are other considerations that will. "It's hard not to wonder," as James Edwards of *Time
Out* did, "how the furniture is going to survive a nightly soaking."
Charles Spencer found all of this "a thrilling theatrical metaphor for
both the transience of power and the fragility of human sanity," and he
thought Ford Davies "one of the most moving and intelligent Lears I
have ever seen" (*Daily Telegraph*). But he was one of few who did not
find that the director's House-of-Usher concept called attention to itself
rather than to the play's protagonist. More typical was the conclusion of
Clapp: "It's hard for anybody to look other than *quaintly dotty* tiptoeing
through puddles in [under]pants and socks" (*The Observer*).[13]

Ford Davies has included detailed rehearsal diaries in his recent
book, *Playing Lear*. These notes let us see the Almeida's storm from behind the footlights. We hear about the production concept in Jonathan
Kent's own words. The idea of producing *Lear* was generated, it seems,
from an image that formed itself in the director's mind. "I first pictured
doing [the play] in a Lincoln's Inn paneled Elizabethan hall, because I
was interested in the whole notion of [the storm] happening to a degree
within [Lear's] own head. The image I had was of a paneled room with
the rain falling through the roof on to a sofa." The opening scene was
to take place in a well-defined room, which symbolized the safe, solid
world of Lear's mind, and, as that mind disintegrated, so would the formal room. What was to be revealed was the void beyond. The play is
about "the thin buttress of our acquired surroundings keeping chaos at

bay, and paneled rooms seem to me an apt metaphor for that." Crucial to the generation of the image were associations Kent made between Lear's deteriorating mind and his grandmother's Alzheimer's disease, "her loss of self, and being in exile from the land of her own intelligence. The terrifying notion of losing the land of your mind is frightening for me." Kent hoped that the collapse of the set would register upon the audience not as a *coup de théâtre*—he never wanted that—but in terms of the metaphor: "it should be the splintering of a place and also a mind."[14] There was an irony to all this. The room in Kent's *King Lear* was meant to suggest the multiple levels on which Shakespeare's action develops by representing not merely a *place*, not only a *society*, but, more importantly, a *mind*. Instead, the exactingly constructed four-wall set signaled to the viewer a production style straight out of Ibsen. It was all so thoroughly realistic.

But let's get back to the topic at hand—the technological creation of a real storm on the Almeida stage. What effect did the staging of the storm inside of a paneled room have on the actor playing Lear? Apparently, the technical dress rehearsal was anticipated with trepidation not only by the Lear but by all of the actors. What will happen to the acted portions of the heath scene—carefully worked out interpretations of the spoken words—when the acting is joined to the collapsing set and the drenching rain? From Ford Davies' commentary on the tech rehearsal itself, we learn of the kind of distractions that the wetting rain created for the actors:

> [I]n the storm we have not just thunder and lightning, but rain with real water. The five of us out on the heath—Lear, Kent, the Fool, Gloucester and Edgar—have been dreading this. Our dread is justified. Though many jokey references have been made to "warm rain", the water is of course icy. I am wearing a shirt, which is quickly sodden, and I then take off my boots and trousers. I am now in a shirt, two pairs of underpants and socks. Quite soon the rain, which is supposed to disappear down the cracks between the floorboards, has formed large puddles, though to my relief my sodden socks seem to grip the floor quite well. It becomes clear however that there are dry "corridors" in between the sprinklers in the ceiling, and if you can manoeuvre yourself into these safe havens you remain relatively dry, while it cascades in front and behind you. Soon I predict the five of us will be strung out in a row across the stage, venturing neither forwards nor backwards. . . . Fortunately [when we come off stage,] our expert dresser, Spencer Kitchen, has a range of hot towels and dressing-gowns ready for us.[15]

Elsewhere, we hear about the demands made upon the actor's voice by sound technician John Leonard's thunderclaps. Ford Davies mentions at one point that, in the small space of the King's Cross theater, he had to use all the vocal power that would have been required had they been playing *Lear* at the Drury Lane.

At some level, apparently, once the production was under way, the rain made things easier: "The rain does a lot of the acting for us," writes Ford Davies. "Glorying in the rain and trying to survive in the rain mingle in what I hope is fruitful combination."[16] But in "Afterthoughts" (this actor's musings on the experience of playing Lear against a background of a collapsing set and beneath a ceiling equipped with sprinklers that spit out icy cold water), Ford Davies reveals that he would have preferred to do his work without all that splashing about: "I never fully came to terms with the set. I think the concept was brilliant, but I found myself having to force certain things to accommodate it, mainly in 2.4 and the *Heath*. At times I felt I was playing my cello, and the orchestra, far from accompanying me, were drowning me out."[17] *Playing Lear* leaves one with the impression that Ford Davies' understanding of Shakespeare's Lear was penetrating.[18] But, alas, my own experience was that the set attracted so much attention to itself that it became difficult to keep one's mind focused on his performance. Distracting questions kept intruding. Where is all that water coming from? Where is it going to? How are they going to get those upholstered chairs dry for tomorrow night?

We come up against this tendency to allow the storm to overwhelm the spoken word in so many productions of *King Lear* that, alas, we never see Shakespeare's *Lear*. The expression that Herbert Blau used in defining the electronic storm created for a production of the play at the San Francisco Actor's Workshop, "chaos dazzled by its own coherence,"[19] is applicable here. Just where *is* the coherence in these overwhelmingly realistic storms? There is so much more of disintegration.

Storming the stage. I would say that the Almeida production pushed the notion of a fully staged meteorological storm as far as it can go. In most areas of artistic endeavor, when that happens there is some reaction—a search by individual artists for purer forms. Is there *hope* on the horizon? *Will* the real rain go away?

"Nothing cosmic about it": *Lear* at Lincoln Center

What hope exists for a change of direction among theater practitioners? Michael Feingold, reviewing Jonathan Miller's most recent *King Lear* for *The Village Voice*, is filled with optimism. He finds Miller

setting a new standard for Shakespeare productions, a return to the
simplicity of the Elizabethan stage such as would delight William Poel.
With what rapture Feingold lauds the revolutionary "gain in dramatic
clarity" he witnessed in the *King Lear* presented under Miller's guidance
first at Stratford, Ontario (2002), and later at Lincoln Center in New
York City (2004). Wryly implying that Miller is charting new ground,
he all but labels as avant-garde Miller's "removal of directorial 'interpretation' as a criterion of value for Shakespeare production." In Miller's production, says Feingold, with undisguised gratitude, "the play is
played for itself, and not for Miller or anyone else's crackbrained notion
of it. As a result, . . . you can actually see *King Lear:* not a concept, not
an update, not a renovation, not a deconstruction; just a very great play
by Shakespeare. What an experiment. And what a relief." Feingold is
exultant about what he clearly perceives as a miraculous and much-
needed corrective in directorial attitudes. "We are back at first principles, and with a play as great as *King Lear*, that turns out to be a very
good place."[20]

Feingold is not alone in applauding the revolutionary "gain in dramatic clarity" achieved by Miller and his collaborator, Christopher
Plummer, the production's Lear, by ridding the Lincoln Center stage of
the encumbrances of twentieth-century realism. Hear Desmond Ryan:
"The advantage of Miller's no-frills *Lear* is that nothing comes between
us and the text in Lear's anguished descent from the palace and pinna-
cle of authority to the humbled and demented outcast wandering the
blasted heath with his Fool."[21] Or hear Gary Smith:

> The essential drama of this production is expressed in the spartan way it
> avoids excess. The storm, for instance, begins as a quavering white light.
> And when its thunder reaches a stirring and sonic height, it escapes any
> necessity for raging theatricality. . . . Jonathan Miller's direction, clean and
> neat, focuses squarely on the text, making no attempt at imprinting debasing
> theatrical clutter."

"Shakespeare's play turns on words," Smith affirms, and what pleased
him most was that Miller allowed his Lear to be heard, heard especially
in Plummer's "glorious voice, singing truth through every brilliantly
enunciated phrase."[22] Or listen to Tony Brown: "Miller . . . manages to
elicit maximum wallop from minimalist effects in the famous storm
scene, limiting his tricks to a few puffs of stage fog and strobe flashes,"
"a frank, unfettered production."[23]

The reviewers are united in applauding the "no-frills" approach adopted by Miller for his most recent staging of *King Lear*. One finds a universal sigh of relief, a unanimous consent that here, at last, is the kind of *Lear* that "we all yearn to see."[24] "Unfettered." Shakespeare, their images affirm, has at last been freed.

Not that the production was without flaws. Most viewers would agree with Feingold that, "[l]ike a defective videotape, the performance surrounding Plummer tends to shift erratically between full color and fuzzy gray."[25] Hilton Als regrets that Miller "neglected to cast actors who could tear through Shakespeare's passion and grief with anything approaching passion and grief of their own."[26] More to the point, there is an irony that no one seems to have noticed, that Miller's return to the Spartan techniques of the Elizabethan stage in itself arises from an attitude toward the play that is as closely bound up with realism as the meteorological storm and creates a different but equally serious impediment to the realization of the transcendent levels of Shakespeare's vision. Miller scorns the cosmic dimensions other producers have sought by storming the stage, but he does so in order to highlight the *mortal* Lear, the worn-out and dying king—in the process letting go any intimations of immortality that might hint at new knowledge won through suffering. One might see Miller's refusal to stage a cosmic storm as the right move made for the wrong reasons.

Miller and Plummer, jointly, are committed in this production to a very contemporary image of the protagonist—what interests both is that aspect of Shakespeare's play that renders the experience of an old man dying. To their credit, they aim to render not an idea but an experience. But the experience they wish to render—and succeed in rendering—is not equivalent to the transcendent experience to which Shakespeare subjected his own King Lear, who journeys from ignorance to wisdom. Far from it. Consider the reason Miller gives for stripping down his production to bare essentials, this in an interview with Anne Cattaneo entitled "Keeping Out of the Rain":

> Some of my colleagues feel that the play is made much more epic or more mythic if it's set in some sort of mythic past. But I feel there's nothing epic or mythic about it, in exactly the same way that I don't think there's anything cosmic about it. People get deluded into the cosmic quality of the play simply because there's a thunderstorm in it . . . You have to have lightning and thunder, but, you know, the storm itself only lasts about five minutes. But people get so excited by it and think that's cosmic."[27]

Miller acknowledges that the "specifically Christian notion—that it's only by enduring the hideous ordeal of loss that any of these people

gain" is written into the play, at least "by allusion." But the gain—
spiritual insight—is not what interests Miller. He goes on to explain
that his work on *Lear* at the Stratford Festival was done under the influence of Michael Ignatieff's *The Needs of Strangers*. Ignatieff, says
Miller,

> talks about how *Lear* is really about homelessness. It's about: Keep out of
> the rain, otherwise you won't be able to go back. Once you're out in the rain
> and you give up domesticity and the civil polity, you are nothing more than
> a "bare, forked" creature. That's what everyone would have thought at the
> time, and that's why it makes no sense to set the play in a primeval world.
> They are not far off from bare, forked creatures anyway.[28]

In giving the play the historical setting of seventeenth-century England,
Miller assumes not so much the multileveled universe implied in Elizabethan stage practice where, through the conventions of the multileveled stage, the macrocosm was shown to reach to and beyond the
canopy of stars. On the contrary, what is assumed is that particular moment in history when people were embracing the Hobbesian notion of a
materialistic universe in which (Plummer speaks of this) life was nasty,
brutish, and short.

What is true of all productions is true of this one: there is no escaping
the fact that the given historical setting will be inescapably imbued with
the worldview prevailing at the time of the production. In the end, one
has to recognize, especially in Plummer's conception of Lear, that element of naturalism that pervades modern thinking. Like Miller, Plummer eschews the "cosmic" aspects of the play. He is at home with the
idea of Lear as homeless, so much so that for the New York revival (as
he tells David Gates in a *Newsweek* interview), he has "settled in to more
legitimately mad behavior, like some old bum on Eighth Avenue."
Plummer's rendering is noted for the realism with which he captures
the forgetfulness, the faltering, the feebleness of the elderly: "Plummer's
Lear comes alive in such details: from the Jacobean hospital johnny in
which he dies ('You *know* he's p——ed in it,' Plummer says) to the med-
ically correct intensification of his dementia. 'There's absolutely no reason on God's green earth why Lear didn't have a couple of strokes.'" As
Gates comments, "Christopher Plummer brings Lear down to earth."[29]
Brantley goes further in describing this production as the "story of
Lear's dispossession"—there seems to be, he says, "a conscious acknowledgment of the nonexistence toward which everyone is
moving."[30]

On the surface, Miller's production appears to hearken back to the seventeenth century, the era in which he has costumed his players. Beyond that, he has rigidly forgone the trappings of the modern realistic stage. Yet, despite all his efforts to evoke an earlier era, his production remains not merely modern but realistic. The visual evocation of an earlier time obscures but doesn't negate the realistic underpinnings on which his production is predicated.

Where the realism informs Miller's production is at the level of how he conceives not just the play but the structure of reality, the nature of the universe. He apparently does not believe that there are dimensions to reality beyond those out of which the quotidian world is constructed. After all, realism is more than an artistic style; it is a concept of the nature of reality. If for Miller and for Plummer there is nothing beyond the material world for symbols to point toward, then to exploit the symbolic levels of *Lear* would be tantamount to endorsing superstition.

Although Jonathan Miller has costumed his production in the seventeenth century, the vision informing the production is as twenty-first century as that behind Jonathan Kent's modern-dress production at the Almeida. Neither director is able to escape from the confines of a worldview that perceives reality from the same vantage point that Lear and Gloucester perceived it in act 1.

In juxtaposing the Almeida production with its ultra-contemporary setting to the Lincoln Center version set in the Jacobean era, one can see that the same difficulties confront both production crews. Both productions assume a finite world in which there is nothing beyond death but a void, that empty, dark, and presumably meaningless space that is perceived when the paneled walls collapse at the Almeida Theatre. Both Kent and Miller talk much of Lear's body, much of the disintegration of his mind, but have little or nothing to say about spirit and less about soul. The vision that informs both productions is that which informs realism. We are material creatures, doomed to live in a totally physical world, and there is no escape. Such a vision is the rejection of and antithetical to the one that lies at the heart of *King Lear*, that through suffering and love, one can find redemption.

NOTES

1. L. C. Knights, *"King Lear* as Metaphor," in Knights, *Further Explorations* (Stanford: Stanford University Press, 1965), 174.

2. Richard David, *Shakespeare in the Theatre* (Cambridge: Cambridge University Press, 1978), 101.

3. *King Lear*, in *The Riverside Shakespeare*, 2nd ed., ed. G. Blakemore Evans (Boston: Houghton Mifflin, 1997), 2.4.280–82. Subsequent references to Shakespeare's plays are from this edition and are cited parenthetically.

4. Richard B. Sewall, *The Vision of Tragedy* (New Haven: Yale University Press, 1959), 77.

5. Harley Granville-Barker, *Prefaces to Shakespeare: King Lear* (1927; Portsmouth, NH: Heinemann, 1995), 36.

6. Ibid., 37–38, 41.

7. Ben Brantley, "A Fiery Fall into the Abyss, Unknowing and Unknown," *New York Times*, March 5, 2004, Weekend, 28.

8. Paul Scofield—*King Lear*, PAL, prod. Michael Birkett and Mogens Scot-Hansen, dir. Peter Brook (1971; London: 4 Front Video, 2002); Michael Hordern—*King Lear*, VHS, prod. Shaun Sutton, dir. Jonathan Miller (1982; New York: Ambrose Video, 1987); Laurence Olivier—*King Lear*, VHS, prod. David Plowright, dir. Michael Eliot (1984; West Long Branch, NJ: Kultur Video, 1989); Ian Holm—*King Lear*, VHS, prod. Sue Birtwhistle, dir. Richard Eyre (1998; Boston: WGBH Video, 1998).

9. Michel Saint-Denis, *Theatre: The Rediscovery of Style* (New York: Theatre Arts Books, 1960), 59.

10. Ibid., 53–54.

11. Anthony Davies, *"King Lear on Film,"* in *Lear from Study to Stage: Essays in Criticism*, ed. James Ogden and Arthur H. Scouten (Madison, NJ: Fairleigh Dickinson University Press, 1997), 263.

12. Patricia Tatspaugh, Review of *King Lear*, *Shakespeare Bulletin* 21.1 (2003): 24.

13. Quotations from reviews of the Almeida production have been drawn from *Theatre Record* 12 (February 25, 2002): 178–85.

14. Oliver Ford Davies, *Playing Lear* (London: Nick Hern Books, 2003), 162–63.

15. Ibid., 155.

16. Ibid.

17. Ibid., 176.

18. Ibid., 184. His book ends with this passage:

[Lear] goes out into the wilderness, and this condemns him to an early death. But he is afforded a curse and a blessing. He goes mad, and he is liberated. He lives for a time in a dream/nightmare, where truths about himself and society are exposed. Things that he had always known, but buried, about sex, power, and injustice are revealed to him. He wakes from the dream, and all that he remembers is the primacy of love. This knowledge won't stave off disaster and death, but it brings him some understanding and healing. The play seems to me to say that life is crippled by a failure of understanding, that inequality and injustice corrode our existence, but that human nature can—even in the most extreme circumstances—rise above this. It feels, despite everything, a hopeful play.

19. Herbert Blau, quoted in Maynard Mack, *King Lear in Our Time* (Berkeley: University of California Press, 1972), 35.

20. Michael Feingold, "Lear as Daylight," *Village Voice*, March 10–16, 2004, C81.

21. Desmond Ryan, "With Few Trappings, Plummer's *Lear* Rules," *Philadelphia Inquirer*, March 7, 2004, H6.

22. Gary Smith, "Plummer Gives Us a Lear for Our Age," *The Hamilton Spectator*, August 26, 2002.

23. Tony Brown, "The Eternal *Lear*," *Plain Dealer*, August 27, 2002.

24. Benedict Nightingale argues that what is wanted are "performances strong enough to overwhelm the imagination, seize the mind and heart, and . . . excite extremes of terror and pity." Actors who may be capable of accomplishing this

> have often become victims of the earnest whims of their directors, the temper of a cynical era, and their own mistrust of raw, bold emotions combined with a determination to explore the complexities of character. . . . there is a *Lear* that continues to prove elusive yet at some unreconstructed level I suspect we all yearn to see. ("Some Recent Productions," in *Lear from Study to Stage: Essays in Criticism*, ed. James Ogden and Arthur H. Scouten [Madison, NJ: Fairleigh Dickinson University Press, 1977], 245–46.)

25. Feingold, "Lear as Daylight," C81.
26. Hilton Als, "King for a Day," *The New Yorker*, March 15, 2004, 151.
27. Anne Cattaneo, "Keeping Out of the Rain: A Conversation with Jonathan Miller," *Lincoln Center Theater Review*, no. 37 (Winter/Spring, 2004): 7.
28. Ibid.
29. David Gates, "He's Every Inch a King," *Newsweek*, March 15, 2004, 62.
30. Brantley, "A Fiery Fall into the Abyss," 28.

Placing the Audience at Risk: Realizing the Design of Massinger's *The Roman Actor*

Edward L. Rocklin

The Roman Actor is indeed a brilliant tragedy (RSC and National Theatre, please note) but perhaps it pleased Massinger as much as it did—"the most perfit birth of my Minerva"—because it is the play in which the related ideas of life as arraignment and as theatre are most elaborately and perfectly conjoined.

—Anne Barton[1]

IT IS A PREMISE OF THE PERFORMANCE APPROACH TO DRAMA, AND A premise realized in reviews published in *Shakespeare Bulletin* during the coeditorship of James Lusardi and June Schlueter, that witnessing a performance always has the potential to revise radically one's understanding of a playtext. For example, after seeing Tyrone Guthrie's production of one of Shakespeare's plays in 1936, John Dover Wilson—who, having edited the text, thought he knew its range of realizations—wrote an essay on *"Love's Labour's Lost:* The Story of a Conversion" in which he thanked Guthrie because the director "gave me a new play."[2] In terms of my own encounter with Philip Massinger's *The Roman Actor*, Wilson's essay points toward a crucial difference between our experience of plays by Shakespeare and plays by other English Renaissance dramatists. On the one hand, the frequency with which Shakespeare's plays are staged seems to increase the likelihood that even those who know the plays in detail will encounter such a revelatory performance—yet our pervasive knowledge of these texts, combined with frequent opportunities to witness performances, may well reduce our chances of having a conversion experience. On the other hand, the fact that the majority of surviving scripts by other English Renaissance dramatists are rarely performed means that even for those who study, teach, and write about these plays, knowledge of the range of performance realizations is relatively narrow—so that any production might give us new understanding of old texts' potentials.

144

When I attended the Royal Shakespeare Company's production of *The Roman Actor*, directed by Sean Holmes and opening in the Swan Theatre on May 22, 2002, I had not re-read the play in over a decade, nor had I taught or written about it. I left the theater with my mind electrified and with the RSC playtext[3] I had purchased in hand. I began making notes in that text that same night. My second and third experiences of the production, on June 10 and June 12, were each more intense, and my sense of the play's potentials was enriched by noticing differences in performance and variations in responses of spectators.

As I have indicated, exploring this production was made easier by the fact that the RSC published a modernized text of the play as performed. This version is an approximate partial acting edition of the play: it omits the lines cut at the outset of rehearsal and includes the original stage directions, but it does not add any details of action invented for this performance. My comparison of this text with the scholarly edition by Colin Gibson in *The Selected Plays of Philip Massinger*[4] indicated that Holmes' RSC production cut about 320 lines, or about 15 percent of the 2,199 lines in the original text. I also noted that at least one speech omitted from the text (1.2.70–73) was restored in performance (10). Almost all the cuts were of classical allusions and references to historical figures or events, and I infer that these were passages that Holmes judged might distract most spectators.

In the course of this immersion, I also developed a formulation of the play's action and plot. The *action* follows how Emperor Domitianus Caesar, through the commands by which he asserts, imposes, and seeks to maintain "The deitie you labour to take from me" (4.1.133 / 54), performs a sequence of what Gibson calls "acts of unexpected savagery" that finally drive the surviving members of his court—particularly the four women who constitute the rest of the imperial family appearing on stage—to assassinate this man they have come to perceive as a tyrant.[5]

This action is embodied in an elegant *plot* that can be summarized as follows: 1) In each of the four acts after the expository first act, Caesar encounters challenges to his self-proclaimed status as a deity that provoke him to perform actions that, from his point of view, demonstrate his godlike power but that, from the point of view of his subjects, demonstrate he is a merciless tyrant. 2) These challenges form a progressive sequence, each more intense than the last. 3) Although Domitian recovers from each challenge and reasserts his status as a deity, each recovery leaves him with more victims, hence fewer allies. 4) As he encounters each challenge, Domitian must repeatedly deny his suspicion that the gods themselves may be ordaining his destruction and, in particular, the ultimate proof that he is not a deity—his death.

This basic plot is made richer by another element of Massinger's design. For woven through the representation of Domitian's reign is the action by which the Roman tragedian Paris and two colleagues perform a sequence of three inset plays that, although apparently commanded in order to divert the emperor from cares of state, actually contribute to Caesar's downfall. These playlets appear in the middle three acts: the *Cure of Avarice* (2.1.287–406 / 29–33), *Iphis and Anaxarete* (3.2.148–281 / 44–47), and the *False Servant* (4.2.241–83 / 64–65). In addition, there is the pivotal scene in which Domitia coercively seduces Paris (4.2.5–112 / 55–59), which functions as a playlet insofar as this scene is observed by Caesar, who interrupts the seduction, condemns Domitia to death, and, casting himself in the role of the vengeful husband, uses a command performance of the *False Servant* as the pretense to murder Paris. These inset plays help propel the plot since the first two produce the betrayal of Domitian by Empress Domitia, lead Domitian to murder Paris, and demonstrate how this murder drives Domitia to join the plot to assassinate Domitian. At the same time, the three plays-within-the-play also provide Massinger's implicit commentary on the play's representation of the relation between power and theatrical performance.[6]

What made the RSC production so powerful was the manner in which it realized and amplified the design described above. In particular, this production superbly incarnated three key elements. The first element is the focus of this essay, hinted at by Barton's reference in the passage quoted below; it is the manner in which Massinger works to place "his audience, too, at risk." In what follows, my objective is to describe how choices made by the RSC production team resulted in a particularly vivid realization of this element of the script. The second and third elements, which I hope to explore in another essay, can be briefly described. The second element, especially prominent at the end of the fourth and throughout the fifth act, is the staging employed to foreground how his enemies remove the despot's props as they engineer his fall. The third element is the manner in which actor Antony Sher realized Domitian as one who, to adapt a phrase from *Hamlet*, put a gigantic disposition on.

PLACING THE AUDIENCE AT RISK: EXPERIENCING LIFE IN THE TYRANT'S COURT

There is a sense in which *The Roman Actor* is more pessimistic about the power of art to correct and inform its audience than any other play written between 1580 and 1642. Yet there was something in Massinger which refused to abandon the effort, while insisting that the game should not be played with marked cards. This is why he places his audience, too, at risk.[7]

In terms of the play–audience relation, an analysis of the text of the play reveals seven moments where Massinger's script either mandates or offers the actors an opportunity to transform the spectators into inhabitants of Rome.[8] This production not only effectively realized all seven moments but also created a new opening that sharpened the pattern even as it prompted the spectators to be more alert to the textually mandated components of that pattern. Furthermore, some time between the opening night of May 22 and the June 10 and 12 performances, the production team revised two of these moments in ways that sharpened the projection of Massinger's design.

(1) Death in dumb-show, or "What doe wee acte today?" (1.1.1 / 1).

The amplifying inventions began with an extratextual dumb-show that functioned as an introduction to Rome and an induction into our

Anna Madeley as Domitia and Antony Sher as Domitian Caesar in the Royal Shakespeare Company's 2002 production of Philip Massinger's *The Roman Actor*, directed by Sean Holmes. Photo by Donald Cooper/Photostage.

role as participant-spectators. For without warning, except for the faint sound of a buzzing fly, two gladiators entered in a violent combat that culminated when the taller warrior disarmed his opponent and cut his throat. As the panting victor stood over the face-down victim, we had a few seconds to wonder if we had become spectators in the Colosseum. Then a third figure entered through the audience, walked up to the dead man, examined him with apparent clinical (dis)interest, and asked "What do we act today?" Instantly, we realized that we had just witnessed a rehearsal-within-the-play. On the one hand, this prologue startled spectators—even a spectator who knew the text could not have been prepared for this extratextual staging of violence. On the other hand, because of the way the dumb-show transformed what appeared to be mortal combat into a joke, the opening words provoked the first of many bursts of surprised laughter that, throughout the evening, prepared us to anticipate unexpected outcomes for each of the plays-within-the-play. And whereas the apparent deadly brawl of this rehearsal proved to be make-believe, each of the three command performances, which should have entertained as harmless theater, precipitated startling acts of betrayal and violence. Moreover, since the victor of this combat proved to be the Roman tragedian Paris, the prologue also foreshadowed the moment when Domitian takes his revenge through the on-stage murder of this actor.

It is worth noting that the opening night performance was slightly different. Here, after Paris cut Latinus' throat, he rose, and Paris repeated the throat-cutting. Aesopus entered as Latinus rose again, and, when he asked his question, he did not evoke any laughter. Whatever motivated this reblocking, I think we can see what made the second staging an improvement. For while the repeated throat-cutting is just as effective in making us aware that we have mistaken pretense for reality, the question "What do we act today?" did not elicit the laughter provoked by addressing that question to an apparent corpse. The alternative version, therefore, functioned to teach us more precisely the agile shifts between mortality and grim mirth that were so essential to the experience of Massinger's complex design.

(2) "may we being alone / Speake our thoughts freely of the Prince, and State, / And not feare the informer?" (1.1.67–69 / 5).

If Holmes' opening action sequence impelled us into a complex play–audience interaction, less than five minutes passed before Massinger's design explicitly began to transform us into Roman citizens and inhabitants of the emperor's court. Three Senators—performed by Keith Osborn, Joshua Richards, and Geoffrey Freshwater—entered and, having glanced around, began their discourse:

> *Lamia.*   What times are these?
> To what is *Rome* falne? may we being alone
> Speake our thoughts freely of the Prince and State,
> And not feare the informer?
>
>   (1.1.66–69 / 5)

Because the glances of the Senators included us, they were, as often happens in English Renaissance drama, making us their confidants— and, as the actors made clear, privy to judgments that rendered the Senators subject to charges of libel and sedition. By the end of scene 1, we could realize the full import of the question facing Lamia: that if we were actually rather than virtually present, we would confront the option of becoming informers. We thereby experienced the dilemma that can confront any person in Domitian's Rome, where being party to a secret conversation, even one you have initiated, always creates an opportunity to become an informer. A world in which one might be tempted to commit preemptive betrayal is the world of twentieth-century police states, and this production repeatedly invited twenty-first-century spectators to make this connection. Moreover, the accuracy of the harsh assessment of Domitian by Lamia and his colleagues was confirmed in the next scene. For here, Parthenius, a freeman of Caesar's, serving Caesar's interests but clearly experiencing his own pleasure in the exercise of power, used the threat of torture to compel Lamia to divorce Domitia so that she might become Caesar's empress.

(3) "Or censure us, or free us with applause" (1.3.142 / 15).

If the first scene invited us to become co-conspirators with the three Senators, the play's next maneuver situated us as members of the Senate meeting in the Forum. Although Holmes cut Aretinus' scene-initiating direct address, "Fathers conscript may this our meeting be / Happie to Cæsar and the common wealth" (1.3.1–2), he achieved the same effect with the Tribune's opening command for "Silence," followed by the speech in which Aretinus addressed us as Senators, inviting us "to give thankes to the Gods of *Rome*" (1.3.4–10 / 11–12) for providing a godlike Caesar to govern us. Furthermore, in another maneuver both mandated by the text and amplified by the performers, we became colleagues of

Sura and Rusticus, who addressed their asides to us from above. The fulsomeness of Aretinus' flattery was enough to prompt us to endorse Rusticus' observation that "This is no flatterie!" (1.3.22 / 12). But even as such an endorsement registered our appreciation of Rusticus' integrity, our response was made more complex by Sura's whispered "Take heed, you'l be observ'd" (1.3.22–23 / 12). Observed by us, their words reminded us how even an apparently privileged position might create potentially lethal vulnerability.

The blurring of this world/stage distinction was emphasized as Paris prepared to defend his profession by beginning an oration that elicited Aretinus' startled yet sardonic question:

> *Aretinus.* Are you on the Stage
> You talke so boldly?
> *Paris.* The whole world being one
> This place is not exempted, . . .
>
> (1.3.49–51 / 13)

"This place is not exempted" is a moment of metadramatic comedy insofar as Paris and Aretinus are both on the stage, and Paris (played in 1626 by Joseph Taylor, a leading player in the King's Men) speaks the part of a celebrated actor who gives the most important speech of his life in a "real" trial. Thus Paris' reply not only emphasized the dissolving boundary between stage and world that haunts this play but also prepared for the most vivid demonstration of that dissolution when Caesar used the staging of a theatrical murder as the pretext for the murder of Paris. When this murder occurred, it demonstrated that if the Roman Senate can be seen as a stage, then a supposedly safe theatrical playing space can become as lethal as the gladiatorial arena suggested by the added prologue. Witnessing his murder, we could grasp the irony that, while Paris saves his life by speaking in the Senate, he loses it performing on the stage.

But what was most immediately striking here was an effect that was only achieved some time between the opening performance on May 22 and that on June 10. For the actors worked at shaping their collective performance so that when Joe Dixon's Paris completed his defense, his appeal "Or censure us, or free us with applause" prompted a round of fervent applause. This was an elegant maneuver since, in acquitting the actors of the charges against them, there was no obvious way to distinguish our applause as spectators for the fine performance of Dixon from our applause as ad hoc Senators for the fine performance of Paris as orator for the defense. At the same time, our applause-acquittal also set us up to make the painful discovery that, as critics such as Barton, Martin White, and Martin Butler (see note 6) have argued, all three of the plays-within-the-play demonstrate the failure of theater to perform the moral functions Paris so eloquently proclaims.

(4) "What Roman could indure this?" (1.4.52 / 18).

But hardly had we given our applause to Paris' apology than our relation to the action shifted again with the entry of Domitian Caesar. This entry also at once embodied and modified Massinger's design; whereas the stage direction specifies that Caesar enter *"in his Triumphant Chariot"* (1.4.13 sd / 17), designer Anthony Lamble created a mobile tower, two stories high and bearing an emblem of Caesar's patron, Minerva, on the front, on which Caesar entered, literally towering over cast and audience. As they hauled the tower on stage, the cast voiced a martial chant, accompanied by metallic music that assaulted our ears with a cacophony of reverberating sound, culminating in ear-piercing unison shouts of "Cae-sar! Cae-sar!" as they abased themselves. Meanwhile, Sher's Domitian stood with his eyes crinkled and lips grinning in a near-rictus smile, his arms raised, palms facing us, as if he were indeed already a god or the statue of a god. His opening words, "As we now touch the height of humane glorie" (1.4.14 / 17), were literalized in his roof-reaching elevation.

In this scene, the first of two key moments in the ongoing development of the play–audience relation came when Rusticus, even as he was prostrating himself at Caesar's feet, voiced his nausea at his own behavior. We thus could share the safety-valve effect by which Rusticus, in an aside, could exclaim "Base flattery / What Roman could indure this?" (1.4.51–52 / 18). On the one hand, we could look across the stage to see the smiles and hear the laughter that Rusticus' subversive speech evoked from our fellow spectators. On the other hand, we saw the only onstage figures so far willing to criticize Caesar demonstrate that the answer to Rusticus' question is "Every Roman must endure this if he or she wants to live!"

(5) "Tis death to him that weares a sullen browe" (1.4.83 / 19).

As the scene ended, we witnessed a second vivid demonstration of precisely how vulnerable everyone is in the tyrant's court. For as the assembled Romans lined up to parade after him, Sher's Domitian spun around to catch out those massed behind him, proclaiming "Tis death to him that wears a sullen brow." We watched as several of the characters did, in fact, alter their expressions—and noticed how Caesar's action also changed the expression on the faces of some suddenly selfconscious spectators. We thus became aware that this was a world in which what are usually thought of as unselfconscious physical responses might become acts we would need to regulate since "a sullen brow" or any other proscribed expression might provoke execution.

(6) Supporting an enemy of Caesar: sharing guilty thoughts
(2.1.228–39 / 27).

Whereas at the end of 1.4 we see Caesar attempting to condemn subjects for not producing an expression that would indicate the presence of a mandated thought or emotion, the next moment in this sequence began as Caesar prepared a trap for his first chosen victim, Lamia, announcing that

> I will blend
> My crueltie with some scorne, or else tis lost.
> Revenge, when it is unexpected, falling
> With greater violence; and hate clothed in smiles,
> Strikes, and with horror, dead the wretch that comes not
> Prepar'd to meete it.
>
> (2.1.174–79 / 25)

This speech not only alerted us to the danger awaiting Lamia but confirmed the Senators' earlier description of Caesar as a sadist:

> *Rusticus.*   In his young yeeres
> He shew'd what he would be when growne to ripenes:
> His greatest pleasure was, being a childe,
> With a sharp pointed bodkin to kill flies,
> Whose roomes now men supply.
>
> (1.1.98–102 / 6)

How thin a margin, if any, Lamia might have was emphasized by the staging of the moment in which Caesar gave a prearranged cue for an offstage Domitia to sing:

> *Caesar.* She does begin. An universall silence
> Dwell on this place. 'Tis death with lingering torments
> To all that dare disturbe her.
>
> (2.1.219–21 / 26–27)

In this performance, Caesar's call for silence was motivated by an offstage crash that sounded as if someone had just dropped a huge piece of metal, while the rage with which he spoke foreshadowed the rage waiting to destroy Lamia and the cascade of victims who followed him. As Lamia nearly wept at the sound of Domitia's voice, Caesar proceeded to torment him with praises of his ex-wife's beauty and sexuality, seeking to provoke him to intemperate speech but, even more cunningly, making it impossible for Lamia not to have subversive thoughts—thoughts that Domitian used to sentence his stunned victim to death:

> *Caesar.* Say *Lamia*, say,
> Is not her voice Angelicall?
> *Lamia.* To your eare.
> But I alas am silent.
> *Caesar.* Bee so ever,
> That without admiration canst heare her.
> Malice to my felicitie strikes thee dumbe,
> And in thy hope, or wish to repossesse
> What I love more then empire, I pronounce thee
> Guiltie of treason. Off with his head. Doe you stare?
> By her, that is my Patronesse, Minerva,
> (Whose Statue I adore of all the Gods),
> If he but live to make reply thy life
> Shal answer it.
> *The Guards lead off LAMIA, stopping his mouth.*
>   My feares of him are freed now
> And he that liv'd to upbraid me with my wrong,
> For an offence he never could imagine,
> In wantonness remov'd.
>
> (2.1.228–42 / 27)

In a world where Lamia might survive only if he could prevent Caesar from even finding an excuse to attribute such "treasonous" thoughts to him, we were also compelled to recognize that the dramatist, like Caesar, had provoked us to think things that would make us eligible for charges of treason. This moment was crucial, furthermore, because the combination of the farcical trap with the lethal consequences elicited a powerful outburst of the incredulous laughter that became pervasive in all three performances I attended—and, for whatever reason, was noticeably greater in frequency and intensity during the June 12 performance. The intensity of our laughter was an indicator, it seemed to me, that Holmes' realization of Massinger's text did indeed make us feel at risk. And that by making us feel at risk, his staging resonated with whatever knowledge each of us might have of totalitarian states and of the ways in which, through secret police, covert surveillance, and networks of informants, such states seek to control not only the actions but the thoughts of their subjects or citizens. The power of Holmes' staging of this scene also made me appreciate the way that Massinger, stimulated by descriptions of Rome under the Caesars and, we might speculate, by his own encounter with Jacobean censorship, proved able to imagine what it would be like to live under such a regime.[9]

(7) Philargus: The spectator who learns the wrong lesson
(2.1.434–47 / 33–34).

The next instance of Caesar's unexpected savagery emerges as an outcome of the first of the three inset plays which are a key element of Massinger's design. By focusing so explicitly on Parthenius' Hamlet-like attempt to use a play to make a particular spectator—his miserly father, Philargus—recognize and reform his folly, Massinger makes this act not only subvert the earlier defense of theater but also challenge the audience to interpret the completed action of his playlet and his play correctly. Much of the power of the scene arises from the way it catches off guard all those who witness it since this time they are not forewarned of the risk facing Philargus and since he is executed for doing what the spectators are doing, namely, interpreting a play.

The meaning of the *Cure of Avarice* is driven home by the explicit statement of its moral in the concluding couplet (2.1.405–6 / 32). Like the onstage audience, we could see and hear that public meaning. Yet because we were more detached, we were also able to realize how it was possible for Philargus to reject and reverse the explicit moral: seeing what was portrayed as a vice as being his virtue. However, it seemed to me that our deeper engagement was with Parthenius. On the one hand, we had witnessed his role in the legal appropriation of Lamia's wife, Domitia, and witnessed his relish in performing this role, which enabled him to compel a man who is his superior to humiliate himself. On the other hand, the present action emerged from his filial piety. And the utter unreasonableness of Caesar's "cure" for avarice demonstrated an abuse of power that overwhelmed Philargus' "mistake" in how he interpreted the action:

> *Caesar.* by *Minerva* thou shalt never more
> Feele the least touch of avarice. Take him hence

And hang him instantly. If there be gold in hell
Injoy it; thine here and thy life together
Is forfeited.

(2.1.437–41 / 34)

Furthermore, the way in which Caesar used the threat of execution
to silence Parthenius after his horrified plea "Mercie for all my service,
Cæsar mercie!" (2.1.442 / 34), even as it provoked incredulous laughter, compelled us to register the appalling shock of this unjust and dis-
proportionate response by Caesar to even this slight resistance by
someone who poses no direct threat to his regime.

A moment's reflection, however, compelled a recognition that Philargus *does* pose a threat to—and a peculiar opportunity for—Caesar. The
threat he posed was to Caesar's premise that, as a god on earth, his
will is omnipotent and that no mere mortal can do other than obey his
commands. The opportunity he offered was a further occasion for Caesar to embody spectacularly the capricious use of power by which a
tyrant creates the fear and uncertainty that sustains his rule, inhibiting
even the most courageous subjects from daring to imagine they might
successfully resist that power, let alone persuade others to join a revolt.

(8) "my synnewes shrinke, / The spectacle is so horrid" (3.2.81–83 / 41).

The pattern of including the spectators in Massinger's onstage fiction
reaches a climax in 3.2, and Holmes emphasized this fact by placing the
interval after this scene. What we witnessed was an explicit representation of the tyrant's wish to control not only his subjects' actions but also
their thoughts and feelings, even or especially at the point of death. We
were thereby prompted to realize that what Domitian embodies is not
only the fantasy of absolute power but also the tyrant's tacit admission
that, while he may proclaim that he deserves universal love, he must
fear that he elicits universal hatred.

Initiating the onstage torture of the Senators Junius Rusticus and
Palphurius Sura, Aretinus once again defined us as participants:

> *Aretinus.* 'Tis great Cæsars pleasure
> That with fix'd eyes you carefully observe
> The peoples lookes. Charge upon any man
> That with a sigh, or murmure does expresse
> A seeming sorrow for these traytors deaths.

(3.2.46–50 / 40)

As he spoke, Michael Thomas' superbly unctuous Aretinus looked around at both onstage subjects and the audience, as if to catch the eye of spectators who might be about to move toward a detachment that would insulate them from what was to follow. A minute later, as the stoic endurance of the Senators being tortured—in this production by having their backs ripped with meat hooks—provoked the infuriated Caesar to cry out "Not a groane, / Is my rage lost?" (3.2.77–78 / 41), their suffering also prompted a striking aside from Parthenius:

> *Parthenius.*   I dare not show
> A signe of sorrow, yet my synnewes shrinke,
> The spectacle is so horrid.
>
> (3.2.81–83 / 41)

The impact of this moment is partly inherent in the incarnational nature of the theater, where the medium is not only the body of the actor but the body of the spectator and where a performance achieves some of its most powerful effects through our response to the physical and emotional experience of the human beings embodied before us. Here Antony Byrne's Parthenius movingly enacted the horrific tension between his involuntary sympathetic response to the suffering of fellow human beings and his knowledge that any visible manifestation of this sympathy might subject him to the same fate. In the Swan, we were close enough to the stage and to each other to realize that our own shrinking responses were indeed visible to Caesar, Aretinus, and the Guards, who—with faces hidden by metal masks that made them safer from the threat of inadvertent self-revelation than we were—continued to stare at all those present, both onstage and off. We were able to see our own horror reflected in the faces of those sitting twenty or thirty feet across from us, even as we could sense the gasps and tensed muscles of those sitting next to us.

Watching Byrne's Parthenius offered us a compelling embodiment of the long-term dilemma confronting anyone living in the court of a tyrant such as Domitian. The dilemma is that either your own body will betray your dissent from the tyrant's willingness to sacrifice any human being who actually resists his whims, in which case you will be executed, or you will survive only by repressing these responses in an act that ultimately deforms your humanity by alienating your mind from your body, in which case you will secure your own physical survival at the cost of obliterating your integrity. It is a moment in which Parthenius may, and a spectator can, realize that if complete suppression of the simplest responses of one's nervous system is impossible, then dissenting from Caesar's will is a physiological inevitability, and providing a pretext for Caesar to execute you may be as inescapable as the need to take your next breath.

I hope that what I have written captures the way in which Massinger's design provides the opportunity for a production to place the audience "at risk" and the way in which Holmes' brilliant realization of that design for the RSC offered us an opportunity to experience the bitter combination of extreme farce and lethal violence that constitutes life at the emperor's court, even as the safety of art protected us. For me, this electrifying performance recalled the words of Gretel Ehrlich, who, in the course of meditating upon her experience of being struck by lightning, wrote, "You don't have to experience everything life can throw at you—torture or ecstasy—to fuel empathy; just a taste is enough."[10] What this production of *The Roman Actor* offered audiences was, indeed, a taste of life in a world governed by torture. Certainly, when I walked out of the intimate and intensely charged atmosphere of the Swan Theatre, I could still taste life in a world of torture—and, therefore, could appreciate vividly indeed the simple pleasure of walking over the river, back to a (rented) room of my own and an opportunity to begin reflecting on this disturbing yet intensely satisfying performance.

NOTES

1. Anne Barton, "The Distinctive Voice of Massinger," *Times Literary Supplement*, May 20, 1977, 623–24. I quote from the version in *Philip Massinger: A Critical Reassessment*, ed. Douglas Howard (Cambridge: Cambridge University Press, 1985), 227.

2. John Dover Wilson, *Shakespeare's Happy Comedies* (Evanston, IL: Northwestern University Press, 1962), 64.

3. Philip Massinger, *The Roman Actor* (London: Nick Hern Books, 2002). The title page announces "This edition prepared for the Royal Shakespeare Company" without naming an editor. Obviously, the director functioned as an editor in terms of the text performed, but it appears that this edition is based on one of the two editions prepared by Colin Gibson (see below, note 4).

4. Massinger, *The Roman Actor*, in *The Plays and Poems of Philip Massinger*, ed. Philip Edwards and Gibson, 5 vols. (Oxford: Clarendon Press, 1976), 3:13–93. Subsequent references are from this edition and are cited parenthetically; they are followed by a slash and page number(s) of the RSC text. I use the page numbers because the RSC text has no line numbers.

5. Edwards and Gibson, *The Plays and Poems of Philip Massinger*, 5:187.

6. In this essay, I do not trace Massinger's representation of the relation between power and theatrical performance and the ways in which the outcome of these three

plays-within-the-play systematically contradict the defense of theater offered by Paris. This topic is sketched in Barton, "The Distinctive Voice of Massinger"; outlined in Martin Butler's Introduction to the RSC edition (xii); and cogently developed in Martin White, "Jacobean Metatheatre," in White, *Renaissance Drama in Action: An Introduction to Aspects of Theatre Practice and Performance* (London: Routledge, 1998), 100–108. See also the comments of G. K. Hunter on this play in relation to Ben Jonson's *Sejanus* in *English Drama 1586–1642: The Age of Shakespeare* (Oxford: Clarendon Press, 1997), 465–66.

7. Barton, "The Distinctive Voice of Massinger," in *Philip Massinger: A Critical Reassessment*, ed. Howard, 231.

8. 1.1.67–69 / 5; 1.3.56–142 / 13–15; 1.4.51–52 / 18; 1.4.84 / 19; 2.1.228–39 / 27; 2.1.434–47 / 33–34; 3.2.46–51 and 81–83 / 40 and 41.

9. See Janet Clare, *"Art made tongue-tied by authority": Elizabethan and Jacobean Dramatic Censorship*, 2nd ed. (Manchester: Manchester University Press, 1999), 195–205, which offers a detailed analysis of Sir George Buc's censoring of the manuscript of *The Tragedy of Sir John van Olden Barnavelt* (1619) by Massinger and John Fletcher. Clare notes that

> Buc's . . . explicit prohibition relates to a passage in which Barnavelt draws an elequent [*sic*] historical parallel between the Netherlands under Orange and the Rome of Octavius Caesar. . . . Buc was intent on removing the analogy between the United Provinces and the Roman Republic transmuted into the Roman Empire: . . . Buc's interference here betrays the censor's habitual distrust of historical parallels drawn by playwrights to comment by comparison or default on the present. Buc has altered the meaning of the passage so that the ideological critique of monarchy—more apposite to the conditions of England than to the United Provinces—is lost. (197, 199–200)

10. Gretel Ehrlich, *A Match to the Heart* (New York: Pantheon, 1994), 49.

"I'm not a feminist director, but . . ." : Recent Feminist Productions of *The Taming of the Shrew*

Michael D. Friedman

DURING THE PAST THREE DECADES, SEVERAL BRITISH PRODUCTIONS of *The Taming of the Shrew* have engaged overtly with the play's "masculinist" conception of the ideal wife in a "feminist" manner. The first wave of performances included the directorial efforts of Charles Marowitz (1973), Michael Bogdanov (1978), and David Ultz (1985), whose work self-consciously invited a feminist categorization. These productions depicted the Paduan community, and Petruchio in particular, as cruel, barbaric abusers of women. They hoped to incite audiences to angry disapproval of any social system that would tolerate such treatment. A second wave of feminist performances of *Shrew* differed from the first. Reacting to the 1980s backlash against feminism, the directors of these productions shunned the feminist label, yet they pursued an agenda that matched the goals of feminism. Female directors Di Trevis (1985), Gale Edwards (1995), and Phyllida Lloyd (2003) diverged from their male predecessors by moving away from harsh, unqualified condemnation of the Paduan marriage market and Petruchio's taming methods. They also employed alternative strategies that evoked sympathy for the shrew's predicament, complicated the intense relationship between Kate and her husband, and satirized the sexist behavior of the male characters. In this way, recent feminist productions of *Shrew* mirror changes in attitude toward the women's movement that have occurred outside the theater.

Marowitz's production at the Open Space in London, entitled simply *The Shrew*, is considered the first British feminist version of the play. Marowitz adapted Shakespeare's comedy into a collage of selected scenes, cut and reordered, but his harrowing reconception of the taming action received the most attention. As John Elsom remembers, the production

> stressed the thuggishness of Petruchio. The result is a nightmare of male tyranny. Petruchio just wants Katherine's dowry, Baptista is only trying to

get rid of a sullen daughter: once the bargain between men has been struck, the process of subjugation can begin. Katherine is starved, manacled, brainwashed, raped anally and finally dragged before a fascist tribunal at which Petruchio presides, to deliver a formal speech of submission.[1]

Graham Holderness records that "Kate delivered her speech of submission mechanically, by rote, 'as if the words were being spoken by another.' Hesitating between complete passivity and hysterical resistance, Kate was constantly prompted and prodded by husband and father to speak out her manifesto of abjection."[2] Marowitz attempted to achieve a feminist effect by portraying Katherine as a victim of male oppression, whose coerced paean to female obedience cannot be accepted by liberated spectators. As Penny Gay recalls, "my own memories of the production remain those of the physical torture and madness of Kate, which placed the play firmly in the emerging feminist context of the 1970s."[3]

Marowitz adapted Shakespeare's text because he wanted to peel away "all those arbitrary layers of gaiety and comedy" to get at "the fable naked and unadorned." In Marowitz's view, the original play

> always leaves a nasty taste in the mouth. Women despise it, because . . . it always smacks of male chauvinism and a contemptible, contemptuous, attitude towards women. The play itself, shorn of the highjinks and slapstick that usually embroider it, is a detestable story about a woman who is brainwashed by a scheming adventurer as cruel as he is avaricious.[4]

For Marowitz, the text's humorous elements are mere embroidery: inessential distractions from "the play itself." Therefore, he stripped away everything that did not smack of a misogynistic attitude and strove to achieve his feminist effect through negative example, portraying "male chauvinism" as an attitude so abhorrent that no spectator could possibly endorse it. Accordingly, Marowitz writes of the "fury" he "hoped women would feel against Petruchio after his debasement of Katherine."[5] However, Marowitz's "mission to infuriate women rather than men" may have backfired as a feminist tactic because it also sent the message that "uppity women get anally raped and brainwashed, so women should think twice before creating trouble."[6]

Like Marowitz, Bogdanov emphasized Petruchio's brutality toward Katherine in an effort to enrage spectators, both male and female, and spur them toward political action. He intended the violence of his production to provoke viewers to ask themselves what makes them "angry." What makes me "want to do something to change the world"?[7]

Thelma Holt as Katherine and Malcolm Tierney as Petruchio (originally played by Nikolas Simmonds) in the Open Space Theatre's 1975 revival of *The Shrew* (1973), conceived and directed by Charles Marowitz. Photo by Donald Cooper/Photo*stage*.

Yet, as Holderness notes, while Marowitz felt compelled to adapt the "repugnant" text severely to achieve his political aim, Bogdanov assumed that the "true meaning" of Shakespeare's play was already "compatible with modern feminist ideology."[8] In scenes like Baptista's bargaining with Bianca's suitors, Bogdanov discovered Shakespeare's compassion for powerless females:

> I believe Shakespeare was a feminist . . . I think there is no question of it: he shows how women are ill-treated. . . . totally abused—like animals— bartered to the highest bidder. He shows women used as commodities, not allowed to choose for themselves . . . and his purpose, to expose the cruelty of a society that allows these things to happen.[9]

Although Marowitz and Bogdanov both highlighted Paduan society's dehumanization of women, Marowitz found this "detestable" element hidden below a layer of comedy, while Bogdanov saw the same abuse as evidence of Shakespeare's feminist sympathies, unobscured by the play's humorous aspects. Therefore, Bogdanov's performance script retained far more of Shakespeare's text and comic features than did

Marowitz's adaptation, but Bogdanov also made selective cuts and interpolations that underscored the play's treatment of gender issues.

In place of the argument between the Hostess and Sly that begins Shakespeare's play, Bogdanov's Royal Shakespeare Company production substituted an altercation between an intoxicated spectator (Jonathan Pryce) and a female usher (Paola Dionisotti), who later reappeared as Petruchio and Kate. Warning her, "no bloody woman's going to tell me what to do," Pryce clambered onto the stage, destroyed the set, and passed out.[10] The rest of the play then became Sly's dream of the "desired but unachievable subjugation of the usherette."[11] Pryce embodied Petruchio as "a male chauvinist pig"[12] who "pinioned Kate's wrists" and "hurled her to the ground" in the wooing scene.[13] This violence continued at Petruchio's house, where his treatment of his wife resembled torture more closely than taming.[14] Although some scenes in the production evoked considerable laughter, the encounters between Katherine and Petruchio displayed no humor, nor a growing bond of love. As in Marowitz's adaptation, "There was certainly no hint of [a] possible relationship, much less affection" between Kate and Petruchio.[15] This lack of warmth foregrounds the mercenary nature of Petruchio's wooing, which aligns him with the avaricious values that rule the Paduan marriage market. According to Peter Thomson, Bogdanov's "real villain is an acquisitive society (Baptista with an adding-machine to calculate the assets of Bianca's suitors) governed by men who carve up first women and then each other."[16] This confluence of greed and the abuse of women was most evident in Dionisotti's delivery of Kate's tribute to obedient wives:

> Katharina's speech began in complete sincerity . . . But each succeeding period carried her into still-grander hyperboles of male dominance, and she kept going long after Petruchio was ready for her to stop. He grew increasingly nervous in the face of this grotesque masque of wifely surrender. Trapped in his role of shrew-tamer, with no choice but to accept her long tribute lest he lose face before the other husbands, he was Frankenstein, appalled by the monster he had created out of the remains of Katharina.[17]

Kaori Kobayashi asserts that Bogdanov's finale shamed both Petruchio and the audience by implicating them in Kate's humiliation: "The scene conveyed a horrible sense of opprobrium . . . [and] ended with the implication of no possible change in the Paduan collective philosophy of mercantilism and male chauvinism."[18] Although Bogdanov intended to incite his audience to political ac-

tion, his indictment of Petruchio, as well as the audience, for their com-
plicity in the systematic debasement of women may have caused
viewers to despair that such institutionalized injustice can ever be overcome. Lorna Sage offers a divided response to the remorseful quality of
Bogdanov's ending:

> It is an interesting and courageous (not to say feminist) way to interpret the
> play, but though it works in theory, I am not so sure in practice. It is very
> difficult to accept an emotional curve that starts with exhilaration and ends
> in depressed deadlock, and I had the feeling that the audience emerged into
> a damp afternoon more simply grumpy than thoughtful . . .[19]

Feminist productions of *Shrew* that operate by negative example, like
Bogdanov's and "the depressing Marowitz collage,"[20] risk failure by potentially disheartening viewers instead of inspiring them to seek
changes in the way society treats women. Furthermore, some conserva-
tive critics balked at Bogdanov's production for its feminist leanings.
In a strikingly sexist phrase, Benedict Nightingale refers to Dionisotti's
Katherine as "a hard-faced bitch with a strident voice."[21] Although this
modern-dress version contained no signals associating Kate with the
women's movement, Nightingale projects the production's gender politics onto Katherine by invoking the negative stereotype of the bitchy
and "strident" feminist.

The backlash against feminism is also evident in some responses to
Ultz's all-female production, which carried the subtitle *The Women's Version*, a phrase that one reviewer described as "implying a lot of loony
feminist nonsense."[22] Unlike Marowitz and Bogdanov, who intended to
anger spectators, Ultz and his actors apparently wanted to express their
own rage at the sexism of Shakespeare's comedy. Michael Coveney
characterizes this rendition of *Shrew* as "a sustained gesture of disapproval for its sexist content . . . done in a spirit of outraged disbelief."[23]
This hostility impelled Ultz to highlight "the element of chauvinist cruelty that is shriekingly evident in any conventional version" of the comedy and to undercut its complexity by "zealously stripping the play of
anything resembling humour."[24] The harshest verdict on Ultz's polemic
came from a female reviewer, who lamented that the director's politics
prompted him to distort Shakespeare's work: "By taking all that is misogynistic and unpalatable in the play and violently wrenching it into
his own concept he robs it of all shade of meaning but the one in
hand—a bitter satirical feminist tract about the depersonalisation of
women."[25]

Ultz, like Bogdanov, stressed the play's contemporary relevance by adapting the Induction to fit a modern locale. He placed the action at "a feminist theatre group meeting" in a room decorated with paper screens listing "the functions of Man (woos, ravishes, achieves) and the characteristics of a Perfect Wife (gentle, yielding, obedient)."[26] He also employed various alienating effects, such as identical costumes and rhythmic verse speaking, to denaturalize the events depicted by his feminist actors. As the play-within-the-play began, each actor portraying a man hurriedly penciled on facial hair and paraded around the stage "with a placard proclaiming her appointed role, striding and swaggering in a parody of masculinity." Systematically, the sexist elements of the play were "hauled up and debunked": the wooing of Bianca had "all the romance of a cattle auction, and any trace of artifice to be found in Petruchio's subduing of Kate [was] displaced by a braggart's unreasoning cruelty."[27] Ultz subsequently followed Marowitz and Bogdanov by escalating Petruchio's domestication of Kate into physical and mental torture. At his home, Petruchio encased Kate "in a muzzle labeled 'Scold'" and subjected her to "a barrage of flashing lights," which underscored "the inherent barbarity of wife-taming."[28] Petruchio's coercive methods eventually drove Katherine insane, and her speech to Bianca and the Widow in the final scene became increasingly frantic. As Kate waxed "more and more eloquent and hysterical," her stage colleagues realized that she was "going out of her mind."[29] The other actors then renounced their roles and ended the play "with embarrassed coughs and shuffling, wrapping [Kate] in a blanket and forcibly removing her,"[30] the blanket serving as a type of "straight jacket."[31] While Marowitz attempted to demonize Kate's doctrine of wifely obedience as the product of a brainwashing campaign, Ultz sought to neutralize the chauvinism of the speech by treating it as the ravings of a mind diseased. The embarrassed reaction of the feminist cast likewise prompted the audience to disavow such regressive sentiments. But due to the production's "lack of subtlety, [and] humour,"[32] some reviewers expressed concern that Ultz's production would give feminist performances a bad name. As Carole Woddis declared, "I am still waiting for the real 'women's version' directed by a woman. This is not it."[33]

Woddis' remark raises the issue of the director's gender as a qualification for an effective feminist production. For her, even an all-female cast cannot perform a "women's version" of the play if the female actors are circumscribed by the authority of a male director. While I reject the notion that male directors, by virtue of their gender alone, cannot produce successful feminist versions of *Shrew*, I admit that the second wave of productions covered in this essay, all directed by women, succeeded in grappling with the sexist elements of the play in a theatrically more effective manner than the productions directed by their male predecessors. However, I would attribute this success not to the director's gender but to alternative staging strategies, which abstain from amplification of the brutality of Petruchio's taming and allow for humor and complexity in the relationship between Kate and Petruchio. Surprisingly, I also observe a comparative reluctance on behalf of these female directors to acknowledge a feminist stance in their work. Although reviewers commonly identify the performances directed by Trevis, Edwards, and Lloyd as feminist productions, the directors themselves do not embrace the feminist label as freely as do Marowitz, Bogdanov, and Ultz. I take this reluctance as a symptom of the backlash against feminism embodied by the phrase "I'm not a feminist, but . . ."

Numerous works about the women's movement refer to a tendency among contemporary females, especially younger ones, to affirm feminist values while concurrently dissociating themselves from the feminist cause. For example, Paula Kamen, who interviewed over a thousand young people about their associations with the term "feminist," reports on their lack of commitment to the women's movement: "Most didn't identify with feminism or want to be associated with it on a personal or political level. The great irony is that although feminism has generally made a tremendous difference in the perceptions and opportunities in many of these people's lives, it is something that they almost universally shun.[34] Likewise, Leslie Heywood and Jennifer Drake write of facing "classrooms of young women and men who are trained by the media caricature of 'feminazis,' who see feminism as an enemy or say 'feminist' things prefaced by 'I'm not a feminist, but . . .'"[35] As Susan J. Douglas explains, this "conversational gambit" means that the speaker supports such things as equal pay for equal work, reproductive freedom, equal access for women to the same educational and professional opportunities as men, and "marriages in which husbands cook dinner and empty the diaper pail. . . . It also means that the speaker shaves her legs, bathes regularly, does not want to be thought of as a man-hater, a ball-buster, a witch, or a shrew."[36] If, as Douglas suggests, a woman who calls herself a feminist is likely to be perceived as a shrew, then a female director of *The Taming of the Shrew* whose production flaunts the mantle of feminism risks her production's damnation by association with the personality of its odious title character. Therefore, the female directors of certain British performances of the play, whose productions directly confront the patriarchal ideology of Padua, distance themselves from the women's movement, apparently as a means of shedding the unwelcome baggage that accompanies the feminist label.

Trevis' RSC Touring Company production of *Shrew* placed a Brechtian frame around the performance of Shakespeare's play: "Her strolling players entered with a vast sackcloth banner, bearing as its strange device the words 'The Taming of the Shrew, A Kind of History.' The unfamiliar quotation (Induction 2.138) was clearly intended to remind us, in Shakespeare's own words, of the feminist argument that history is all too often 'his story.' "[37] In contrast to the cheerless renditions directed by her male predecessors, Trevis delivered what was generally considered a "good-humoured" feminist production.[38] She did not make expressing or provoking anger at the inequities depicted in the play her primary goal; rather, Trevis fostered the play's comedic elements at appropriate moments, even within the Katherine/Petruchio plotline. As Geraldine Cousin writes, the production "was very moving and, though funny only intermittently, the laughter when it came was of a particularly satisfying kind. It didn't evade the question of the play's contemporary relevance, but found instead a way of confronting its difficulties."[39]

Trevis handled the play's intersection with modern concerns about the role of women by exploiting the metatheatrical opportunities provided by Shakespeare's Induction. After the Lord's men changed Sly out of his rags into a rich man's clothing and provided him with a Lady (the transvestite page), the poverty-stricken players reentered with their ramshackle cart to perform in tattered costumes. Trevis recalls how she linked the penury and subjugation of Sly to the identical conditions suffered by the women in the acting troupe:

> I realised that I could draw a parallel between the powerlessness of the women in the play and the powerlessness of that beggar. And I didn't have to do that terrible thing of making Katherine send up the last speech because I had a structure whereby, after the ending of the play within the play, I could then make a theatrical comment about the position of the actress playing Katherine in the inner play—she and the beggar were finally left alone on the stage together and one saw that they were fellows.[40]

The scene between Sly and the actress playing Katherine occurred at the end of Trevis' production, after Kate and Petruchio exited together and the traveling players took their bows. Having observed Petruchio leading his bride to bed, Sly turned to embrace his own "wife," but the page removed his wig and laughed mockingly as he ran off the stage. The Lord then cast a few coins contemptuously at the feet of the beggar, who began to perceive the cruel joke that had been played upon him. At this point, the actress portraying Katherine returned to the stage:

> She looked humble and downtrodden now. There was no trace of her cour-
> age and vivacity as Kate. In her arms she held the baby she had carried at
> the beginning of the performance as she pulled the cart. As the lights faded
> for the final time, Sly stretched out his hand to this actress, offering her as
> a gift one of the coins that had been tossed at him.[41]

Sly's gesture of fellow-feeling toward the humble actress elicits sympathy for her plight, as a feminist production might be expected to do. However, by connecting the woman's powerlessness to Sly's own "downtrodden" condition, Trevis highlights the distress of all people, male or female, whose poverty disempowers them. In fact, in published interviews, Trevis distances her socialist reading of *Shrew* from the feminist movement. In one newspaper, she declares, "This play is about power, not gender"; in another, she asserts that the play "isn't just about gender and teaching a girl how to behave, but is actually about class and economics."[42] Downplaying the importance of gender in her public comments about the play, Trevis apparently seeks to avoid the feminist stigma that her production's pro-female stance might otherwise attract.

Trevis' production also differed from the openly feminist versions directed by her male counterparts by dramatizing a growing mutual affection in Kate and Petruchio's relationship. The success of this portrayal depended upon Alfred Molina's depiction of Petruchio not merely as an insensitive brute but as a three-dimensional human being: "Molina was not afraid of showing the audience the unpleasant aspects of Petruchio. . . . But neither did he show Petruchio as an unpleasant man, with whom it was unnecessary to sympathize."[43] Once the action shifted away from Padua, "The taming was in no way softened by . . . Petruchio, but beneath the bullying there was a bond of shared adversity."[44] Since Petruchio was not just a cruel, mercenary swine, spectators could accept the possibility that Katherine might come to love him. Despite Trevis' remark that she didn't have to make Katherine "send up the last speech," Cousin perceived "a certain ambiguity" in Kate's account of the duty wives owe to their lords that seemed to be designed "to show its absurdity":

> The speech was partly tongue-in-cheek, but it also clearly showed Kate's
> new-found love for her husband. Petruchio listened with growing emotion

to Kate's words, and at the end wiped away a tear. . . . He picked up the cap which he had ordered Kate to throw down, put it gently on her head, and then jokingly placed it on his own. The two of them ran off with their arms round each other, laughing at the folly of the other characters.[45]

Trevis' Kate, Sian Thomas, delivered her troublesome speech in such a way that it expressed affection for her husband, yet she also drew attention to the ridiculously imbalanced marital relationship that the lines describe. Thus, Trevis incorporated into her production a feminist critique of patriarchal marriage without sacrificing the comic tone of the play or dispiriting her audience.

One decade after Trevis' touring production, Edwards became the first woman to direct *Shrew* on the RSC's main stage. Like Trevis, Edwards altered and expanded upon Shakespeare's Induction; however, instead of focusing on the traveling players, Edwards emulated Bogdanov by having actor Michael Siberry double as Sly and Petruchio, who recoils in shame at his degradation of Katherina in the final act.[46] Edwards' controversial innovation was to match Siberry with television star Josie Lawrence as both Kate and Mrs. Sly, an interpolated character. A plot summary in the production's program announces that Sly falls asleep after arguing with his wife, then dreams of himself as "a cavalier fortune hunter" named Petruchio, who eventually realizes his offenses against Katherina and that his dream "has become a nightmare."[47] When Sly awakes as himself, he kneels and contritely embraces his wife; so "Petruchio has gone too far and blown it, but Sly can still make amends. . . . Presumably, an unacceptable 1590s ending has herein been made palatable for the 1990s."[48] Siberry's own comments about this conclusion confirm that the company intended to make the production "palatable" by balancing a comic tone and a feminist perspective on the play's events: "We were determined . . . to be entertaining, to make people laugh, so long as, at the end of the play, it was clear that certain parts of the behaviour the audience had been watching were unacceptable. But we wanted to state this only at the end, not lay it on with a trowel from the start . . ."[49] In contrast to the previous wave of feminist directors, who chose to "lay it on with a trowel from the start . . . ," Edwards endeavored to express her gender politics more subtly and to cause spectators to reevaluate their responses to earlier events based on the production's conclusion.

In interviews, Edwards dissociates her production's reading of the taming plot from earlier renditions that heighten Kate's torment: "Edwards laughs: 'Can you imagine doing a tortured victim interpretation

of this play with Josie?' That bleak, black view of the play with Petruchio as 'such a terrible bastard and a Kate learning how to love violence and oppression' would be completely abhorrent."[50] Edwards links
this "abhorrent" interpretation, which she disavows, to the women's
movement: "Obviously no one is interested in a deeply feminist, editori-
alised version of the *Shrew*."[51] Despite her disinterest in a "deeply feminist" version of the play, Edwards made several performance choices
that invited spectators to see events from the shrew's point of view, including a single-line cut at the beginning of 4.3 that granted Kate her
own soliloquy.[52] Some reviewers complained that this female perspective, a by-product of Edwards' "natural feminist instinct," ran counter
to the macho dream structure established by the Induction,[53] but Sarah
Werner argues that such contradictions were part of a deliberate attempt to create a different type of feminist production of the play than
had ever been staged before. Observing that the production vacillated
between "forcing the audience to recognize the violence of the taming"
and "encouraging them to approve the love story," Werner claims that
Edwards both critiqued and endorsed "the patriarchal politics of the
playscript"[54] until the end of the play, when Sly's recognition of his mistake prompted viewers to share his contrition:

> We realized that our desire for a happy ending implicated us in a regressive
> and harmful ideology, and thus we recognized the danger of consuming
> Shakespeare blindly. In this way, Edwards' *Shrew* offered a feminist produc-
> tion that could be presented on the RSC main stage without succumbing to
> a passive acceptance of its politics.[55]

Eight years after Edwards transformed theatrical strategies used by
Bogdanov, Lloyd, at Shakespeare's Globe, renovated the all-female approach employed by Ultz and finally produced what might be called
"the real 'women's version' directed by a woman."[56] Lloyd's Company
of Women, with its all-female cast, generated widespread anticipation
of an old-school feminist rendition of the play, but most reviewers were
pleasantly surprised at the playfulness of the Globe production:

> So what on earth would the ladies make of a comedy that shows a macho,
> mercenary brute employing sleep deprivation and starvation to crush the
> rebellious spirit of his bride? I feared a dour, stridently feminist staging,
> heavily underlining the fact that all men are bastards. I should have known
> better.
> Phyllida Lloyd is a director with an infectious sense of fun, and the mere

fact that all the men here are played by women highlights the absurdities of
the male of the species without any need of overt editorialising.[57]

Like Edwards, who disclaimed any interest in "a deeply feminist, edito-
rialised version of the *Shrew*," Lloyd abstained from a "stridently feminist staging" with "overt editorialising" in the style of Marowitz,
Bogdanov, and Ultz. In place of harsh condemnation of the Paduan
marriage market, Lloyd elected to lampoon mercenary behavior with
more subtlety: "As Janet McTeer (Petruchio) commented, the point
was 'to gently satirize men by exaggerating male behavior' in 'a macho,
competitive society in which marriage is a matter of mercantile transaction.'"[58] McTeer played Petruchio as a vulgar, money-grubbing, but not
entirely unlikeable man, and he and Kate "were mutually smitten from
the moment they laid eyes on each other."[59] Combining gentle parody
and romanticism, Lloyd's production evaded a belligerent tone yet succeeded in striking the target of its satire. As Nightingale wrote, "we
aren't watching some shrewish revenge on the Bard, still less a feelbad
production. . . . Speaking as one of the Lords of Creation under sly
female attack, I enjoyed myself."[60]

  Abigail Anderson, the production's assistant director, maintains that,
although Lloyd "has an interest in telling women's stories," she would
not "explicitly state" that she is a feminist. Anderson believes, moreover, that Lloyd would not characterize her version as a feminist production but, rather, as "a look at the play, and men as portrayed by the
play, from a woman's point of view." Describing the cast and crew's
interpretive process, Anderson recalls, "We spent the majority of our
time working out what it meant that women were performing these
roles, rather than working from the idea of a feminist perspective." This
"exploration of the portrayal of gender" reached its apex in the staging
of Kate's final speech:

> The production really pushed the confidence, bordering on boorishness, of
> the men in the play as portrayed by women, and this came to a head in the
> final scene. The men were drunk, loud and very laddish: banging the table
> and cheering each other on. Katherine's speech was presented as playing
> into the hands of the men and then subverting their expectations by continu-
> ing to speak long after it had ceased to be appropriate. She danced on the
> table and raised her skirts to show the softness of her body and vulnerabil-
> ity, embarrassing all the "men" present on stage but delighting the audi-
> ence.[61]

Reviewers record that Petruchio's mortified reaction to Kate's "obedience" clinched a female victory in the battle of the sexes: "Petruchio

clearly wanted his tamed wife to say a few words to those present, but her long-winded stop-start diatribe clearly took him aback. Unable to stop her, he became embarrassed and . . . almost cried. Clearly, Kate was the boss now. It was a neat reversal of their relationship and turned a deadly ending into a comic triumph."[62]

As the productions directed by Trevis, Edwards, and Lloyd demonstrate, one may deliver a stage version of *Shrew* that questions patriarchal assumptions about the role of women without necessarily angering or disheartening spectators. Petruchio need not be portrayed as a cruel, male chauvinist pig, nor must his relationship with Kate be devoid of genuine affection. The inequities of the Paduan marriage market may be comically satirized rather than indignantly denounced, and performance choices that draw sympathy to the shrew's plight within this mercantile transaction may be successfully utilized. However, female directors who have employed such techniques have also felt obliged to distance themselves from the same feminist movement whose agenda, by all external accounts, they appear to be pursuing. Distinct from their male predecessors, who wore their feminism on their sleeves and risked disapproval for their "strident" and "depressing" political stance, the new wave of "feminist" directors of *Shrew* in Britain have been reluctant to align themselves with the women's movement, lest their productions be thought as shrewish and unpleasant as their heroine. In this way, such female directors behave like many contemporary young women of the "I'm-not-a-feminist,- but . . ." generation, who support the aims of feminism but shrink from the stigma attached to "the f-word."

NOTES

1. John Elsom, "Shrews," *Listener*, December 20, 1973, 864.

2. Graham Holderness, *The Taming of the Shrew*, Shakespeare in Performance (Manchester: Manchester University Press, 1989), 93. Holderness quotes from the stage directions in the published version of Charles Marowitz's *The Shrew*, in *The Marowitz Shakespeare* (New York: Drama Book Specialists, 1978), 178.

3. Penny Gay, *As She Likes It: Shakespeare's Unruly Women* (London and New York: Routledge, 1994), 104.

4. Marowitz, "Shakespeare Recycled," *Shakespeare Quarterly* 38.4 (1987): 471.

5. Marowitz, *The Marowitz Shakespeare*, 21.

6. Elizabeth Schafer, ed., *The Taming of the Shrew*, Shakespeare in Production (Cambridge: Cambridge University Press, 2002), 38–39.

7. Michael Bogdanov, interviewed by Christopher J. McCullough, in *The Shakespeare Myth*, ed. Holderness (Manchester: Manchester University Press, 1988), 92.

8. Holderness, *The Taming of the Shrew*, 91.

9. Bogdanov, interviewed by Christopher J. McCullough, 89–90.

10. Holderness, *The Taming of the Shrew*, 76.

11. Kaori Kobayashi, "Can a woman be liberated in a 'chauvinist's dream'?: Michael Bogdanov's Production of *The Taming of the Shrew* in 1978," *Shakespeare Studies* (Tokyo) 35 (1997): 79.

12. Michael Billington, "A spluttering firework," *Guardian*, May 5, 1978, 10.

13. Gay, *As She Likes It*, 105.

14. Kobayashi, "Can a woman," 80.

15. Roger Warren, "A Year of Comedies: Stratford 1978," *Shakespeare Survey* 32 (1979): 202.

16. Peter Thomson, "Shakespeare and the Public Purse," in *Shakespeare: An Illustrated Stage History*, ed. Jonathan Bate and Russell Jackson (Oxford: Oxford University Press, 1996), 166.

17. E. A. M. Colman, "Autumn Leaves on the Avon: The Royal Shakespeare Company's 1978 Season Reviewed," *The Literary Half-Yearly* 20 (1979): 150.

18. Kobayashi, "Can a woman," 84–85.

19. Lorna Sage, "The Shrew's Revenge," *Times Literary Supplement*, May 19, 1978, 555.

20. Schafer, *The Taming of the Shrew*, 39.

21. Benedict Nightingale, "Wiving It," *New Statesman*, May 12, 1978, 649.

22. Unsigned review of *The Taming of the Shrew: The Women's Version*, directed by David Ultz, Theatre Royal, Stratford East, London, *Standard* (London), March 12, 1985. Reprinted in *London Theatre Record*, February 27–March 12, 1985, 227.

23. Michael Coveney, Review of *The Taming of the Shrew: The Women's Version*, directed by David Ultz, Theatre Royal, Stratford East, London, *Financial Times*, March 13, 1985, 15.

24. Billington, Review of *The Taming of the Shrew: The Women's Version*, directed by David Ultz, Theatre Royal, Stratford East, London, *Guardian*, March 12, 1985. Reprinted in *London Theatre Record*, February 27–March 12, 1985, 227.

25. Suzie Mackenzie, Review of *The Taming of the Shrew: The Women's Version*, directed by David Ultz, Theatre Royal, Stratford East, London, *Time Out*, March 14, 1985. Reprinted in *London Theatre Record*, February 27–March 12, 1985, 227.

26. Coveney, Review of *The Taming of the Shrew*, 15.

27. Alastair Goolden, "A Woman's Place," *Times Literary Supplement*, March 29, 1985, 358.

28. Billington, *London Theatre Record*, 227.

29. Unsigned review of *The Taming*, *London Theatre Record*, 227.

30. Goolden, "A Woman's Place," 358.

31. Mackenzie, review of *The Taming*, *London Theatre Record*, 227.

32. Ros Asquith, "Women only," *Observer*, March 17, 1985, 23.

33. Carole Woddis, review of *The Taming of the Shrew: The Women's Version*, directed by David Ultz, Theatre Royal, Stratford East, London, *City Limits*, March 15, 1985. Reprinted in *London Theatre Record*, February 27–March 12, 1985, 227.

34. Paula Kamen, *Feminist Fatale: Voices from the "Twentysomething" Generation Explore the Future of the "Women's Movement"* (New York: Donald I. Fine, 1991), 23–24.

35. Leslie Heywood and Jennifer Drake, eds., *Third Wave Agenda: Being Feminist, Doing Feminism* (Minneapolis: University of Minnesota Press, 1997), 4. Although most writers discuss the use of this equivocal phrase in the United States, Yvonne Roberts

offers evidence that the "I'm not a feminist, but . . ." phenomenon occurs in Britain as well by referring to the cliché in her work *Mad about Women: Can There Ever Be Fair Play Between the Sexes?* (London: Virago Press, 1992), 242. Among British feminists, the tendency of young women to steer clear of any overt connection with feminism is more frequently evoked by the term "the f-word." As Imelda Whelehan observes in *Over-loaded: Popular Culture and the Future of Feminism,* "Yet somewhere along the line, feminism has become the 'f-word,' perceived to be an empty dogma which brainwashed a whole generation of women into false consciousness of their relationship to power": (London: Women's Press, 2000), 16.

36. Susan J. Douglas, *Where the Girls Are: Growing Up Female with the Mass Media* (New York: Times Books/Random House, 1994), 272.

37. Nicholas Shrimpton, "Shakespeare Performances in London, Manchester and Stratford-upon-Avon 1985–6," *Shakespeare Survey* 40 (1988): 171.

38. Gay, *As She Likes It,* 9.

39. Geraldine Cousin, "The Touring of the Shrew," *New Theatre Quarterly* 2 (1986): 277. My account of the details of Di Trevis' production is highly indebted to Cousin's essay.

40. Quoted in Schafer, *Ms-Directing Shakespeare: Women Direct Shakespeare* (New York: St. Martin's Press, 2000), 59.

41. Cousin, "The Touring," 281.

42. Quoted in Schafer, *Ms-Directing Shakespeare,* 61. Schafer's first quotation of Trevis comes from *Time Out,* September 12, 1985, and the second from *City Limits,* August 23, 1985.

43. Cousin, "The Touring," 280.

44. Thomson, "Shakespeare and the Public Purse," 168.

45. Cousin, "The Touring," 281.

46. Critics who note the similarities between Gale Edwards' and Bogdanov's approaches include Billington, *"The Taming of the Shrew*: Royal Shakespeare Theatre," *Guardian,* April 24, 1995, T10; Coveney, "Theatre Dominance and Submission," *Observer,* April 30, 1995, 13; Peter Holland, "Shakespeare Performances in England, 1994–1995," *Shakespeare Survey* 49 (1996): 257; and Jackson, "Shakespeare at Stratford-upon-Avon, 1995–96," *Shakespeare Quarterly* 47.3 (1996): 324–26.

47. Quoted in Alan C. Dessen, "Improving the Script: Staging Shakespeare and Others in 1995," *Shakespeare Bulletin* 14.1 (1996): 8.

48. Ibid.

49. Michael Siberry, "Petruccio in *The Taming of the Shrew,*" in *Players of Shakespeare 4: Further Essays in Shakespearian Performance by Players with the Royal Shakespeare Company,* ed. Robert Smallwood (Cambridge: Cambridge University Press, 1998), 46.

50. Kate Alderson, "Whose Shrew Is It Anyway?" *Times* (London), April 21, 1995, features section.

51. Quoted in Clare Bayley, "The Return of the Shrew," *Independent* (London), April 20, 1995, 26.

52. Gay, "Recent Australian Shrews: The 'Larrikin Element,'" in *Shakespeare and the Twentieth Century: The Selected Proceedings of the International Shakespeare Association World Congress, Los Angeles, 1996,* ed. Bate, Jill L. Levenson, and Dieter Mehl (Newark: University of Delaware Press, 1998), 177.

53. Billington, *"The Taming,"* T10.

54. Sarah Werner, *Shakespeare and Feminist Performance: Ideology on Stage* (New York: Routledge, 2001), 84.

55. Ibid., 87.

56. Although I will attribute the final state of this production to Phyllida Lloyd's direction, it took shape as a result of decisions made by several individuals, some of them men. Mark Rylance, the Artistic Director of the Globe, wished to redress the scarcity of acting opportunities for women exacerbated by the theater's frequent all-male productions, so he made the decision to employ an all-female cast for the show even before a director was chosen (Abigail Anderson, e-mail message to author, May 9, 2004). Barry Kyle was first given the job, and the production's casting and original conception may be attributed to him (Coveney, "Shakespeare's sisters get to grips with *The Shrew*," *Daily Mail*, August 29, 2003, 54). Kyle eventually left the production because, once the actors moved into the no-man's land of the women's dressing room, he felt alienated from the cast. Lloyd was asked to take over the production in mid-stream as a result of her personal connection to cast members Janet McTeer and Kathryn Hunter; due to these unusual circumstances, she did not seek out public opportunities to discuss her vision for the production (Anderson, e-mail message to author).

57. Charles Spencer, "Gender bending revives dying art," *Daily Telegraph* (London), August 25, 2003, 16. For similar accounts of defeated negative expectations, see Coveney, "Shakespeare's sisters," 54; Rhoda Koenig, "All-female *Shrew* emasculated by mannered male impersonations," *Independent* (London), August 22, 2003, 9; and Nightingale, "The shrew has a sting in her tale," *Times* (London), August 23, 2003, 23.

58. Quoted in Susan L. Fischer, Review of *The Taming of the Shrew*, *Shakespeare Bulletin* 21.4 (2003): 83. Fischer quotes McTeer from the production's Program Notes, 16.

59. Fischer, Review of *The Taming of the Shrew*, 85.

60. Nightingale, "The Shrew," 23.

61. Anderson, e-mail message to author.

62. Louis Muinzer, "The 2003 Season at Shakespeare's Globe," *Western European Stages* 15 (2003): 68.

"So What?": Two Postmodern Adaptations of Shakespearean Tragedies

Naomi C. Liebler

During the last decade or so of the last century, Jim Lusardi, as theater review editor for *Shakespeare Bulletin*, often sent me to remote hole-in-the-wall performance venues (some without walls altogether) ostensibly to assess, but principally to archive, productions of Shakespearean and other early modern plays. On some of these occasions, I was privileged to see and hear an extraordinary version of one or another Shakespearean play that in itself did more to answer the question my students never ask—the one about Shakespeare's relevance to our time—than any series of lectures could have done.

Two such productions, Rome Neal's *Julius Caesar Set in Africa* and Linda Mussmann's *M.A.C.B.E.T.H.*, both coincidentally staged in 1990, permanently reshaped the way I (and presumably the other members of their audiences) respond to two of Shakespeare's most frequently performed/taught/read tragedies; moreover, they offered exquisite evidence, if any were needed, that the Shakespearean vision of the tragic episode speaks and works today with only a slight flexion of perspective. Both of these productions made radical interventions in their source-text plays; both were much more than interpretations in the way that many current productions interpret and translate Shakespeare for our time. Both altered the text while simultaneously retaining a powerful fidelity to the text's rich implications. Neither, to the best of my knowledge, was recorded on film or video in any form of performance publicly recoverable.[1] Thus, what follows here may seem unfairly chosen: unless one has seen either of these productions, one would be unable to verify or challenge (as one can do with a printed text or a filmed version) what I will say about them. Nevertheless, I risk the charge of "no fair"; if in what follows some sense of the profound excitement and merit of these productions comes through, then I will have discharged my intention to explore the ways in which intertextuality can both rewrite and celebrate the original.

175

Before turning to these two performances, it is useful to ask some questions about the different kinds of affects that are possible in adaptations. Some of these arguably are meant to achieve other ends than the popularization of Shakespeare *per se*; some, to be sure, are opportunistic appropriations. Because Shakespeare sells tickets at playhouses and movie-houses, producers of this kind of appropriation count on the embedded appeal of a Shakespearean narrative to underpin a film or a stage production with, perhaps, a different or additional aim besides promoting an understanding of Shakespeare. I am thinking of such recent instances such as the condescending teen fodder—even my students disdained these—of Tim Blake Nelson's *O* (2001)[2] or Gil Junger's *10 Things I Hate About You* (1999).[3] I am also thinking of Gus Van Sant's rigorous, remarkable, and, in my view, brilliant *My Own Private Idaho* (1991)[4] and William Reilly's 1989 *Men of Respect* (the Henriad and *Macbeth*, respectively).[5] Both of these genuinely, and in ways that are artistically authentic, reconfigure the Shakespearean source to offer social and political commentary on significant segments of American demographics in the late eighties and early nineties. These latter films do not pretend to be mere adaptations of Shakespeare's plays; Shakespeare is barely identified as a source, and Van Sant's credits cite only "additional dialogue by William Shakespeare." Such films offer not only a new way to see that source but also new ways of seeing our own contemporary issues via the Shakespearean lens.[6] When we are assessing adaptations, among the questions we might ask is "why?" or, as I usually put it to my students, "so what?" Are these adaptations merely opportunistic instances of plagiarism, or are they indicators of immense possibility? How do such new ways of seeing/hearing Shakespeare "bend" the earlier text's models so that the postmodern instance not only makes its own statements but simultaneously revivifies the sixteenth- and seventeenth-century matrix? Both Van Sant and Reilly offer what we might call "translations" of Shakespearean texts; I have not asked them, but I would guess that assisting viewers in understanding the Shakespearean text was *not* among their foremost intentions in producing their films. That is, recuperating Shakespeare for an American public was not the *raison d'être* of either film; if that happened, it happened as a bonus, not as an intention.

Nor was recuperation of Shakespeare the motive of the two *auteurs* whose works I examine in this essay. Something else, perhaps undefinable and certainly unspecified by either Neal or Mussmann, is at the heart of these endeavors. Shakespeare in such performances becomes something-other-than-Shakespeare and also, I would argue, something

more than just the appropriation of "cultural capital" so famously identified by John Guillory,[7] although the works certainly do that to some
extent. In the sense of a Hegelian synthesis, they become something
other and larger than the sums of their parts. I confess that I am still
not sure exactly what to call it and hope that an examination of these
performances will lead readers to formulate their own terminology for
classification.

As a way of explaining what I mean, I refer to the Winter 2001 issue
of *Shakespeare Quarterly*, which took as its theme the rubric of "Dislocat-
ing Shakespeare." This project emerged from a July 2000 conference
(bearing the same title) held by the Australia and New Zealand Shakespeare Association. The guest editor, Michael Neill, writes compellingly
of "cultural reinscription[s] of the Bard."[8] As I understand his point,
this is not just about "making Shakespeare relevant" to an historically
disenfranchised population, nor is it the patronizing "Shakespeare Para
Todos" that was the theme of the New York Shakespeare Festival's
"Free Shakespeare in the Park" production of *A Midsummer Night's
Dream* done in Portuguese during the summer of 1991. Such transcultural adaptations, which are different matters from dressing up Shakespeare in modern or even postmodern guises, are somewhat separate
issues from my scope here, although they are not entirely incompatible
with the present discussion.[9] According to Neill, the Maori translation
of Shakespeare's sonnets by Merimeri Penfield, celebrated at the conference and accompanied by a tattooed version of the Martin Droes-
hout engraving and a "refiguring" of the Claes Jancz Visscher *Long View
of London* from the viewpoint of Polynesian navigators sailing on the
Thames, both designed to publicize the conference, taken together signaled a complex range of meanings:

> . . . for New Zealanders nowadays it is impossible to look at such images
> without remembering how early European contact turned formerly revered
> *moko mokai* (tattooed heads) into commodities . . . So that the very gesture
> that relocates Shakespeare within a distinctively Maori *whakapapa* (geneal-
> ogy) also marks his role alongside the Bible and the gun as an instrument
> of cultural hegemony.[10]

Obviously, the relocation of Shakespearean texts into cultures and
esthetic frames quite distant from their early modern inscriptions is a
compelling and difficult matter, one that speaks differently to audience
members according to their own specific relations to the context as well
as to the text. That is, audiences watching these productions reflected

inwardly upon their own relations not only to the texts but also to the historical and political affects associated with those texts and to the ways in which the texts and the culture they represent were forcibly inserted into the indigenous culture. An audience's answer to "so what?" depends crucially and entirely on who sits in that audience.

A similar important distinction was made in an essay by the late Nicholas Visser, reporting on his experience in teaching *Julius Caesar* during the schools boycotts in Rhodes in 1980. His essay narrates two kinds of exposures to the play: white university students were shown Joseph Mankiewicz's 1953 film starring James Mason, John Gielgud, and Marlon Brando.[11] Black students boycotting the schools but seeking to pass their exams through independent study successfully petitioned the university to allow them to see the same film. Visser described the different responses of the two groups of students: for the white university students, "the scenes of crowd activity confirmed several unquestioned assumptions: crowds are easily swayed, irrational, prone to violence, prey to 'mob psychology'"; for the black matriculation candidates, on the other hand, "there was nothing at all 'realistic' about the presentation of the crowd [in the film]." The reason for such divergent views was obvious, he said: "the [white] Rhodes students in all likelihood had no personal experience of political crowds, and could not have imagined that alternative perspectives on the matter were available. They were operating from a set of beliefs so socially and historically entrenched as to constitute a form of 'knowledge.'" The black students, in contrast,

> were living through a formative political experience of mass meetings, demonstrations, "freedom funerals," and other forms of mass political action . . . For them there was nothing irrational about the actions of political crowds, nothing fickle about their commitment to certain courses of action. The notion that a political crowd would be swayed by whomever happened to be addressing them, far from confirming prevailing "wisdom" on such matters, seemed ludicrous.[12]

Visser concluded this section of his essay by noting that

> Through these strikingly different receptions, we are provided insight into *how formidable an ideological signifier* the crowd is, how deeply embedded in middle-class mentality are "commonsense" beliefs about the crowd, and how successfully literary and dramatic works—or, more accurately perhaps, the receptions, productions, and reproductions of literary and dramatic works—serve to codify and confirm these beliefs."[13]

The crowd, or any selected element in a play, becomes a "formidable ideological signifier" in its reflexive relation to its particular audience, and such responses will never be the same for any audience in the aggregate or for different audiences in various times and loci. Even the most dispassionate critical reception of this or any Shakespearean play is inevitably shaped by one's own experience and understanding of words and actions imitated onstage. Visser's strong-voiced critique of audience and reader perspective is important here: in the light of recent work by social historians who have focused attention on "the view from below" and called for a radical revision of our understanding of collective political activity, "pronouncements today about the aptness and astuteness of Shakespeare's depiction of the plebeian crowd . . . are shown up for the class-based prejudice they are instead of the certain knowledge they purport to be."[14] Shakespearean performances or adaptations in Auckland or Rhodesia produce very different kinds of responses from those done in America for American audiences. But the affects of the first group should not be presumed to be entirely and irredeemably alien to those of the second group.

The two performances to which I now turn are American "reinscriptions" of a slightly different kind, but the points just made about affect and recoverability apply. The first, *Julius Caesar Set in Africa*, performed by the Nuyorican Poets Café Theater Company, located in the Lower East Side neighborhood of New York City, looks on the surface like the transcultural adaptation explicit in its title. The company consisted entirely of African and African-American performers: actors, dancers, drummers. The only slightly revised plot located the play's action in Mali, West Africa, in the year 1242 CE: the country newly formed by Julius Caesar's defeat of Sumanguru (for Pompey) attempts to unite Mali and Old Ghana. But the new hybrid nation, by definition, threatens Malian autonomy, especially since the now-doubled population appears to choose Caesar for its king, chanting "Caesar Kayamaga! Caesar Kayamaga!" during the sacred festival of Odwira, or Feast of the Yam (the replacement for the Lupercal). The Ides of March are called here the 7th of Odwira, which eliminates the troublesome conflation, in the Elizabethan version, of the month's time from the mid-February Lupercalia to the mid-March of Caesar's murder. Cassius wants to retain Mali as a democracy and enrolls Brutus in the cause. From then on, the Shakespearean plot is clearly visible as the ground upon which this production rests. But the theatrical event emerges not so much as an adaptation as an apotheosis; I came away from this production temporarily persuaded that *Julius Caesar* was perhaps a thirteenth-century West African play later adapted by an Englishman from Stratford-upon-Avon. The question upon which this adaptation depends for its resonance is the one I suggested above in regard to any adaptations, and indeed one that we might (or should) easily suppose that some of Shakespeare's audience might have asked in 1599: "So what?" The oscillating "tide in the affairs of men" can occur anywhere and anytime when despots and orators strive to capture people's bodies and minds, and this has never been more apparent, or more important to recognize, than in this first decade of the twenty-first century. The "translation" of a Shakespearean text across times and spaces is—or can be when properly handled—more than a *jeu d'esprit*. We need to ask of such productions whether they condescend to their audiences through claims upon their notions of "relevance" or cultural capital (although I do not think that either of the two productions I describe here did that). What do they say about Shakespeare's "portability"? The answers to these questions seem to me less important and less compelling than the questions themselves, which we are made to ask by performances such as these.

Elements of Neal's production made neutrality an impossible response. The audience was never allowed to sit safely behind an imagined fourth wall, in part because the performance space was so small and the audience's chairs stopped no more than a few feet from the performers' arena. The brick walls of the Café were hung for the event with a few ceremonial spears, a few parchmentlike skins with a shield painted in the center of each, and several wooden masks; a painted flat tree occupied the space stage left; a totem stood stage right. The audience sat level with and at the boundaries of the playing space; they were at once part and partners of the action. We were in the marketplace, among hawkers and buyers who gave way shortly to dancers, who in turn became the advance guard announcing "Caesar Kayamaga's" arrival. The festivity was aborted by the entrance of the tribunes, Flavius and Marullus, who latched onto the unfortunate cobbler ("naughty Oroko") and literally arrested the popular celebration in order to make room for the more formal hierarchy of Caesar's procession amid bushels of strewn flowers. The formal Lupercal-Odwira rites were pantomimed in what seemed to be a physically impossible slow-motion, accompanied by equally slow-motioned applause pantomimed by the full company ranged along the back wall as the observant community.

In a textual economy, while Cassius recited his recollections of Caesar's swimming difficulties in the Tiber, there was another dumb-show in which Caesar first declined and then accepted the crown passed to

Keith Johnston as Metellus Cimber, Ed Sewer III as Decius Brutus, Chris Adams as Servant, Rick Reid as Cinna, James Garrett as Casca, and Renauld White as Caesar (seated) in the Nuyorican Poets Café's 1991 production of *Julius Caesar Set in Africa*, conceived and directed by Rome Neal. Photo by Gregory Mink.

him. The semiotics of this "split-screen-without-a-screen" action, requiring simultaneously separate attentions of the audience, spoke more eloquently for the play's multiple contestations than many analytic essays have done for the multiple registers of the play's political implications; Caesar's public acclamation competed visibly with Cassius' private recollection of "this god's" infirmities and effeminate ("like a sick girl") call for rescue. While Cassius interrogated Brutus about the implicit value of the "name of Caesar," we saw (again in slow motion) Caesar pull a dagger across his own throat (as Brutus-whose-name-equals-Caesar's would later likewise offer to do), then fall into his epileptic seizure while Cassius recited, "'Tis true, this god did shake." The scene between Portia and Lucius took place stage right and upstairs, while Trebonius delivered the warnings from the flies toward stage left, again reinscribing the alternating voices of private domesticity and public (or cosmic) resonance. The female Soothsayer was pitted against Calphurnia as, eye to eye, they competed for Caesar's fate.

Further stage economies included the expansion of Casca's role, while

Cassius appears more Brutus-like than in Shakespeare's text; here it was Casca who incited both Cassius and Brutus to rebel against Caesar Kayamaga, suggesting, perhaps, that such conspiracies require more than two instigators. While Cassius importuned Brutus to join the conspiracy, the other five conspirators debated the direction of the sunrise, that is, the East, from where they are standing, thereby underscoring the sacramental nature of the assassination. Amidst all this power, there was room for humor: when Caesar "pluck'd me ope his agbada [cloak]" and offered his throat to be cut, says Casca, Cicero spoke. But, of course, Casca could not report what Cicero said, as "it was all Yoruba to me."

With its attention to ceremonial detail, the production privileged the ritual underpinnings of Shakespeare's play, which are focused primarily in the assassination scene itself. As the conspirators "stoop, then, and wash" their hands in Caesar's blood, their faces registered combinations of awe, fear, and sheer terror. They understood the necessary urgency, and the danger, of what they had done. When Antony delivered his eulogy over Caesar and offered to shake hands with the conspirators, he did so in true *de casibus* tradition, and the handshaking itself had all the solemnity of a ritual; only Casca, declining to shake Antony's hand, stood apart and enacted a private, more omophagic, ritual, licking the "blood" off his own hands. There were other remarkable transcultural moments in this event: when the spirit dancer who accompanied Brutus' dream of Caesar's ghost promised to "see thee at Sahara" (for Philippi), Brutus showed fear for the first and only time: the spirit world has more power over the traditional hero in an African setting than it does over the Stoic Cato's pupil and son-in-law in Rome.

The difference that this reinscription makes, it seems to me, is in its potent foregrounding of elements, especially the ritual-based armature of the play, that are often lost to or on a modern audience but that, as I have argued elsewhere,[15] would have resonated well with Shakespeare's Elizabethan audience. What matters most in a production such as this one is not only its appeal to one or another represented population on the Lower East Side nor its topical "relevance" that for many of us is not in question (and in any case would not have been illuminated by "translation" to thirteenth-century West Africa). What matters most is the way in which such a transcultural restaging serves to highlight frequently overlooked vibrations in the text that we study as academics.

I want to make a similar case for the different kind of "transculturation" from the macho feudal world of Shakespeare's *Macbeth* to a postmodern feminist "reading" of the play in Mussmann's *M.A.C.B.E.T.H.*, as performed (like *Julius Caesar Set in Africa*) not in a conventional theater but at the Merce Cunningham Dance Studio, Westbeth, New York. Mussmann's rewriting responds to the pervasive unease that many feminists experience in reading, teaching, or seeing filmed or staged performances of the Shakespearean play. Critically and performatively, Lady Macbeth is almost universally demonized, either through a hypersexualized "Eva Prima Pandora" reading as the cause of (one) man's downfall or, at the very least, as a co-conspirator in Macbeth's treason and murder of his king and kinsman. Mussmann sees her as the hero of the play. "Balls!" said the Queen. "If I had 'em, I'd be King!" This punch line from an old joke crystallizes the monologue; the entire performance is a monologue, assisted on occasion with taped crowd noises and whispers and a wide range of visual and musical effects incorporating slide-shows, stills, and backdrops. This multi-media event hews to the Shakespearean text, occasionally quoting verbatim and at other times adapting the lines to a modern semantics. In so doing, it recuperates the Shakespearean design, not only the text but its arguable import. But in a time when everybody and his kinsman is adapting, updating, reformatting, and otherwise surgically altering Shakespeare's plays, Mussmann's effort deserves to be taken on its own terms. It is not so much an adaptation of the Scottish play as a fantasy of the fiend-like queen's ruminations. I was reminded of John Gardner's *Grendel* (1971), the Beowulf story told from the monster's point of view.

What if Lady Macbeth got to tell her side of the story? How much power and feminine heroism have we missed seeing in this play in the last 400 years? The spirit of the queen, confined to a room furnished with a small butcher-block table (which seemed remarkably appropriate) set for one, a dressing area with makeup table, and a sideboard laden with sound (and fury) equipment, moved around in this limbo-space talking mostly about her late husband, mourning and missing him. Assisted by slides and projected film, various kinds of music, song, little made-up poems, and dance (all performed by one actor, Claudia Bruce, with Mussmann handling most of the electronics), Lady M. tells us how she would have done things better if she had had not balls, perhaps, which she has in abundance, if only metaphorically, but opportunity and recognition:

> Oh, what did you write, Billy Boy, Billy Boy?
> Oh, what did you write, charming Billy?
> You described the victory day,
> But the lady had no say.
> She's been waiting without consideration.

(294–98)

One does not evaluate such a performance for its fidelity to the original or for the rendition of character, or for any of the standard theatrical apparatus but for itself, for the ways it directs our attention to implications we have too long missed. The bare floor space was enclosed on three sides by white screens, the upstage one serving as a projection base for various graphic and photographic images during the piece. At the back stood a plain pine bench, with the aforementioned dressing table off to the left rear and the high-tech sound equipment filling the right side. Downstage were the little butcher-block-for-one and, in front of all, between performer and audience, a television screen that carried the projections of a punctuating set of projected stills. The upstage and downstage projections were Bruce's supporting cast, telling their own stories, as it were, a visual chorus to her songs and dances. On the TV screen, for instance, appears a plain white china plate; after a while, a knife appears on top of the plate, then knife becomes scissors, then revolver, then a red lipstick. Meanwhile, on the rear screen, the word "RED" appears, in red of course, written three times on a transparency by Mussmann, sitting downstage in full view, who then colors in the whole transparency while Bruce chants "ALL IS RED" and the

Claudia Bruce as Lady M. in Time & Space Ltd.'s 1990 production of *M.A.C.B.E.T.H.*, conceived and directed by Linda Mussmann in collaboration with Claudia Bruce. Photo by Mussmann.

recorded music pumps out bagpipes playing "Amazing Grace" and "Over the Sea to Skye." During all of this, Bruce as Lady M. has emerged from behind the screen, applied her makeup at the upstage dressing table, and come to life before us. She comes down to the little dining table set with stacked plates, a huge red apple, which she slices and eats, and a glass of red liquid, which she drinks. This physical symbolism was laid on with a shovel, but no matter.

Lady M. talks about her late husband, familiarly referred to as Macky: "Macky said . . . Macky said . . . Macky had a way with words." On the rear screen, we see a birch tree, leaves flapping in a high wind, replaced in time with the legend "FIX HER CAN'T YOU. SHE'S BUSTED." Meanwhile, on the TV screen, the knife appears again on the plate, then the lipstick; then, what looks like a pool of blood fills the plate, while Lady M. chants things like "Is-was-will be." And that, dear reader, was only the first half-hour.

The rest of the performance went on more or less in the same way, the debt to Shakespeare occasionally acknowledged in screen-projected legends ("WHO WOULD HAVE THOUGHT THE OLD MAN TO HAVE HAD SO MUCH BLOOD IN HIM"), TV images of sand filling the plate, and back-screen images of birches turning to a single blasted tree on (what else?) a blasted heath, the sounds of dripping water providing the back-beat. Lady M. complains that she had "no say" in Shakespeare's play:

No one knows what I was doing
   While I was waiting for Macky to come home.
What was the little lady doing at home all alone?
Was she washing?
Was she ironing?
Was she reading?
Was she mending?
Was she knitting?
What was she doing on that victory day?
. . . .
It was I who had the time to wait . . .
It was I who could claim the time, not Macky.
Now here, I have not been given credit—for it is impossible to wait without
having a thought—or an idea. . . .
Is a woman who plans the murder more than a man, or less than a woman?
Is she a fiend . . . ?
Does she transcend her role? Is she the tragic hero of the show?
No, she deserved what she got—they say.

No, I deserved what I got—they said.
He is the tragic hero, not I—they said.
Why is that? Why?
If you pity failure, then you should pity him.
If you celebrate success, then you should pity me—for I am the
unacknowledged hero of the story.
I am the brains behind the act.
I am the one who wanted to transcend her role.
I am the one who wanted to move on.
I am the one who wanted to be more than Macky's wife.
I am the one who wanted to be King!

(300–334)

The performance lasted for about an hour and a half. The visual and
auditory fields clashed and converged. Mussmann's feminist statement
could not have been made minimally. "Question: Who understands
this? / Answer: . . . The rich privileged men" (371–79).

At other moments, Mussmann appropriates Shakespeare's text more
literally for this modern "Wife's Lament": for instance, a tape recording
speaks the line "If chance may crown him king" while Bruce answers it
with "Not chance, ambition. Today, Macky, today." Then she "speaks"
to Duncan, explaining how she worked hard to get Macky to keep his
promise:

Well, Duncan, I could not believe what I was hearing.
WHAT! I said to Macky.
WHAT? YOU CAN'T DO IT? YOU CAN'T KILL DUNCAN?
.   .   .   .
Then, Macky says to me:
    Prithee peace. I dare do all that may become a man.
    Who dares do more is none.
Oh, Duncan, was I in a state over this!
He promised me he'd kill you . . . and now he breaks the promise.
This MAN thing is too much.
.   .   .   .
Now get it together, Macky, I said to him.
Now listen to me, I said.
Duncan, listen to me.
I am but a mere woman but *I have given suck* to a babe.
I *know how tender it is to love a babe that milks me.*
But listen up, Macky, I said.
I know *I would, while it was smiling in my face,*
    Have plucked the nipple from his boneless gums . . .

I know I would have *dashed the brains out of its head* . . .
Had I so sworn as you have done, to me, Macky, to kill the King.
Then Duncan, Macky gets all squirmy looking . . . little boy like . . .
    Looking at his Mama . . . and says to me in a whimpy manner:
    But if we *fail*?

(486–520)

Mussmann's creation demanded much from her audience. There was no sitting back here (literally, as the audience sat on backless benches in the Cunningham studio) to be entertained. The audience was assaulted, bombarded with multiple images and sounds, music, language, humming, whistling that flew around in the boxed space. Lady M.'s recollections of the "battle lost and won" were accompanied by martial music, "Over There," with sounds of explosions and machine gunfire, and the rockets' red glare, and bagpipes coming in underneath it all. On the video monitor, the knife-candle-plate becomes a spinning egg, which then cracks and spills its yolk and white, broken and smeared by the knife that constantly returns, a dominant and dominating image.

Somewhere underneath all of this was the mentor, Shakespeare. Who can guess what he might have said about this event? Maybe: "It ain't Shakespeare, but these days what is?" Can post-colonial or post-feminist audiences *not* see Shakespeare against the backdrop of their own political/critical persuasions? How many of us have wondered how to read Lady Macbeth or Brutus, Cassius, and Casca when not following another generation's no-longer-satisfying critical precepts? Against the grain of even my own habitual responses to refashionings of Shakespearean texts, I would here suggest that certain kinds of outside-the-box imaginings sometimes do more good than harm, if they (as I think the two productions I describe here have done) invite a fresh examination of our author's vision by asking uncomfortable questions. This is a different matter from dressing Shakespeare in borrowed *agbadas*. Neal's *Julius Caesar Set in Africa* and Mussmann's *M.A.C.B.E.T.H.* interrogate what has been occluded through centuries of academic and scholarly study, elements that are revealed only through performance and perhaps only through radically reinscribed performance. How have we failed to notice Lady Macbeth's protagonism, her heroic status, or the permanent political apocalypse of *Julius Caesar's* revolution? (To be fair, this last point has been noticed and indeed debated but not, I think, often enough, and rarely in performance.) And what is the consequence of noticing such things in the evaporating moment of performances?

As a partial answer and as a way toward closure here, I refer to a well-known essay by Francis Barker and Peter Hulme, "Nymphs and Reapers Heavily Vanish: The Discursive Con-texts of *The Tempest*," in which the authors suggest the term "con-texts" for "the precondition of the plays' historical and political signification."[16] Barker and Hulme argue for reading "Con-texts with a hyphen, to signify a break from the inequality of the usual text/context relationship. Con-texts are themselves *texts* and must be *read with:* they do not simply make up a background."[17] On this view, the performances I have described coalesce with their respective Shakespearean matrices to produce reciprocally referential "texts," each serving as "con-text" with the other. To put it a bit differently, in both of the 1990 performances, the Shakespearean text is always in the background, or present the way an afterimage is present in a photograph: seeing it alters the way we see the foregrounded image, and neither can be seen without reference to the other. What we would understand as the Shakespearean "source" text becomes part of the new image, and inseparable from it, which leads or even forces the viewer to consider each in light of the other. As Barker and Hulme explain it, "each individual text, rather than a meaningful unit in itself, lies at the intersection of different discourses . . . the text must still be taken as a point of purchase on the discursive field—but in order to demonstrate that, athwart its alleged unity, the text is in fact marked and fissured by the interplay of the discourses that constitute it."[18] The performances I have discussed here are in themselves worthy of attention as unitary texts, informed and supported by the Shakespearean "sources" that become their "con-texts" (or perhaps their hypertexts). At the same time, those very "con-texts" are reanimated by the performance pieces so that we are compelled to read them forever differently as a result of the photographic effect I have suggested. The performance of a Ghanaian takeover of West Mali at a time somewhere between the setting and the writing of *Julius Caesar* does not bring us closer to the Shakespearean play in any meaningful way; instead, it accomplishes a Brechtian alienation that refigures both text and reciprocal con-text. Similarly, a postmodern radical feminist speculation on the interiority of a heroic female protagonist who demands her place in the pantheon of tragic heroes reconfigures the claims that the "butcher and his fiend-like queen" have on our attention. These adaptations do not steal (from) Shakespeare; they return him with interest.

NOTES

1. I thank Linda Mussmann and her company, Time & Space, Ltd., of Hudson, NY, for providing me with a script of *M.A.C.B.E.T.H.* (1990). Quotations from the play

refer to this text, or, where the script differs from my notes taken at the time of the production I saw, to my review in *Shakespeare Bulletin* 9.4 (1991): 8–9. Parenthetical references are to line numbers.

2. *O*, VHS, screenplay by Brad Kaaya, directed by Tim Blake Nelson (2001; Los Angeles: Lion's Gate Films, 2002).

3. *10 Things I Hate About You*, VHS, screenplay by Karen McCullah Lutz and Kristen Smith, directed by Gil Junger (Touchstone Pictures, 1999; Burbank, CA: Buena Vista Home Entertainment, 2002).

4. *My Own Private Idaho*, VHS, prod. Laurie Parker, dir. Gus Van Sant (1991; Los Angeles, CA: New Line Studios, 1996). Writing credited to William Shakespeare and Gus Van Sant.

5. *Men of Respect*, VHS, prod. Ephraim Horowitz, dir. William Reilly (1991; Culver City, CA: Columbia/Tri-Star, 1996). Writing credited to William Reilly and William Shakespeare.

6. See, inter alia, Paul Arthur and Naomi Conn Liebler, "Kings of the Road: *My Own Private Idaho* and the Traversal of Welles, Shakespeare, and Liminality," *Post Script* 17.2 (Winter/Spring 1998): 26–38.

7. See John Guillory, *Cultural Capital: The Problem of Literary Canon Formation* (Chicago: University of Chicago Press, 1993), esp. 3–82.

8. Michael Neill, "From the Editor," *Shakespeare Quarterly* 52.4 (2001): iii.

9. On this topic, see *Shakespeare and Cultural Traditions: The Selected Proceedings of the International Shakespeare Association World Congress, Tokyo, 1991*, ed. Tetsuo Kishi, Roger Pringle, and Stanley Wells (Newark: University of Delaware Press, 1994).

10. Neill, "From the Editor," v.

11. *Julius Caesar*, VHS, prod. John Houseman, dir. Joseph L. Mankiewicz (1953; Los Angeles: Warner Home Video, 1992).

12. Nicholas Visser, "Plebeian Politics in *Julius Caesar*," *Shakespeare in Southern Africa* 7 (1994): 22.

13. Ibid., 22–23; emphasis added.

14. Ibid., 23.

15. Liebler, *Shakespeare's Festive Tragedy: The Ritual Foundations of Genre* (London and New York: Routledge, 1995).

16. Francis Barker and Peter Hulme, "Nymphs and Reapers Heavily Vanish: The Discursive Con-texts of *The Tempest*, in *Alternative Shakespeares*, ed. John Drakakis (New York: Methuen, 1985), 195.

17. Ibid., 236 n. 7.

18. Ibid., 197.

Shakespeare's Body:
Robert Lepage's Slippery *Dream*

Samuel Crowl

Shakespeare is a sculpture and you've got to make him revolve.
— Robert Lepage

A SINGLE BARE BURNING LIGHT BULB HUNG SUSPENDED OVER A ROUND glassy surface. From stage left, a small, androgynous figure dressed in red walking, crablike, on its hands scurried out and gently splashed into the pool of water. It stopped under the light bulb, glanced left and right, then slowly reached up and turned the light off. How fast this old moon wanes . . . how quickly will we dream away the time. This lively image opened Robert Lepage's production of *A Midsummer Night's Dream* at the Royal National Theatre in 1992, the most controversial and daring Shakespeare to open in London in the last decade of the twentieth century.[1]

Lepage, the French-Canadian theater artist and director, primarily known for creating his own stunning theater pieces like *The Dragon Trilogy, The Tectonic Plates, The Seven Streams of the River Ota, Needles and Opium,* and *Elsinore,* had been recruited by the new director of the Royal National Theatre, Richard Eyre, to work his particular magic on one of Shakespeare's comic standards. By inviting a radical North American outsider to the National, Eyre was trying to place his own theatrical stamp on an organization already firmly defined by its first two artistic directors: Laurence Olivier and Peter Hall. Eyre clearly got more than he bargained for, including the one and a half tons of mud (actually a mix of ligonite and bentonite) that Lepage's design team used to create Puck's Pond.

Lepage's production was distinguished by his bold decision to utilize fully the Olivier Theatre's potential to release Shakespeare's text into the wonders of three-dimensional space. With a global cast whose origins ranged from England to Quebec to Africa to India to the Carib-

190

bean, Lepage fashioned a production, rare for British Shakespeare, that privileged seeing over hearing and body over voice. As Barbara Hodgdon documents, in an essay devoted to a cultural reading of the production's reception, most of the English reviewers, with a few noted exceptions, were hostile to Lepage's conception and execution.[2] They faulted the production for drowning the music of Shakespeare's most lyrical comedy in a cacophony of accents from his multinational cast and swamping the delicacy of many of Shakespeare's images like "I must go seek some dewdrops here, / And hang a pearl in every cowslip's ear"[3] with a setting that most resembled "the nine men's morris . . . fill'd up with mud" (2.1.98).

For instance, Michael Billington objected strenuously to Lepage's approach: "In the theatre, . . . directors who bypass [Shakespeare's] language or treat it as a springboard for their own invention miss the point: witness Lepage's wet *Dream* with its total absence of comic joy."[4] "Nonsense," replied Robert Hewison, defending the production: "The visual poetry surpasses any music the rhetoric misses. [Peter] Brook's *Dream* set a standard aimed at ever since. Dark against the light, but no less true to the magic of the piece, Lepage's stands beside it."[5] The critical response to the production was as intense and confused as the experience of the lovers in the woods, with those supporting Billington's negative judgment in the clear majority. The passage of time has not been kinder to Lepage's achievement, and so this is an appropriate moment for a reassessment of the production's theatrical vitality.

Many reviewers echoed Hewison's evocation of Brook's famous 1970 white box circus *Dream* to praise or damn Lepage's. Curiously, not one of them thought to recall Hall's series of Stratford *Dreams* in the late 1950s and early 1960s that culminated in his 1968 film of the play shot in the Warwickshire woods in the wet and cold September of 1967.[6] Not even Jay Halio, in the best recent account of the production, makes the connection with Hall's film even though he has provided a full and sympathetic reading of Hall's film earlier in his book on the *Dream* in performance.[7] Those Hall productions, on stage and film, were meant as a break with the balletic tradition of staging the play defined by fairies in tutus and Mendelssohn's famous score—a conception mocked and parodied in a high-spirited production of the play directed by John Caird for the Royal Shakespeare Company in 1989—in order to stress the play's Elizabethan social milieu and festive ritual (C. L. Barber)[8] and its darker sexual confusions (Jan Kott).[9] Brook's high-flying, colorful, exuberant production emphasized the play's buoyant theatricality as a response to the natural world that Hall placed at the center of his interpretation. More than two decades later, Lepage's production sought to link the two approaches by plopping a mud-banked pond down on the Olivier stage and by casting a circus acrobat and contortionist (Angela Laurier) as Puck to scuttle through and sail above it.

Lepage's production was driven by its landscape. Once you put a muddy pond on stage, no theatrical magic can suddenly whisk or dream it away. As Lepage humorously remarked in response to Eyre's query concerning the production's lack of a court setting to contrast that of the woods: "We had tons of mud on stage, and you just don't strike mud."[10] Lepage's production began as a week of open workshops — with a future production of *Dream* in mind — on the theme of forests conducted at the RNT in the fall of 1991. Lepage's design partner, Michael Levine, reports that they immediately transformed their elaborate forest plans when water, not wood, became the actors' central preoccupation: "What the actors were doing was more interesting than my designs. When things go wrong in woods and forests there is usually water involved. Rain. Discomfort."[11] The muddy pond provided Lepage and his actors with a landscape that not only grew out of the play's imagery — Titania's "forgeries of jealousy" (2.1.81) speech on the disruptions and dislocations in nature caused by her quarrel with Oberon and Puck's "dank and dirty ground" (2.2.75) description of Lysander and Hermia's forest bed — but also gave them a brilliant physical access to Kott's Freudian understanding of the play's dream/nightmare translation of awakening adolescent sexuality into bestial images and actions.

Lepage was quite aware of how his landscape served his approach to the play: "We have balanced nightmare and nice dreams. . . . The summer fantasy is fine, but there are deeper, darker areas. . . . The forest represents a slippery environment; full of traps. The play is full of mirrors, doubling, coupling, seeing images and reflections."[12] Lepage's production had Shakespeare's lovers quite literally falling in love, losing their balance, slipsliding painfully and comically in the muck of their emotions gone wild in the night. Water is a key property in metamorphosis, and the production sent me back to Ovid, who glistens behind Shakespeare's invention, to discover again the key role played by rivers, streams, ponds, and pools in his often brutal and nightmarish tales of transformation. Freud, Jung, and Kott, as well as Ovid, lurked behind Lepage's landscape. Lepage was clearly exploring a psychological territory, which Barbara Freedman rightly sees, in her work on *A Midsummer Night's Dream*, as equating dream work with performance.[13]

After Puck's initial foray into the pond, the play opened with Theseus and Hippolyta, dressed in flowing white gowns more suggestive of

Bombay than Athens, seated statuesquely on the headboard of a grey iron bedstead. The bed was situated in the center of the pond, its mattress loaded with bodies huddled together. As Theseus launched into his instructions for the nuptial revels, Philostrate—with his back placed up against the corner of the headboard—began to push and pole the bed in a circle through the water as Egeus registered his complaint about Lysander while standing on a wooden kitchen chair. This bizarre sight not only provoked a gentle smile but suggested something of the Ganges and the spiced Indian air and so provided the first resonance of the play's mirroring of the human and spirit worlds. Such associations between the rivalries and confusions of the play's day and night worlds were reinforced as three of the four young lovers (dressed in pajamas) tumbled out of the revolving bed when called for by Egeus, awakened from the dream of sleep to the realities of patriarchal power.

After the exit of the court and Lysander and Hermia's exchange about the bumpy road of love—taken with both of them now sitting on the bed's headboard with their silhouettes projected on three huge rear panels that were often used to catch the giant shadows of the protagonists or shimmering reflections from the pond—the bed was tipped on its end to reveal the last of the lovers, Helena, clinging to its frame. She peered through the bed's now perpendicular springs to spy Hermia and Lysander sharing a farewell kiss and then opened the springs, as if it were now a garden gate, to join the space occupied by her friends. This was only one of the many ingenious transformations that Lepage and his actors discovered for this central prop. Later, placed in the same upright position at the edge of the pond, it served as a perch from which Oberon and Puck could observe the fond pageant that they oversee and complicate; back in the center of the pond, it became again a doorway or gate through which the mechanicals entered to rehearse and then, with a red blanket draped over it as a curtain, it became the exit that gave Bottom access to the brake; in 4.2, now turned upside down and covered with the blanket as a tarp, it became the hut in which the mechanicals huddled around a coal brazier lamenting the fate of their star performer; later still, it served as the stage for their production of "Pyramus and Thisbe."

One of its most inventive uses was as Titania's bower. At the end of 3.1, the fairies—adult creatures with their faces painted blue, who seemed only recently to have wriggled up out of the ooze—carried Timothy Spall's braying Bottom off on the bed's springs. Sally Dexter's wonderfully powerful and sexy Titania—the power and the sexuality brilliantly expressed in her delivery of a single command, "Out of this wood do not desire to go" (3.1.152)—then lowered herself into the pond, where she delicately anointed her body—as with a perfume—with its waters. Then she sinuously swam after Bottom, slithering to her knees at the pond's edge to crush a fistful of mud over her breasts. She rose and, while beating her hands to her chest, gave out with a mighty female version of Tarzan's jungle call. She stalked off after her man as the interval lights came up and the house exploded with whistles and cheers.

At the end of the next scene, the bed frame (sans mattress and springs) was again at center stage, and Puck led each of the four lovers into it as she put them to sleep after their long and confusing journey into the night. Lepage then complicated this tidy image of bringing the lovers full circle back to the bed from which they had tumbled in the opening scene, by having the fairies restore the mattress and springs to the bed on which Titania and Bottom were soon vigorously coupling. Here Lepage's staging not only linked all the marvelous contrasts between spirit and flesh, imagination and reality, beauty and beast that Shakespeare locates at the center of his tale but made the union of Titania and Bottom a part of the lovers' dream as well.

Another, and perhaps even more startling, device was Lepage's use of Puck literally to accomplish Bottom's translation. When Bottom reappeared from the brake, Laurier's Puck was suspended from his back with her feet making his ass's ears. Laurier's remarkable acrobatic abilities were repeatedly put to exciting use throughout the production. When Oberon sent her after the little western flower, she shinnied half way up the light cord, anchored her foot in a loop, and twirled her body above Oberon's head, thus putting a girdle round the earth right before our eyes. Her body was small and lithe with an androgynous quality, radiating a strangeness heightened by her costume's exposure of her right breast. Spall's body made a stunning contrast in its earthy amplitude. Spall gave his Bottom a wonderful walk—appropriately a cross between a prance and a swagger—with a tan leather coat hanging from his shoulders, a large chain and medallion around his neck, with his shirt unbuttoned almost to his navel, exposing with every step the jelly bounces and quivers of his amorphous flesh. Bottom and Puck represent the widest extremes of this wide-reaching play, yet both are incorrigible actors; willing agents of transformation; stars constrained only by productions controlled by others (Quince and Oberon). Each wants to play all the parts.

In a production concerned with the release of the actor's body as a means of articulating text—Lepage's insistence on three-dimensional

Shakespeare—the sight of Puck stuck on Bottom's back like a burr was perhaps its signature image. If this *Dream* emphasized Hall's earth and water rather than the fire and air of Brook's high-flying circus, clearly Laurier's Puck was Lepage's acknowledgment of elements above the swamp and an imaginative nod to Brook's trapezists. But not even Brook's synthesizing imagination found a way to link the worlds of spirit and flesh, air and earth, in the single image achieved by Lepage's fusion of Bottom and Puck—adding a new creature to Shakespeare's bestiary.

Lepage, following Kott, understands that Puck is as much devil or hobgoblin as benign fairy sprite.[14] In a largely monochromatic production, Puck was the only character dressed in red. Oberon and Titania were in black, the lovers—before becoming mud splattered—in white, the mechanicals—with the exception of Bottom's tan leather coat and platform shoes with Cuban heels—in various shades of grey. Puck is seen by Lepage as the crucial connection between the human and fairy worlds; so her red costume linked Cupid and the devil, passion and violence, blood and fire. When Puck's mischief-making ended and she brought the lovers to peace and reconciliation, Laurier unscrewed the suspended light bulb and found it filled with milk. She took a mighty drink and then spread the milk into the pond, creating a fog through which the lovers wearily stumbled and collapsed as the night's confusions gave way to the restorative powers of sleep. Puck is now imagined as a nurturing spirit leading her charges safely to bed.

As Theseus and Hippolyta entered for the hunting scene, the three large black rear panels earlier used as screens to capture shadows were each raised about three feet to reveal the yellow-red glow of a sunrise (a neat conflation of Oberon's description of the eastern gate all fiery-red turning Neptune's salt green streams into yellow gold) on the far horizon. As the cast sat in front of the center panel and gave out with a series of exotic chants, Philostrate again began to pole Theseus and Hippolyta about, and, as the bed swung in its circle, the lovers were exposed huddled beneath it in parallel with the play's opening moments.[15] As Demetrius reached the climax of his description of the night's experience, Hippolyta got down from her impassive perch on the bed's headboard and slowly crossed to the lovers. It was her movement and strong glance back at Theseus that triggered his decision to overrule Egeus. This time his "Come, Hippolyta" was met by her willing cross to take his hand. As they exited, the center rear panel was raised to reveal a gentle rain falling behind it, and the four lovers, still shaking the dewdrops and cobwebs from their eyes, moved to stand under its refreshing and cleansing powers. Lepage's device, perhaps straining a bit to provide a visual equivalent for the quality of Theseus' mercy, nevertheless always provoked a wonderful gasp and then applause from the audience.[16]

The joy released by this moment was in stark contrast to Lepage and Spall's handling of Bottom's awakening. When Oberon released Titania from her spell, the fairies had unceremoniously dumped the sleeping Bottom off the bed, where he rolled over several times before coming to rest at the stage left edge of the pond. He remained asleep there until the lovers had departed into their tropical shower. Spall, having played so much of his pre-Titania Bottom for broad humor, resisted the temptation to return to that mode here. As memory began to intrude upon consciousness, he appeared to be both dazed and shaken by what he thought he was and what he thought he had. His bray, disconcertingly, began to creep back into his voice, first on "Heigh-ho" and again on "Methought" (4.1.202, 207). Spall's Bottom was touched and troubled by his vision rather than lewdly exultant as its rare details reappeared in his replay of the dream. In fact, there was something tentative and uncharacteristically reserved about Bottom's return to the bosom of his pals, and it wasn't until he was well launched into "Pyramus and Thisbe" that his spirits and former self were fully restored: theater as therapy.

Lepage's visual conception of the *Dream* was built around the bed and the pond. As I have indicated, the bed was put to protean use not only as a bed but also as a throne, a door, a gate, a hut, a forest perch, and, finally, as a stage for the mechanicals' play. The red blanket, associated with both the lovers and the players, became, in its final incarnation, the floor covering for the stage. As the pond's mud had kept the lovers perpetually off-balance — mirroring the instability of their emotions — so playing "Pyramus and Thisbe" on a set of bed springs gave a similar unpredictability of footing to the tragic parody of their struggles. It also allowed Bottom, the most earthbound and solidly rooted of mortals, a sense of the imagination's weightlessness as he enjoyed experimenting with the bounce of his dramatic environment even as his vocal tones as Pyramus seemed to echo and parody Olivier's heroic tenor trumpet.

Lepage, following his fellow internationalists Peter Brook and Ariane Mnouchkine, had a special Javanese gamelon created for the production and then augmented it with flutes and percussion instruments from China, India, Africa, and South America as well as with violin and cello so that sound mirrored cast and setting. Music played a prominent role in the production, often underscoring long speeches and exchanges

Mark Hadfield as Starveling, Brian Pettifer as Snout, Adrian Scarborough as Flute, Timothy Spall as Bottom, Steven Beard as Quince, and John Cobb as Snug in the Royal National Theatre's 1992 production of *A Midsummer Night's Dream*, directed by Robert Lepage. Photo by Neil Libbert.

rather than just setting mood or covering scene changes. Some instruments were used to establish themes for individual characters: the cello for Hermia, the flute for Helena, percussion for Oberon. Lepage and his music director, Adrian Lee, gently mocked their own efforts by allowing the mechanicals to fashion their own gamelon, consisting of several pots, a muffin tin, a washboard, and a bottle used quite effectively as a flute.

For all the imaginative liberties Lepage took with the play's landscape and action, he remained quite faithful to the text. He made only one significant transposition, and that he saved for the play's conclusion. As a *Bergomask* performed on a bed or in a pond was out of the question, Lepage cut directly from Theseus' praise of Bottom and company to the entrance, upstage right, of Puck, Oberon, and Titania. As they circled round the pond performing their rites of housekeeping and house blessing, the bed underwent its final transformation by being moved stage left and placed on its head with the springs once again made to function as a door. As the fairies made their rounds, the cast in single file walked backwards across the pond and out through the door.

As Oberon and Titania made their exit, only Theseus, bringing up the rear, was left standing at the portal. From that liminal spot, he delivered "The iron tongue of midnight" (5.1.363) speech and exited while Puck shut the door behind him and propped his broom against it. She then reappropriated center stage and acrobatically spread her body out into the pond with her head resting on her hands just above the water as she delivered the final word from the world of shadows before returning to the elements.[17] Lepage's textual transposition lost Shakespeare's sweet irony in having the rationalist Theseus' tossed-off use of " 'tis almost fairy time" (5.1.364) immediately followed by the arrival of the fairies, but it did allow the reconciled court world a stately exit, through the play's central prop, from the end of one dream into the beginning of another.

As this account has indicated, the landscape of Lepage's *Dream* made for a very physical production. British Shakespeare is almost always a triumph of voice over movement. Lepage, recognizing that productions of Shakespeare in other cultures are often highly visual, has drawn attention to an interesting linguistic insight: "when I was rehearsing *A Midsummer Night's Dream*, an actor said it's strange, in French you don't say an audience, you say 'spectateurs.' For him it defined very clearly how in the English culture the word is important. The word audience has to do with the ears, and the word 'spectateurs' . . . has to do with the eyes."[18] Lepage's production not only demanded that we be *spectateurs* but that we also realize theater is not like painting or film, where the flat image is all, but depends for its joy upon the release of the actor's body in space. I have rarely seen a Shakespeare production where the actors' bodies were so central to conveying meaning.

For instance, the physical contrast between the rulers of the day and night worlds was immediate and vivid. Theseus and Hippolyta were middle-aged, wrapped about in white drapes, and largely immobile. They were moved, literally and figuratively, by others, suggesting the aridity and rigidity of the court world. In contrast, Oberon and Titania were sexy, vibrant, and physically riveting. Jeffrey Kissoon's Oberon moved with the grace of a panther, and his speaking of the verse was equally exotic. He had a powerful upper torso that allowed him to make a remarkable gymnastic backswing and roll to gain the perch he shared with Puck above the pond. I have already described Dexter's sinuous swim and the obvious pleasure she took in her body as she prepared herself for her rendezvous with Bottom. She, too, had to perform several gymnastic feats on the slender cord that almost, but not quite, connected the human and fairy worlds—it took the actor's body to complete the link. Laurier's abilities as an acrobat and contortionist were at the heart of her performance; her brilliant control of her body, in water or in air, was in stunning contrast to the lovers' negotiation of the night world.[19]

For it was into Puck's world that the lovers, as unsure of their bodies as their emotions, tumbled. Much of the humor that resulted from their romantic confusions was created and expressed by their bodies. Their initial embarrassment about being "exposed" was shared by the audience, but, as they hurled themselves physically into the desperate expression of their painful pubescent turmoil without care or concern for their physical selves, we were treated to a rare comic release. Lepage's actors took full advantage of the Olivier Theatre's spaciousness from the moment Helena (Rudi Davies) and the bespectacled Demetrius (Simon Coates) arrived in the woods. Round and round the huge path circling the pond, Helena chased Demetrius, which brought laughter from the audience unaccustomed to seeing bodies moving at full gallop in the theater and the woman in active pursuit of the man: "Run when you will; the story shall be chang'd: / Apollo flies, and Daphne holds the chase" (2.1.230–31). Before Oberon and Puck had begun to do their work, Helena was already evoking and reshaping one of Ovid's transformations. As our eyes followed her dizzy chase, they also caught Puck's body spinning fifteen feet above the pond. Lepage's production did not retreat from the potential destructive consequences of this whirling world. As Helena finally became weary of her chase, she expressed her physical exhaustion with masochistic frustration: "I am your spaniel; and, Demetrius, / The more you beat me, I will fawn on you" (2.1.203–4), causing Oberon to intercede to protect her from Demetrius' blows. How quick bright things come to confusion.

Lysander (Rupert Graves) and Hermia (Indra Ove) entered the woods more confident of their mission. Lysander cleverly thought to bring along bedding (a sheet and the second red blanket), which he quickly spread out and proudly presented to Hermia. She popped under the covers and removed her pajamas. Lysander eagerly followed her lead. The initial titters and giggles from the young in the audience (particularly at the school-kid-packed matinees) simply presaged the explosion of nervous embarrassment and delight that followed as Hermia foiled Lysander's pretty advances and banished him from her bower. Graves, with naked sullenness, arose from her side—snatching his pajama trousers at the last instant and pressing them fig-leaf fashion to his groin—and slowly backed away from his ungenerous love, providing the now squealing house a prolonged view of his backside. The

tease of this pants humor continued when he soon awoke—having
put his trousers back on—to greet "Transparent Helena" (2.2.104). As
Graves began to slip and slide through the mud in pursuit of Helena,
he repeatedly allowed his trousers to slip low on his hips before pulling
them up. Hermia experienced a similar physical, though less comic, exposure when she awoke from her fearful sexual nightmare and found
herself alone and abandoned. The emotions of these lovers get rubbed
raw in the night, and Lepage's production was willing to explore the
physical chaos engendered by those passionate confusions.

Davies, Ove, Coates, and Graves gave themselves recklessly to their
environment. Their verbal insults were immediately translated into
physical ones. There was a physical progression to the collapse of their
inhibitions. First they slipped, then they fell down, then they whomped
each other with gobs of mud, then the men wrestled while the women
quarreled, then the men engaged in a group grope with Helena as Hermia stood alone crying out her despair about her size, and finally—after
attacking Hermia and shoving her face in the water—Lysander did a
full belly dive sliding back across the pond to arrive in Helena's lap
just as he delivered: "Be not afraid; She shall not harm thee, Helena"
(3.2.321).

I should add that, like Dexter's sexually triumphant Titania, Helena
and Hermia, once freed by their amphibian environment of their
maiden modesty, gave as good as they got in their battles with Lysander
and Demetrius. Both Helena and Hermia managed to score direct mud
hits on both lads as retaliation for their abuse. Let me describe one such
moment during the first meeting between Hermia and Demetrius in 3.2.
As her hysterics over Lysander's disappearance grew, Hermia backed
Demetrius across the pond, where he slipped and fell on his bottom.
Laugh. Then he responded with nonchalant disdain to her fury ("You
spend your passion on a mispris'd mood" [3.2.74]), and she socked him
with two large balls of mud. Bigger laugh. She then turned and haughtily stomped and splashed her way across the pond ("from thy hated
presence part I [so]" [3.2.80]), almost losing her balance and compo-
sure by slipping in the muck on the far bank. More laughter. Pause—
allowing us to swing our attention from the departed Hermia back to
Demetrius and his mud-splattered face and spectacles. Slowly, he
turned directly to the audience and, with a look worthy of Jack Benny
("Would you believe *that*"), deadpans: "There is no following her in this
fierce vein" (3.2.82). Long pause as the house exploded with laughter
on this carefully crafted comic climax. Admittedly, there was broad

slapstick comedy at work here, but it was all built toward maximizing, rather than undercutting, the pleasure of Shakespeare's punchline.

Lepage made his *Dream* revolve and in that revolution discovered new surfaces of shimmering pleasure in Shakespeare's art while providing radical reassessments of the play's gender relationships. Lepage's work has often been linked to film because of the power of his images, but film images are flat, and Lepage is a sculptor. His theatrical genius is to discover the stunning images made by the actor's body as it explores the relationship between space and text. Lepage has remarked: "We have a vertical relationship with theatre . . . film is horizontal. The camera is always moving horizontally and people rarely dare to make the camera move vertically because the language of cinema says it goes horizontally. So you never have the contact [in film] with above, whether it's with a god or . . . with your aspirations. . . . That's why we wanted to draw a line in *A Midsummer Night's Dream* with the light bulb, because that's where theatre starts."[20]

Lepage's *Dream* rediscovered theatrical space as a machine for playing and making joy in and, in the process, gave us a *Dream* that challenged and revised the work of Hall and Brook and aided Eyre in revitalizing England's Royal National Theatre. Eyre offers a fitting comment on Lepage's theatrical genius: "Robert has the ability to render the theatre poetic: images, verbal and visual, succeed one another, and accumulate resonance; they grow and harmonise, threads become themes, themes become narrative."[21] But howsoever, strange and admirable, as Hippolyta might respond.

NOTES

1. I owe much, including a revived interest in this essay, to Jim Lusardi. I spent 1992–93 in London beginning work on a sequel to *Shakespeare Observed: Studies in Performance on Stage and Screen* (Athens: Ohio University Press, 1992) intended to chart developments in English stage Shakespeare in the post-Brook-Hall-Nunn era. I was particularly interested in the work of Richard Eyre, Adrian Noble, Michael Bogdanov, and Declan Donellen. Robert Lepage's production of *A Midsummer Night's Dream* opened at the Royal National Theatre in June 1992 and played in repertory there until January 1993. I saw the production several times during its run and quickly concluded that I wanted to include an account of it in my new study. In April 1993, Jim Lusardi wrote to me asking if I would be interested in reviewing Kenneth Branagh's new film of *Much Ado About Nothing* for *Shakespeare Bulletin*. I jumped at the chance, and that review became the first of many I did for the journal as one new Shakespeare film after another emerged during the decade. Those reviews became the starting place for *Shakespeare at the Cineplex: The Kenneth Branagh Era* (Athens: Ohio University Press, 2003),

devoted entirely to a consideration of the fifteen major Shakespeare films that appeared between 1989 and 2001. The conclusion of that project has led me back to Shakespeare on stage and a return to the Lepage essay (and others), fittingly revised and expanded for this volume to honor Jim Lusardi's powerful contribution to making Shakespeare in performance a vital area of the contemporary critical dialogue about Shakespeare.

2. See Barbara Hodgdon, "Looking for Mr. Shakespeare after 'The Revolution': Robert Lepage's Intercultural *Dream* Machine," in Hodgdon, *The Shakespeare Trade* (Philadelphia: University of Pennsylvania Press, 1998), 171–90.

3. A *Midsummer Night's Dream*, in *The Riverside Shakespeare*, 2nd ed., ed. G. Blakemore Evans (Boston: Houghton Mifflin, 1997), 2.1.14–15. Subsequent references to Shakespeare's plays are from this edition and are cited parenthetically.

4. Michael Billington, *Guardian*, October 24, 1992, in a column discussing the re-release of Orson Welles' film of *Othello*.

5. Robert Hewison, "Such Stuff as Dreams Are Made On," [London] *Sunday Times*, July 12, 1992, Sec. 7, 6.

6. A *Midsummer Night's Dream*, VHS, prod. Michael Birkett and Martin Ransohoff, dir. Peter Hall (1968; New York: Water Bearer Films, 1993).

7. See Jay L. Halio, A *Midsummer Night's Dream*, Shakespeare in Performance, 2nd ed. (Manchester: Manchester University Press, 2003), 122–33.

8. C. L. Barber, *Shakespeare's Festive Comedies: A Study of Dramatic Form and Its Relation to Social Custom* (Princeton: Princeton University Press, 1959).

9. Jan Kott, *Shakespeare Our Contemporary* (New York: Anchor Books, 1966), 213–36.

10. *Platform Papers 3: Directors* (London: Publications Department, Royal National Theatre, 1993), 35.

11. Heather Neill, "Dream and Nightmare Meet" [Interview with Robert Lepage and Michael Levine], [London] *Times*, July 2, 1992, "Life and Times" sec., 3.

12. Ibid.

13. Barbara Freedman writes, "Play production, like dream production, is a matter of translation that effaces as it reaches toward an original": *Staging the Gaze* (Ithaca: Cornell University Press, 1991), 178.

14. Kott, *Shakespeare Our Contemporary*, 213–15.

15. The National Theatre's stage management for the production responded to my inquiry about the origins of the chant by indicating it was a Balinese monkey chant called "The Catchak."

16. That applause (but not the gasp) might as easily have been triggered, I realize, by the audience's relief in getting these Woodstock muddied kids cleaned up and presentable.

17. Here is the stage manager's detailed description of Angela Laurier's final contortion taken from the production's promptbook:

> At first Puck slowly handstands in "normal" fashion—head always looking directly out at the audience. Slowly she brings her legs over D/S so that her feet rest over her shoulders. Then she lowers her body to support her weight on her forearms. Finally she "snaps" her feet behind her armpits and drops onto her chest. Her body is now completely doubled but her head and arms remain quite free for movement so that she may rest on her elbows, hands under her chin, head cocked cheekily to one side. Blackout. End.

18. *Platform Papers 3: Directors*, 33.

19. Laurier's centrality to the production was confirmed when she was injured in an accident several months after it opened. While her understudy spoke the part with élan, she was incapable of performing many of Laurier's physical feats, and the production lost much of its animating spirit.

20. *Platform Papers 3: Directors*, 37.

21. Richard Eyre, *National Service: Diary of a Decade* (London: Bloomsbury, 2003), 132.

Trevor Nunn's *The Merchant of Venice:* Portia's House of Mystery, Magic, and Menace

Kenneth S. Rothwell

TREVOR NUNN'S TV MOVIE OF *THE MERCHANT OF VENICE* (2001)[1] PROBES the darkest secrets of the play's magical "casket plot," in which vessels of silver, lead, and gold signal false messages about their true nature. Each of the caskets embodies a major trope of the play. Antonio and Bassanio are sealed in the silver casket, as their troubled friendship turns each into a "blinking idiot";[2] Shylock earns the leaden casket for his outer nastiness and inner integrity ("An oath, an oath, I have an oath in heaven" [4.1.228]); and, as Morocco and Arragon discover, Portia's golden Belmont conceals an inner cache of menace and death. Although some critics have despaired of locating any unity in the play's disparate tales of the caskets, the bond of flesh, and the ring tangle,[3] the interpretive key, which Nunn turns with aplomb, lies in the caskets.

By good fortune, Nunn's cinematography preserves this antique vision for today's electronic universe. While his minimalist *Merchant of Venice* cannot match the visual splendor, even opulence, of Michael Radford's big-screen 2004 film of *Merchant* starring Al Pacino as Shylock,[4] it far transcends the narrow constraints of a photographed stage play, such as the Stuart Burge/Laurence Olivier 1965 *Othello*.[5] To claim filmic credentials, even as the opening credits roll, he introduces a flickering montage from old movies of Venice between wars—sidewalk cafés, wining and dining, heroic mahogany bars with bartenders energetically shaking cocktails in silver pitchers, and then a close shot of the dancing feet of carefree merry makers.[6] Subsequent clips show the dark side: a street with aged orthodox Jews living in the shadow of Nazi terror. This celluloid dumb-show flickers out, having served its purpose of impressing the audience with images of bourgeois society enjoying the high life juxtaposed with specters of doomed Jews, a crude but effective evocation of the central tension in *The Merchant of Venice*. Nunn's extratextual opening also anticipates the roaming, interrogative camera, which makes each frame revealing but nevertheless tantalizing. There is always an invitation to wonder what lies beneath. While Nunn's is not the "acrobatic" camera of robust cinema (there are no elaborate panoramic, crane or very long shots), it is certainly a "roaming" one. As the camera deftly highlights and underscores the feelings of Portia, Shylock, and Antonio with "Rembrandt" shots, as they came to be called in the classical Hollywood films of the thirties, and matching reverse shots, it in itself becomes a mute character in the play. The integration of word, image, and sound embraces *mise-en-scène*, thespian talents, cinematography, editing, blocking, etc., each deserving its own in-depth analysis. The gazing camera morphs into an invisible narrator that defines and redefines the *diegesis* in myriad ways.

Nunn's special touch derives, however, from the close-up. As Russian film director Grigori Kozintsev once wrote, "The advantage of the cinema over the theatre is not that you can even have horses, but that you can stare closer into a man's eyes; otherwise it is pointless to set up a cine camera for Shakespeare."[7] The ability of the camera to peer, pry, and poke into the innermost being of a character gives new life to Sir Philip Sidney's defense of poesy as "a speaking picture."[8] Analytical close shots can speak volumes, such as one in the courtroom that shows Shylock depositing his yarmulke and tallith at each end of the scale as metonymy for the loss of his integrity. Equally unforgettable is the specter of Shylock in close-up sharpening his knife on the sole of his shoe. As Ernst Lubitsch became famous in Hollywood for his "touch" with icons like white telephones on boudoir bed stands, Nunn also focuses his camera on key symbols to suggest far more than meets the eye.

Like all filmmakers, Nunn needed to make over the stage script into a movie scenario. Average in length for a Shakespeare play at 2,546 lines, *The Merchant of Venice*, in Nunn's treatment, loses about 735 lines, or about 29 percent of Shakespeare's text.[9] The greatest casualty is Old Gobbo. Some indelible language that also winds up on the cutting room floor includes Salerio's graphic description of how the stone on the side of a church makes him think of "dangerous rocks" (1.1.31) splitting the hull of Antonio's vessel and "enrob[ing] the roaring waters with my silks" (1.1.34). The trial scene remains intact, but the poignant fifth-act love duet of Jessica and Lorenzo about world famous lovers like Dido and Aeneas suffers grievous harm. To sustain the interest of a television audience, Nunn and his codirector, Chris Hunt, needed the continuity and seamless narrative of a classical film[10] (no Orson Welles stunts here).

Gains balance losses. The clever set design executed at Pinewood Studios by Hildegarde Bechtler turns a single studio space into a palimpsest for a raucous cabaret, a city street, a sidewalk café, a room in Portia's chic Belmont digs, Shylock's dingy house, and a courtroom. Venice has been jettisoned in favor of 1930s Weimar Germany, a period of such gleeful decadence that to make it surrogate for Venice's Belmont is to condemn by guilt-through-association the friends and associates of Antonio.

The rowdy cabaret, at once moody, shrill, jangling, amusing, escapist, and menacing, becomes the ship of fools for Antonio and his cronies, whose roles as blinking idiots link them firmly to the silver casket. The cabaret environs especially offer exactly the atmosphere for David Bamber's Antonio. A bland, passive-looking person with a brushed back "pompadour," spectacles, and a roundish face, Bamber's fleshy Antonio is precisely the kind of lonely man who would seek diversion in the bar scene. Unable to arouse the libido of young women, he is free for his male friendships, including the phlegmatic Bassanio's.[11] The flamboyant club itself becomes a macroexpressive object in the way that its materiality frames the wistful Antonio and his parasitical cronies.[12] Nunn stocks the scene with multiple signs and talismans for Antonio's chronic depression ("In sooth, I know not why I am so sad" [1.1.1]), a melancholy induced no doubt by an imbalance of humors and a lack of Prozac. He confides to Gratiano that "I hold the world but as the world, Gratiano, / A stage, where every man must play a part, / And mine a sad one" (1.1.77–79). In a shadowy corner, he moodily plays passages from a Brahms sonata on a battered piano, under an array of pendant chandeliers while his roistering cronies giggle and shriek around him. The ribald young men, the "Salads," are a choreographed ballet in the chromatic shades of their black dinner jackets with sparkling white dress shirts and black ties. British bathroom humor intervenes when Gratiano, played by Richard Henders as a vulgar clown, comes staggering out of the men's room with his trousers dropped around his ankles. Thirties-style bimbos are decoratively scattered around the club's small tables as congenial companions to the young men.

Gratiano, still in a state of semidishabillé, functions as *allegro* to Antonio's *penseroso* with his "Let me play the Fool" (1.1.79); with "mirth and laughter" (1.1.80), he attempts to divert Antonio. Playing the stand-up comedian, he squawks into a primitive microphone that squeals, shrieks, and wheezes until, between that and his hysterical laughter at his own feeble jokes, he becomes unintelligible. When the oafish Gratiano, of whom Bassanio says he "speaks an infinite deal of nothing" (1.1.114), declares his love for Antonio and drunkenly kisses him on the cheek, poor Antonio shows every sign of distress. But Antonio's melancholy and Gratiano's frivolity set the tone for the bipolarity between Venice and Belmont, between the appearance and reality of the caskets, between the banter about a "merry bond" (1.3.173) of a pound of flesh and the ugly butchery it almost leads to.

The considerable acting skills of the cast hone the issues. When Antonio questions Bassanio—"Well, tell me now what lady is the same / To whom you swore a secret pilgrimage?" (1.1.119–20)—his manner becomes subtly feline. When he toys with Bassanio's hair, a crossover begins from Platonic friendship to eroticism; even when Bassanio sits down on a chair and takes Antonio's hand in pleading for a loan to help him woo Portia in proper style, Bassanio seems more interested in obtaining the money than in reciprocating Antonio's crush. Antonio then caves in to Bassanio's whining. He removes his glasses, glances upward, rolls his head, and reluctantly grants authorization to look for a loan: ". . . go forth, / Try what my credit can in Venice do" (1.1.179–80). No one can outdo Bamber in the art of inventing significant tics, nods, eyebrow archings, brow furrowings, hand gestures, and facial spasms. It all might be thought of as flagrant scenery-chewing were it not so organic to the role that Shakespeare has Salerio mimic Antonio's mannerisms in the second act. When a grateful Bassanio embraces him, Antonio looks as if he is desperately trying to appear indifferent. The insult added to injury, the *coup de grâce*, occurs when Antonio, the world-class loser, puts his glasses back on just as the waitress stiffs him for the bar tab, his gaggle of cronies having faded into the night.

Later in the cabaret, Launcelot Gobbo takes over the bandstand microphone as the stand-up comic for a lengthy speech from 2.2, only to be caught *in flagrante delicto* mocking his master when Shylock unexpectedly appears. In the smoke-filled *mise-en-scène*, in mid and long shot, the club throbs with hysterical revelers. Before a raucous male audience, two chorus girls shriek out their period-piece Rudy Vallee, "Everything I Have Is Yours," and end by flipping up their skirts in a saucy lingerie peep show. In a Nunn touch, one elderly and doubtless impotent man, sitting slumped with his potbelly and white boiled shirt projecting over the tablecloth, raises his fist in an obscene gesture. The cabaret exists in a haze of tobacco smoke that acts as a gauze curtain between the characters and the audience.[13] The theatrical polish of the cabaret scenes illustrates Nunn's ability to move in the realms of both low and high culture.

Just as the ribald nightclub atmosphere reinforces Antonio's psychological issues, so Shylock's drab, "leaden" domicile provides the correct venue for stormy scenes between Henry Goodman's formidable Shy-

lock and his Gabrielle Jourdan's Jessica. Shylock's house occupies the
same all-purpose studio space, but it has been transformed into a barren
shell, something like a cinder-block school cafeteria in a slum neighborhood. The shabbiness of Shylock's lifestyle, despite his prosperity, signals his miserliness. Contradictions proliferate. He is at first shown
snarling and raging in Yiddish at his abject daughter for not having
washed the pots thoroughly. His emotional fragility is caught, however,
when the camera moves in on a framed picture of his lost wife, Leah,
whose absence defines Shylock's misery. When Tubal informs him that
·Jessica has sold Leah's turquoise ring for a monkey, Shylock's anguish
is unspeakable: "I would not have given it for a wilderness of monkeys"
(3.1.122–23).

And yet Shylock can become manic again when Launcelot Gobbo,
the black servant who is present while his master is railing at Jessica,
lets slip that there will be a masque that evening. The Jew becomes
deranged, the mere thought of Christian hijinks driving him crazy. "Let
not the sound of shallow fopp'ry enter / My sober house" (2.5.35–36),
he shrieks. In a shocking transgression that Nunn may have borrowed
from John Barton, Shylock slaps a stunned Jessica across the face. The
close-up magnifies Jessica's hurt and bewilderment.

The roving camera documents these manic-depressive phases. Nothing, for example, could be more poignant than the contradictory but
unscripted moment when Shylock draws "my girl" close to him and
father and daughter sing a duet in Yiddish from the ancient song "Eshet
Chayil" ("a woman of virtue"), in which "a husband and children pay
tribute to the woman of the house on the Sabbath, praising her as provi-
dent and hard working."[14] The image redomesticates Shylock as human,
not a monster, something more than a M. Verdoux or Jekyll-and-Hyde
figure. Little wonder that Jessica is motivated to cry out to her only
friend, the servant Launcelot Gobbo, "Our house is hell" (2.3.2). To
put a different spin on it, Shylock remains another version of the ob-
sessed humor figure, a type of Jonsonian puritan, like Zeal-of-the-Land
Busy in *Bartholomew Fair*,[15] whose Christian fundamentalism was rooted
as much in the Old as in the New Testament. Regardless of the nearly
unanswerable question of how profoundly anti-Semitic the play is in
the post-Holocaust era, in Shakespeare's time it was really Portia's, not
Shylock's, play.

Belmont as presided over by the imperturbable Derbhle Crotty's
Portia becomes a macrometaphor for the golden casket, rich in superfi-
cial brilliance but inwardly booby-trapped. The same studio space that
held Shylock's wretched domain now acquires a sleekly minimalist

décor in a frigid Nordic modernist vogue, bare of furniture except an Ikea-style glass rack for the magic caskets. Portia's disciplined maids — looking like matrons in a Victorian reformatory; dressed in uniforms of oversized white oval-shaped aprons over black dresses, stockings, and shoes; and commanded by the haughty butler Balthazar—animate the inanimate décor.

Crotty's Portia, an Italian "lady richly left" (1.1.161), follows the grand tradition of *la belle dame sans merci*, not because she is endowed with stunning beauty but because, under the eagle eye of the camera, she radiates a smarmy charisma. Her short dark hair, high forehead, fresh white complexion, and blazing eyes summon up faint echoes of Egyptian goddesses, and the insecure Bassanio even reinvents her as a dominatrix, who is a "torturer" inflicting "happy torment" (3.2.37). The inscrutable Portia and the solicitous Nerissa mirror the relationship between Antonio and Bassanio. Like Antonio, Portia also complains of chronic depression: "By my troth, Nerissa, my little body is a-weary of this great world" (1.2.1–2). Nerissa, in turn, seems to own a direct line into the invisible world inhabited by Portia's control freak of a father so that she can put the right "spin" on why Portia has been afflicted with the bizarre casket riddle: "Your father was ever virtuous, and holy men at their death have good inspirations" (1.2.27–28).

Nerissa obligingly orchestrates an audio/visual program with a 16mm film projector featuring Portia's forlorn suitors. Insouciantly, Portia ticks off the inadequacies of her unlucky supplicants as their wraithlike shadows flicker across the screen. Portia elevates the selection of the caskets by Morocco, Arragon, and Bassanio into a ceremonial rite, the squad of obedient maids, functioning as her acolytes. When Portia haughtily dispatches Morocco to choose a casket, she kneels on a prayer cushion, her back as stiff and erect as a guardsman's and, in at least one instance (when Bassanio chooses the casket), ostentatiously crosses herself. The extradiegetic music lends sonic support to an eerie sense of inscrutable but portentous forces. As has been observed by Charles Edelman, Derbhle Crotty's Portia is attracted to the dark complexioned Moroccan prince, elegantly attired in a sharply tailored double-breasted pinstripe suit and white spats.[16] When he chooses the wrong casket and discovers that "All that glisters is not gold" (2.7.65), she can barely contain herself. Shattered, the Moroccan bursts into tears, embraces Portia fervently, and stomps out of the chamber, leaving Portia to extend "a gentle riddance" to "all of his complexion" (2.7.78–79). Nunn quietly excises that racist line.

The Prince of Arragon's wrangle with the casket unveils a comic subtext. The Spaniard, who shows an enviable talent for the rhythmical choreography of flamenco dancing, arrives in the high style of a toreador with his own personal guitarist. In addressing him, Portia condescendingly uses gestures as well as words as if he were some kind of third-world servant who could not possibly otherwise understand English. When he stumbles over the word "chooseth," the ever-helpful Portia corrects his pronunciation, meanwhile exchanging furtive glances of shared amusement with Nerissa over her quarry's dilemma.

Portia's robot maids bustle about, carrying out their well-rehearsed roles in preparation for Bassanio's bout with the caskets. Nerissa hovers, or flutters, on the edges while Balthazar, the snooty butler, keeps a wary eye on the caskets. An unusually emotional Portia urges Bassanio to ". . . tarry, pause a day or two / Before you hazard" (3.2.1–2). As her praetorian guard of household retainers watches her, she seems almost ready to betray her father's trust by nudging Bassanio toward the prized casket of lead. As Bassanio approaches the caskets, Portia kneels, crosses herself, and clasps her hands in prayer. Nerissa's piercing contralto, accompanied by a harpsichord, trills out the fateful song: "Tell me where is fancy bred, / Or in the heart or in the head?" (3.2.63–64). Kelly handles Nerissa's plaintive song admirably, though perhaps not quite so spectacularly as the world-class delivery by the two shrieking viragoes (played by Clare Walmesley and Laura Sarti) in Jonathan Miller's 1973 Precision Video production.[17] Bassanio again hits on the play's major theme when he remarks of the golden casket "there is no [vice] so simple but assumes / Some mark of virtue on his outward parts" (3.2.81–82).

An overjoyed Portia then presents her fiancé with the lethal ring. She holds it aloft in midshot as she admonishes him that to lose control of it would "presage" nothing less than ruin. The normally reserved Bassanio lets out a war whoop of joy, and a defrosted Portia fiercely smashes the caskets against the wall, yet the joyousness conceals Portia's plan for setting up a loyalty test with the ring. This enigmatic woman harbors a fleet of secret agendas. The camera also makes possible an *Upstairs/Downstairs* silent subplot involving the servants as it shows one of the maids clearly agitated, then distressed, over the playboy Gratiano's selection of Nerissa as a wife. It would appear that Gratiano had been spending too much time downstairs.

As in other episodes, Nunn thriftily furnishes forth the same studio space to create the neutral environs of a courtroom for Antonio's trial, a milieu in which there is no room for color-coded caskets, only the transparency of truth. The duke enters, and in a flurry of reverse and over-the-shoulder shots, exchanges greetings with Antonio, who is clearly a member of the in-group of old boys. Antonio has by now pulled himself together after his ignominious arrest and is nattily turned out in a dark blue suit with vest, handkerchief in breast pocket, light pink shirt, and grey power tie. He calmly tells the duke how he is "arm'd / To suffer, with a quietness of spirit" (4.1.11–12) and, with a confident toss of his head, fetches a Bible out of his coat pocket. Shylock's friend, Tubal, suddenly enters, his face showing no expression, his long black overcoat and wide-brimmed fedora stigmatizing him as an outsider.

Shylock then appears wearing a black suit with a conspicuously large white handkerchief dangling from the breast pocket, the fringes of his prayer shawl hanging from under his suit jacket. An officious bailiff seats him in the same row as Antonio. At the close of the duke's lengthy appeal to Shylock for compassion ("We all expect a gentle answer, Jew!" [4.1.34]), everyone applauds—a pretty good index to Shylock's unpopularity. When Bassanio offers Shylock a draft for six thousand ducats, the camera moves in closely as he vindictively shreds the document. The anxiety escalates as Shylock stubbornly defends his rejection of a cash settlement: "So can I give no reason, nor I will not, / More than a lodg'd hate and a certain loathing / I bear Antonio" (4.1.59–61). Nerissa, looking like a small boy, enters just in time to witness her own Gratiano throwing a temper tantrum, "O, be thou damn'd, inexecrable dog!!" (4.1.128), induced by Shylock's insolent whetting of his knife. This volatile moment in the courtroom privileges the law over illusion and exacerbates the tension between mercy and justice, gentile and Jew.

When Portia enters the courtroom, the trial scene generates a kinetic flow, which allows full display of Nunn's (and Hunt's) genius in pointing a cine camera. Portia, dressed in a plain business suit with a no-nonsense vest, her hair brushed well back over her forehead, and wearing round plain spectacles, has been disguised as the very model of an earnest young barrister. Her enunciation becomes deliberate, even halting. In long shot, she stands directly in front of first Shylock and then Antonio, making an earnest effort to identify them: "Which is the merchant here? and which the Jew?" (4.1.174), she asks, as if distinguishing between a puritan and a Jew were a problem, which it may well have been according to James Shapiro's account of Jews in Shakespeare's England.[18]

Directors over the years have squeezed every last drop of inventiveness out of Portia's speech on mercy to avoid making it sound like a

Henry Goodman as Shylock, Derbhle Crotty as Portia, and Michael Wildman as Stephano in the Royal National Theatre's 1999 stage production of *The Merchant of Venice*, directed by Trevor Nunn. Photo by John Haynes.

classroom set piece. Crotty follows a stage tradition at least as old as Sarah Siddons' 1786 performance at Drury Lane by turning it into a direct answer to Shylock's question "On what compulsion must I [be merciful]?" (4.1.183). At "the force of temporal power" (4.1.190), she draws up a chair and, moving very close to Shylock, becomes a surrogate for the probing camera as her brief for mercy swirls toward Shylock's impervious face. At "enthroned in the hearts of kings" (4.1.194), she adroitly gestures toward Shylock's heart, then gently waggles her finger at him. Meantime, the maddening self-righteousness of Portia's homily on human decency curdles Shylock's soul. Finally, pushed over the edge by Portia's insistence that "We do pray for mercy" (4.1.200), unable to stand it for even one more second, Goodman's Shylock lifts his head in despair, buries his face in his hands, stands up, his eyes brimming over with rage, and cries out to the court, "I crave the law" (4.1.206). A quivering Antonio sits terrified at the prospect of the sharp knife slicing into his exposed flesh. In a tender *tableau vivant*, Antonio and Bassanio sob in each other's arms.

Nunn knows exactly how to tease out the suspense even when the audience knows full well how it will all turn out. The camera lens drags the spectators into a virtual reality of pathological sadism. When, finally, Shylock must cut into Antonio's bared bosom, the on-screen spectators cover their faces. From a low angle shot, Shylock, his expression demonic, prays "Shemah Yisroel" ("Hear O Israel"), then the camera moves back and forth between Shylock and Antonio, who is hysterically murmuring the Lord's Prayer. A sweating and shaking Shylock, perhaps unnerved by Tubal's previously abrupt exit from the courtroom, falters. The razor-edged knife hovers inches above Antonio's chest, only to be abruptly withdrawn when Portia discovers the statute in Venetian law abjuring Shylock from taking even a jot of blood. She holds the legal tome high over her head as if she were a priest about to read from the Gospel. A berserk Gratiano leaps around the courtroom crying out for joy over Portia's being "A second Daniel!" (4.1.333). In low angle shot, the sphinxlike duke of Venice stares down at a groveling Shylock still seated but rapidly losing *sangfroid* as his ego crumbles.

In the graphic culmination, Shylock is defeated by Antonio's demand that he convert to Christianity and by his surrender. A broken man, he staggers out of the room, while a close shot of Antonio's face shows him enjoying his victory a bit too much. When the duke declares the proceedings ended, the spectators break into applause as if they were creatures at a play. As a visual coda, a long shot creates an emblem of justice: Antonio seated in the background in deep focus and the scales of justice suspended in the foreground.

Nunn's fifth-act version skips forty-five lines of the lyric duet between Jessica and Lorenzo ("In such a night as this" [5.1.1]) to reveal them lying side by side on the deck looking up at "the floor of heaven / . . . thick inlaid with patens of bright gold" (5.1.58–59). The focus becomes increasingly on Jessica. She and Lorenzo move gracefully like ballet dancers to the accompaniment of a piano nocturne, but her cry of guilty horror when she recollects the betrayal of her father by literally becoming Lorenzo's torchbearer ("I am never merry when I hear sweet music" [5.1.69]) dampens the ardor of romance.

Portia and Nerissa, after their successful courtroom appearance as men, return to Belmont as though reborn. Literally coming out of the shadows, Portia wears a stylish blue crepe or silk suit with a long skirt and boa neckpiece of fur or feathers, matching straw cloche, and beaded necklace. Her bright red lips, mascaraed eyes, and lightly rouged cheeks offset her raven black hair. An echo of her mistress, petite Nerissa affects a blue dress with a white scarf and matching pillbox hat. The women embody thirties high fashion, with Portia a veritable Duchess of Windsor. To lighten the occasion, the austere butler serves glasses of champagne from a silver tray. In the midst of this genteel merriment, however, Portia is never more sadistic than when she torments Bassanio about the loss that she has herself engineered of the ring ("By heaven, I will ne'er come in your bed / Until I see the ring!" ([5.1.190–91]). The camera moves in for an analytical close-up of their hands when Portia, relenting of her Catch-22 snare, returns the ring to Bassanio's finger. For a light moment, both the outer and inner Belmont look golden.

Nunn brings some fresh ideas to the notorious ambiguities of the play's closing moments. Jessica's remorse over becoming a female Jazz Singer replaces Antonio's lonely homosexuality as the center of interest. Dismayed and uneasy, her Christian friends look on as she chants a lamentation of several bars from "Eshet Chayil." They stand in long shot around Jessica, as if to protect her, until in close shot, Portia, dropping the play's last few lines, simply says, "It is almost morning" (5.1.295). What Portia omits to say is that no one is really "satisfied / Of these events at full" (5.1.296–97).

Nor are we. Like Bassanio, we still must heed Antonio's warning, against the seductiveness of false appearances, for "The devil can cite Scripture for his purpose . . ." and appear "like a villain with a smiling cheek, / [and with] A goodly apple rotten at the heart. / O, what a goodly outside falsehood hath!" (1.3.98–102).

Nunn's distinctive treatment of each of the caskets reflects his understanding of their figurative power and his own interest in the blend of mystery, magic, and menace that sustains the play. Under his nuanced directorial hand, the dilemmas, the doubts, the uncertainties, and the ambiguities linger in a "residual text," reminding viewers of the subliminal mysteries that Shakespeare's play explores.

NOTES

1. *The Merchant of Venice*, DVD, prod. Chris Hunt and Richard Price, dir. Trevor Nunn (2001; Chatsworth, CA: Image Entertainment, 2004). See "Trevor Nunn," http://pro.imdb.com/ (accessed March 19, 2004) and the Public Broadcasting System's "Essays and Interviews" at http://www.pbs.org/wgbh/masterpiece/merchant/ (accessed April 23, 2004).

2. *The Merchant of Venice*, in *The Riverside Shakespeare*, 2nd ed., ed. G. Blakemore Evans (Boston: Houghton Mifflin, 1997), 2.9.54. Subsequent references to Shakespeare's plays are from this edition and are cited parenthetically.

3. See Joan Ozark Holmer, *The Merchant of Venice: Choice, Hazard and Consequence* (New York: St. Martin's Press, 1995), ix, for a concise statement of this problem.

4. *The Merchant of Venice*, feature film, prod. Cary Brokaw and Michael Cowan, dir. Michael Radford (2004).

5. *Othello*, VHS, prod. John Bradbourne and Anthony Havelock-Allan, dir. Stuart Burge (1965; Los Angeles: Warner Studios, 1996).

6. Charles Edelman describes a similar opening for the 1963 modern dress production directed by Richard Baldridge at the University of Michigan, which affected a Federico Fellini-like *dolce vita* attitude, though, of course, Nunn moved his setting from Venice to Weimar Germany, presumably Berlin: *The Merchant of Venice*, ed. Edelman (Cambridge: Cambridge University Press, 2002), Introduction, 62.

7. Grigori Kozintsev, *King Lear: The Space of Tragedy: The Diary of a Film Director*, trans. Mary Mackintosh (Berkeley: University of California Press, 1977), 55.

8. Philip Sidney, "An Apology for Poetrie," in *Elizabethan Critical Essays*, ed. G. Gregory Smith, 2 vols. (Oxford: Oxford University Press, 1904), 1:158.

9. The printed text (Edelman) and the video text (Nunn) have been collated on the split screen of a computer monitor. Nunn's complicated transpositions, especially in the second act, make the process vulnerable to minor errors. Absolute accuracy demands participation of two researchers side by side, an arrangement I was unable to organize.

10. David Bordwell, Janet Staiger, and Kristin Thompson exhaustively define the classical Hollywood film: *The Classical Hollywood Cinema: Film Style and Mode of Production to 1960* (New York: Columbia University Press, 1985).

11. Robert Smallwood observes that Antonio looks like "a self-made provincial," which would account for his awkward "nerdy" style: "Shakespeare Performances in England, 1999," *Shakespeare Survey* 53 (2000): 268.

12. The "expressive object," somewhat analogous to the stage prop, functions like a

character in the film, a classic example being the smoking gun. See V. I. Pudovkin, *Film Technique and Film Acting*, trans. and ed. Ivor Montagu (New York: Grove Press, 1970), 143.

13. Nunn also employs this trick in his TV movie of *Othello* (DVD, prod. Greg Smith, dir. Trevor Nunn [1990; Chatsworth, CA: Image Entertainment, 2004]), where a film of smoke underscores the complexity of ferreting out true identity, of piercing through surface appearances to inner reality, when Ian McKellen as Iago intones "I am not what I am" (1.1.65). An identical trope frequently occurs in Akira Kurosawa's preoccupation with smoke, mirrors, and haze, in *Rashomon* (1950), *Throne of Blood* (1957), and *The Bad Sleep Well* (1960). See also Yoshio Arai, "Kurosawa's Shakespeare Films," *Journal of the Faculty of Letters, Komazawa University*, December 1997, 1–36. For many years, I have owed a debt to Professor Arai for his help with Japanese film.

14. *The Merchant of Venice*, ed. Edelman, Appendix 2, 265. Edelman's commentary on this episode in Nunn's production is definitive.

15. Ben Jonson, *Bartholomew Fair*, in *Ben Jonson*, ed. C. H. Herford, Percy Simpson, and Evelyn Simpson, 11 vols. (Oxford: Clarendon Press, 1925–52), 6:19–141.

16. *The Merchant of Venice*, ed. Edelman, 84–85.

17. *The Merchant of Venice*, VHS, prod. Cecil Clarke, dir. John Sichel (1969; Santa Monica, CA: Artisan Entertainment, 1999). A television version of Jonathan Miller's 1970 staging for the National Theatre at the Old Vic, with Laurence Olivier, Joan Plowright, and Jeremy Brett. First distributed as a video in Great Britain in 1974 by Precision Video; previously distributed in the USA as *The Merchant of Venice videorecording/ITC* presents a Jonathan Miller Production by LIVE Home Video of Van Nuys, California (1993).

18. James Shapiro, *Shakespeare and the Jews* (New York: Columbia University Press, 1996), 32. As suggested in an unpublished paper delivered by Janet Adelman at the 2004 New Orleans Shakespeare Association of America meeting, one means of ethnic identification would lie in looking for evidence of circumcision, though this could hardly be carried out on stage! The real point seems to be the overlapping ethos of puritanical Christians and Jews.

The Lady Vanishes or,
the Incredible Shrinking Gertrude

THE EXISTENCE OF VIDEO PRODUCTIONS MARKS A NEW EPOCH IN THE study of Shakespeare's plays in performance, especially plays for which many different versions are already available, such as *Hamlet*. Even if stage productions of *Hamlet* are "always going on somewhere,"[1] their virtues and defects fade quickly from memory except for the few details preserved in such records as reviews, memoirs, biographies, and performance studies.[2] Videotape and DVD are, in contrast, nearly permanent, making the details of performance easily available for leisurely study and heightening their influence as models for future performers. I will consider four such productions of *Hamlet*,[3] produced over a span of nearly fifty years, which, in their variety and despite their shortcomings,[4] offer a fair sense of the range of character readings and performance choices allowed by the text. That range of choices is evident for Hamlet and every other principal character except Gertrude. Her character and importance are uniformly diminished, despite clear textual signals for her to be an independent moving force in crucial situations. In consequence, film/video renditions all tend to ignore Gertrude in the same way, while admiring Hamlet in many different ways. The resulting video-world orthodoxy of dismissiveness toward an important female character should not go unnoticed.[5]

I am an unrepentant admirer of Gertrude, for what I think of as her unappreciated qualities of boldness, imagination, and dramatic importance. Yet if the idea of *"Hamlet* without the prince" is proverbially unthinkable, the importance of Gertrude remains dishearteningly problematic. It seems only too thinkable to treat her as largely a device for developing the "big" characters, Hamlet and Claudius. Her small number of lines, only 157, is no measure of her importance, and Marvin Rosenberg warns us not to think of her as weak, passive, or lifeless: "Gertrude needs an identity that interacts positively with the other characters and the court. In pivotal situations, speaking or silent, she

Eileen Herlie as Gertrude and Laurence Olivier as Hamlet in the 1948 film version of *Hamlet,* directed by Laurence Olivier. Photo courtesy of MPTV.net.

must affect the action."[6] We can see that identity unfold in a special way over the course of seven scenes, not through words alone but through a repeated pattern consisting of situation, words, and accompanying movement. The full "Gertrude pattern" consists of her (a) encounter with discord, present or potential; (b) intervention, usually physical; and (c) conciliatory but false statement of the facts, intended to restore harmony. Not all of these elements are obvious every time; sometimes the situation is most important, sometimes the false statement, sometimes the intervention; this pattern is one that works cumulatively to define her character and to give meaning to what earlier seemed either obscure or insignificant.

As a group, the video versions under consideration here fail to satisfy the test advanced by Jim Lusardi and June Schlueter, who tell us to evaluate performances of Shakespeare's plays by asking "Does it read?" Does the "written text and its realization in performance at one and the same time" achieve a coherent "relationship between signals in the text and their translation into representation on the stage?"[7] "Reading" in this sense means close reading of both the text and then the performance, in order to form an opinion as to the nature of the signals and then of the representation. Here, it requires a brief detour to explain the textual pattern against which I will "read" the video productions.

In adopting a "Gertrude pattern" of my own invention as the standard for "signals in the text," I am not claiming that it is the exclusive or best reading. I maintain only two things: first, the pattern derives exclusively from the text, independent of extrinsic information or theory. Second, its repeated occurrence in different situations from beginning to end suggests that it expresses something fundamental, sufficient to give Gertrude a style and character of her own. This makes it useful for studying otherwise dissimilar productions, in order to uncover common biases in the matter of translating from written text to representation on stage. Note that "useful" does not mean exclusive or reductive, nor does it require any particular view of Gertrude. It leaves an actor with freedom of interpretation; she may be a loving wife or mother, sensual, repressed, authoritative, morally dense, or anything else. This constant, however, holds: in the presence of social discord or awkwardness, it is Gertrude's characteristic to respond quickly if not wisely to resolve it. Her response takes the form of a physical and verbal intervention, during which she typically restates the facts in a way that effaces the reason for conflict and substitutes an uncontroversial alternative. Indeed, the practiced ease by which she restores harmony time and again may explain why it is so easy to overlook her part in doing so.

The first scene to consider is Gertrude's first appearance, in 1.2. Claudius has just refused to let Hamlet return to Wittenberg, but he tries to soften the disappointment with affectionate words, "my cousin Hamlet, and my son," to which Hamlet's answer, "A little more than kin, and less than kind," is "pure rebuff."[8] When Claudius follows patiently with "How is it that the clouds still hang on you?", Hamlet's reply, "Not so, my lord, I am too much in the sun,"[9] is equally offensive, and the king often shows his displeasure openly.[10] Generations of performers have read the scene as a growing crisis, at which Gertrude is the "one person . . . able to avert a clash . . ."[11] The situation and dialogue call for Gertrude to move toward Hamlet, as she generally does, and then convince him to remain by speaking of her own prayers for him to stay in Denmark. However, the king must have already made his irritation clear if her movement is to be seen as an intervention "to avert a clash."

The video versions all do the opposite, excluding any need for intervention by minimizing the grossly offensive nature of Hamlet's replies. Consequently, all their Gertrudes are left with a choice of two passive roles: either to play the loving mother speaking what she feels or to play the dutiful wife speaking in support of her royal husband. In the BBC production, Derek Jacobi's Hamlet's "too much in the sun" reply leaves Patrick Stewart's Claudius unruffled and Claire Bloom's Gertrude passive; she remains seated and static next to him, and it is Hamlet who approaches her rather than the other way round. Only when Claudius rises to assure Hamlet that he is the "most immediate to the throne" (1.2.109) does Gertrude, clinging to the king, rise to add her own request in support. The closing insult to Claudius in Hamlet's consent to obey *her* passes unremarked, and mother and son embrace and kiss.

In Laurence Olivier's film, Herlie's Gertrude is more demonstrative toward Olivier's Hamlet, reflecting the director's view that the mother-son relationship was strictly Oedipal.[12] In an implausible reversal of the protocol of rank and dignity, both king and queen rise from their thrones to approach the kneeling Hamlet and address him, Basil Sydney's Claudius facing him from the right, Gertrude behind him with hands affectionately on his shoulders. What follows next, and would require movement on stage, is accomplished instead by film technique. All three are seen in head and shoulders close-up, so when Gertrude makes her deeply felt plea for Hamlet to stay, the focus simply shifts to her; she slides over somewhat between the two to caress Hamlet's face and, when he accedes, kisses him on the lips at length.

The Tony Richardson production conveys a similar effect. It emphasizes the mutual affection between king and queen and, in disregarding the patent insolence of Nicol Williamson's Hamlet in his replies to the king, deprives Judy Parfitt's Gertrude of any motive to intervene except to support her husband. Kenneth Branagh's production, like the BBC version, cuts relatively little from the text but follows the others in disregarding all indications that Gertrude's intervention averted a crisis. Adopting Olivier's odd conceit that the king and queen would leave their thrones of state in order to approach Hamlet, Branagh has Jacobi's Claudius and Julie Christie's Gertrude move in concert to kneel submissively before addressing him, she from the right and he from the left, and their symmetry of movement confirms their unity of purpose.

The meeting with Rosencrantz and Guildenstern in 2.2 presents a socially awkward moment rather than a conflict, but another opportunity for Gertrude to notice, step in quickly, and smooth things over. As the two men take their leave, Claudius salutes them, "Thanks, Rosencrantz and gentle Guildenstern," and Gertrude famously reverses the order, "Thanks, Guildenstern and gentle Rosencrantz" (2.2.33–34). It is generally assumed that the king got the names of these two nonentities wrong, and Gertrude stepped in graciously to rectify his error; but another view is that she is engaging in an elegant royal courtesy to ensure that each is accorded equal precedence.[13] In either case, she has noticed an awkward lapse in decorum and moved immediately to correct it. Her natural gesture, to move toward the courtiers and away from the king, draws their attention to her. It also connects her behavior here with the earlier scene and begins to build a picture of Gertrude as an individual with a style of her own and a natural intervener in awkward situations.

The scene is omitted by Olivier, perhaps for its lack of any Oedipal relevance. The BBC production shows the king and the two courtiers talking in close profile—here and always, a camera technique that reduces that sense of movement through space through which an intervention becomes manifest—with Gertrude facing the camera in the background, slightly out of focus. When the time comes, she reverses the order of names without appearing to correct the king, but the young men make it clear that something awkward has been resolved by responding with titters of gratitude. Richardson uses the scene to emphasize Gertrude's sensuality, as she and Claudius receive the two courtiers while they sit in bed eating away happily at what looks like pieces of chicken. When she corrects the king in the matter of names, she does so casually but not out of concern for the young men's feelings. Branagh's production is not much different, as Gertrude greets the two with extended hands in the manner of a gracious hostess. At the end of their interview, she and Claudius leave hand in hand walking briskly ahead of them, and she corrects Claudius with wifely good humor while ignoring them.

Polonius' instruction to Gertrude just before Hamlet arrives in her chamber draws further attention to her penchant for intervention: "Tell him his pranks have been too broad to bear with, / And that your Grace hath screen'd and stood between / Much heat and him" (3.4.2–4).[14] Nothing so far makes it credible at this point for Gertrude to remind Hamlet of her steadfast loyalty to him; on the contrary, the whole tenor of Hamlet's complaint against her is the accusation that her "[o'erhasty] marriage" (2.2.57) to Claudius was in some way grossly disloyal to him.[15] For Polonius' advice to make sense, as Gertrude seems to accept, the idea of her as someone for whom the behavior described—screening and standing between, and intervening to cool the heat of discord— must already be established as so typical that the description strengthens her credibility so that Hamlet will believe what she says afterwards.

The image proposed by Polonius to Gertrude in order to disarm Hamlet is the key to understanding how her subsequent description of Polonius' death is meant to disarm Claudius, whose first words in the next scene make it clear that Gertrude has drawn his attention with her loud sighs and moans: "There's matter in these sighs, these profound heaves—/ You must translate, 'tis fit we understand them. / Where is your son?" (4.1.1–3) and then, "How does Hamlet?" (4.1.6). What she reports is notably different from what the audience just saw: "Mad as the sea and wind when both contend / Which is the mightier. In his lawless fit, / Behind the arras hearing something stir, Whips out his rapier, cries, 'A rat, a rat!' / And in this brainish apprehension kills / The unseen good old man" (4.1.7–12).

There are some who accept the report as essentially correct and credible. Others note the inaccuracies but excuse them as evidence of Gertrude's intense mental distress. Her description of Hamlet as mad has even been viewed as a denunciation and evidence of continuing loyalty to her husband.[16] However, the prevailing view is that her report is materially and intentionally inaccurate, an obvious cover-up to protect Hamlet; it follows, therefore, that Gertrude has taken the initiative. The whole performance, including her sighs and heaves, must be a quickly conceived device for getting to Claudius first and privately with her own sanitized version of the facts, before he sees the body and draws his own conclusions. And so the situation resolves quickly into the familiar pattern: a scene of imminent discord, followed by intervention on her part, and accompanied by a substitute version of the facts.

However one wishes to explain it, her story is clearly neither complete nor accurate, much less a fair summary of what just happened on stage. It does not report that Hamlet thought or hoped that his victim was Claudius: "is it the King?" (3.4.26) or describe his reaction after seeing whom he killed: "heaven hath pleas'd it so / To punish me with this, and this with me" (4.1.173–74). It disregards Hamlet's convincing insistence that his madness was feigned, that he was "mad in craft" (3.4.188) but completely sane in fact and willing to be tested for it. It omits both his accusation of murder against Claudius and his warning to Gertrude to keep quiet for her own safety. Nor do we hear how she confessed her own sense of guilt and asked Hamlet for instructions what to do next. Even her report of Hamlet's "A rat, a rat!" distorts and sanitizes what the audience just heard him say: "How now? A rat? Dead, for a ducat, dead! . . . is it the King?" (3.4.24, 26).

Gertrude's capacity for quick thinking deceit is by now evident, and the attentive reader can no longer afford to take her words at face value without exercising critical judgment; later events will only confirm the importance of attending closely to what she says. And now that we know Gertrude can be devious, shouldn't we reconsider her supposed first act "prayers" for Hamlet to remain in Denmark? Would Gertrude have been hoping for Hamlet to stay while believing that his foul mood was directed at her and fueled by the "o'erhasty marriage" to Claudius? Looking back critically and in context, we see how implausible those prayers are, no more than an excuse of the moment to justify her intervention in the clash between her husband and son. Against all odds, the video versions are in agreement here, but not in a positive way. They resist every textual indication that Gertrude is quick-witted, deceptive, independent, or anything more than a dutiful spouse.

Olivier and Richardson, with their Oedipal and sensualist ideas about Gertrude, find nothing useful in her narration of Polonius' death, and both omit it. Gertrude's straightforward report of the killing in the BBC production has been interpreted as evidence of her ambivalence in the conflict between two loyalties,[17] but I see no on-screen indications to support the idea. Branagh introduces a bit of stage business to negate any suggestion of Gertrude's independence or reduced loyalty to Claudius. When the king closes the scene—"Come, Gertrude, we'll call up our wisest friends / And let them know both what we mean to do / And what's untimely done . . . O, come away! / My soul is full of discord and dismay" (4.1.38–40, 44–45)—he hugs her with deep emotion, and she responds to him at length, with apparently sincere affection.

The most extreme breach of decorum to confront Gertrude is Laertes' rebellion, when he breaks angrily into the royal presence, often with sword drawn. When a messenger arrives a moment earlier to warn of the insurrection, she is the first to react: "How cheerfully on the false trail they cry! / O, this is counter, you false Danish dogs!" (4.5.110–11). Then, when Laertes bursts in, she is the only one to speak "Calmly, good Laertes" (4.5.117) or take action to intercept his advance, as indicated by Claudius six lines later, "Let him go, Gertrude, do not fear our person: / There's such divinity doth hedge a king / That treason can but peep to what it would, / Acts little of his will. Tell me, Laertes, / Why thou are thus incens'd.—Let him go, Gertrude" (4.5.123–27). Whatever manner Gertrude adopts toward Laertes, be it imperious, soothing, or anything else, the important fact is that the stage direction implied by Claudius' words requires her to have intervened between the king and Laertes.[18]

It may be attractive here for dramatic effect to show Laertes as posing a clear threat of murderous violence, but not for textual reasons. Nothing in the text requires Laertes to brandish a drawn sword, although he often does, and nothing in Gertrude's earlier behavior suggests she possesses the sort of physical boldness required to subdue an armed man. More than most readings, Branagh's staging of the moment fails the Lusardi-Schlueter condition that it *read*, that it fairly express what the text requires. All the text gives the actors to work with is the situation; and the bare fact of Laertes' bold intrusion is shocking enough, as an inexcusable display of lèse-majesté.[19] That breach of decorum is, setting aside the small matter of capital treason, quite enough to stir Gertrude into decisive action. If the story of Polonius' death is the clearest example of outright fabrication by Gertrude, this is the clearest example of physical intervention in the context of the "Gertrude pattern." And it is the pattern, in turn, that shows her intervention here to be characteristic and inevitable rather than unaccountable and incongruous.

Except for the Olivier production, which omits the confrontation, the screen renditions depict Gertrude as a bravely loyal wife but not much more. In the BBC production, she steps forward quickly but regally to rest her hands on Laertes' shoulders, restraining him gently at first and then more forcefully as he hears that his father is dead. Her intervention is bolder in the Richardson production, where she steps forward to bar the way of an armed Laertes. Then, as Laertes and the king confront each other in profile and we see her between them facing the camera, Laertes' mood of outrage dissipates almost magically. By the time Gertrude denies that Claudius is responsible for Polonius' death—"But not by him" (4.5.129)—there is little sense that she is needed to keep order. The Branagh film (using a rare long shot of the kind that would have made Gertrude's interventions noticeable) shows Laertes burst violently into the royal presence and charge down a long and empty room, with sword drawn and pointed at Claudius. Gertrude leaps forward boldly to seize Laertes' arm and, although her action is not especially muscular, it suffices to halt his charge, just as in the Richardson production. She remains between him and the king, although now no longer required to prevent violence, and the dialogue between Laertes and Claudius is simply allowed to proceed.

Gertrude's lyric and graphic (and often tedious) description of Ophelia's drowning is so powerful and well known that it is easy to enjoy it out of all context, as an isolated set piece. However, the situation in which she delivers it shows it to be something different, and another example of the "Gertrude pattern." It is clear from the stage direction "Enter QUEEN" that she has broken in on a conspiratorial Claudius and Laertes, and their discomfiture at her intrusion is sometimes shown on stage by having one of them tuck the telltale poison hurriedly out of sight.[20] What are the signals to be "read" in this situation, as Gertrude delivers her speech?

To her eyes, the scene itself must appear distinctly ominous, not because Claudius and Laertes are in postures of guilt or confusion—that is a performance choice the text allows but does not demand—but because of their surprising intimacy. A short time ago, it was all Gertrude could do to restrain Laertes from attacking Claudius, and now she finds the two of them conferring privately on some matter of shared interest. Knowing what she does, one thing is apparent: any rapprochement between them is sure to be bad for Hamlet. Something has to be done, and intervention is what Gertrude does best. In this case, her need is to separate two people who are probably planning harm to her son and to come up with a story that will not only allow her to move them apart but will also disguise the incendiary fact of Ophelia's suicide. It may well appear that her sudden flight into lyricism is out of keeping with what we know of her but, read in light of the situation and with the "Gertrude pattern" in mind, her great set piece appears surely to be a brilliant and extemporaneous fabrication.

The improbable vividness of her description makes it seem to be an eyewitness report, at least to those who take it for the truth. And this, in turn, has led many to denounce Gertrude for having watched the girl drown without trying to rescue her, a distracting issue some actors try to negate by arriving wet or bedraggled from their supposed rescue efforts. Other productions show Gertrude to be working through her own shock at the terrible event. Many Gertrudes, paying closer attention to the text as a whole, signal that they are obviously fabricating the whole story, "disguising an action that we will learn in the graveyard scene was almost certainly a suicide."[21] On stage, she generally moves slowly toward Laertes, to comfort and commiserate. But as simply another spur-of-the-moment fabrication in aid of another intervention, the distracting style and length of her story are not a dramatic weakness but a clever device that enables Gertrude to control the scene and give her time to move between the two as she speaks. If she approaches Laertes, her intervention will seem a gesture of sympathy and comfort; if she moves alongside the king, it emphasizes her queenly status and lends royal authority to a report that we will all soon discover to be false.

With all the variety shown by their Hamlets and other male characters, none of the video productions even hints at Gertrude's capacity to take the initiative or control events. Olivier continues to erase her when he can by reducing the report of Ophelia's drowning to a voiceover and then silently confirms the truth of her story by showing the drowning on-screen. He even relocates the conspiracy to follow her report, inverting the crisis-intervention sequence that is central to Gertrude's role and isolating her report from the sequences of onstage events. The BBC, Richardson, and Branagh productions all show the king drinking amicably with Laertes at a small table, but Richardson is the only one to emphasize the conspiratorial nature of their meeting; his Claudius and Laertes stop talking abruptly when Gertrude arrives. None of the Gertrudes shows any surprise at their new intimacy, nor any intention other than to tell the sad news. Branagh even follows Olivier in discouraging any reflection on the truth of her report, by showing the drowning take place as she describes it.

In the text, but not the screen versions, Gertrude and her familiar pattern are much in evidence during the last act, twice in the graveyard scene and again at the fatal duel. First, Laertes rails at the officiating priest for curtailing his sister's funeral rites: "I tell thee, churlish priest, / A minist'ring angel shall my sister be / When thou liest howling" (5.1.240–42). The altercation continues until Gertrude steps forward to declare how she had hoped for Ophelia to marry Hamlet: "Sweets to the sweet, farewell! / I hop'd thou shouldst have been my Hamlet's wife. / I thought thy bride-bed to have deck'd, sweet maid, / And not have strew'd thy grave" (5.1.243–46). Because the priest drops out of sight at this point without explanation, the implied stage direction is for Gertrude to step forward between him and Laertes, distracting the one and allowing the other to retire into the darkness. And, if we detect the "Gertrude pattern" in the situation and intervention, it makes sense to ask if her words are not just one more fabrication. After all, how could she possibly have hoped for a marriage between her son and Ophelia without Polonius or Laertes knowing? How could Polonius, as chief royal advisor, have been so ignorant of the queen's favor toward Ophelia as to forbid her to see Hamlet or describe him to Gertrude as "a prince out of [Ophelia's] star" (2.2.141)? Would Laertes also have had no inkling that royal good will had made Hamlet's courtship respectable? Surely, this is another on-the-spot invention, designed only to keep things from getting out of hand (and to prevent Laertes from realizing that her touching portrayal of the drowning as a sad accident was false from start to finish).

A second crisis breaks out moments later, with Hamlet and Laertes at each other's throats at (or in) Ophelia's grave. She and the king intervene quickly, but, when Hamlet resumes his verbal assault, "I'll rant as well as thou" (5.1.294), the Q2 and F versions differ importantly in describing the action. In Q2, the queen, and in F (and Q1) the king, delivers the important lines "This is mere madness, / And [thus] a while the fit will work on him; / Anon, as patient as the female dove, / When that her golden couplets are disclosed, / His silence will sit drooping" (5.1. 284–88). The Gertrude who heard Hamlet's assurances of sanity in the closet scene and then promised to do as he instructed surely doesn't believe Hamlet is mad. But if we remember that Gertrude is intervening to quiet a brawl, a *false* statement is exactly what we should expect from her. In other words, the Q2 version conforms perfectly to the "Gertrude pattern" and helps her to stay in character throughout. Admittedly, there is nothing intrinsically wrong with the F version, which may be taken as evidence of Gertrude's earlier success in convincing Claudius that Hamlet killed Polonius in a fit of madness.[22]

The video productions give minor attention to these details during the graveyard scene. The BBC Gertrude strews flowers in the grave and speaks "This is mere madness" but without a hint of intervention between Laertes and either the priest or Hamlet. Olivier's production makes little of the flower strewing and gives "This is mere madness" to

Claudius. Oddly, his Gertrude places herself in front of Laertes in a real gesture of intervention, but her part has been already so far reduced that there is nothing with which to connect the gesture. Richardson deflects any interest in Gertrude's behavior by reducing the episode between Laertes and the priest to spoken words without showing them in confrontation, and he cuts "This is mere madness." Branagh preserves the line for Gertrude, but nothing in her delivery or the circumstances makes it purposeful.

The climactic fencing match displays the "Gertrude pattern," in circumstances like its first occurrence, as a grand public spectacle with king and queen in state and the court in attendance, all to the sound of trumpet fanfares. Claudius offers the poisoned goblet after Hamlet scores the first hit, but Hamlet turns it down unceremoniously: "I'll play this bout first, set it by awhile." Gertrude apparently sees a breach of decorum here, a repetition of Hamlet's public bad manners in the first act. The ceremonial presentation of the goblet earlier, amid the sounds of trumpets, drums, and guns, to say nothing of the precious pearl thrown in for good measure, surely demanded at least a sip, if only for form's sake. So when Hamlet scores the next hit, Gertrude takes matters into her own hands with a last, and fatal, intervention: "He's fat, and scant of breath. / Here, Hamlet, take my napkin, rub thy brows. / The Queen carouses to thy fortune, Hamlet" (5.2.287–89). And she drinks. Reading the text with critical attention, mustn't we suspect that Hamlet is neither fat nor scant of breath and that this is one more fabrication to accompany the last intervention? Hamlet is so little in need of refreshment and so eager to get back to the match that he rejects her offer, too—"I dare not drink yet, madam; by and by" (5.2.293)—and turns to tease Laertes: "You do but dally" (5.2.297). In fact, he has "been in continual practice" (5.2.211) since Laertes left for France more than four months earlier, and, as we see, he never loses a bout.

At this point, Gertrude takes the goblet meant for Hamlet but embarrassingly untouched by him and, reconceiving the king's treacherous offer as a general invitation to drink up, she drinks it herself. Her last intervention is the most promptly disastrous of them all. It places her fatally "Between the pass and fell incensed points / Of mighty opposites" (5.2.61–62) through an impulsive but thoroughly characteristic action through which the whole pattern culminates by uniting Gertrude's story with the well-recognized thematic pattern of self-destruction by one's own device.

The video productions again uniformly reduce Gertrude's role to a passive one, principally by ignoring the discourtesy inherent in Hamlet's refusal of the king's goblet. Hamlet rejects it politely in all the videos, leaving Gertrude with nothing to smooth over and turning her decision to drink into a random stroke of bad luck, with no dramatic justification beyond making the tragic disaster as complete as possible. In Olivier's production, with Gertrude's prior opportunities for independent action all cut or negated, she shows her loyalty to Hamlet with a pair of loving (but seemly) kisses, presumably in furtherance of the Oedipal reading. Shakespeare gives Gertrude something consequential to say as the poison overcomes her, but Olivier perversely takes it away from her. He cuts her last speech to end with the conveniently Oedipal "O my dear Hamlet" (5.2.309) and transfers to Laertes (in slightly altered form) her dramatically important revelation of the king's perfidy: "No, no, the drink, the drink . . . I am pois'ned" (5.2.309–10). In Branagh's production, there is at least some notice of the rejected goblet, but it is Claudius and not Gertrude who sees that things are going wrong. He is disconcerted and troubled after Hamlet declines the drink, and he remains so as the bouts continue, while Gertrude follows Hamlet's successes with increasing pleasure and throws him a loving kiss. When Gertrude takes up the goblet to drink, Claudius grips it firmly and forces her to pull it from him with force; she stares into his face with an intensity that looks like a clear statement of independence on her part, but what it reveals is impossible to say.

There is a fault line that separates stage performances from screen renditions, to which Gertrude's character has proved especially vulnerable because of the extent to which her onstage movement helps define who she is and how she affects the action. The stage accommodates large movements across open space, the dramatic choreography of exterior and social relationships, and it is simply one technique in the complex art of stagecraft of which Shakespeare was a master. The close-ups and camera techniques of film and video emphasize interior and psychological dimensions of character and relationship. To the extent that Gertrude's character is bound up in her willingness to take the initiative, in her interventions, and in her physical movements in space, it is not even visible in the body of work contained on film and video. In consequence, the screen productions of *Hamlet* most likely to be seen by the public contain undesirable barriers to a full appreciation of the nature and importance of her role.

NOTES

1. *Hamlet*, Shakespeare in Production, ed. Robert Hapgood (Cambridge: Cambridge University Press, 1999), 1.

2. For accounts of various productions of *Hamlet*, see Marvin Rosenberg, *The Masks of Hamlet* (Newark: University of Delaware Press, 1992); Raymond Mander and Joe Mitchenson, *Hamlet Through the Ages: A Pictorial Record from 1709*, 2nd ed., ed. Herbert Marshall (London: Rockliff, 1952); and *Hamlet*, ed. Hapgood.

3. *Hamlet*, VHS, prod. and dir. Laurence Olivier (1948; Santa Monica, CA: MGM Home Entertainment, 2000), with Olivier as Hamlet, Eileen Herlie as Gertrude, Basil Sydney as Claudius, and Jean Simmons as Ophelia; *Hamlet*, VHS, prod. Hans Gottschalk et al., dir. Tony Richardson (1969; Culver City, CA: Columbia/Tristar Home Video, 1998), with Nicol Williamson as Hamlet, Judy Parfitt as Gertrude, Anthony Hopkins as Claudius, and Marianne Faithful as Ophelia; *Hamlet*, VHS, prod. Cedric Messina, dir. Rodney Bennett (1980; New York: Ambrose Video, 1987), with Derek Jacobi as Hamlet, Claire Bloom as Gertrude, Patrick Stewart as Claudius, and Lalla Ward as Ophelia; *Hamlet*, VHS, prod. David Barron, dir. Kenneth Branagh (1996; Beverly Hills, CA: Castle Rock Entertainment, 2000), with Branagh as Hamlet, Julie Christie as Gertrude, Jacobi as Claudius, and Kate Winslet as Ophelia. Limitations of space force me to ignore other versions available on video including Grigori Kozintsev's Russian film *Gamlet* (1964), with Innokenti Smoktunovsky as Hamlet; Franco Zeffirelli's film, with Mel Gibson as Hamlet and Glenn Close as Gertrude (1990); the video version of John Gielgud's stage production (1964), with Richard Burton as Hamlet and Herlie as Gertrude (as she was in Olivier's film); and Michael Almereyda's movie (2000), with Ethan Hawke as Hamlet and Diane Venora as Gertrude.

4. Olivier's famous voiceover—"This is the story of a man who could not make up his mind"—has established Hamlet, however wrongly, as a universal icon of indecision. A newspaper reporter summarizing the 2004 World Series referred to a player's "moment of Hamlet-like indecision on the basepath": *New York Times*, October 31, 2004, Week in Review section.

5. Ellen J. O'Brien, "Revision by Excision: Rewriting Gertrude," *Shakespeare Survey* 45 (1993): 27–35. This study focuses on eighteenth- and nineteenth-century stage productions with particular reference to the way promptbooks either cut or disregard textual indications, such as the manner in which individuals address one another and stage directions for entrances and exits, that reveal allegiances between and among Gertrude, Claudius, Hamlet, and Laertes. Despite using different methods and materials than here, she also concludes that producers and directors have regularly overruled Shakespeare in deciding what to make of Gertrude.

6. Rosenberg, *The Masks of Hamlet*, 71.

7. See James P. Lusardi and June Schlueter, *Reading Shakespeare in Performance: King Lear* (Madison, NJ: Fairleigh Dickinson University Press, 1991), 17; Maurice Charney, "*Hamlet* without Words," in *Shakespeare's More Than Words Can Witness: Essays on Visual and Non-verbal Enactment in the Plays*, ed. Sidney Homan (Lewisburg, PA: Bucknell University Press, 1980), 24, quoted in Lusardi and Schlueter, *Reading Shakespeare in Performance: King Lear*, 15.

8. Rosenberg, *The Masks of Hamlet*, 191.

9. *Hamlet*, in *The Riverside Shakespeare*, 2nd ed., ed. G. Blakemore Evans (Boston: Houghton Mifflin, 1997), 1.2.64–67. Subsequent references to Shakespeare's plays are from this edition and are cited parenthetically.

10. *Hamlet*, ed. Hapgood, 112 n. 79b, 113 n. 94b, 113 n. 106b–8a.

11. Rosenberg, *The Masks of Hamlet*, 200.

12. Olivier has stated his lifelong adherence to Ernest Jones' reading: *Confessions of An Actor: An Autobiography* (New York: Simon and Schuster, 1982), 102.

13. *Hamlet*, ed. Hapgood, 152 n. 34.

14. Rosenberg remarks that, if Gertrude has secretly been defending Hamlet against a raging Claudius, "she has been more mother to Hamlet than Hamlet knows." By emphasizing the absence of textual support for Gertrude to protest her loyalty to Hamlet, he supports my belief that the statement must be plausible for other reasons: *The Masks of Hamlet*, 649.

15. I have argued elsewhere that, under widely known legal principles, Gertrude defeated Hamlet's right of inheritance when she married Claudius during the forty-day period she could retain possession of her husband's lands, before selecting and moving to her dower estate. See J. Anthony Burton, "An Unrecognized Theme in *Hamlet:* Lost Inheritance and Claudius's Marriage to Gertrude," *The Shakespeare Newsletter* 50.3 (2000): 71, 76, 78, 82; 50.4 (2000–2001): 103–4, 106; and "Laertes's Rebellion: Further Aspects of Inheritance Law in *Hamlet*," *The Shakespeare Newsletter* 52.3 (2002): 63, 66, 78, 80, 88, 90.

16. Rosenberg, *The Masks of Hamlet*, 727–28.

17. *Hamlet*, ed. Hapgood, 220 n. 7–12.

18. It is tempting at this point to wonder what to make of Claudius' serene confidence in his personal safety. If Gertrude's decisive action has blunted the immediate threat of violence, then he seems to have waited behind Gertrude until she stopped Laertes' advance. Perhaps his "divinity" speech is meant to be taken for hypocrisy— coming as it does from a regicide—rather than an authentic belief that his kingship could count on divine protection.

19. Burton, "Hamlet, Osric, and the Duel," *Shakespeare Bulletin* 2.10 (1984): 5–7, 22– 25. The point is made there that, in rebuking Laertes, Claudius' description of the rebellion as "giant-like" immediately characterized it as an act of lèse-majesté.

20. Rosenberg, *The Masks of Hamlet*, 822.

21. Ibid., 823.

22. Hapgood interprets Q2 as a show of maternal affection and F as an intervention by the king: *Hamlet*, 260 n. 251b–5a. In my view, Q2 is just as much an intervention as F, even if Gertrude is motivated by maternal affection.

Childhood Dreams and Nightmares:
Children in Productions of
A Midsummer Night's Dream

Miranda Johnson-Haddad

OVER FORTY-FIVE CHILDREN APPEAR IN SHAKESPEARE'S PLAYS, BUT I am interested here in children who never appear at all—or rather, they appear in production but not in Shakespeare's text. It is not unusual to see extratextual children appear onstage and function as active presences in a production.[1] Some of these "shadow children"[2] are characters who are mentioned in the text but whose physical presence onstage is not dictated: for example, we often see more than one of Macduff's children during the murder scene. By far the most familiar and explicit of this type of shadow child is the Indian Boy in *A Midsummer Night's Dream*. Puck tells a wandering fairy in act 2, scene 1 that Oberon, the fairy king, is furious with his queen, Titania, "Because that she as her attendant hath / A lovely boy stolen from an Indian king; / She never had so sweet a changeling."[3] Examples abound, both onstage throughout the centuries and in films, of productions in which the Indian prince makes an appearance, though often a brief one, when no such literal appearance is described in the play. Similarly, many directors over the years have chosen to cast some or even all of the fairies as children.[4] In most twentieth-century stage productions, however, particularly those since the 1970s, the use of children in these roles, and the appearance of the Indian Boy, have been rare.[5]

More recently, at least two directors have experimented, one on film and one on stage, with including another type of shadow child—an extratextual child who is neither the changeling or a fairy—who manages to be simultaneously outside of the action of *Dream* and integral to it. Such is the case with Adrian Noble's film (1996).[6] Although largely based on his earlier stage version, in which no child appeared, the film version introduces a child who becomes the central unifying figure, the only character who exists in both the human and the fairy realms as the same person. A similar choice was made by Sands Hall, the director of the Lake Tahoe Shakespeare Festival Summer 2003 production of the play. These and other recent productions seem to be using the presence of a child to suggest the roles that fantasy and imagination may play in *Dream*. In this essay, I will be focusing on these two productions within the context of twentieth-century film renditions of the play, in which children have tended to figure prominently. In doing so, I hope to demonstrate that the more recent trend (within roughly the last decade) toward using extratextual children in productions of *Dream* appears to be going beyond the familiar uses to suggest a more specific link among children, their imaginations, and the adults in their lives.

As early as Max Reinhardt (1935),[7] screen versions include representation of the Indian Boy, a practice that continues in the Noble and Michael Hoffman (1999)[8] films. In Reinhardt's version, Titania's many attendants include children as well as adults. We see her embracing a richly attired and Caucasian-appearing Indian Boy (after all, this was the 1930s), and a young Mickey Rooney plays a childlike Puck. Throughout the film, she is surrounded by a lavish train that includes many children, but they do little besides follow her around. Over thirty years later, in Peter Hall's 1968 film treatment,[9] children are featured throughout, although the Indian Boy himself does not make an appearance. The first child we see in the film is the First Fairy, played by Clare Dench. The child tosses silvery glitter into the air and talks playfully with Ian Holm's Puck throughout their scene together; at times, she giggles at what he says or tickles his nose with a spray of roses. Occasionally, she shows concern or even fear at Puck's words: Oberon's name causes her smile to vanish and an anxious expression to appear on her face, as does Puck's account of the ale pouring down the "withered dewlap" of the old wife as a result of his antics.

The trains of both Oberon and Titania are composed entirely of children in Hall's film; none of the fairies is an adult. Dench's almost bare breasts, her nipples tastefully covered with leaflike pasties, may suggest Titania's maternal as well as her erotic nature,[10] and, indeed, she is frequently surrounded by a crowd of children. She delivers her 2.2 speech ("Come, now a roundel and a fairy song . . ." [2.2.1–8]) to this crowd and the children "pipe" on reed pipes and sing a version of the "Philomel" song that is alternately frantic and harmonious.[11] At the gentler harmonies, they stroke Titania's hair, but then they surprise her with sudden louder and faster singing at "Weaving spiders, come not here" (2.2.20); Titania smiles fondly after her initial startled reaction. The children place leaves on her sleeping form as Oberon and his fairies, all played by young boys, hide in the forest and observe. In their wildness and woodland skills, they recall the Lost Boys of *Peter Pan;* they gaze resentfully at Titania and her attendants. (Are they also, like the Lost Boys, longing for a mother?) The fact that Oberon's attendants are all boys in this production offers a possible explanation of why he is so eager to obtain the changeling child from Titania and make him "Knight of his train, to trace the forests wild" (2.1.25) — a desire that is otherwise open to a variety of interpretations. The boys are not above rough play: Titania's sentinel is dispatched with a blow to the head by one of Oberon's boys, thereby enabling Oberon to approach Titania's bed with the love juice. Titania's fairy children, however, are a gentler crew: they clearly do not like Bottom's jokes about their names and are not used to such crude humor. Nevertheless, at the conclusion of the film, Titania's fairies and Oberon's Lost Boys all join with Puck, Titania, and Oberon for the final scene. This time, they all sing the harmonious "Philomel" together as they hold lighted tapers and listen attentively to Oberon's blessing before scampering throughout the house to bless all the lovers. Hall's treatment clearly suggests that not only Oberon and Titania but their entire respective retinues of Lost Boys and fairy children (and the opposing sensibilities that they may represent) have been reconciled by the play's end.

A similar reconciliation takes place at the conclusion of the 1981 BBC version directed by Elijah Moshinsky,[12] in which the presence of children is even more pronounced. Nearly all of Titania's fairies are children, who range in age from toddlers to teenagers. They constantly hover around Titania (Helen Mirren), who is here unmistakably maternal. She holds the sobbing Indian Boy protectively in her arms, defending him from Peter McEnery's sinister Oberon as she delivers the "forgeries of jealousy" speech (2.1.81–117), during which she is surrounded by children, some of whom cling fearfully to her, some of whom smirk at Oberon. She delivers the speech about the child's mother directly to the boy, playfully holding him on her lap facing her and bouncing him gently up and down and then embracing him.[13] When she goes to her bower to sleep, she kisses each fairy goodnight and snuggles down to sleep with several of them nestled around her. In contrast, Oberon's forbidding attendants resemble a seventeenth-century Spanish court, with black-clad boys and henchmen wearing exaggeratedly large ruffs; there is even a dwarf, who at one point darts at Titania as if to snatch the changeling child from her. (The dwarf may represent a kind of parody of the children who surround Titania.) Nevertheless, at the conclusion of Moshinsky's video production, Oberon's attendants (mostly boys at this point) unite with Titania's Elizabethan fairy children to run together through the house, blessing the inhabitants.

In contrast, Hoffman's film version of *Dream* is notably child-free. We receive two brief glimpses of the Indian Boy, once on a pony and once in Titania's (Michelle Pfeiffer) arms. He appears with long unbound hair and covered in blue body makeup. But aside from these brief appearances, there are no other children in this production, and the fairy attendants of both Oberon and Titania are all adults (albeit, in some cases, rather goofily childish ones).

Perhaps the ultimate example of children appearing in a film rendition of the play is *The Children's A Midsummer Night's Dream* (2001), directed by Christine Edzard.[14] The cast is composed almost entirely of children who, for the most part, had no previous acting experience. The results are what one might expect, and the reviews of the production were decidedly mixed.[15] Despite the amateur quality, however, as a production this version holds some interest. The performance begins as a marionette show, with adult voices speaking the parts. The feisty audience, composed solely of schoolchildren, sits in a small imitation of an Elizabethan theater. Halfway through the first scene, a young girl whom the camera has already picked out from the crowd suddenly stands to deliver the line "I would my father look'd but with my eyes" (1.1.55). The marionette portraying Theseus pauses and turns slowly toward the girl in the audience before the actor (Derek Jacobi), after a brief hesitation, delivers Theseus' reply in the girl's direction. The audience responds by applauding Hermia and hissing Theseus' pronouncements. For the remainder of this scene, various children stand up in the audience, and we realize that they are Helena, Lysander, and Demetrius. They interact with the puppets, but, when the scene ends and the audience begins to wander out, the characters come together, the puppets disappear, and the action moves outside the theater into the "real" world of a school. The production is contemporary (Helena prepares to notify Demetrius of Hermia's impending flight by picking up the telephone), although old-style touches abound, most notably in the fanciful Elizabethan costumes worn by the children portraying the fairies.

Although Edzard's film incorporates children into the performance more literally and more thoroughly than any of the other productions that I examine here, it is, by its nature, outside the scope that the other productions represent when we observe their inclusion of children. *The Children's Dream* is in most respects quite traditional: the Indian Boy does not appear; the fact that the fairies are children in no way distinguishes them from the fairies in several other versions or, indeed, from the other cast members; and the overall staging contains no radical departures from more traditional interpretations. To find a truly innovative production in terms of the presence of an extratextual child, we must turn to Noble's film.[16] The film adheres faithfully to the stage production, including using the same cast but with one striking example: the remarkable inclusion of an extratextual child, who provides the frame for the play.

The film opens with the camera panning across a starry night sky, down through clouds, to a lighted window and into a child's bedroom—(*Peter Pan* again). The camera moves slowly around the room, taking in a number of children's toys, which include numerous teddy bears as well as several vaguely creepy, old-fashioned toys. Finally, the camera falls upon a boy (Osheen Jones)[17] asleep in bed, with a copy of *A Midsummer Night's Dream* falling from his hand. His bedside clock points to midnight. We then see the child, clad in striped pajamas and evidently dreaming, open his bedroom door and walk down a green hallway. At the end, he opens a door and finds himself in a red hallway. Both hallways contain a threatening statue next to the door of the adjacent hallway. At the end of the second hallway, the child encounters another door. He peers through the keyhole and sees the backs of Theseus, standing over a seated Hippolyta (Alex Jennings and Lindsay Duncan, double-cast as Oberon and Titania) and eavesdrops as Theseus delivers the opening lines of the play. As Theseus caresses Hippolyta in a somewhat sinister way and then bends down to kiss her, we see the child's eye through the keyhole widening in surprise and alarm. The suggested image is that of a child receiving his first glimpse of parental sexuality, and he is disturbed by and even resentful of what he has seen.[18]

For the rest of the production, this child remains as a wordless though strongly reacting presence in virtually every scene. He observes and overhears—from under the table, or seated at the table, or seated on the floor next to a despondent Helena—all of the action and plotting of the rest of the first scene. At the scene's conclusion, we see him falling down a deep tunnel that inevitably recalls Alice falling down the rabbit hole and her dream of Wonderland. As he falls, there is a brief moment when we see him sitting up in bed in what we recognize to be his bedroom, screaming "Mummy!" He then pops up from inside a pot-bellied stove that is located in a humble building where the mechanicals soon arrive.

As the play progresses, we begin to see the child as an integral part of the action, usually as an observer but occasionally as the controlling force, as when he manages Oberon and Puck (Barry Lynch, double-cast as Philostrate) on a miniature stage as if they were puppets. He briefly sees himself as the Indian Boy, wearing a jeweled turban and suspended in a bubble that Puck has blown from a drop of water plucked from the large upturned green umbrella on which he floats. When the child himself blows bubbles at the same little stage, the fairies appear inside the bubbles and descend gradually to earth (recalling, at least for me, Glinda the Good's arrival in the 1939 *The Wizard of Oz*). The child sits with the mechanicals in the forest and watches their re-hearsal. He rides off with Titania and Bottom (the alternate father fig-ure) on a motorcycle silhouetted against an enormous moon. Significantly, when Titania and Bottom make vigorous and noisy love in an overturned umbrella, it is not the child who is shown watching them but Oberon and Puck.

In the latter part of the film, however, the child again becomes di-rectly involved in the action of the play, specifically as an opposing force to Oberon. The two confront each other silently across a moonlit body of water at the conclusion of Oberon's "But we are spirits of an-other sort" speech (3.2.388–95), and we are given a close-up of their eyes, their gazes locked. The child then spins around joyfully as he imagines the happy reunions of the lovers; then we see him turning what appears to be a gigantic, darkened globe. Next, he closes one of the fanciful doors that define the forest outside of Athens and opens another door that leads into the palace and the wedding feast. The lov-ers and the wedding guests turn toward the camera; the impression given is that they turn to look at the boy as he enters. He listens with slight hostility to Theseus' dismissive speech about poets and lovers (5.1.2ff), and, at the end of the speech, Theseus raises his hands, curv-ing them into claws, then lunges at the boy on the word "bear," which he exaggerates. Hippolyta shakes her head at him as he strides off, then gives the boy a reassuring and motherly smile.

Puck leads the child into the theater, where the boy pulls up the cur-tain on "Pyramus and Thisbe," to which he is shown reacting through-out the performance. The Bergomask ends suddenly with the clock striking twelve. All of the characters stand still and look out at the the-ater attentively, almost tensely. We then are presented with a rapid se-ries of images: the child's bedside clock; the child again sitting up in bed and screaming for his mother; then a truly frightening Oberon who crawls, snarling, toward the camera and, by implication, toward the child and us. Then we are back in the theater, where everyone exits except for Puck, who delivers the "Now the hungry [lion] roars" speech (5.1.371–90) to a darkened theater while the child watches from the balcony.

But then a profound reconciliation occurs. Puck takes the child's hand and leads him through yet another door to the backstage area. They join hands and see the entire company—fairies, mechanicals, lovers—floating toward them across a body of water (the same across which Oberon and the boy faced off earlier) while Oberon speaks his "Now, until the break of day" (5.1.401–22). When Puck and the child reach the others, Oberon picks up the boy and speaks directly to him for the blessing ("And the blots of Nature's hand / Shall not in their issue stand" [5.1.409–10]), then hands him to a loving Titania. Oberon, continuing with his speech, also speaks directly to the child at "And the owner of it [this palace] blest / Ever shall in safety rest" (5.1.419–20). The blessing of the lovers has also become a benediction for the child. Puck then takes the child's hand once more, and all the characters run back through the door and onto the stage, where they lift the child up above them, pass him gently overhead, then place him down between Titania and Oberon. All gaze wonderingly out toward us as the film ends. The reunion with the "good" parents is complete, and the Oedipal nightmare of the "bad" parents is over. The snarling Oberon and the diffident Theseus were temporarily replaced by the affectionate and fun-loving Bottom (and we recall that the child never sees this "good" father making love to the Titania/mother figure); but Bottom will ultimately not do as a father figure either. Nevertheless, because of the journey into his own unconscious, which he must take alone (note that we never see the mother respond to the boy's nightmare cries), the boy is able to reconcile with Oberon, who is finally revealed and understood as a loving father figure with the power to bless his son.

The idea of the play as a process of reconciliation between the Theseus/Oberon father figure and a child featured prominently in a remarkable production of the play presented at the 2003 Lake Tahoe Shakespeare Festival. The very location of the Lake Tahoe Shakespeare Festival guarantees a magical setting for *Dream:* the open-air stage is built on the northern shore of the lake; with the lake beyond the stage and the mountains behind the audience, an evening production begins with sunset and ends with moonlight. In this production, a young girl (Lauren D. Berti) played the role of an extratextual child, who, like Jones' character, served as a nonverbal observer of and participant in the play. Her particular identity, however, as Hippolyta's child soon became apparent from their gestures and obvious connection, and the journey that she took during the course of the play was a somewhat

Amy Gotham as a fairy and Lauren D. Berti as a child in the Lake Tahoe Shakespeare Festival's 2003 production of *A Midsummer Night's Dream*, directed by Sands Hall. Photo by Michael Okimoto.

different one from that of Jones' child. Although her presence was not
so consistent as Jones' in the Noble production, this girl was an active
character with whom the other characters, whether those at court, the
fairies, or the mechanicals, interacted constantly. Like the boy in the
Noble production, she was the only character in this double-cast production besides the mechanicals (who here did not double as fairies)
who consistently appeared as herself in both the fairy and the courtly
worlds.

I spoke with director Hall during the fall of 2003,[19] and she discussed
her decision to include an extratextual child in her production. She told
me that she had originally planned to show the changeling child and
had even designed a costume for him; but then Hall found herself pre-
occupied with a different child, the child Hippolyta might have had.
She found herself speculating about this child, who would move from
the "fraught court" to fairyland—in this production, a nurturing environment where everyone gladly takes care of the child—and who would
then be able to return to a court where all dilemmas, including her own,
had been resolved. Therefore, Hall concluded, this child's "arc" could
be summed up as "because I got to meet Oberon [who is her projection
of Theseus], I can come back to the world of the court and have him
become my stepfather." Consequently, when we first saw the child in
the opening scene of the play, she was more or less ignored by those
around her, including Theseus, who spared her only a passing and not
particularly friendly glance; but at the end of act 4, she and Puck together turned a large crescent moon that stood above the stage and that
Puck had wheeled into a different position at the beginning of act 1,
scene 3, when the action first moved to the forest. After this act of control, which we understood as returning us from the forest to the world
of the court, the girl willingly reentered that world, and she and Oberon
greeted each other with a warm embrace. She was now welcomed into
a relationship that time and understanding had resolved.

Hall noted that she had ultimately decided not to include the changeling child because she did not want Hippolyta's daughter to become
that child. Hall noted that the "stakes" become much higher for Hippolyta "with a child in the mix, especially in the opening scene." She went
on to discuss how she had been influenced in her interpretive choices
by current social and cultural concerns and noted that she had wanted
to have a "contemporary take" on the play. She remarked, "I see the
world we live in, and how hard it is to be a child, and that there are
parents who can't parent. I see how hard that plays out on a child."
She noted the importance of the child's loving relationship with Bottom

(signaled from the opening scene, in which the mechanicals were present as musicians). The significance of Bottom as the "good" father who enables the child to reconcile with the "bad" (that is, threatening) father or stepfather clearly interested Noble as well, as seen in Bottom's fun-loving interactions with the boy and Oberon's subsequent change from the snarling menace of the child's unconscious to the loving father who appears at the play's conclusion.

Hall's production was the one that got me thinking about this topic in the first place, and productions like hers and Noble's lead me to conclude that a sea change is occurring in how children are incorporated into productions of this play. The concept of "childhood innocence" no longer seems so uncomplicated as it once did, given what many children go through, every day, in every part of the world.[20] Similarly, our understanding of *A Midsummer Night's Dream* has become more sophisticated in recent decades, thanks largely to innovative productions and to feminist and psychoanalytic criticism, including essays such as Louis Montrose's seminal article. Montrose's insights are relevant here; he observes that "Oberon's blessing of the marriage bed of Theseus and Hippolyta evokes precisely what it seeks to suppress: the cycle of sexual and familial violence, fear, and betrayal begins again at the very engendering of Hippolytus."[21] Both Noble and Hall allude to these darker themes (the child's hostility when confronted with parental sexuality; Oedipal anxieties; the potential for familial violence) in their productions, but both choose to resolve these issues happily by focusing on the dream world of the unconscious in which the child is able to work through the fears and hostilities that trouble him or her.

Nevertheless, as harshly realistic as our understanding may have become of the challenges that can affect a childhood, children remain, culturally speaking, metaphorically linked with imagination and creativity. Using the presence of extratextual children to emphasize the dreamlike qualities and psychological significance of *A Midsummer Night's Dream* makes sense, given these associations. In the past, the casting of children as the fairies may have suggested this idea rather prettily; in these postmodern times, we are more concerned with children's unconscious desires and fears than with their prettiness. As the Noble and the Hall productions make manifest, the dreams of childhood, once decoded, often prove to be nightmares, but the nightmares themselves can lead to resolution and even harmony. We recall Theseus' remarks that ". . . in the night, imagining some fear, / How easy is a bush suppos'd a bear!" (5.1.21–22)—the line that Jennings delivers as a mock threat to Jones. But the corollary to this truth is that often the bear, or monster, of a nightmare turns out to be only a bush, or even a loving father, and the nightmare itself evolves into a mere dream, as it does for the lovers and for the shadow children of these productions—a dream of reconciliation, and of hope, that promises to overcome the darker emotions that sometimes lurk beneath the surface of family relationships.

Finally, another meaning for these extratextual children also suggests itself. It seems apparent that children in these productions may also exist as the embodiment of an external shaping force beyond the play itself—the director or the audience, perhaps. If we understand at least some of the action of the play to constitute a child's dream, or nightmare, as these directors imply, can we also equate that dream with the director's vision of the play, or with our own understanding of it?[22] As Hall's evolving viewpoint of the changeling child illustrates, directors' convictions about a play develop as a given production takes shape, and the finished product (which most directors will point out can never be said to be finished) ideally will represent a harmonious whole and a resolution of the director's sometimes conflicting views about the play. Similarly, the audience members bring their own understanding of a play to bear on the performance they witness; and they, too, will hope to find a harmonious resolution to their questions by the end of the performance. Seen in this light, the extratextual children in these two productions, even more than any fairy children or the Indian Boy, can be understood to represent all the creative and imaginative forces that are at work in any production of a play, whether it be a director's vision, an audience's comprehension, or the creative power embodied in the play itself. In a certain sense, these extratextual children are not extratextual at all; rather, they are the reification of many seemingly disparate elements that are inherent in the playtext and essential to it. And, perhaps because they are the literal embodiment of forces within the text, the presence of these children in productions such as Noble's and Hall's feels indisputably and literally right, as well as wonderfully imaginative and dreamlike.

NOTES

1. A particularly good example of an extratextual child occurred in a production of *As You Like it* by The Shakespeare Theatre (Washington, DC) in the late 1990s, in which a young boy joined Duke Senior and his band of merry men in the forest of Arden. The duke and his followers were solicitous of the child, who eventually befriended the melancholy Jacques and ultimately helped him to become far less melancholy.

2. I have been influenced in my choice of this term by the novels of Margaret Haddix, who uses the phrase in a different context.

3. *A Midsummer Night's Dream*, in *The Riverside Shakespeare*, 2nd ed., ed. G. Blakemore Evans (Boston: Houghton Mifflin, 1997). Subsequent references to Shakespeare's plays are from this edition and are cited parenthetically.

4. For a history of casting children in productions of *Dream*, as well as a history of the appearance of the Indian Boy, see Gary Jay Williams, *Our Moonlight Revels: A Midsummer Night's Dream in the Theatre* (Iowa City: University of Iowa Press, 1997), passim.

5. Alan C. Dessen, private e-mail communication, May 28, 2004. See also *A Midsummer Night's Dream*, The New Cambridge Shakespeare, ed. R. A. Foakes (Cambridge: Cambridge University Press, 1984), esp. 12–24. A notable exception was Joseph Papp's 1982 production in New York's Central Park, in which the Indian Boy (played by a young African American child) appeared throughout, including in the final scene. For a brief overview of the presence of children in early productions, see *A Midsummer Night's Dream*, Shakespeare in Production, ed. Trevor R. Griffiths (Cambridge: Cambridge University Press, 1996), 8, 15.

6. *A Midsummer Night's Dream*, VHS, prod. Paul Arnott, dir. Adrian Noble (1996; Burbank, CA: Miramax Home Entertainment, 2002).

7. *A Midsummer Night's Dream*, VHS, prod. and dir. Max Reinhardt (1935; Los Angeles: Warner Home Video, 2002).

8. *A Midsummer Night's Dream*, VHS, prod. Michael Hoffman and Leslie Urdang, dir. Michael Hoffman (1999; Beverly Hills, CA: Twentieth Century Fox Corporation, 2001).

9. *A Midsummer Night's Dream*, VHS, prod. Michael Birkett and Martin Ransohoff, dir. Peter Hall (1968; New York: Water Bearer Films, 1993).

10. She is maternal in her treatment of Bottom as well.

11. The children appear to be lip-syncing to music sung by a boys' choir.

12. *A Midsummer Night's Dream*, VHS, prod. Jonathan Miller, dir. Elijah Moshinsky (1981; New York: Ambrose Video, 1987).

13. Papp, in his 1982 New York Public Theater production, made a similar choice: Titania delivered her speech to the child, who then went to sit on Oberon's lap. Two lines were altered to accommodate the staging: Titania observed that the boy's mother, "being mortal, of *this* boy did die"; and Oberon likewise urged Titania to "give me *this* boy" (emphases mine).

14. *The Children's Midsummer Night's Dream*, VHS, prod. Oliver Stockman, dir. Christine Edzard (2001; London: Sands Nut Films. 2002). For more information on this production, including director's notes and production information, see www.sandsfilms.co .uk/midsummer/midsummer.htm.

15. For a complete listing of these reviews and review articles, see www.world shakesbib.org (Index Location: 30.52.10.30, Individual Works—Plays; *A Midsummer Night's Dream;* Productions and Staging; Film, Cinema, Radio, Television).

16. For a useful cinematographic summary of Noble's *Dream*, see Michael Anderegg, *Cinematic Shakespeare* (Lanham, MD: Rowman & Littlefield, 2004), 144. For a decidedly negative review of the stage version, see Williams, *Our Moonlight Revels*, 255–57. For a more positive one, see *A Midsummer Night's Dream*, ed. Griffiths, 76–78.

17. Astute viewers will also recall Osheen Jones' remarkable performance as Young Lucius in Julie Taymor's *Titus* (1999), in which his textual character also plays an extratextual role that functions as a narrative framework for the play.

18. Cf. Louis Montrose, "*A Midsummer Night's Dream* and the Shaping Fantasies of Elizabethan Culture: Gender, Power, Form," in *New Historicism and Renaissance Drama*, Longman Critical Readers, ed. Richard Wilson and Richard Dutton (London and New York: Longman, 1992): "Yet 'jealous' Oberon is not only Titania's rival for the child but also the child's rival for Titania: making the boy 'all her joy,' 'proud' Titania withholds herself from her husband; she has 'forsworn his bed and company,'" 118.

19. I interviewed Sands Hall by telephone on September 19, 2003. She has been with the Foothill Theatre Company (the parent company of the Lake Tahoe Shakespeare Festival) for almost ten years as actor, director, and playwright. In addition to plays, she has written one novel, *Catching Heaven*. I thank her for taking the time to speak with me about this production.

20. Several of the reviews of *The Children's Dream* commented on the "innocence" of the production. Hall also observed that "I love having kids in the cast for what they do to everyone else—their wide-eyed innocence, and so on," although in her case it seems to me that she is commenting on something different—the benefits of having children in the cast and what they contribute to the theatrical experience for the actors and others involved in production.

21. See Montrose, "Shaping Fantasies," 120–21.

22. See *A Midsummer Night's Dream*, ed. Griffiths, 64:

> It is a peculiarity of the stage history of *A Midsummer Night's Dream* that few directors have explicitly related their own theatrical practices to the element of "dream" in the play's title and that the rise of modern psychological thought has had such limited overt effect on productions of the play. However, the relationship between the conscious and the unconscious was to become the key factor in interpretations of the play in the last decades of the twentieth century. . . . Obviously . . . the idea of exploring the "dream" elements . . . was [not] new. What was new was the application of ideas about the therapeutic nature of the experience in the wood to the framing relationship between Theseus and Hippolyta as well as to the four lovers, so that the play's psychological journey begins to be seen as involving all the mortals.

Griffiths includes the Noble stage version in this category of new interpretations of the dreamlike qualities of the play. In the film version, as I have suggested, the notion of a journey, and a framing character who makes that journey, becomes even more pronounced.

Teen Shakespeare:
10 Things I Hate About You and *O*

Alexander Leggatt

TWO RECENT MOVIES, GIL JUNGER'S *10 THINGS I HATE ABOUT YOU* (1999)[1] and Tim Blake Nelson's *O* (2001),[2] transfer Shakespeare plays—respectively, *The Taming of the Shrew* and *Othello*—into the world of the contemporary American teenager. To call either of them a production of the play in question would be misleading; they are independent works, following their own agendas. But in each case, the agenda includes a conscious awareness of the Shakespearean original and a dialogue with it. An important part of that dialogue is in an interplay between Shakespeare and the teen world, with its volatile mix of rebellion, conformity, insecurity, self-consciousness, competitiveness, and hormonal energy. Even a so-called straight production of a Shakespeare play will be a product of its own culture and medium, revealing as much about its own context as it does about the play; and it will slant the play accordingly. With a world as strongly defined as that of the teenager, the self-revelation and the slanting are bound to be particularly strong.

10 Things I Hate About You approaches *The Taming of the Shrew* in a spirit of free play. The Shakespearean plot is twisted, fragmented, and, for long stretches, disappears completely. Many of the characters have no Shakespearean counterparts, and the overt references to Shakespeare are mostly jokes. *O* treats *Othello* with what looks on the surface to be greater respect: the contours of Shakespeare's plot are visible throughout, all the principal characters have clear counterparts in the play, and many crucial passages of dialogue are recognizable paraphrases of the original. If rebellion and conformity are the poles on which adolescence turns, then *10 Things* rebels against its artistic parent and *O* conforms: except that the free play of the comedy is in the spirit of the original; and the way *O* conforms to an existing structure gives it a self-conscious, formal control that is powerful in itself but arguably un-Shakespearean.

The central love story of *10 Things I Hate About You* is that of Katarina

Heath Ledger as Patrick Verona and Julia Stiles as Katarina Stratford in the 1999 film *10 Things I Hate About You*, directed by Gil Junger. Photo courtesy of Richard Cartwright/MPTV.net.

Stratford, generally known as Kat (Julia Stiles), and Patrick Verona (Heath Ledger). Their surnames suggest a coming-together of England and Italy, and what could be more Shakespearean than that? But calling their relationship a love story signals a crucial difference between the movie and the play. Whether Katherina and Petruchio can really be called lovers is debatable, and to do so may be the triumph of hope over close reading. But *10 Things* is unequivocally a romantic comedy that aims to work within the audience's comfort zone.

The movie opens with two cars stopped side by side at a crosswalk: in one, four girls listening to music and bouncing up and down to the beat; in the other, Kat Stratford, listening to *her* music, absolutely still. Immediately we get the message: she's different. Refusal to conform is her mantra, repeated with variations throughout: "I don't like to do what people expect. Why should I live up to other people's expectations instead of my own?" The paradox is that she has a clear reputation in the school and lives up to it. The guidance counselor, Ms. Perky (Allison Janney), warns Kat, "People perceive you as somewhat . . ." "Tempestuous?" Kat offers; "Heinous bitch is the term used most often." Elsewhere, she is (of course) "the shrew." In a rough echo of Shakespeare's plot, Kat's overprotective father insists that her sister Bianca cannot date unless Kat does; he assumes she never will. When Cameron (Joseph Gordon-Levitt), the Lucentio figure, plots with his friend Mike (David Krumholtz) to find someone to date Kat, they assemble an unprepossessing lot of youths and ask them how they feel about the idea. One screams loudly, and another replies, "Only if we were the last two people alive, and there were no sheep." Patrick Verona, accepting the assignment, sees his job as "to tame the wild beast."

Kat's role as rebel follows established lines. In English class, she denounces Ernest Hemingway as "an abusive alcoholic misogynist" and complains of "the oppressive patriarchal values that dictate our education." When we first see her at home, she is reading Sylvia Plath's *The Bell Jar*. All of this creates the impression (not quite accurate, as we shall see, but close) that Kat is a type and her feminism comes from her reading. When Mike introduces Cameron to the school, he gives him a tour not of the rooms but of the groups: the basic beautiful people, the coffee kids, the white Rastifarians, the cowboys. This is a coded world in which teenagers typecast themselves and each other as a way of controlling the amorphousness of adolescent identity. When Kat tells her friend Mandella (Susan May Pratt) that they should not go to the prom—because not to go is making a statement—Mandella ironically retorts, "Oh, goody! Something new and different for us!" Kat is just amused enough to show she has taken the point.

Petruchio comes into Shakespeare's play with a macho swagger: he has heard lions roar, he has heard the sound of battle, he does not fear a woman's tongue. Patrick enters the film surrounded by legends: he sold his liver on the black market to buy speakers, he did a year in San Quentin, he once ate a live duck. It proves dangerous to be around him when he handles power tools; at one point, he drills a neat hole in Cameron's French textbook. Like Kat, he seems to have his role firmly in place. But—far more quickly than she does—he reveals a soft center. For example, we learn that the year he allegedly spent in San Quentin was actually devoted to looking after a sick grandfather. Petruchio's taming of Katherina is done, he claims, "in reverend care of her."[3] The veracity of this claim is debatable; for many readers, as for Katherina, it is outrageously ironic. Patrick's caring streak is real, and it develops as a crucial part of his relationship with Kat. At the wild party that forms a set piece scene halfway through the action, Kat, drunk on tequila, dances alone on a table, egged on by the crowd. Then she falls, stiff as a board, and Patrick catches her. "You okay?" "I'm fine." "You're not fine, come on." He takes her outside and, for the next few minutes, does everything he can to keep her awake, afraid she might have a concussion. Patrick's actions convey the genuine concern that the most optimistic readers would like to see in Petruchio. Caring in play with sparring marks at least the first encounter of the couple. Patrick first approaches Kat as she is coming off the soccer field. To his greeting, "How you doing?" she replies, "Sweating like a pig, actually. And yourself?" His response, "Now that's the way to get a guy's attention," tells her where the conversation is going, and she backs off: "Do you even know my name, screwboy?" The Shakespearean equivalents are Petruchio's steering the conversation to the physical, and Katherina's insistence on not being called Kate: "They call me Katherine that do talk of me" (2.1.184). Patrick later describes the source of her appeal: "Who needs affection when I can have blind hatred?"

The ice cracks, in stages. After Patrick has dragged Kat away from the party and they are sitting outside on a pair of swings, she leans toward him and makes her first romantic statement: "Hey, your eyes have a little green in them." Then she vomits. Later, in the front seat of the car in which he has driven her home, she goes a step further: "You know, you're not as vile as I thought you were." But when she leans forward to kiss him, he is the one who withdraws: "Maybe we should do this another time." She walks off in chagrin. They finally get together when they play paintball, a form of mock combat that turns their verbal sparring into a physical game and leads to their first kiss — in the most traditional of situations, lying on a pile of hay. They are in an open space (the paintball arena is outdoors, away from the school-and-house settings of the rest of the movie) and dressed in white uniforms. Away from the rest of their lives, in a play area, they can come together, turning the fighting into teasing and, finally, into shared affection.

There are reasons, however, why Patrick withdraws from the first kiss. In Shakespeare, the aim of the plot is marriage, and marriage in the play's society is for money. Petruchio has come "to wive it wealthily in Padua" (1.2.75), and Bianca is auctioned off like property. Whatever a modern audience may think, no one in the play is shocked or uncomfortable about this. But *10 Things I Hate About You* is about dating, and, when the financial motive enters, dragged in by Shakespeare's plot, the effect is disquieting. Cameron needs someone to date Kat so that he can have a chance with Bianca Stratford (Laura Oleynik); having no money of his own, he has to use the obnoxious Joey (Andrew Keegan), a full-of-himself fashion model, as a backer. Joey agrees, having his own designs on Bianca. Patrick — caring, sensitive, and good-natured though he may be—dates Kat for money. Petruchio's financial motive invades and complicates the film's romantic comedy.

Joey offers Patrick twenty dollars; they both glance at Kat, and Joey immediately raises it to thirty. Patrick asks for seventy-five, and they settle for fifty. After a couple of encounters with her, Patrick raises the price to one hundred dollars per date, in advance. As he gets to know her he tries to back off, telling Joey, "I'm sick of playing your little game." But he accepts three hundred dollars to keep going. He looks unhappy about it, but he takes the money. Kat, in turn, suspects his motives, despite her growing attraction to him. When he asks her to the prom, she asks, "Why are you pushing this? What's in it for you?" Touched on a nerve, he retorts, "You need therapy, did you know that?" On the dance floor, Joey, annoyed at seeing Bianca with Cameron, confronts Patrick: this is not why he paid him to take out Kat. Kat, of course, hears this and storms out: "You are so not who I thought you were." Teenagers play roles, and for Kat the role of the caring, affectionate Patrick has been exposed as a fake.

A payoff saves Patrick for the audience. Immediately after he accepts three hundred dollars to keep going, we see Kat in a music shop, trying out a guitar, with Patrick watching her. He knows she wants to start a band. At the end of the movie, she goes back to her car, and there is the guitar. Patrick explains how he got it: "Some asshole paid me to take out this really great girl"; he adds, "But I screwed up; I fell for her." If this were what brought them together at the end, we might say that Kat, like Patrick, could be bought. But it is preceded by the set piece that gives the movie its title. The English teacher has asked the class to write their own versions of Shakespeare's "Sonnet 141," which begins, "In faith, I do not love thee with mine eyes, / For they in thee a thousand errors note" and moves to a confession: "But my five wits nor my five senses can / Dissuade one foolish heart from serving thee." Kat offers to read her poem, which picks up the idea of noting a thousand errors, beginning: "I hate the way you talk to me, and the way you cut your hair." The list continues, "I hate your big dumb combat boots, and the way you read my mind" and gets closer to her own situation with, "I hate the way you're always right, I hate it when you lie. / I hate it when you make me laugh, even worse when you make me cry." At this point, the tears start, and at the end the meter breaks down and so does she: "But mostly I hate the way I don't hate you, not even close, not even a little bit, not even at all." She runs out of the room. Given the cool, don't-mess-with-me persona that Stiles normally projects, the breakdown is startling. She runs to her car and finds the guitar; Patrick (who has listened to the poem with pain and surprise in his eyes) joins her, and we have the romantic finale. It has been set up not by the revelation about the guitar but by Kat's public confession of feelings she hates and cannot control. Her self-created role has cracked wide open.

This scene is the equivalent of Katherina's lecture on wifely obedience in *The Taming of the Shrew*, another set piece that comes at the end. In both cases, a character takes a position that surprises everyone who thinks they know her. One preaches submission to men; the other confesses vulnerability to one particular man. But Kat's poem is in several respects the reverse of Katherina's speech. Kat is personal where her Shakespearean counterpart is general. Katherina's façade never breaks; it may not even be a façade. Kat's façade breaks quickly and completely. Her loss of control reverses her predecessor's rhetorical command. She might even paraphrase Patrick's confession: "I screwed up; I fell for him."

The movie also resolves Kat's relations with her sister Bianca, something Shakespeare refuses to do. At the beginning, Kat sees Bianca as a spoiled princess, while Bianca's endearments for her sister include "loser," "mutant," and "bitch." But Kat goes first to a party, and then to a prom, with the result that (given their father's rules) Bianca can go too. She also tries to keep Joey away from her sister, something Bianca initially resents. But there is a reason. Kat tells Bianca that in ninth grade she went out with Joey for a month, and they had sex: "Just once, right after Mom left. Everyone was doing it, so I did it." He dropped her when she refused to do it again. Her refusal to conform dates from this incident: she conformed once, and decided it was a mistake. This is one of the film's sharpest departures from Shakespeare, who does not look to past events to explain his characters.

The revelation sets up Bianca's final emergence, which roughly equals the sudden independence her Shakespearean counterpart shows at the end, but put in a context that gives it a different effect. In his subplot, Shakespeare reverses the usual story pattern, so that Lucentio's troubles with Bianca begin at the end. Pursuing its romantic agenda, *10 Things I Hate About You* switches back to normal, putting Cameron's troubles with Bianca at the beginning. She is unattainable; the group she belongs to, according to Mike, is the "Don't even think about it" group. For a while, Joey is a serious rival, and Cameron retreats, discouraged. But Bianca gets Cameron to drive her home from the party and, in a scene that follows immediately on Kat's failure to get a kiss from Patrick, Bianca kisses Cameron. She goes to the prom with Cameron; Joey, who thought Bianca was going with him, gets angry and takes her friend Chastity instead. In the ladies' room, Chastity tells Bianca why Joey wanted to take her: he had bet his friends that he would "nail" her that night. A brawl breaks out on the dance floor: Joey knocks Cameron down; Bianca responds by hitting Joey three times, once for Cameron, once for her sister, and once for herself. The third is a knee in the crotch. She is not only avenging Kat (and Cameron, and herself) but following in a sisterly tradition: at the beginning of the film, when the guidance counselor refers to one of Kat's previous victims, Kat replies, "I still maintain that he kicked himself in the balls." The subplot ends romantically with Bianca and Cameron comfortably together and with the sisters reconciled. Shakespeare's ending is much tougher: besides the falling-out between Bianca and Lucentio, Katherina uses her last speech in part to score off her sister.

Kat's recoil from her brief affair with Joey reflects the movie's general treatment of sex. There is a lot of raunchy talk. In our introduction to Patrick, he has been summoned to the guidance counselor for exposing himself in the cafeteria. He replies, "I was joking with the lunch lady. It was a bratwurst." Ms. Perky's response surprises him: "Bratwurst? Aren't *we* the optimist?" In fact, jokes about bratwurst are about as far as it goes. There is never a suggestion (despite in some showoff dialogue to the contrary) that Kat and Patrick—much less Cameron and Bianca—will actually have sex. Couples kiss (or fail to kiss) in the front seats of cars, just before saying goodnight. It is as though the film shares, and respects, Kat's caution after one bad experience. The film takes an equally mild stance on drugs. The teacher in the detention room confiscates a package of pot and a package of snacks, and they seem equally serious. As we shall see, *O* goes much further in both cases. Sports—taken seriously in *O*, where life centers on the basketball team—are just sports here, taking place on the sidelines of the story.

As part of the general lightness, the authority figures are mostly caricatures, beginning with Ms. Perky, who demonstrates less interest in her clients than in the soft-porn novel she taps out on her laptop. During an archery class, a misdirected arrow from Bianca hits a bystander; we later notice that the teacher in the detention room has trouble sitting down. The key authority figure is, of course, Daddy. While Baptista sets his Katherina-first rule to make sure both his daughters get married, Walter Stratford (Larry Miller), who as a doctor sees too many teenage pregnancies, sets his rule to prevent both daughters from dating. His protectiveness plays as a comic tic, the equivalent of the cartoon roles some of the teenagers play. As Bianca and Cameron go off together, he calls out, "I know every cop in town, bucko!" But, like

Patrick, he has a soft center. Kat desperately wants to go to Sarah Lawrence (she screams when she gets her letter of acceptance); Walter wants her to stay close to home. In the end, he and Kat come to a gradual reconciliation: he admits he is impressed that Bianca, following Kat's footsteps, "beat the hell out of some guy," and goes on to explain his own behavior: "Fathers don't like to admit it when their daughters are capable of running their own lives. It means we've become spectators." He then reveals that he has just written a deposit check for Sarah Lawrence. Kat hugs him, and he touches her arm awkwardly.

This is, in the end, a film teenagers could recommend to their parents (after warning them about some of the language). It is a romantic comedy in which teen behavior, and parental behavior, are finally good-natured and reassuring (and the one obnoxious character gets kicked in the balls by a girl). Neither rebellion nor oppression needs to be taken seriously; it is, if you like, *The Taming of the Shrew* with the gloves on. The happy ending for this shrew is that she goes to the college of her choice on her father's money.

But *10 Things I Hate About You* does more with Shakespeare than soften him; it plays games with him, and these games have a rough equivalent in the original play. Anyone who has trouble taking the play straight has the option of using the Induction to say that we don't have to: as a play-within-the-play, the main story has a quality of meta-theater, which can give it an air of "just kidding, folks." Shakespeare jokes are scattered through the surface of *10 Things I Hate About You*, and, given the Shakespearean source of the story, their effect is meta-theatrical, metafilmic, or, as the characters might say, metawhatever. As Bianca walks into his gaze for the first time, Cameron's language suddenly skips periods: "I burn, I pine, I perish." For a moment, he is Lucentio, until Mike brings him back to the screenplay. The English teacher, Mr. Morgan (Daryl "Chill" Mitchell), delivers a rap version of "Sonnet 141." Kat's friend Mandella has Shakespeare's picture in her locker and declares, "We're involved." Mike's reaction to the picture is "What's that collar for, is that to keep him from licking his stitches?"

While *10 Things I Hate About You* plays fast and loose with *The Taming of the Shrew*, and with Shakespeare himself, *O* sticks close to *Othello*. Directed by Tim Blake Nelson, *O* features Odin James (Mekhi Phifer), star of the basketball team in a residential private school in the south and one of the few black students. He is going out with Desi (Stiles again), daughter of the Dean (John Heard). Hugo Goulding (Josh Hartnett) has reasons to resent Odin: Odin has picked Mike (Andrew Keegan—"Joey" in *10 Things*) to share the Most Valuable Player award with him, an honor Hugo feels he himself deserves. Hugo's father, Duke Goulding (Martin Sheen), the coach of the basketball team, compounds Hugo's problem by the way he favors Odin. Hugo uses the dumpy, unpopular Roger (Elden Henson), who wants Desi for himself, to get his plot going, telling him he has a plan to break up Odin and Desi. Roger, standing in the shrubbery outside the dean's house, makes an anonymous call to the dean on his cell phone: "I don't know how to tell you this, sir, but someone sort of stole something from you . . . your daughter." Odin, with Duke supporting him, finds himself up before the dean defending his relationship with Desi. Hugo then provokes a drunken brawl in which Mike injures Roger, and Duke suspends him from the team. Hugo then tells Mike that the way to get back is to work on Desi, who will talk to Odin, who will talk to the coach. Odin gives Desi a one hundred-year-old silk scarf: "It was my great-grandmother's; it's always been in my family." Hugo's girlfriend Emily (Rain Phoenix) steals it and gives it to Hugo, who wants it for "a little prank." The plot unfolds as we expect, and, when Emily tells the truth about the scarf, Hugo shoots her dead. In the final movement, Roger ambushes Mike on a country road but bungles his attempt to kill him; Hugo knocks Mike out with a tire iron and shoots Roger dead. Odin strangles Desi, then shoots himself.

If we can think of the characters of *10 Things I Hate About You* as free to move in and out of *The Taming of the Shrew* as it suits them—and that the time they spend outside the play far outweighs the time they spend inside it—we can think of the characters of *O* as trapped in the story of *Othello*. They are also trapped in its dialogue. Odin's attempt to reconcile himself to the dean is only loosely connected to what Othello says to Brabantio: "You've got a great daughter there. . . . And I really, really care about her. . . . What we have is beautiful." But the dean's reply directly paraphrases Brabantio: "No. She deceived me. What makes you think she wouldn't do the same to you?" In other words, "Look to her, Moor, if thou hast eyes to see; / She has deceiv'd her father, and may thee" (1.3.292–93). It is as though Odin is trying to get out of the play and the dean pulls him back in. We feel the same entrapment in the temptation sequence, which sticks closely to the original: "Did Mike know that you and Desi were gettin' together?" "Yeah, he knew. Why?" . . . "Mikey is the one who kinda hooked us up." "Do you trust Mike?"

The temptation sequence is set in an exercise room whose dominant color is grey. Odin and Hugo are seen through the bars of an exercise machine; they look like caged prisoners. The school in *10 Things* is pastiche Gothic, in keeping with the surface layer of Shakespeare jokes; the school in *O* is neoclassical, with imposing pillars. Shot from below against the sky, it looms oppressively. Just before Hugo plots the final murders, the camera, aimed straight up, cranes to simulate circular motion up a spiral staircase, at the top of which is an oval skylight. The effect differs significantly from the ending of *10 Things*, where the camera swings around a band playing on the school roof, finally pulling away into the distance, a shot that must have been done from a helicopter. Here we are trapped in the building just as we are in the plot, and the only movement possible is in one direction, within closely defined boundaries. The same sense of entrapment is created by recurring shots of trees, taken from below, laced against the sky.

While the students in *10 Things* dress any way they like, the students in *O* spend much of their time in uniforms, in shades of dark blue and grey. The formality of the compositions, and of the uniforms, is part of a general cinematic strategy of control. At ninety-one minutes, *O* is three minutes shorter than *10 Things I Hate About You*. *Othello*, by comparison, is over nine hundred lines longer than *The Taming of the Shrew*. In keeping with the school's neoclassical architecture, the Shakespearean sprawl of the original has been trimmed to the length of a Greek tragedy. There is only one opening title: the single letter O, white on black, filling the screen. Appropriately, the film's structure is circular. It begins with a shot of white doves while a female voice sings "Ave Maria" and we hear a voiceover ("All my life, I always wanted to fly . . ."). The voice, we later learn, is Hugo's. Over the final scene, with police cars and ambulances surrounding the school and bodies carried out on stretchers, we hear the same singer and the same voiceover from Hugo, repeating the opening words. The effect achieves formal closure, more rigorous than Shakespeare's ending.

With formality goes concentration. While in *10 Things* we see a variety of school activities, Palmetto Grove Prep school is about one thing: basketball. Duke, the coach, is the only character in the film whose role expands far beyond his Shakespearean original. School authority and family authority are fused. The dean is Desi's father; Duke is Hugo's father; Roger's father, who never appears, is a major donor to the school. Mike feels the disgrace of the brawl that leads to his suspension from the team because "My parents always talk about reputation." Up to a point, the authority figures loom as formidable, in a way that they do not in *10 Things*. Odin would be in serious trouble with the dean if he did not have Duke on his side. Duke himself, alternating generous enthusiasm with volcanic anger, is as powerful a figure on the basketball court as any of his players. Yet the dean is seriously challenged from the beginning, and, in the end, he and Duke are both shattered. When the dean learns for the first time that Odin and Desi have been together for four months, he confronts his daughter: "Together? What does that mean, together?" Her reply is cool and uncompromising: "Dad, that's none of your business." Walter Stratford feels he has been reduced to a spectator and ruefully accepts it; the dean is simply shut out. Later, Desi describes her father as "scared." He has reason to be scared. The forces at work in this school are far more dangerous than the innocent role-playing of *10 Things I Hate About You.* In the final scene, Duke sits on the porch of the dormitory, surrounded by the flashing lights of police cars and ambulances, gasping for breath, possibly having a heart attack; and the dean slumps in grief over the stretcher that carries his daughter.

Drugs in *O* are seriously represented. We see Hugo, wincing in pain, get a steroid injection in the stomach while the dealer warns him of the danger he runs. Hugo's hold over Odin is dramatized when we see Odin, at Hugo's urging, inhaling two lines of cocaine. Sex, confined to one bad memory in *10 Things*, is more pervasive and disturbing here. When Odin goes to bed with Desi early in the film, he says, "We're not going to do anything. I just like feeling your skin next to mine." However, once his jealousy has taken hold, we witness a scene in a motel in which Odin's love-making becomes angry and violent; Desi, in obvious pain, begs him to stop, but he takes no notice. In the mirror, he sees Mike, not himself, on top of her—the equivalent of images Iago plants in Othello's mind.

Odin has always had a dangerous streak. After his interview with the Dean, we see him beating Roger for lying about him, a moment for which there is no equivalent in the play. But for the most part, his manner at the beginning is easy, confident, and humorous. In bed with Desi, he jokes with her about the word "nigger": he can use it and she cannot. In the same scene, he seems to be poking fun at Othello. "You asking me how I got that scar on my back?" he says, setting Desi up. Her reply brings her close to Desdemona: "You do have the best stories." He tells her, first, that he was a C-section baby and the knife cut too deep; his mother couldn't afford a good doctor. Then he laughs and admits that he fell off his skateboard. He acknowledges, briefly, something like Othello's insecurity: he was scared when he first talked to Desi. But he goes on to insist that he could handle the pressure. The star of the basketball team, he feels at ease with her as he is in his world generally.

Hugo, of course, destroys his confidence as Iago destroys Othello's.

The n-word ceases to be a joke when Hugo tells him that Desi and Mike call him "the nigger." His jocularity turns into smoldering anger. Odin departs from his Shakespearean original in his relative lack of authority, a minor element throughout the action that becomes more prominent at the end. He is associated with the hawk that is the team's mascot; his name is that of a god. But it is Duke who bears the responsibilities of leadership, the one who has to make the decision to suspend Mike. Odin, in the early scenes, is beholden to Duke, under his authority. And when he comes to kill Desi, he is not so much a powerful force unleashed as a stricken young man. As he strangles Desi, he whimpers, "I want to be able to let you go, but I can't . . . I can't, I can't." He pleads with her, just as helplessly, "Go to sleep, go to sleep, go to sleep." The power of his last speech is also reduced from the original: the effect is equivalent to the contrast between Katherina's rhetorical control and Kat's breakdown. While Othello in his last moments commands eloquence, Odin's equivalent speech is broken, distraught, slurred. The echoes are as clear as usual. He tells his hearers that when they recall "the nigger that lost it back in high school . . . you make sure you tell 'em the truth. You tell them I loved that girl. I did." But while Othello judges himself, Odin judges Hugo, focusing on him as Othello at this point does not focus on Iago: "He twisted my head off. He fucked it up. . . . It was this white prep-school motherfucker standing right there." While Othello, with a terrible final clarity, judges and kills himself in the form of the Turk, Odin's last words before he shoots himself are not only brief but cryptic: "You tell them where I'm from that'd make me do this."

The control that Othello has in the last moments of the play passes in the end of the film to Hugo. Nothing I have said intends to denigrate Phifer's performance as Odin: he is intense, accomplished, and persuasive throughout, in all the shifting aspects of the character. But for all the dominance he achieves, the film's most urgent concern is finally with Hugo: what makes a nice-looking, popular boy from a good family do something like this? We see where the trouble comes from at the beginning as the crowd surges around Odin after his latest triumph on the basketball court, while the camera picks up Hugo, alone, watching from the sidelines. It doesn't help when Duke, during the awards presentation, hugs Odin and declares, "I love him like my own son." We see Hugo in the stands, not looking happy. Later, in a naked appeal for approval, Hugo tells his father that he is getting As in English; Duke's response shows he is pleased, but also that he takes Hugo rather for granted, and, in any case, he has other things on his mind. After Odin's behavior on the court turns violent, Hugo mutters to himself, "Yeah, Dad, who's your favorite now?" Kat's disruptiveness is comic role-playing that has a source she herself understands, and she is not finally committed to it. It gets attention, but that is not why she does it. The danger Hugo presents comes from a compulsive need for attention, over which he has no control.

Though Hugo echoes Iago's final vow of silence, the film breaks that silence, at a point where, in the play, Iago is sidelined. Hugo's is the last voice we hear, as well as the first. His opening voiceover, before we know whose voice it is, declares, "All my life, I always wanted to fly; I always wanted to live like a hawk. I know you're not supposed to be jealous of anything; but to take flight, over everything and everyone; now that's livin'." In the end, as he is walked off to a police car, we hear the same words in voiceover. Now we know whose voice it is and what the words mean. The voice continues, this time making a final statement about Odin, more articulate than the statement Odin made about himself, giving him an Othello-like stature that the terms of the film never quite allowed him: "But a hawk is no good around normal birds. . . . They hate him for what they can't be. Proud, powerful, determined, dark. Odin is a hawk. He soars above us. He can fly. But one of these days everyone's gonna pay attention to me. Because I'm gonna fly too." As we hear this, Hugo is looking through the back window of a police car, which drives away. He has been given the equivalent of Othello's last speech, a clear and deliberate summing-up.

In performance, Iago often steals the play from Othello; it is easier to cast Iago, and the role, though challenging, is less difficult. Hugo's final dominance is not a matter of the relative strengths of the two perform-ances, which are, in fact, evenly matched. It has to do with the effect of the final scene, the crowd of police cars and ambulances in front of the dormitory, the bodies carried out on stretchers. In *10 Things*, Patrick and Kat have their final embrace in the school parking lot; the camera pans back to show orderly rows of cars, with students strolling about. It is a normal day; everything is all right. *O* ends by shattering that sense of the normal in a way that has become all too familiar. And it has all happened because of the handsome, seemingly normal young man we see being escorted into a police car. While *10 Things I Hate About You* sees the disruptiveness of adolescence as harmless role-playing, linked to its own playful attitude to Shakespeare, *O* uses its serious concentra-tion on *Othello* to touch on deeper fears about what lies behind the pic-tures in the yearbook. While *10 Things I Hate About You* keeps its audience happy and comfortable, the release of *O* was delayed in the wake of the Columbine massacre.

NOTES

1. *10 Things I Hate About You*, VHS, prod. Andrew Lazar, dir. Gil Junger (1999; Burbank, CA: Buena Vista Home Entertainment, 2002). Screenplay credited to Karen McCullah Lutz and Kristen Smith.

2. *O*, VHS, prod. Eric Gitter and Anthony Rhulen, dir. Tim Blake Nelson (2001; Los Angeles: Lion's Gate Films, 2002). Screenplay credited to Brad Kaaya.

3. *The Taming of the Shrew*, in *The Riverside Shakespeare*, 2nd ed., ed. G. Blakemore Evans (Boston: Houghton Mifflin, 1997), 4.1.204. Subsequent references to Shakespeare's plays are from this edition and are cited parenthetically.

Contributors

FRANCES K. BARASCH, Professor emerita at Baruch College, The City University of New York, is author or editor of studies on the Grotesque, the Romantic poets, Shakespeare, and Commedia dell'Arte. Recent articles have appeared in *Shakespeare Bulletin*, *Shakespearean International Yearbook*, *Shakespeare Yearbook*, *English Literary Renaissance*, *Intertestualità Shakespeariane*, and *Henry V: Critical Essays*.

J. ANTHONY BURTON is an independent scholar. Author of articles and book reviews for *Shakespeare Bulletin*, *The Upstart Crow*, and *The Shakespeare Newsletter*, he conducts a Shakespeare seminar at The Center for Renaissance Studies at the University of Massachusetts in Amherst and occasionally acts as dramaturge for the Hampshire Shakespeare Company.

MAURICE CHARNEY is Distinguished Professor of English at Rutgers University. He is author or editor of over twenty books, including, most recently, *All of Shakespeare* (1993) and *Shakespeare on Love and Lust* (2001). He has been President of The Shakespeare Society of America and the Academy of Literary Studies. In 1989, he was awarded the Medal of the City of Tours.

SAMUEL CROWL is Trustee Professor of English at Ohio University, where he has taught since 1970. He is the author of *Shakespeare Observed* (1992), *Shakespeare at the Cineplex* (2003), and the forthcoming *Citizen Ken: The Films of Kenneth Branagh* (2006). He has published widely on all aspects of Shakespeare in performance and has won numerous teaching awards.

ALAN C. DESSEN is Peter G. Phialas Professor emeritus of English at the University of North Carolina, Chapel Hill. He is the author of eight books, most recently *Recovering Shakespeare's Theatrical Vocabulary* (1995), *Rescripting Shakespeare: The Text, the Director, and Modern Produc-*

tions (2002), and *A Dictionary of Stage Directions in English Drama, 1580–1642* (1999, with Leslie Thomson).

MICHAEL D. FRIEDMAN is Professor of English in the Center for Literature and Performing Arts at the University of Scranton. He is author of *"The World Must Be Peopled": Shakespeare's Comedies of Forgiveness* (2002), as well as several articles on Shakespearean stage performances and Shakespeare on film.

ANDREW GURR is Professor emeritus at the University of Reading and, until recently, Director of Globe Research at the Shakespeare Globe Centre, London. His books include *The Shakespearean Stage 1574–1642* (1970), *Playgoing in Shakespeare's London* (1987), *The Shakespearian Playing Companies* (1996), and *The Shakespeare Company 1594–1642* (2004). He has edited several Renaissance plays, including *Richard II, Henry V,* and the Quarto *Henry V.*

MIRANDA JOHNSON-HADDAD is Visiting Lecturer at the University of California, Los Angeles. She has published articles on Shakespeare, Spenser, Dante, and Ariosto, as well as numerous theater reviews in *Shakespeare Quarterly* and *Shakespeare Bulletin.* She has been Scholar in Residence at the Folger Shakespeare Library and was affiliated for many years with the Shakespeare Theatre in Washington, DC.

JAY L. HALIO, after nearly fifty years of teaching, thirty-five at the University of Delaware, took emeritus status in 2003. He is the author or editor of more than thirty-five books, including several editions of Shakespeare's plays as well as books and essays on modern authors. He recently updated his edition of *King Lear* and, with Patricia Parker, is currently editing a five-volume Shakespeare encyclopedia.

CHARLES A. HALLETT is Professor of English at Fordham University. He is the author of three books, including *The Revenger's Madness* (1980) and *Analyzing Shakespeare's Action* (1991), both coauthored with Elaine S. Hallett. He has also published numerous essays, mainly on drama.

ROSLYN L. KNUTSON is Professor of English at the University of Arkansas at Little Rock. Her books include *The Repertory of Shakespeare's Company 1594–1613* (1991) and *Playing Companies and Commerce in Shakespeare's Time* (2001). Her long-term project is a search for the narratives behind lost plays of the Admiral's Men in Henslowe's diary.

ALEXANDER LEGGATT is Professor of English at University College, University of Toronto. Publications include *Shakespeare's Comedy of Love* (1973), *Shakespeare's Political Drama: The History Plays and the Roman Plays* (1988), *English Stage Comedy 1490–1990: Five Centuries of a Genre* (1998), *The Cambridge Companion to Shakespearean Comedy* (editor, 2002), and *Shakespeare's Tragedies: Violation and Identity* (2005).

NAOMI C. LIEBLER is Professor of English and University Distinguished Scholar at Montclair State University. Her books include *Shakespeare's Festive Tragedy: The Ritual Foundations of Genre* (1995), *Tragedy* (coeditor, 1998), and *The Female Tragic Hero in English Renaissance Drama* (editor, 2002). Current projects are a critical edition of Richard Johnson's *Seven Champions of Christendom* and an edited collection on early modern prose fiction.

EDWARD L. ROCKLIN is Professor of English at California State Polytechnic University, Pomona. He is the author of *Performance Approaches to Teaching English* (2004) and is at work on a book on *Measure for Measure* for the "Shakespeare in Performance" series. He has been a fellow of the American Council of Learned Societies, a participant in the Folger Institute on Shakespeare Examined Through Performance, and a director of the California Reading and Literature Project site at Cal Poly Pomona.

KENNETH S. ROTHWELL is Professor emeritus at the University of Vermont. He has published in a broad spectrum of anthologies and scholarly journals. The second edition of his *History of Shakespeare on Screen: A Century of Film and Television* (1999) was published by Cambridge University Press in 2004.

JOHN TIMPANE is the Commentary Page Editor of the *Philadelphia Inquirer*. Before coming to that position, he taught English for seventeen years at institutions including Rutgers University, the University of Southampton, and Lafayette College. A reviewer for *Shakespeare Bulletin* since 1981, he is the author of four books, including *Writing Worth Reading* (1994, with Nancy H. Packer) and *Poetry for Dummies* (2000, with Maureen Watts), and articles on Spenser, Shakespeare, Tennessee Williams, and August Wilson.

Index